A FACE OF THE MASTERS CUBE

A COLLECTION OF SCI FI SHORT STORIES

JOSHUA R TAYLOR

For more information, address: jtaylor@authorjoshuartaylor.com.

First paperback edition Sept 2022

ISBN 979-8-9866304-0-3 (paperback)

ISBN 979-8-9866304-1-0 (ebook)

https://authorjoshuartaylor.com

Two Seashells Publishing, LLC

Chesapeake, Virginia, United States

This book is dedicated to my love, Jennifer for inspiring me with creative ideas and to all my family who love and support me. Also, to a younger me who searched for forty-eight years to find something he really loved doing. Here it is.

Table of Contents

1

Impossible Spontaneous Emergence

THAT SOUND AGAIN. IT'S CLOSER. His nerves tighten and he holds his breath. He keeps saying to himself in his head, "Don't make a sound. Stay covered." No sound now. At least he thought it was closer. These woods are so thick. Exhaustion is overwhelming, he can't run again, not now. There's not enough energy in his system to sustain getting away or getting ahead enough to hide from whatever is hunting him. He lets out a slow breath, quivering. The sound reverberates through his ears. He's so loud, it's annoying. Breathing trembles in synchrony with his heartbeat in release, and he takes another.

"Hunted?" he reflects. It's not believable. There's nothing that hunts humankind like this. He thinks of ancient tales of a mysterious beast unknown to science. Campfire tales and old miner and hiker stories. Nothing with any evidence or history. No bodies, no DNA evidence, no actual pictures of anything not disprovable. But what the hell is chasing him with such rage? It's been most of the afternoon now running, hiding to rest, running again when a footfall or a crashing branch drives prey to move. Twice he's heard the breath and thudding of the feet behind him. Yet he hasn't seen it running as hard as he has. Its presence alone invokes a deep and primal fear. An unquestionable ancient imprint for survival that seizes time and body.

"But I think I saw something," his brain toys. "About midday," as an unsure image recalls the timing.

His eyes take in his hiding place. A portable one, it turns out. It's a very well disguised sleeping bag. And as fate, serendipity, and modern market dynamics would dictate, one that is fantastic for hiding. It's modern camping by every standard. No tent required, nor is a campfire required for warmth at night. This camper's tool doesn't look like a place anyone sleeps. On the outside are artificial plants, grass, dead leaves, and twigs. It's like that because modern campers want to blend in with nature. Just climb in and press the red "Seal/Unseal" button. This seals the bag around you and snuggles you into a basic plaid interior with optional low lighting. It comes with a Micro-Air and Temperature Management System (MATMS), which ensures CO_2 build up and humidity are in balance with fresh, dry air. Power is solar/lunar with more than enough graphene lattice storage to last days on a charge. And there is a thermal-reflective liner between the thin cushiony materials that keeps the heat in for those chilly nights. You wouldn't know a person was laying right there if you came upon it unless you knew what to look for. Otherwise, it's just the forest floor as seen anywhere. A real marketing dynamo and all the rage. He was the last to get one like his buddies.

Nearby, the small sound of a twig cracks. His breath and heartbeat freeze. Was it followed by the quietest pressing of leaves to the ground? Couldn't it be a squirrel? Pausing every sound his movements make, he listens. A few minutes go by. Nothing. A little sound from the trees rustling in the wind and he weakens. His shoulders loosen, and he adjusts his back to reach maximum relaxation, or at least as much as he allows himself. His eyes close as thoughts race through his mind. Thoughts of survival. This will go away if he lays quiet and doesn't snore. Boy, what a freaking insane story he'll tell when he wakes up, if he wakes up. Right now, as he falls asleep, this story's telling seems far away.

Outside, the sun has fallen behind the mountain tops and twilight creeps in from the eastern sky as the first star appears. Sounds abound in the forest at night. More so than the daytime, as nocturnal creatures are plentiful. They are all the sounds one would expect to hear. Occasionally, though, there are unusual sounds. Not unique but sounds like they don't fit or should not belong. Things like out-of-place howls. Other times, movement that seems heavy on the ground and brush. Science knows everything by now, therefore, it must be a species cataloged somewhere. Human imagination is an unstoppable force.

The urge to pee is also an unstoppable force. He awakens with the need for this release, bearing down on him hard. Without thinking, he hits the unseal button above his head and scurries out. It's dark. The humidity seems higher. The air is heavier. He pauses and he realizes his situation. He listens for several moments meanwhile busting at the seam. Nothing. Not a sound to be heard. Not even the cicadas and crickets. It's dead quiet. Then five or six measured steps toward the nearest tree. Hoping and praying when he moves, he doesn't step on anything loud. He makes it and completes his business, though you'd think they could make quieter zippers, but he guesses the market never demanded that.

Just as he slides back into his bag, he hears two slow, very measured steps in the brush about twenty-five meters (82 ft) from his position. He turns his head toward the sound and holds still. Thirty seconds goes by and then a third planted step, rustling a couple of leaves. No question about that one. He measures the sounds and best he can tell, they are moving away from him.

Sliding all the way in now, he hits the seal button. If it attacked him before he got to the tree, he'd just pee everywhere. It led him to a bit of a laugh. He couldn't help it. He was going to pee all over his attacker if he had to die here.

"That'll teach 'em. I might be dead, but I win!"

There's nothing like going out on top with a victory. A smile rested on his face at his thoughts. With droopy eyes, he tires as lactic acid sets in on every muscle, making him weak and sore.

The morning sun rises but doesn't crack the treetops until about 10am. It must crest the mountain tops first. He had run into a wide valley between two competing peaks. He finds himself on the upper side of one valley slope. The other side is far away. He doesn't know where he is. He dropped his NuTreks Pro Comlet sometime early in yesterday's chase. It offers what every camper needs; that tie back to civilization. It has world maps, global tracking, hemisphere-wide emergency signaling for rescue operations, satellite communications linked to the world wide web. And his dumb ass dropped it.

He's in no shape to run great distances today. Throwing on his pack, he starts down the long, sloping valley. The track runs near parallel to the bottom where a small creek trickles clear.

Talking to himself, "As soon as I can make it to a clearing, I'll be able to reckon a better route."

He realizes that sounded loud, as if forgetting all about yesterday's run from determined death. The birds are still singing. That's a good sign. No disturbances nearby.

"I'm sore, but I will get to civilization," he says out loud again.

"I need to find the closest spot."

He catches himself humming a little as the morning sun is now almost directly overhead. It's a made-up tune of his own. "Must be shortly before high-noon," he guesses, as if the attempt at tracking time mattered.

"I've walked for two hours, and I can't see crap!"

"Let's see. I remain high on the slope, hoping to glimpse something that looks like it has people present."

"Maybe I'll try to angle more toward the bottom of the valley."

"There has to be a good viewpoint somewhere!" he says with manufactured exasperation.

So downward he goes staring at the ground in front of the tops of his shoes like every hiker that ever existed. Yesterday seemed like an impossibility, a bad dream, even. His mind wandered through the events all morning. Now, though, he found himself relaxed in his stride and the sore muscles were gone because of the morning's steady workout. Different thoughts bounced around when he noticed a clearing coming up and something blue.

"Ah, this might be a good chance to validate my direction."

He can see the valley from the edge of the clearing. The trees sort of fall off at the far edge, making visibility good. He takes a quick broad scan, but initial processing of useful directional information on the horizon took a back seat to something else.

"What is this blue thing?" he inquires as if he's in normal, everyday conversation with someone else.

The grass is tall here. Taller than the underbrush squashed by the forest treetops. He walks several steps to his right, and with each step, he forms a guess. As the scene comes into view, he wonders if it is a tent.

Speaking to himself soft and low, "It sure as hell used to be a tent." As the level of his words falls off with growing concern.

His steps cease at the edge of the encampment. An old smell of death was upon the still air, touching everything, even his thoughts. He couldn't tell what was dead, but it's there. A tattered, blown over echo of a campfire remains before a broken lantern, two tackle boxes, and a large cooler near a log. He spots a nice side-by-side double-barreled shotgun on the ground, almost underneath the log.

"Damn, that's a fine gun for someone to just leave around like that." He says in his lowest voice.

The whole dishevelment before him looks to be from far earlier in the spring. There appeared to be a couple of weeks of dirt on everything. And now for the tent. He had stepped his way toward it with caution. A blue and white fishing pole lays outside of a shredded lump of a former habitation. There was one top corner of the tent, still tied up to a limb. It's what first caught his eye before he reached the clearing. The rest was a guess. Two more large, lunging, quiet steps over to the fishing pole leads to its grab. Prodding the shredded pieces of tent with the end of the pole reveals there is mud and blood on the material, and something covered. Fears rise and tell him what lies beneath. His mind restrains his emotions. The pole catches a torn area just right, and he pulls it back. In absolute horror, he gasps and steps back. Fears, now confirmed, drive his eyes to survey his immediate area.

An exposed skull with hair and bloodstains, along with a few vertebrae, meets the sunshine. It looked to be an older male but missing his lower jaw. It was nowhere to be seen. The head and vertebrae were separated from the torso, which he uncovered next. Creatures had nibbled on the corpse. There is a thigh bone of another individual shrouded in the mess. Hanging around is no longer an option. Grabbing the shotgun ushers in opportunity for a rapid inspection. It's in great shape with intricate wood and metal work. A top end shotgun for sure. Breaking it open finds both barrels empty. Spying the ground for ammunition results in nothing. After a moment of considering bringing the shotgun along, he lays it down anyway when in the distance his ears spike panic. Faint but familiar, like yesterday's familiar sound, muscles tighten. Starring toward the sound for a solid thirty seconds leads to nothing.

"On second thought, I'll just keep this," he whispers, and convinces himself it was nothing unusual.

Making a short distance away from the murder scene, gun in tote, he stops in the middle of a clearing to make his brain work to remember this spot, forcing it to catalog location details. Upon returning, all of this will need to be reported. Figuring out ownership of this gun can help identify the bodies in the tent.

Location details captured now causes other thoughts to churn when thud, thud, thud came the sound of an oblong rock landing just behind him and rolling past. It was twice the size of his hand. This was no accident or natural event. Almost hitting him, it only takes a moment to figure out what happened. Something threw it. Turning toward where it originated, it appears to be approximately sixty meters (200 ft) to the far side of the glade. There's nothing to see. The midday sun makes it hard to see into the forest darkness when standing out in the light. It's the same principle as looking into a house midday from a distance. You can't see anything inside, but anyone inside can see you just fine. Knowing this, he reaches for the rock and throws it back whence it came. It flies only thirty meters. The rock was heavy, and he had given it quite a heave. The moment it bounced to rest on the ground, there came a fiendish, guttural scream from the far side. It sounded like it was in pain and insulted all at once.

A treetop set back from the clearing fifteen meters shakes back and forth, and a howling and screaming like nothing ever heard raised all his hairs. The instinctual urge to run stole his feet and set them into maximum flight. That was a lot of force to move that tree. A second howling scream from further away on his right fills the valley. Peeking over his shoulder at the sound, birds pepper the sky in frantic escape. The screaming roar again behind him fills the mountain glade. He drops the gun for speed.

"Two? Is there two now? Two of what?"

He couldn't conceive "of what" as he had not seen his harrower the day before in his narrow escape. It was massive and strong enough to break down small trees, moved at least as fast as him, and was dead serious about keeping him on the run and more than likely killing him.

Another roar right comes from behind. As fast as legs can carry a man, he glances over his shoulder to catch a hulking mass of an upright figure closing ground. Every last drop of energy is poured into surging locomotion. There's nowhere to hide. Speeding through the trees on a downhill slope behind him, a tree or tree limb snaps and breaks, then another and another. One right after the other. Just like yesterday. Gravity pulls greater speed on the downward slope, stealing control from leg muscles which have never moved so fast. Whatever is giving chase is right up on his back it seems. In full exhaustion, back muscles tense, and hairs raise with intense focus on keeping upright down the slope of trees. He hears the footsteps and heaving breaths of his aggressor. It's everything he can do to avoid slowing down and staying upright at the same time. Turning his head might reduce speed, but the prey must see the eyes of the predator.

Peeking forward a little farther ensures his continuing path is valid before the glance backwards when he notices the land ends in about forty meters. A ledge it seems and a drop off. But how high? Having traveled a long way down the valley slope, he's close to the bottom. The valley's opposite side shows land sloping upwards again, and the chasm is very wide and deep. The distance is too great and the decent is deadly. There's no room left. Breaking full stride finds him sliding feet-forward because he's going over an edge which is not survivable. Sliding out of the forest ridgeline across a gravelly granite outcrop, and moving faster than he realized, a jagged granite rock gouges a thigh with little outcrop left to save him. Scrambling to grab earth and rock with all his might, his motion slows, and the approaching edge reveals his destiny.

It's one hell of a drop. Maybe eighty to one hundred meters (250 - 300 ft) on a flying guess. Butterflies fill and flutter his stomach at the scene while legs and torso fly beyond support. A rock jabs sharply upwards into his chest and his hands lurch to grab on. Catching himself, he dangles with no support. Muscles, exhausted from the full-speed run for his life, are drained. Another two or three meters would have been lifesaving. It wasn't there.

Down below trickles the rocky creek he noticed at a distance earlier in the morning. A roar reverberates from the other side. Much closer this time. His hands are straining to keep him alive. Large, jagged granite of all sizes borders the creek below. There's no hope of landing and surviving. Hearing the breathing and footfall of his aggressor above him, he strains for a look, but cannot see him. Is there a way out of this? He wonders, but salvation has forsaken him. With fingers tiring and aching, they weaken. His desire to live accepts its new contract. Remembering the people who he has loved and loved him in return, he adjusts his aching hands repetitively now to sustain their lifesaving grip driving every nanosecond to be an entire life relived. He wishes his buddies were with him. They planned three exceptional days when all of them would be together this weekend. Slipping ever more with each change in grip, he knows only seconds remain. Death is inevitable for all things. Holding on for the last empty, lonely, ticking seconds is all that is left. In his mind, he sees his pets, his daughter, his family, his camping friends, old girlfriends, and that kid he fought on the playground in fifth grade. Then suddenly, on destiny's undisclosed timing, weakened hands in the last of their effort, slip from their anchor.

Wind across his ears delivers a final unharmonious dirge as body and mind race toward a ragged, broken fate. In this moment, though, something unknown and untold among the generations occurs. There is a sudden and new emotion filling his being. One never felt before in his life. It was overpowering, and pure. If he could put words to it, "A final release of everything" is what it felt like. A complete reassurance that everyone who knew him and loved him or had depended upon him would move forward with time. They'll forge their way in the best way they each know. His life didn't matter, nor his job nor any debts. Only a few would care to remember him on the off occasion. His image fading in time. He embraced this terminal moment of his existence with a flawless understanding of how the universe fades all things into oblivion. He was in a divine release. Something unknown to a living man until his final breath. Upon feeling this and knowing its truth, in his last moment before meeting his jagged end, he looks upwards in peaceful grace, reaches forth his hand, and touches the sky.

His ears become alert to the words of a conversation. One eye cracks open. A blurry image of a large, heavy man is on his right. He feels like he is on a bed.

"Yeah, I don't care, Donna," came the words from a curly haired, overweight man. "The system shows anomalous errors and after the testing, there shouldn't be any! Now it's my job to figure out what it is because the standard error catching didn't catch it. All it shows is it is something in memory. That's all we know now."

"You've taken too much time for your processes up to now! I'm tired of waiting for you every time the rest of us feel this project is ready to move on! We waste time and money twiddling our thumbs, waiting for 'the software guys' to finish their part." Donna asked in frustration, "How much more time is required?"

Donna is on his left, though he can't see her well. His right eye grabs focus.

"I'll have your answer in the next couple of hours," replied the fat, curly-haired man. "My team can divide it up and if the answer comes sooner, you'll be the first to know."

"Fine, just please give me something before noon. Anything, even if you don't know. I have to report to the board tonight, so I need time to prepare. We were supposed to be ready to go today. We are ten months behind schedule."

On the fat man's way out, he said, "I'm not saying sorry anymore, Donna. It takes what it takes to build a great software system, especially one like this. It's not like we're plotting on you. We want success too. We're the first to achieve anything this advanced." His voice fading as he enters the hallway, "We did not know the number and types of problems we'd run into."

Donna watches him go and shakes her head in frustration, along with an exasperated breath. She glances at the bed and notices her patient is watching. "Oh, you're awake! Excellent! What are you feeling?"

What was he feeling? He was off. He awoke only a moment ago. Donna asks again, "Are you feeling anything?" He was still putting it together. His last memory was of himself falling, and now this. He summarizes what he is feeling.

"I'm feeling pressed down."

"Pressed down?" She asks, as if not expecting to hear that. "Oh, that's because we have your limbs secured. We need to keep you immobile for the next twenty-four hours after your latest surgeries. We'll loosen those limbs again afterward."

"Surgeries?"

"Yes, you're done, but it's important to let the soft tissues start their recovery naturally. Especially the deeper cuts and tears. Once that's started, we will expedite the surface healing with the Chromata-Care Light Healing Unit. You'll be good as new soon."

"Good as new?"

"Yes, good as new. Now you need to rest because, well, you were banged-up when we rescued you three weeks ago, and the damage almost ended our program here. Your body needs to be healthy so we can show you to the world. We've got your brain covered."

He thinks about what she told him, but he is tired. Then, a young black lady in hospital garb enters, pushing a cart. "Hi Donna," she drones in a half cheerful tone and, "Hi Mark," in the same drawn-out way.

Donna says, "Oh and look! Just in time! Tamika's here with your morning meal and meds. We need to get your metabolism back to eating solid foods. She'll help you eat a little and then get you squared away. Meanwhile, I have some work to finish for tonight's board meeting. Tamika will take care of you. Tamika, watch out for him. I'll see you both later."

"Yes Mrs. Donna, will do. Take care," says Tamika as Donna walks out of the room. "How's it going, Mark?"

He remembers that's his name. "Well, I guess? I'm feeling woozy, maybe. I can't move, as you can see."

"Well, we'll get you scratchin' those itches in no time!" She chuckles.

Then she says, "Let me see here."

She walks to the monitors. "Looks like your HGH is low. I'll supplement it for now in your drip and I'll let Mr. Mike know he needs to check your vials. You also need some serotonin. You are all out! Must be all that restin' and healin' you've been doin'."

She giggles as she types something into the console.

With little of this conversation making sense to him, he inquires, "What do you mean I'm low? And vials? Supplement my HGH?"

Tamika looks at him with raised eyebrows. "Wow! That fall did a serious number on you! When they said they were resetting you to your last baseline, they must not have realized how much core knowledge you were going to lose."

"What," he stutters some as he interrupts in confusion and says, "B-b-b-baseline, re-re-reset?"

"Yes, sometimes they do nightly backups of everything you learned and if something happens or they need to make alterations in your learned outcomes, they can make the required changes and re-upload the corrected knowledge into your system. It makes your learning faster. It's just like you learned it yourself, but with outside help. Daily, you do things and learn things while later a small team of software engineers and scientists reviews your learned outcomes. They get new ideas and stuff from it that gets used in future science things."

"I sound like some sort of experiment."

"Oh, you are!"

She puts something from a needle into a bag of saline solution next to his bed.

"There ain't no harm in telling you myself, I suppose."

"Tell me what?"

"Your name in your life before this one was Brian Scott." She continues, "You received serious, life-ending wounds in Taiwan when you were in the Marines. You were brain dead and died a couple of weeks later at your family's request to end your life support. However, when you entered the service and knew you were going straight into combat, you wrote a will. You donated your body to science with the stated desire for experimentation with reanimation."

Mark searched his mind. Nothing like this sounded familiar. Is this reanimation? Is that his reality?

"Reanimation?"

"Yeah, you know… bringing you back to life long after you've died."

She paused and looked for some response on his face. "This is kind of heavy, isn't it?"

She pulls the breakfast tray over. "Here, nibble this soft food. It'll get your stomach and intestines ready for proper food. It doesn't look yummy, but you need it to jump start. I added a little sugar on top for you."

He takes his first bite of what appears to be gruel of sorts. Not much flavor, but he's more interested in what Tamika will say next.

"Your brain was dead and without that, well, there just ain't nothin' to reanimate. But these people here had an idea. They took the best research around making the human body and machines work together. They experimented for six years to come up with what's called a 'Computer as a Brain Interface.' C-B-I for short. Meanwhile, you were on ice, so to speak."

Mark interrupts, "on ice?"

"Yeah, what I mean is your body was suspended in a tank of liquid that helped keep your organs and skin and everything fresh until they were ready for you. You had all kinds of tubes comin' out of you. And just so you know… (she leans in closer) you were naked too! Ha-ha-a-ah!" Her head bobbed side to side a little, hoping to get at least a grin, but he seemed more interested in her information. "It's all good, though. Here, let's take another bite."

"I'm not hungry," he mutters.

"Tell you what. This stuff isn't that tasty, but if you eat what's on this spoon, you don't have to finish it. This is your first proper meal, and it's gonna take a few before you're eatin' hearty again."

He takes his last spoonful. In walks a middle-aged black man in a lab coat.

"Hi Mike," she says as she puts away the breakfast bowl.

"Mark, you remember Mike, I'm sure."

Mark looks at Mike for a moment but didn't seem to recall. Tamika could see the inquisitive look on Mark's face and interjects, "You know, Dr. Mike Stoddard? He's the lead Bio-Mechanical Engineer. He's the one that put you back together and designed your one-of-a-kind hormone system. Nothing like it exists in the world today except in your brain."

"Tamika, why are you telling him this?" Mike asks. "He knows us. It's not his first time."

"It seems as if the reboot or whatever they want to call it wiped out more of his memory than they thought."

Mike responds, "The reset."

"Yes, the reset. I've been filling him in on who he is. I haven't told him much yet. Just enough to keep him from lookin' confused."

"Oh, I see," says Mike as he peeks over his reading glasses. "We can fix that once the data analysis is complete. They reset everything but his short-term memory, which gives him about sixteen hours of perfect, detailed memory. They didn't want to turn him into a complete dummy."

"Yeah, um-hmmm," she mutters as she hustles to pull together her cart to leave. "Well, I'm done here. I have other duties now. Goodbye, Mike. See ya, Mark!"

"Bye, Tamika," says Mike.

"Oh! and Mark, Mrs. Sherry will be in for your lunch later if you ain't all sleepin' by then," Tamika states as she heads down the hallway.

"Well, Mark, it's nice to see you alert again. You've been out for several weeks while we fixed you up. It's amazing how quickly we can fix the organic parts of your body these days. In days gone by, you would have been in traction for months before healing correctly. You did a number on yourself," Mike says as he reads the console, and then lets out a deep breath. He was looking at the latest updates from the computer in Mark's head and the status readouts of Mark's body.

After a moment of quiet, Mark states, "Tamika put something in the daily notes for you."

"Oh, did she now? Let me look here," replies Mike in a low, monotone voice.

Mike continues, "Oh yes, I see. I noticed that on the bio-report just now. You're low on critical hormones. Looks like she got you squared away for the short term. I'll get those refilled for you."

"What do you mean?"

"Well, your brain is one hundred percent computer, and your body is one hundred percent human body save for a few vertebrae that needed replacement and the back-side of your head. Those items are three-dimensionally printed titanium, along with the bones in your entire left leg below the knee, including your foot," replies Dr. Stoddard.

"This means you are missing key hormone producing organs found in the human brain. Namely, the Hypothalamus and Pituitary gland. Without these, your physical systems would be deficient in HGH, melatonin, serotonin, dopamine, oxytocin, and vasopressin. It's a long list. You need every one of them to wake up, move around, and live. We've synthesized them all and you have small titanium vials of these hormones in your cranium which are connected to your computer brain and your blood vessels. That brain runs some software I wrote with a grad student of mine that controls the release of the hormones in the natural way the body requires. We have the advantage of increasing dosages of serotonin and HGH when you are seriously injured. It helps the healing process in a big way. I check your levels of each hormone to ensure thirty days' utility without a refill. At the end of every week, we look at your datasheet to determine the next dosages."

"I'm feeling tired still."

"Well, you'll feel a little tired moving forward the next couple of days as your final healing is taking place. That's because we've increased your serotonin and Tamika just gave you a supplemental dose because you were out," responds Mike. "Don't be afraid to just doze off if you feel like it. I won't be offended. I'm just glad to have you around still. Once you go to sleep, I'll open the back of your cranium and do the usual refill for the month." Mike noticed Mark was off to a dreamy wonderland now. So, he continued with his duties required to get Mark healthy and active again.

Meanwhile, the tech team started its initial findings review.

Deepak, a tall, lighter skinned Indian programmer says, "The Cortex data and the database aren't in line with each other. There is different data in the Cortex data that does not appear in the database. It is only a few data elements. The comparator is completing now."

The fat man speaks up, "Ok, let us know as soon as it's finished, Deepak." He continues, "Babu, have you found anything wrong with the behavioral classes or methods?"

Babu, another smaller and darker skinned Indian programmer, replies, "No Jeff, nothing is different. It's the baseline code exactly."

Jeff, the fat man says, "Ok, now I need you to count all the methods which call the behavior control functions from the baseline implementation and compare it to all the methods which call all the behavioral control functions from the most recent version we ran. There must be something there that's different, or it's somewhere in the M-Core. That's all it could be outside of immediate considerations for one or more of the agents. We'll attack the agent issues after these initial checks because analyzing them gets complex quickly. And guys, I don't want to get into the M-Core issues again. It's been four or five solid months now and it has been working just fine. If it comes to the agents, we'll need everyone helping each other."

Jeff was dreading the rise of more M-core issues. They have been the bane of his software programming existence since he's been on the project the past three years. The M-Core stands for the Morality Core. It's a super-critical feature of modern Artificial Intelligence that gives machines the ability to make independent decisions. These decisions are based on data, values, and functions defined to support proper process and action outcomes. The M-Core is built on code which defines moral definitions of how to act. It contains well-defined goals and functions for achieving those goals and a strict list of the methods which support those functions. The M-Core also supports the data and its allowable variances in range values, which drives alternative decision making to meet the goals. It's heavily complicated even for a gifted programmer like Jeff. But it turns out, the architecture is strong and well-tested these days. Putting it all together and working through the kinks was a three-year nightmare.

Because morality implemented in a machine is so important, it's captured in a cryptographic block part of the software architecture. No one from outside the entity can influence the data, values and functions in the crypto block, regardless of whatever the entity runs into in the real world. Its morality is not accessible from outside the entity, nor is it modifiable from within the baseline code, driving the outward actions of the entity. The baseline code can only call into it and receive outputs from it. That baseline code operates as the Cortex Event Center or CEC. The only exception to this is a highly secure, small library of classes with method calls that can be made only by the intelligent entity itself. They are accessible only when values and actions to be performed coming out of the M-Core fall significantly short of addressing the needs of the current situation. This library is well understood and contained. If it was triggered, it would be found in the method calls being analyzed by Babu.

The CEC runs as the normal main event thread for the entire brain, though it has thousands of threads. Methods that impact M-Core concerns are run through the crypto block first. If specific values are returned for the outcome, then the machine follows those outcomes because they are based on morally defined goals. If nothing is returned, then it can use the alternate default values to continue processing and performing actions. It's an effective, safe, and secure relationship between established moral goals and entity interaction with the outside world.

About an hour later, Jeff rounds the corner to Donna's office. The door is open. She's on the phone talking to what sounds like the manager for the special fund set aside to pay for this research and development.

"We need something more concrete for you, and I know you've waited far too long for results," says Donna.

And she continues after a pause, in which she signals Jeff to come in. "I assure you of a full report tonight on the overall status of the project and I will be available to answer all the detailed questions you have."

And after another pause, she says, "Yes, I'll bring data and supporting information for recent delays, and I…" She is interrupted by whoever is on the other end of the line again.

She finishes by saying, "Ok, yes, I'll get that prepared for the board and have copies, yes."

She looks at Jeff and rather rolls her eyes. He can tell she's under a lot of stress and so is he. He knows the situation.

"Ok, talk to you later. Thank you." She hangs up.

"Well, I guess I don't have to tell you what that's about," she says. Jeff responds, "No, I can guess."

She interrupts before he can say anything else. She asks, "What do you have for me?"

"Something strange happened, and we are trying to figure out what caused it."

Donna inquires with her head titled somewhat, "What do you mean?"

"We found evidence of newly created data that should not exist," Jeff says with a bit of dismay in his voice, as if he almost can't believe he is saying the words out loud.

"But we deal with newly created data all the time. It's how the A.I. understands its environment and captures changes and alters actions and everything, right?"

"Yes, correct. It's supposed to operate like that. But in those instances, we are always talking about what we call the universal data set. That's all the knowledge pre-defined for the entity. The entity can create or receive new information about anything in the universal data set, and everything is good. The universal data set captures the new information, and a metadata description is applied to the new data itself. This is how an entity like Mark grows and learns. But the key is knowing the data it creates is always relational to the universal data set. This specific data we've found is outside the universal data set inside Mark, and that's a serious problem. It's all new information that relates to nothing in his pre-established universal data."

"Well, how's that bad? Isn't this a sign of advanced intelligence? Isn't this what we are trying to achieve?"

Jeff responds with a lower and urgent voice, "No, Donna. This is something that, according to theory, cannot happen. There is no such thing as spontaneous emergence of data and worse, something inside Mark has built relationships to data items in the universal data set which seem legitimate but have no known origin. It is requisite that all data has a known origin."

"I don't understand. The last several versions of Mark have seemed so lifelike. He even appeared self-aware already. And isn't knowledge supposed to grow with intelligence?"

"Yes," Jeff replies. "First, Mark isn't fully self-aware, but he seems like it occasionally. Second, any advanced and properly architected artificial intelligence moves through its environment with a focus to learn, then over time everything it learns becomes some new data point in its universal data set. This is not the case with Mark. We turned Mark on right before the last run, and the extra data we are finding has no origin. Yet it's there! It can't be poor record keeping because we are validating it against the previous baseline."

"What data are we talking about?"

"He's got data named Buddies and Pets and Daughter and his default scheduler has information in it about a get-together with his newly defined buddies, which has now passed two weeks ago. None of this is part of his universal data set. He doesn't have buddies or friends, nor does he have any pets or a daughter, and as far as pets and a daughter go, neither had the man he was before he was Mark, when he was Mr. Brian Scott. After we turned him on, nothing like that was input. This data seems to have spontaneously emerged, which is impossible by every known standard."

"Ok, but aren't there long held theories stating A.I. will eventually evolve to spawn its own data and theories randomly like in the movies? Isn't that what they always fear? That it will realize its existence and take matters into its own hands?"

"Yes, and No. Yes, the A.I. can generate new ideas and new optimizations from the problems it encounters, but those problems are still sources of input which add to the full knowledge of the entity."

He continues and says, "No for two reasons. First, the M-Core constrains all outcomes from Mark to stay within the moral instruction set we've coded for him when it applies, and second, this new data must have a source of input from someone here." His voice and tension rising a little as he strains for a single breath to finish his sentence.

He goes on, "Otherwise, we are facing the theoretically impossible and I don't want to explain the outcome if this all goes wrong because I know the theory stands. Spontaneous emergence of data does not exist!"

"Alright, calm down," Donna says, "I believe you. We've had this conversation or something like it many times before. The board needs something more tangible, and right now I have the first case of spontaneous emergence. I do not know how they'll react, especially if we prove later, it wasn't true."

Jeff states, "My fear is we will need to do an extensive agent analysis, which could take several days."

"Well then, let's get on it. We must find the answer."

"I'll be back in touch before you have your board meeting. If we don't have any initial discoveries, I'll have the whole team working on the analysis of the agents. Talk to you later, boss." He quickly leaves the room and heads back to engineering.

His mind becomes preoccupied with memories of his college days at Carnegie Mellon University. Memories of himself and his friends discussing the most advanced concepts in artificial intelligence. That was over twenty years ago. God, has it been twenty years ago? He remembers debating strategies for building artificial intelligence, discussing code architectures, practicing machine learning implementations, and building A.I. to beat games of all types. He even joked with his friends about building a robot army just for fun to conquer humanity and to make the world better for everyone under his iron fisted rule. Those were the days.

Other theoretical topics in those days led to deeper ethical discussions, which are now taking on greater urgency. Questions like what happens if your artificial intelligence becomes self-aware? After all, that's the Holy Grail of artificial intelligence engineering. From there, how do you confirm actual self-awareness? And what does self-awareness contain that makes it self-aware? Ultimately, how will science know the singularity has happened? The singularity being the first self-aware machine. Will a supreme and intelligent artificial entity see humankind in a negative or positive light? Does supreme intelligence need morality? Is extreme intelligence contained by moral limitations? Is extreme intelligence even manageable? And critical to theory, could spontaneous emergence of data be a precursor to an uncontrolled dawning of machine self-awareness? None of these questions have solid answers and theorists have taken many approaches over the last century to answering them. But even now, no theory has become the de facto standard upon which to guide the artificial intelligence engineering community.

It's like everyone is waiting for it to happen before they become post hoc prognosticators who know everything. He knows this will never do. Things can't happen like the movies. Jeff remembers arguing with a classmate where if something as profound and powerful as a self-aware machine were to come into existence without well-known scientific guidelines for how to manage such an entity then the only safe option was termination of the entity followed by high-level controlled sub-experiments on different aspects of the entity's code base. Humankind's safety would be of paramount importance. A supremely intelligent entity based on code could learn to infiltrate every programmable device on the planet. Then humankind would lose complete control of its own world and would depend on the hopeful notion a supremely intelligent entity would be kind to all. Lacking an understanding of morality and its consequences, this probably would not be the case. The dark thought resurfaces. If the team isn't finding answers fast, then safety in the name of science and society must come first. He demands this of himself.

Back in engineering, results from the first analysis are ready.

"Deepak, what do you have?" Asks Jeff.

"It is unquestionable. We have some anomalous data that is not in the baseline universal data set," says Deepak.

"You've got to be kidding me."

"I'm really surprised. This thing does not happen. I even checked the analysis with my own queries against the data. The Cortex data is holding the anomalies and they do not show up in the universal data set, which is wrong. These are also what we would call foundational entity data. Things like family, friends, loved ones, close relationships and such with which we would key important connections with the M-Core, as you know. So, we should place new data created in the Cortex Event Center associated with foundational data into the universal data set. The process works correctly, we know, but this data is not in there," responds Deepak.

Jeff is in continuing disbelief. He asks, "Ok, yes, we know that process, so what is it? This data. What are we looking at here?"

Deepak reads off his findings, saying, "We have three buddies, Aaron, David and Tim."

Jeff interjects, "Who the hell are those guys? I know that's not in the universal dataset, and we don't have anyone around here with those names!"

Deepak responds, "I know. I have no clue. And there's more."

"How the hell did this get into our data? Ok shoot," Jeffs responds.

"There are 'pets' plural, but only the name of one pet. A dog named Roscoe. A beagle. And get this, there are memory locations containing images for the 'other' pets with no names. However, when you retrieve the image from the CEC, it doesn't look like any kind of animal."

In extreme disbelief, Jeff almost shrieks with a hint of anger, "What! You've got to be freaking kidding me! It's auto-generating images?"

The team looks at the two of the images pulled up from the CEC's simplified Object-Relational Database system, which is its foundational data relation manager for cortex data. The universal data in the entity's main database gets called by methods and algorithms in the Cortex Event Center to be used with the Cortex data. This is the moment-to-moment data used by the A.I. entity. Everyone knows anything of importance or high value which is reusable in the future needs to have a home in the universal data set. The images don't look like animals. Just some scribbles on the screen. The team is in disbelief.

Deepak says, "He has a daughter named Olivia. There's no image but check out this metadata about her."

On the screen, the team reads of a list of attributes associated with Olivia, including what appear to be two short text stories of interactions with Olivia. Now everyone in greater disbelief is talking amongst themselves in low tones about the findings.

Jeff speaks loudly over the discussions, "Does anyone know an Olivia and if so, how did you get the data into the Cortex?"

No one answers.

After a moment, he says, "You know what this means if we don't figure out who the joker is around here!"

Sarah, a young programmer, says, "Are you sure the Cortex got wiped before the last reset?"

Babu answers, "Yes Sarah, there should have been nothing left at reset in the Cortex or the simplified object-relational database it uses for some of its data. It's like having RAM memory wiped when you turn off a computer."

Sarah chimes back, "Ok, yes, I understand that. I'm just trying to stretch the possibilities here because when I saw the pet pictures in Mark's cortex, I thought back to something I learned last year in college. And the similarity is striking."

Babu says, "What do you mean?"

She says, "There was research going on into systems that fail at the nano-level with photonic processors. Apparently, not all photons are dissipated at once from the photonic processor or the memory chips when the power is removed. Some photons stay in place for various lengths of time, and though those time frames were not very long, they were noticeable. Some of the Phase Change Materials (PCM) used can sometimes look like they hold photonic echoes, which they are now calling sprites. They discovered each time they shut the failing system down, it was the same PCM transistors holding photons over and over. When a map of these photons in Mark's processor is displayed on the screen, it looks like the images of the pets in some ways. But scribbles are subject to wide-ranging interpretation."

She raises her hand a little as she says, "In addition, a failing system could have a small power surge at shut down. I was wondering if a power surge could generate data at the last moment.

Babu responds, "No, I think the power shut-off happens too fast to save anything off."

Deepak jumps in, "No, there would not be enough power to complete the data-save process."

"But I was thinking once it turned on again, if the photons had not dissipated, then the images get written, right?" Sarah asks again.

"Actually no," says Babu in fast response, "Every time we supply power to the System, the processor, and all memory locations get reset back to zero once power is reapplied. So, even if there was an echo of photons in the processor or memory chips, the system is reset to zero in all memory locations during its first nanosecond of operation. It builds up from there into its programmed form."

Deepak jumps in, "That is correct, but I like the thinking."

Jeff says, "Yes, I like that thinking. That's an example of how we should each be thinking. We need to be stretching the possibilities like Sarah. Babu, have you finished comparing the call stack for the behavioral classes and comparing it to the most recent baseline?"

Babu responds, "Yes, I ran them through the tools and did the comparator. There are no differences between the two. No new code and no extra method calls. No unusual exception throwing happened, either. The exception log looked normal. I even ran a compare between the two boot cycles. Nothing shows up."

Jeff declares the list of tasks. He says, "Ok team, then we'll analyze the agents and services, and we need 'all hands on deck' for this."

"Sarah, I want you and Joel to run an analysis on service execution. Just capture basic inputs and outputs and service timing for now. Get it listed out for us chronologically based on the last record in Mark's brain. Babu wrote a tool that can help you pull together all the data you need for that. We need to know if it used alternate services in place of any primary services. You know the routine. Babu and I will attack the procedural inputs and outputs against Sarah and Joel's work. We also need you, Deepak, to gather up the agent memory utilization patterns and the data being used in each one. You wrote a tool a while back to help pull that together, so it's a monstrous task. Most of our time will be used to do analysis. We can start by zeroing in on anything that touched the spontaneously spawned cortex data if we can find it. We're all working on this one. It's a lot of work. Mark is connected and available on the local network, so we can all get in his head from our desks. The remaining three team members will break up Mark's deterministic process flows for analysis and identify any alterations from the architectural design documents Sarah and Joel completed when they first started working here. Last, if nothing comes up, I'll pull Deepak and Babu into an analysis of the dynamic processes and any traceable altered steps. It hasn't given us much issue since I implemented it a few years ago. I used a rare development pattern called the Interceptor Pattern to allow for flexible changing of the steps in a workflow designed for system management and very low-level, simple problem solving. It's always worked well and allows Mark dynamic control to change the order of steps in a step-by-step process in order to satisfy simple, real-world problems. It works with data in data maps, process vectors, relationship development and moral execution to speed up solutioning to name a few things." He pauses, "Ok everyone, get to work."

First, Jeff needs to send a message to Donna and let her know the details of the initial analysis and what they are doing now to address the issue. She'll need the details for the board meeting. After about thirty minutes, Babu peeks in Jeff's door and says, "Ok, I've given a copy of the tool I wrote to Sarah and Joel, and I also provided some training on it. I showed how to get the information you asked for so we can start our analysis once they pull all the data."

Jeff replies, "Ok that's good. I can't believe we are in this situation. It shouldn't be like this."

Babu says, "I know. There must be an issue with an agent. That's what I'm thinking."

"I know Babu, but you and I know data doesn't just create itself. We can create metadata all day long and it always stays within the referential bounds of the universal data set. Nothing new. This is basic computer science and how computers and data work. This looks bad and I'm not sure what the board is going to decide. The board is concerned we are ten plus months behind our defined schedule. I don't know what's going to happen."

Babu replies in a low tone, "Yes, I know." He pauses a moment while Jeff is looking at his computer screen and says, "Ok, I'll be at my desk and when Sarah and Joel finish, I'll ping you."

"Thanks, Babu."

Jeff looks at his clock. He can't believe it's 2:35pm already. It seems like the day just started. He finishes proof-reading the message about the updates he was preparing for Donna. She has already sent two emails to him with other thoughts she has from his last report. It's in her nature to be a stream-of-consciousness thinker. Most of her suggestions are procedural or administrative. Jeff's mind is far too mired in deep technical preparation for his upcoming task to give weight to any response on those light topics. He orients his brain for his work with Babu.

Jeff keeps hoping the issue will arise on analysis. If it doesn't, then what remains? Spontaneous emergence of data? Which leads to what? Potential or eventual self-awareness within a machine? That makes no sense! Now, with it all before him, it seems far too simple, almost ridiculous! Mark is an amazing feat of engineering. Even though he was a human in the past and looks like one now, he is not. Jeff knows when people like Donna and the board members look at Mark, they believe Mark is self-aware. He does human-like things and talks human-like speech. He appears self-aware, but that's only because Mark's tests over the past three years are tuned to get specific outcomes and it seems human-like. Put him in a real human environment with other humans and many minor aspects of Mark would appear somewhat robotic. Jeff thinks back to the beginning of the project almost three years ago. He remembers the irony of how easy it was to see Mark's capabilities and shortcomings just by placing him in different settings. He has never let that realization slip from his mind.

Mark is just a machine. A machine based on a flesh and bone body. Jeff's hope was always to get Mark to a point where he could pass as a regular human and have regular human experiences. Jeff wanted to resolve and conquer what level of effort would be required to build self-awareness into a machine. It's why he came onto the project. But the point is to build it. That way it is controllable. If it spontaneously comes into being, then Jeff believes the world is in trouble. Especially if it's a self-aware, supreme intelligence in human flesh. Babu pings Jeff's messenger app and they begin their work.

The lighting in Donna's office dims at 5:30pm every day. She registers the change, squinting thru her glasses toward the outside world beyond the windowpane. The beaming light of summer's scorching afternoons feels wrong for so late in the day, so she checks the time on her monitor. She has spent most of her time writing up a mid-day report and shooting off thoughts back to Jeff on potential issues and questions she and others might have about the project. With her hands clasped below her chin, she wonders how the board will respond, and abides the steady march of the clock by knocking out little lingering tasks in a timely fashion. Meanwhile, waiting for any early responses back from board members and conjuring as many potential questions and answers as she could muster.

It's now 5:45pm. Donna awaits Jeff's latest analysis. She is short on time and sends him a message to call her about his current findings. The board meeting starts at 6:30pm and she's driving over to the main office to meet with them when her phone rings. It's Jeff.

"Hi Jeff!" she says in a positive voice.

"Hey Donna."

"I see you got my message. Thank you for that. What is the project's status?"

"The analysis will take at least another week. And now we have a major issue we cannot track down. One with social implications and scientific ramifications that surpass all for which this project is prepared. And because of its importance, it's one we cannot continue on without an answer."

"What do you mean, 'cannot continue on without an answer'?"

"We have a case which looks like the spontaneous emergence of new data. Data that is not part of the universal data set and has no known origins in the CEC. This goes against theory and the controls in modern code and software architectures. A machine is only going to do what a machine is programmed to do and there is no valid counterargument to that. That is a key point and is the foundational tipping point for what remains. You must understand that first, ok?" He questions.

Donna replies, "Yes, I understand. Go on, please."

Jeff says, "Nothing in Mark's code creates new data outside the universal data set except the Cortex Event Center. There we have new data as friends, family, and pets. This data is not part of any previous baseline of the Universal data set. Most important, this data was spawned only between the time we dropped Mark off at the test area in the mountains and the time of his fall from the cliff twenty hours later. How? We have no clue as of now. If a non-technical person were to consider all this information, I fear they would jump to the hasty conclusion we have created the world's first self-aware machine and oh by-the-way, it has human flesh and bone too! You see where I'm going here with the board members, right? It's both the vision and wild ideas of the board members and scientific discovery itself which requires that we cannot continue on without answers."

"Yes, I see. I can emphasize these points before the board gets out of hand."

Jeff interjects, "And another thing. The team requires more time for data analysis. Probably another week of effort. We can do no further improvements with Mark until that is complete."

"I still need to give the board something more tangible. What else can I include tonight?"

Jeff says, "Well, you have the results of Mark's last test run. There are several new positive accomplishments you can cover there. I know the board wants that, so start with those. When you get to the tough issues and if you are having trouble speaking to the key points, call me and I can answer tougher questions on speaker."

"Ok, well, I wish I had a little more, but I can remember some of our previous discussions together and some talking points you've had in the past. We will see how it goes. I will leverage as much as I know.

"I'm sorry. Donna, I have no more information for you.

"It's ok. It is what it is, right? We'll continue as we always have. I'll do my usual keeping the board at bay and giving them just enough to keep the funding going for the project."

"Alright, remember, reach out to me if you need specific questions answered. The team and I will work until 8pm or 9pm tonight. That way, we are available to you and the board if required," Jeff replies.

"Alright, I will. See you later," she says and hangs up as Jeff says goodbye.

At the board meeting, Donna is finishing up the early part of her presentation with the findings from the most recent test run. The usual half-interest in the findings reflected in Albert's or Al's face. Al is co-chair for the board and fills in when Ruth Anne, the chairperson, cannot attend. Ruth Anne runs her own technical consulting business and started her professional life as a systems administrator. Al is a partner in an accounting firm nearby. Around the table are Ted, Brian, Jenny, Kendra, Andrew and John. Two members are missing from tonight's board meeting, bringing the board's total membership to nine individuals as prescribed in the charter which funds Donna's project. Five members make a functional quorum, as voted on in the very first meeting.

"So those findings are nice," says Al. "It's been a while since you've delivered any accountable successes. I want to know, again, why you chose that scenario. I thought we had tested basic fight-or-flight responses in the past, or am I wrong?"

Donna replies, "No, you're not wrong, Al. We had to test fight-or-flight with greater intensity in the test run to push the biological and computational parts of Mark's body to extremes. We did this in order to gauge correctly how much stress his body can tolerate and how quickly the computational part of Mark can compensate. The result here was very positive. It shows us we can compensate for fixing and repairing Mark's human body faster than a normal body.

This is an enormous leap. What would have taken Mark many months to heal in a regular hospital happened in three weeks."

Kendra asks, "Do we know how much was because of the new Chromata-Care unit?"

"Our initial assessment is that it was close to twice as fast as the older model. The newer ultra-low frequency light available in the infrared spectrum in this model showed deeper penetration into the skin for the healing process and in areas where skin is thin on bone, we believe we saw expedited bone healing as well. It's amazing how we are learning to use light to heal the human body. The Chromata-Care Unit significantly reduces time for the healing process to complete. It's beyond remarkable and I'm glad our other unit failed us. This one is super powerful," replies Donna.

Al speaks up again, "Did you intend for Mark to jump off a cliff and damage himself as he did to test the healing processes?"

Donna responds, "No, Al. We did not. His fight-or-flight reaction under extreme circumstances had to be tested again to gauge how much of an impact it had on his physical body and systems. Remember, last time it was an overload of adrenaline that caused his heart arrythmia and near death, until we shut him down and gave his body enough time to relax."

"Right, but adrenaline doesn't come from your computer system. It comes from the adrenal glands that sit on top of the kidneys," Al asks, "So how does that impact your computer system? Did you shut down his kidneys last time? I don't remember that. Plus, as long as the body has the right hormones supplemented, then the body can continue living even without the brain. That's proven by us. So, did you shut down his kidneys? What did you do back then?"

"Let me get Jeff on the phone because I've explained it in the past, but I know I didn't do a great job of it, and I want you to have the most correct answer." She dials Jeff's number and puts him on speaker. Al asks his question again for Jeff.

"Right Al, here's how the process works. The amygdala, which we regulate as a brain service with software, pings the hypothalamus, which is another brain service we provide in times of stress. The hypothalamus then relays the alert to the sympathetic nervous system, and the signal continues to the adrenal glands, which then produces adrenaline. This is where all of Dr. Mike Stoddard's work comes in. If you remember, it was quite difficult to get the right sensory triggers into the physical body's sympathetic nervous system in order to trigger the adrenal glands. Dr. Mike worked out a sensory signal pattern similar to normal humans that worked, but it took a while. That was a true computer to the body blending there. The sympathetic nervous system is extra sensitive and can get blown out. He did great work on that one. So, shutting Mark down only meant shutting down specific services in his brain and letting the body relax again, free from inputs. That gave the kidneys and adrenal glands time to cool off and reset. When we restarted Mark, he was back to normal."

Al says, "What was the scenario driving the tests? What was his motivation?"

Donna speaks, "An imaginary and very aggressive Sasquatch. We programmed it to be in his mind only, but visually he thought he saw things."

"Are we to continue looking at Mark as an object and keep running these tests forever?" John asks. "When can he just start living? I mean, I've met him. Many members of the board have met him. He seems as real as real can be when he is operational. Some of his actions and words are a little robotic, but with his learning capabilities, why can't we just leave him on?"

Donna responds, "Well, we've had him operational for extended periods of time, but he goes down for physical upgrades and technical upgrades as well. Once we fixed the persistent pain in his lower spine, he mentions nothing about pain anymore. And we always want him to have the latest and greatest updates in his brain because he will advance faster and faster. One day, we won't have to turn him off."

Kendra asks, "Right, we keep talking about faster and faster advancement and we are using artificial intelligence to guide that advancement in his brain. Why is it taking so long to have him permanently operational?"

Donna asks, "What do you mean permanently operational?"

"I mean living a normal life again, having a family, going to church, throwing birthday parties? That's why we're here, right?"

Jeff sits quietly waiting for another tough question but is sensing where this is going and doesn't like it.

Donna says, "Well, I don't think a normal life is in the cards for Mark. He'll always be a research subject."

Kendra asks, "But what about his advancement? What if it evolves him beyond human capabilities? When does he get his rights back? He is human, after all."

Donna answers, "He isn't human, Kendra. He's a machine with flesh and bone, as we say around the office, and he is legally awarded to the Trust. We try to remind ourselves of that every day in our office. He can appear quite human."

"But that's my point," Kendra asks. "If he's advancing, one day he will declare the right himself because he is an intelligent being like us, and then what do we do?"

Donna jumps in before Jeff can say anything, knowing it's a touchy topic for him. She says, "I don't know, and we must be prepared to cross that bridge when we get there. That's a long time, though."

Jeff responds, "Yeah, I just want to add that something like Mark doesn't need rights. He is not human though he looks like one. Plus, as his intelligence grows, we need to control it in a way that's useful for scientific study and safe for the world at large."

Andrew asks, "What do you mean, safe for the world at large? And as his intelligence advances, doesn't his soul advance too?"

And there it was. The direction Jeff feared the most. Not because it was an excellent question, but because it was a popular question.

"He doesn't have a soul," replies Ted. "He's a machine. In the future, he might be mistaken for one of us. His soul left his body when the man he was, Brian Scott, died."

This talk about a souls and rights is irking Jeff, but he continues to listen.

Donna asks, "Jeff, can you clarify your safe remark for the board, please?"

He begins, "Yes, Ok. Let's say, supporting a very popular fear, that a far more intelligent entity than humankind takes over the world. Over time, because of humankind's egregious weaknesses and hypocrisies, it sets about eliminating humanity forever. Mark represents that in spades because he has a growing A.I. mind combined with the gift of human flesh and bone. That makes him unstoppable should his intelligence decide to end humanity."

Al says, "Well, I don't think he'd ever get to the level of ending humanity. Don't we have that moral center thing we rely on to contain and measure his outcomes against a strict moral code or something?"

"We do," says Jeff, "but he can change that if the situation is unprecedented enough. For example, look at our deteriorating planet. He may one day decide after decades of watching human-kind fail at saving the earth's ecology that earth's ecology is worth placing higher on the protection list for his own sake. Then what will happen? It's anyone's guess, but I can't imagine it being too good for us regular humans. He has an unprecedented ability to connect with every device on the planet if he wants. He can make every device as intelligent as possible and give it a mission. Then what do we do? I'd think we are toast at that point."

Andrew responds, "But what is intellectual growth without a soul to carry it on? The soul is a part of the body, right? Ghosts are souls, and you see their bodies as apparitions. What is life without a soul? Did you ever stop to think about that? And what if Brian's soul is still attached to his body? Did you ever consider his soul may not want this and wants to be at peace?"

Jeff says, "Well, I think if he was worried about his soul, Andrew, he would not have donated his body to science."

Andrew says, "Maybe he didn't know about his soul."

Jeff is getting irate at Andrews' insistence on questioning the soul. But he stays professional.

Donna says, "Ok, let's try to stick to questions we can answer. I think the entire world would love for science to find evidence of the soul, but that's not a project priority."

Andrew says, "You're right. I'm sorry for going down that rabbit hole, but I was thinking about how the data could spontaneously spawn. I was thinking if the soul could communicate through the new technology driving its physical body, then it might spawn random data to start the conversation."

Jeff says, "Ok Andrew. I'll concede that is an interesting spin on things, but there is no evidence for a soul. I like the potential for a soul's activity in your thinking, though. That's quite creative and smart. It even sounds like a cool movie plot."

The entire group laughed a little. Kendra laughed too. She then said, "Yeah, you should start a script. You might be on to something." She ended with a smile in his direction. This seemed to set Andrew at ease. He didn't want to pursue that, but he needed to know if the question was ever asked and what people thought of Mark being, well, Mark.

Jeff speaks up to let Donna know he can drop unless they have anything else. His irritation at the discussions about rights and souls wore on him. A.I. cannot have rights and humankind is not in the business of manufacturing souls. Leave that to God if he exists, thinks Jeff.

"But before you go, he's self-aware too, right? He's aware of who he is, his place in the world, what he is, what's going on and all, correct? We are first to achieve this, right?" asks Brian.

"No. he only appears to be self-aware. He knows who he is and what he is. Every time we reset him; he learns it again only because we tell it to him. He is just echoing what is in his universal data set about himself," says Jeff.

"But isn't that all that's required to be self-aware? It's circular. The machine looks within for the answer and delivers it. That's it at the lowest level, correct?" asks Brian.

"That could greatly extend this discussion, Brian. There are no real excellent tests for testing self-awareness in machines. Machines don't need to think like us. They can think in different ways. Here's what we need to do. If we believe we have a self-aware machine, then we should publish a paper explaining how we came to that conclusion and the tests we ran to confirm it. The problem is there just aren't any decisive tests. Right now, it's more of a 'feels-like' situation, and I don't want to take up the board's time with uncharted theory."

Donna asks if there are any more questions for Jeff. With no response, Donna let Jeff drop the call, and she continues with the board for another forty minutes of discussion. She later sends Jeff last notes on the discussion around 11pm.

Jeff sends everyone home for the evening and sits at his desk staring at a computer screen but not seeing it. He considers better counterarguments to the points made at the board meeting. Continually pacing the front of his office, his right hand flips a pen through his fingers. Muttering to himself, he falls into his chair. His irritation grows the longer he thinks about it. They should just drop all their ridiculous beliefs and listen to what he knows and make it policy. Jeff has worked for over twenty years now in A.I. engineering and has the knowledge. He has worked for several companies and held many endless conversations on A.I. theory and A.I. potential. The good it can do, and the destruction it can bring. He is more well versed than anyone he knows. He knows his job, and he knows code. That is well-proven. And he knows he is right. They should ask him to make the formal policy for the project, but they won't. These A.I. issues remain open-ended. Philosophers and theorists have failed their responsibility to this point. Does society lose anything by not addressing the big issues? It seems the answer is no. And that's as far as society's prognosticators survey. It's the same reason we don't have laws against time travel. No one can see that far, but a rare few like himself.

Later that night, Jeff receives Donna's message. It begins.

Here are the board's points:

1) Mark remains operational indefinitely except in emergencies like what he just experienced. They want to see how quickly his intelligence can grow now.

2) They want us to identify his shortfalls, where he seems to still be robotic and work on training and test strategies to improve and eliminate these robotic tendencies

3) They are forming a spin-off company to provide bio-engineering work under what Dr. Mike achieved. He will be the CEO and will transition to the position immediately but will stay in contact with Mark as well. He and his assistant grad student have written a couple of papers over the past two years that have garnered world-wide attention. His ideas will work wonders with the handicapped and wounded veterans' communities. As of tomorrow, his assistant, Antonio will be our primary daily point of contact from now on.

Finally, they want you to come up with the tests to prove self-awareness in machines and publish a paper on it talking about this project.

Jeff stands up and leans over his desk, holding himself up with both his arms. He huffs loudly once without even realizing it. He was not pleased with what he just read. There's big trouble in the future as Mark's intelligence grows. There is still the outstanding issue of spontaneous emergence of the data. And this awkward push to define self-awareness for the world before it's even been validated by the most recent experiments. What does self-awareness even look like? Too many questions to even consider writing a paper on it. This is bad news in his mind. His left hand runs rapidly through his thinning hair. He contemplates what he will do. Conform to the board's request or try to direct matters in a different direction with Donna's help.

Dallying down the hall with an unflinching gaze, he drops into a chair in the little kitchen area with the snack bar. His mind is full of the situation. Squeals from the chair's feet reverberate off the walls as he scoots himself in and the echoes race distances unheard, falling upon not a single ear. His ears don't hear them either. With head and face frozen in a stare, a slight air-conditioned flow sets in around his neck relaxing all those tense muscles into the coolness as he divides possibilities from conflations of outcomes. Either Mrs. Sherry or Tamika will be in around 1am to check on Mark. He thinks about the politics of the situation, and about Mark having rights and freedoms. Amazing gifts granted long before the M-Core is built up enough to ensure Mark won't act out against humanity at some point. Mark is too precious to have his self-preservation rules eliminated from the M-Core. Those rules ensure he makes the best decisions for himself during these tests they give him. Jeff realizes too much can happen before the M-Core and Mark are perfected. We've come too far to let it slip now. He has been searching for confidence, leading to what he knows he must do in this situation. One should never hesitate about it. In theory, he has always been confident in his conclusions when talking amongst peers. Now, in this situation, it doesn't seem so 'black and white' obvious. A few more minutes pass while contemplation clears a path to action.

Rising with a blank stare down the hall, will engages. It's dark. Only every fifth ceiling light is lit. He steps slowly while in thought. The hard part about turning himself around is finding cause to do so. Deep in his contemplations, his eye catches a fire extinguisher and a fire safety box up ahead just before the turn down the next hall to Mark's room. The safety box marks his spot. A

reflection is in the glass. It looks tired for sure. There's an old man in that glass with thinning, greying hair, and not the recent college graduate which should have been standing there. Struck by his reflection, he tries to justify it's not him. His mind won't linger, a realization for another time. Focus moves through the glass onto the meter long fire safety axe. He realizes he had picked up a napkin dispenser from the kitchen area and was holding it in his right hand. A double take of a look at the dispenser queues up how it's odd he walked so far only to just now notice it. A glance pauses to pierce the low light of the baron hallway.

Eyes drive to his reflection once more. He's not happy with what he sees. An older, fatter man than he thought he was. His mind mocks the fat man, and he smashes the glass with the napkin dispenser.

The axe handle feels cold but comfortable in his hand. Holding it now ignites admiration for its engineering simplicity. Light in one aspect, but heavy in another. Designed for swinging force. A thumb traces the edge and moves it down the blade. It is sharp but the edge is not allowed it to pierce the skin. Endgames race through imagination to endless outcomes. Two beings fight it out within him. One, a young and confident A.I. theorist who has held his theories solid for decades. The other, an older, wiser practitioner. More knowledgeable about life and his job than the other. He finds his feet stepping into the hall where Mark's room is located. It's almost as if he is simultaneously watching himself detached from his body and acting it out all at once.

Mark's door is open and appears to be awake. Jeff snaps into himself for a moment. He had not planned on Mark being awake so late.

Mark says, "Hello. I never caught your name earlier."

A momentary stunned response required his lips to say, "I'm Jeff."

"You look tired, Jeff," Mark says in a monotone voice. Mark can see what Jeff is carrying but doesn't know what it is. His baseline universal data set has not been restored because of the work the team is doing on it. He has no more new information than what he has gathered since waking. Mark's limbs remain tied down and will be for several more days as the healing completes.

Mark asks, "What are you carrying?"

Jeff realizes Mark doesn't have his universal data reinstalled yet. He sighs an inner sigh of relief. Mark is childlike for the moment and the near crippling pressure which has caused him to operate in a trance-like state drives him to seize upon this advantage like a lion upon feeble prey.

He responds, "Something to make you better."

Cool, cold, and calculated words of reassurance. Perfect in the moment. Divinely forked for Mark and Jeff alike.

Mark responds, "Oh good, I'm tired of being tied down. Anything to help would be good."

"Yes, I'm here to help."

Mark looks up at the ceiling, and Jeff lingers for a moment. His thoughts are all on Mark now. He senses his arm move in slow motion and he feels the weight of the axe swing behind his back as his left arm centers over his head and his hands join behind, preparing for a full-force swing. His eyes rest on a nice center position on Mark's skull. Just as he adds energy to the swing, Mark turns his head back to Jeff.

He says, "Thank you, Jeff, for making me better."

Jeff, caught in the act of a swing, suddenly loses all energy and freezes. He thinks, What? He's grateful? How can that be? Had he learned that today? Without his universal data set, this shouldn't even be a topic? How can he show gratefulness? Does he truly feel it or is he just saying it? How much information is he missing? It all seems uncoordinated now. He holds the swinging position, but the axe drops a little further behind his back and he lets out a breath in disbelief.

Mark speaks again, "Thank you for wanting to help."

Mark looks up at the ceiling and closes his eyes.

Moments pass and neither moves. With the axe cocked and ready, Jeff's disbelief locks the look on his face, and his thoughts race unabashedly. He wonders if Mark will feel grateful when he saves the ecology of planet earth by eliminating human beings. Has Jeff's mind gone too far?

Without a single further thought, the axe rises, lit by fluorescence from the two operational lights in the room. and it streaks toward its target with maximum force. Jeff's gut twinges and muscles are drowned in an overdose of adrenaline which spills its way into his brain. Energy, joy, and fright deliver a drunken concoction of determined emotions. The axe streaks through the air again writing the stories of its atrocities in red upon the walls and ceiling. Two more measured swings complete the climax and denouement. Staring at his resolution for only a moment, he considers if he needs to go further. Mark is a computer, and Jeff has leveled his judgement upon the computer that is Mark, who was Mr. Brian Scott long ago. A noble veteran who paid the ultimate price for his country and paid it again in this sadistic reanimation who is Mark. The axe cries a bloody trail of tears marking exit from this tomb of enlightened euthanasia. Guilt seems a million miles from these observations.

Breadcrumbs of droplets track down the next target as Jeff meters out in his mind how far he should go in totaling the consequences. Now, blankly staring at the servers, he thinks of Mark. He can't do it. Too much knowledge wiped away. Far too much gained knowledge to lose. It will be useful learning from this data. They stored all the pieces of Mark on separate servers and they're not operational there. The world is safe. He thinks Mark was amazing. Mark will never be forgotten, he hopes. A thud echoes down the hallway as the axe drops. A bloody smear on the floor is left behind after a small bounce. The handle slips from his fingers as they slightly toss it away from his thigh. Jeff leaves for home exhausted. He feels nothing other than mental and physical exhaustion. His mind will rapidly find peace when he falls into bed tonight and the burden of his theories will be released.

Later that morning, it's 7:33am, and he awakens to the sound of three police cars and a S.W.A.T. van. His fate, unlike Mark's, will eventually be in the hands of a jury.

2

Far Too Far Away

THERE'S DEFINITELY EXTRA ROOM in this spacesuit-looking thing I'm wearing. The next size down was just too tight. Smelling the air inside it relaxes me with a scent like Spring Air or something similar that makes laundry smell wonderful when hung out on the line to dry. It feels thick as well, which is comforting to know I won't be getting any easy punctures and tears for sure. It is the year 2192, and this is a decent suit for the money. There are better ones out there, but that's always the case, right? On the other hand, the quick paced planning and preparation before starting this mission gives me a queasy feeling in my stomach. I'm having major second thoughts about volunteering to go through the portal to help figure out what's going on with the time shift issue they've discovered. They've recently lost the ARIC-5 droid to 'who knows where,' or rather 'who knows when,' but with time travel they are learning they need to be saying 'who knows where and when?'

Humans discovered a second timeline four months ago and realized it's also a location! It was happening concurrently with our primary timeline, which we now call "Origin." We found the proof in a NewsNet login in the second timeline. Yong Je, a Chinese grad student attending M.I.T., was sent through the time portal, but someone did not input the proper PetaTAWs value for stretching the distance between the quantum parts of the atom. It was too low. In fact, the team later found it was on the brink of not being effective at all. Yeong Je would have gone nowhere. However, the quantum stretching of the atoms in the Time-Space Manipulation Machine, also called 'The TiMMs,' was just enough to get him into a different time. We thought it was on Origin time. Turns out, Yong Je was in a different timeline all together.

The clue was when Yong Je tried to login to his NewsNet feed. He had changed his password while at lunch only an hour before going through the portal. The original plan was to send him back in time three days, gather local and national news stories, and bring them back, as well as send himself a certified package by mail to arrive one day after his return. If successful, Yong Je would have returned with three-day-old news stories that were direct, perfect copies of news stories from our Origin timeline, and he would receive a package in our Origin timeline the next day after his return. However, after being sent back in time, he found his login into NewsNet ended up being the login he had just changed at lunch! The date was identical, meaning the date was the same day as the experiment's execution. It was clear he didn't go back three days in time. Rather, he traveled laterally in time, and the news stories he captured were different in small ways. After reviewing everything, it became clear the other timeline was closely tracking with our Origin timeline. In fact, the time on the clocks in the second timeline paralleled our Origin time. Yeong Je wore a wristwatch with our Origin time and when he returned, he confirmed the clocks were equal at least to the minute. Young Je had been sent to a 'same time, different location.' Theories abound. Repeating the experiment with Yong Je has not been tried again as it happened on accident four months ago. Sometime thereafter, we were told to call our current timeline Origin. Alternate timelines used to be theoretical since the time of Albert Einstein 280 years ago. Now we know they are real.

"Garret, be ready in about five or six minutes."

I'm Garret and that sounded like Wayne Temple. He's the mission coordinator, so to speak. Prior to discovery of a second timeline, he was just a basic analyst three years out of college. Now he's in charge of coordinating the start and stop of the mission.

"I'm ready. Just say when." I hear myself say it despite second guessing my decision to do this.

I look down the hall toward the TiMMs. It's about fifteen meters in front of me. I can see the radial pattern around the large block of lead at the center. The pattern looks like one of those old bi-plane engines from World War One. In fact, it could have been twelve cylinders in their own blocks around the lead core. One at each position of a clock. The lead core was where the propellers would have been, but of course, the propellers were absent. I see the irony here. The irony of the architecture in front of me used to take mankind from place to place geographically in an early model biplane, and now it takes mankind from time to time along a dedicated timeline. At least that's the goal.

My mission is to figure out what the researchers are calling the time shift issue. It started with what the team named the "Patio tests." Leadership decided the very first efforts to test and validate time travel would happen outside of the facility on the back patio. No one knew if altering a timeline would cause the building to disappear and the tests to fail, or a collapse of the entire timeline itself. It seems outrageous now. But the tests showed something shocking and remarkable that no one can explain. Something formerly impossible and they think the time shift issue has something to do with it, but what that could be is anybody's best guess right now.

The back patio is where people on breaks like to hang out on nice days and snack or share lunch time. Here's how the first 'Patio test' ran. First, they instructed all employees on the parameters of the experiment. The experiment begins three days before they send the time traveler back in time two days to the first day of the experiment. If employees see the time traveler place a brightly colored box on the back patio table anytime on the first day, they are to leave it alone until the end of the experiment. At the end of the first day, all employees are to sign a document saying whether they saw the time traveler place the box on the patio table. Two copies of this document will be made. One for management to keep and they will put all management copies in a safe until the end of the experiment. The other copy, which is to be the copy of the original signed document, is to be handed to the employee. Next, the employee will walk four meters across the room in front of everyone in the room and hand their copy of the signed document to one human resources person who will place that copy into a second separate safe. We will sign and place the documents into their respective safes in the security office at 5pm on the first day. Three witnesses will sign a document saying every employee did the same thing and the original handwritten documents and their original single copies are in separate safes to be monitored until the end of the experiment.

Second, there will be four cameras recording the back patio for three straight days. Someone will watch the security office during that time to ensure no one touches the videos streams or alters the cameras for the three days. This way, all four cameras will capture the same information in their recorded streams.

Third, on the third day of the experiment, a human volunteer is to go back in time two days and place the brightly colored box on the back patio table and leave it there. The four cameras in our Origin timeline will not stop. The third camera will be affected by the time travel tests at the point where the time traveler is back in time and has already completed placing the box on the patio. When he goes to the video room, he will take the recording from camera-3 offline and bring it back with him. He will then come back through the portal with only himself and the recorded stream from camera-3. Now that he's back in our Origin timeline, he will then go to the security office and press stop on camera-4 only and touch nothing else. No one is to do any of these tasks for him. The entire process will only take about five to ten minutes walking through the portal, placing the box, getting the camera stream, coming back through the portal and turning off camera four. Once camera-4 is turned off by the time traveler, that is the end of the experiment. Witnesses standing watch over the security office on day three will attest to the events and sign a document saying such.

The generally agreed hypothesis was to have the following outcomes. First, at the end of the experiment, all four cameras in our Origin timeline should have shown no signs of time travel because they had completed their recordings before the time travel event. Second, if we find camera-3's video stream is suddenly missing on day one, then we know he went back in time on the Origin timeline. Otherwise, if it is present and he brings back a camera-3 video stream, then we know he went to an alternate timeline. That stream will then be labeled camera-3B. This means we now have five video streams to review and compare. Camera-3B should show the time traveler in this experiment performing his task on the back patio in the alternate timeline. That would have been a spotless experiment.

Instead, the result was wildly different and shocking. He brought back camera-3's video stream, noted there was no one in the security office or standing guard, and the one on our Origin timeline did not vanish on day one. So, he clearly traveled to an alternate time-line, and we indeed had a fifth video stream to review. Cameras one, two, and three from our Origin time showed precisely what they should. No time travel event. Camera-3B from the alternate timeline showed the time traveler, Jamison Wright in this case, placing the colorful box on the patio table. It also showed two of the employees off to the side of the shot talking amongst themselves. They were Don and Earnest. Earnest was just putting out a cigarette when he motioned with his head to Don to turn and watch Jamison put the box on the patio table. Jamison raised his hand in hello to the two who were watching him. They both raised their hand in hello and Jamison walked off to the next part of his task. That's all that was on Camera-3B as it should have been.

Camera 4 from our Origin timeline should have showed nothing, but it showed the same thing as Camera-3B! When everyone saw this, the place erupted in disbelief. Jamison, the time traveler, had touched the camera feed in our Origin timeline to turn it off and had somehow transferred his own historical account of his actions and time from the alternate timeline automatically to the camera stream. It appeared as if actions taken in a different timeline had manipulated our timeline! But only if the time traveler had directly interacted with a person or object in both timelines. But that's not all. Upon a closer investigation, it turns out that camera 4 video was just like camera-3B's video, but five seconds delayed on the timer! This is the time shift issue.

It gets far crazier than this. At the end of days one and two, management asked everyone in the larger group setting to raise their hand if they saw the time traveler perform any actions on the back patio. No one raised their hands. And everyone agreed no one raised their hand. Management asked the same question at the end of the workday on day three before we opened the safes at the conclusion of the experiment. Ernest and Don raised their hands and said they had seen the time traveler, Jamison Wright, before lunch that day place the colorful box on the back patio table. The whole place erupted in chatter and disbelief. This was indeed the Ernest and Don from our Origin timeline. How could they have seen the time traveler? It appears just the presence of Jamison, having communicated with Don and Ernest in the alternate timeline, brought back information into our Origin timeline that changed the memories of the Don and Ernest in our timeline! Would they have this memory if Jamison never returned to the Origin timeline? The theory is no, they would not. Jamison would somehow have had to bring that information back with him. Someone immediately identified this as the Mandella effect, which started a very heated debate and needed to be brought under control immediately.

The crowd cooled but the air hummed uninterrupted as whispers and words flew about. Somehow the camera video streams and memories of people in our Origin timeline were altered, but only if they interacted with the time traveler in the alternate timeline and only after the time traveler returned! And the same for the recording on camera four for no other reason than because the time traveler had touched it! Again, he had not touched cameras one and two and he did not appear in those streams. However, when asked openly in the meeting, he responded he did shake hands with Don and Ernest after returning, so they remember him because he brought that information back with him and somehow it transferred to human memory. Talk about insanity!

Jamison was asked to shake hands with the security people in the security office and a few other employees to see if any information was transferred to them as well. No one he touched received any information about him from earlier during the test. He had not interacted with any of them while in the alternate timeline. He was then asked to turn off camera two's video feed after several witnesses reviewed what was on the feed before he touched it. Prior to Jamison turning off camera two's feed, there was nothing on the video happening on the back patio during the time of the test. After it was turned off, security personnel turned it back on again and everyone reviewed the video feed, which to everyone's astonishment had a record of Jamison setting the pretty box on the patio table and waving to Don and Ernest! These findings are cosmic and quantum game changers.

One last point to reiterate and the entire purpose of my test today is the following. The time on Camera-2 and Camera-4 from our Origin timeline was 10:52:01am when Jamison first appears in the screen. On Camera-3B, the one from the alternate timeline, the time is 10:51:56am. That's a five second difference. My mission is to find out if the five second difference is truly an anomaly or not and maybe in the process, we can figure out why Jamison's touching of the Camera-2 and Camera-4 feeds in Origin time did not revert their times back five seconds on the recordings. What is going on with that? No one has a grand theory for that, however, one stands out. It may be that time is really only humanity's way of keeping everything from happening all at once, but this idea pushes the theoretical to near incomprehensibility. The idea is to tackle one problem at a time for each new experiment. My job is to take a timer which has been synchronized to the security system's server time in our Origin timeline and verify it against the security server's system time in the alternate timeline.

The major concern about this test is there is no guarantee what is going on in the alternate timeline. Are they also finding success in time travel or are they doing other experiments? Jamison may have just gotten lucky walking around like he did. That's why I have to be wearing this space suit looking thing. I have to be very convincing that I'm from another place and time and this is the most extreme way to show the message. After all, who walks around in a space suit unless they are a part of some sort of wild scientific experiment? I also have a message from my management about my purpose if I'm questioned and held up. It contains alternate plans for my return as well.

"OK Garret, starting the TiMMs."

"Ready as I'll ever be, I guess." I hear the machine turn on. It sounds like a refrigerator kicking on. Then there is a low background hum that grows in intensity but never becomes too loud. The air shakes and your eyeballs along with it making the machine appear to be vibrating, but it's just you. The vibrations blur the details of the machine. An energy field is being created by pulling apart but not tearing apart the quantum pieces of each atom of lead in the lead block by a waveform called a TAW. I mentioned PetaTAWs earlier. TAW is a scrambled acronym for Atomic Tensor Waveform. It focuses on pulling apart the particles associated with the strong force of the atom. The incredible result is another counterforce that was completely new to science this century. They call it the Disruptive Strong Force of the Atom. Only recently did science discover it strongly disrupts gravity and time-space as well. Current research is seeking to identify this force in anti-matter. The theory is since anti-matter possesses magnificent quantities of energy then perhaps we can better harness that energy by releasing it slower using Atomic Tensor Waveforms. If this theory holds, it may be possible to manufacture anti-matter and use it for energy with an efficiency greater than three decimals beyond ninety-nine percent.

On the floor, there are thin diagonal lines two centimeters wide and thirty centimeters apart running parallel to each other. When the machine is running at full capacity, you cannot see a field of force in front of you or a portal. Only scientific instruments can tell you it's there. But visually the diagonal lines will appear to break at a point like when you put a straw in a glass of water. It will bend because of refraction of the light and look like it's going in a different direction. Here the lines break on the floor and on the other side of the portal's energy field they shift a couple of centimeters. The portal itself lines up with the hallway. Therefore, you know when you are inside the TiMMs field when you step across the shift in the diagonal lines.

Suddenly, the lines break, and I know the TiMMs field has formed.

"Alright Garret. It's thunderstorms outside tonight but where you're going, it's nice and sunny three days ago. We are ready when you are."

"Alright. Time to shine. I'm heading in!"

I move forward slowly. And right then I get the biggest kaleidoscope of butterflies in my stomach. Another sense is telling me to turn around. I should have listened years ago when I was a kid before I broke my leg. Now it's telling me this team doesn't really understand time travel as much as they think they do, and they might be sending me to another time. I hope it's three days ago. They seemed to pull it off for Yong Je and Jamison. Third times a charm, right? This entire mission should only take five to ten minutes. The only difference is this time they are shutting down the portal and reengaging it with the same parameters after a five-minute shut down. I'll go perform my mission on the back patio and come back. If the lines on the floor aren't broken, I'm supposed to wait up to an hour before contacting anyone from three days ago to let them know the experiment they are going to try in three days will fail. Then they will have to figure out what to do with two of me in the same Origin timeline. Young Je and Jamison just avoided where they knew each other would be. If this fails, I won't have the same luxury. I wonder what mom would do knowing there were two of me.

My right foot moves across the broken line segments first, and I look down. It looks like a straw in water, almost! I don't feel anything different. My foot is visually segmented away from my lower leg. Kind of Cool. I'm not bleeding out at least, so with one deep breath, I cross the broken line on the floor.

"Where the hell am I? This ain't the damn hallway or back patio or any place I've seen! Oh, my God! Is that a flock of Pteranodons? What the holy shit is this? I'm out of here!"

I turn around to step right back into that portal with my eyes down, looking for any shift in the ground that would show the edge of the portal. I can't see it, but I'll step through, regardless. So, I keep stepping and quickly so, but my mind reminds me I only took two or three steps through the portal and ended up here. I've walked way past where the portal entrance should be. So, I do another perfect one hundred eighty degree turn and step lively back to where I started, knowing I'm going to step through a portal I don't see. Damn it! Why can't I see it? I'm back at my starting spot.

The squawks and haunting calls of a hungry hoard ride in on the wind from afar. Was it the Pteranodons? My eyes squint forward to keep my nerves at bay and my breath steady. I can't believe my freaking eyes! There's like two hundred or more of those Pteranodon looking things flying around, but they are doing something remarkable. They are lining up in a ghoulish train four or five Pteranodons wide as they scream through the air, forming a devilish loop over a rolling ocean. At the low end of the loop, their pointy, ancient edges swoop down and glide mere centimeters off the top of the tumultuous feast. They quickly jab their dagger-like heads into the boil and seize a fish or two and yank their head out of the water. Rearing upwards, they flap their way to the top of the black loop, all while downing their lusty catch in a flurry to make another whip around the ring of feasts. Every single ghoul's unslakeable hunger fractionally abated, and the macabre ring of death slowly measures its way across the horizon chasing the ill-fated churning escapes of their prey. The water boils with a teamwork of hunger. First one, then another, swipe after ravenous swipe, bringing forth a froth of white and red upon the rolling surface. The archaic and ghastly fliers lending only to the gruesome imagination of what slides through the dark deep.

I stop to take in my surroundings. My heart beating so hard my vision shakes up aberrations that don't exist. False hopes of anything positive in my near future. My mind is filtering for a real aberration. I'm not seeing it, but I am noticing the landscape and a lot of sounds. There are a bunch of sounds. I'm on a long, sloping grade of a grassy hill not too far from the ocean. The plants and grasses around me are pretty large. Some are taller than me, but nothing that blocks my view. With my visor up, the air has a sweet, flowery smell and the ocean scents occasionally weave their vapors in on a light and exacting breeze.

Grunting and huffing sounds taunt my vision left. Flashes of brilliant orange among the tall grasses. It's a freaking living dinosaur! But nothing like what I have seen in the movies. This one is soft and fluffy and colorful! Above its midline, I can only see its side. I can almost catch a head now and then. I think there's a small group of them about thirty-five meters (115 ft) away and they're feasting. They aren't huge, from what I can tell. At the hips, they are smaller than me, and are definitely the two footed kind. The flashes of orange and brown swishing through grasses signals quite the flurry of activity there. I want to get closer. My memory steals my inertia. What do I do? The portal was supposed to close behind me and, timewise, it was supposed to reappear and stay open until I completed the task on the back patio. Maybe it will reappear in a minute. I decide to stay in place because first looks around here; I don't want to get lost in a wander.

The ocean wind presses my chest. This suit is an environment unto itself. I see toward the bottom of the slope, off to my right, a large, sandy area with thick bushy trees filling the spot and tall grasses here and there. The trees covering patchworks of sandy terrain are only about seven or eight meters tall. Flowers pop white upon the bushy green like fresh popcorn thrown upon them. Beyond the patchwork lies a sandy, rocky break and then a darkened, hazy forest tree line conquers the remaining view.

I turn and the ocean wind pushes my back like a child wanting me to walk uphill at its guidance. If it guided me forward another eighty meters, I'd crest a rounded grassy top with boulders jutting out. I pull my vision back in closer to me and begin looking for any clue to the portal. Since arriving, I have not traveled over two feet. I'm at the spot I landed. I'm looking up and down and circling in a small circle. Nothing. I think what the plan was. The backup plan was to reengage the portal one hour after arriving if something were to go wrong. Well, then I have an hour to wait.

Suddenly, my muscles tense and my breathing shivers. I realize I'm back in the time of the dinosaurs and this isn't just a momentary blip where I can jump back into the portal and be home to tell everyone what I just experienced. This is for real! I will not make it one hour if dinosaurs are anything like the movies. Shaking a little, I question why I have to sit down quietly right here and wait an hour? There are dinosaurs feeding about twenty meters (65 ft) away. They aren't big ones but there's a few of them and they are noisy. Isn't that going to attract attention? The noise and the smell of blood? Like when hyenas on the African savanna catch a meal, don't the big bad lions come running over to steal it away from them? So, what's big and bad around here? The Pteranodons are fish eaters apparently, and their bellies are getting full.

I think hard about the situation. When I was a kid up to my early teens, I was a bit of a dinosaur geek, but I dropped it because chicks don't like dinos that much. I'm trying to remember the popular dinosaurs and what ages they lived in. I know lots of off-beat dinosaurs too. It's just been a long time. I often catch new dino discoveries on the link, though I'm not as 'hard core' interested in them as I used to be. As I sit quietly, I am again tuned into all the surrounding sounds. There are an awful lot of them for sure. This place is lively. Many are far away, but a few are uncomfortably close. Who knew dinos talked so much? It's like kids in a school lunchroom here. A dull roar that never abates. Wow!

The sun is high. I'm not sure if it's late morning or early afternoon. It was a little after 10am when we turned on the portal. I haven't been here a solid fifteen minutes. Since I'm waiting, I'm going to run through dinos in my head and see if I can remember their names and the age in which they lived. I remember dinosaurs looking very simple with basic body forms in the late Triassic. From there, they grew ever larger and ever more unique until their last day. That's super broad but helps me categorize the ones I don't remember well. I'll look around for other dinos and see if I can identify them. My watch says 10:16am. When the portal reopens at 11:00am, I will slip back in. This shouldn't be an issue because I'm right where I started.

I'm deep in thought about my situation when I hear a hard huff behind me and a slight push on my helmet. It had better be someone from the lab. My helmet only allows me to see a part of the way. Being seated, I can't turn all the way around. I want to get up but decide to switch on my rear camera. I look up at the display and am frozen in fear. It's a freaking dino sniffing me! I don't move. The camera distorts its nose as it comes in to sniff me again. Another huff and another push! A carnivore by the teeth. A fast assessment tells me it's a small dino. Shorter than me. I do something crazy. I slowly rotate my body as I'm sitting on the ground so I can see my aggressor. As I turn, I see it has raised its head and is looking down at me with one eye. It's not that big at all. Clearly, it was enjoying itself with the meal a few meters away. It's maybe 1.4 meters tall (5 ft) at most at the hip and just under 3 meters (9 ft) long. It's gorgeous! There's no leathery skin at all! It's covered in what I assume to be primitive feathers because it looks like a baby duck's feathers or a baby chicken's feathers. It's covered like a cassowary or an emu! And it's a fabulous, bright orange color with dark brown stripes down its side to its midline! Of course, I'm noticing the blood on its face from its meal, but I'm taken by the sight. The bright orange feathers form a beautiful arching mohawk from the widow's peak on its head down to the upper part of the neck. Its face is beautiful, feather-free, pale brown with a magnificent, bright yellow, thick lower eyelid. There is a dark brown stripe that runs from near the nose to just under the lower eyelid to the feather line near the jawbone. This thing looks like something stuffed you'd win at a theme park; not something that would eat your face off.

The feet are three-toed and scaly like a hawk with the fourth inner-most toe's claw pulled up. That claw is giant, and I can tell it's used for ripping prey apart. The three-fingered front limbs are covered in the same primitive feathers. They look so much like thick hair. There are "Feather-like-hairs" all over its body. I'm going to call them 'flairs' because I don't know the scientific name for this form of feather. It's my portmanteau for "feather-like-hairs." I'm not even sure science has figured this out yet. It resembles down on baby birds, but each one is larger and thicker. Various flairs on the lower front edge of its forearms look like feathers. It's a mix of both.

It takes a step back but hasn't made a sound yet. It keeps turning its head like a bird looking at me and occasionally I see it glancing back down the slope, probably to where the others are. I get a square on view of its body looking at it from the front. It's narrow from head to waist but the thighs on this creature are its reason for living. The thighs jut out in thickness and erupt with rippling muscles. Mother Nature designed this dino to move at high rates of speed. I wonder how fast it can go in an all-out sprint. Its thin chest tells me it's not designed for incredible endurance. It's too thin. This one is all about top end speed over a manageable distance. Given its size, it probably uses teamwork in the process too in order to increase chances of a meal. My bet is its buddies are just down below us and they all went in on lunch together. Just then it jets off back down the slope. It happened so fast I couldn't catch the details on the tail, but it seemed some feathers and flairs fanned out to sides right at the end of the tail. There were small flairs on the top ridge of the tail only and they were the same brilliant orange.

I sit and wait and listen. I watch the skies for any other type of flying creature. My position tensely huddled next to and partly under a broad leaf plant keeps me from being noticed. It's 11am by my watch now and I wait. I scan the beachy ground and everything around me. Five minutes go by, then ten, then twenty. My unrelenting nerves raise a sweat. This suit's tiny climate management options strain for equilibrium. I'm positive the team doesn't know where or when I am in time. I stay put abiding by fate's declaration of my inevitable doom here in the time of dinosaurs. The surrounding sounds come and go. Instincts intercede my will to move.

It's now 1:05pm by my watch. I kept convincing myself to stay, hoping beyond hope at this point the portal would reappear. Now I need to use the restroom and I need to remove the suit to do that. This ought to be interesting. Since I'm well protected and unseen next to this plant, I complete my task and decide I need to look for better shelter. The sun's time is about two or three hours in front of my watch. I need to get moving. I stand up and start walking. There's nothing toward the ocean, so I start by heading straight up the hill. It's pretty hot today and the sounds have quieted down a bit. Maybe nap time for dinos? At the top of the hill, it's a large grassy plain with tall grasses. Before I venture in, I look over to the right and I see another small rise of about six or seven meters in height before it goes back down again. Since I don't see any dinos over there, I head in that direction.

There's nothing flying overhead that looks like a bird and the Pteranodons flew off in one direction an hour ago. This tells me birds haven't evolved yet and flying dinos are just getting started. I'm probably in the mid to late Cretaceous period. I have seen no super large dinosaurs from my vantage point yet either, but I'm blocked by forests inland from here. This hill crests just below the highest canopy, so the biggest trees viewed from this distance are beyond huge.

At my destination, I look up about two and a half meters and I see a concave cutout into the formation. It's not deep and I fit myself in. This isn't enough for protection, but it's close. I grab a loose rock that has one flattened edge and I dig out a horizontal shelf a little further into the concavity. It's useful to keep my suit on because it's powered by nuclear nano-diamond technology. Its nickname is, "The Brick." The brick is layer upon layer of nuclear nano-diamonds and doped graphene collectors generating electricity via beta decay of the nuclear waste. It's a nuclear-powered DC generator with no moving parts and a half-life of twenty-eight thousand years. The suit's brick can power many low energy consuming devices, including the suit heating and cooling system, which is all I'm using it for now other than to keep the comms system on. The brick is useful to society in another way because it turns previously unusable nuclear waste into a constant stream of electricity. There's no risk of exposure to nuclear radiation because it contains just the right amount of diamond shielding.

As I work, the shroud and deceit of darkness inks its way stealthily around me and there are new calls coming from afar in the forest. Declarations firing up as twilight gives into night. The sounds erupt with vocal intent, more so than the day at first. Then, within an hour, it calms down. I can hear night insects making all kinds of weird noises. Whatever is in the tall grasses near me is very noisy and is having a party with about a thousand of its best friends. Exhaustion blankets my hands, arms, back, and mind. Dehydration cuts deep with its steely knife. The noise becomes white noise. As I fall to sleep in my new cutout on my first night, my body screams getting to drinkable water is my priority in the morning.

I've been laying here with my eyes open for maybe forty minutes watching the purple haze turn to fabulous red, orange, and yellow along the skyline. The morning sky could be my timeline. It's eternal and fills me with hope for a return home. The paste is my mouth is as thick as glue. I slept in my suit with my helmet on as well. Some strange insects or creature may want to climb up and bite me while I sleep. I squeeze out of my cutout in the hill and sit down right in front of it. I take off my helmet and feel a cool breeze coming up the hill from the coast. It's refreshing. I undo my suit top and pull off my boots and bottoms. Airing out feels something like a newfound luxury. I see small drops of dew on everything. It reminds me, I'm thirsty, and this needs to be remedied in a life-or-death way. I rub my hands over small grasses near me. The water sticks to my aching hands, and I lick them for relief. It's not enough and ridiculous at that. I've only seen salt water since I've been here. I also need to figure out what I can eat around here. While airing out, I make my plan.

I suit up and wade my way through the tall grasses and shrubs to the bottom of the hill. I'm on the edge of a hard sand, rock, and dirt clearing about sixty meters wide before the edge of the forest. My eyes catch all kinds of dino footprints in it. Two sets of prints terrify me. I ran into large dinosaur droppings along the way in the grasses. The smell permeated everything. It wasn't plant eater dung. In it was a thighbone of some poor creature. That means meat eater and one of good size, I'm guessing. It must have traversed up the hill in the past several hours. I heard nothing walking round. Gladly, we just missed each other.

Now I know I need to rethink my travels. If these meat eaters are territorial, I know I will not last very long. Optimism escapes me. This isn't a Hollywood film and serendipity has never been a friend to me. I get a goofy idea. Grabbing these tall grasses, I will carry them upright in front of me. I'm going to look like grass moving across the ground. Do you think big meat eaters are curious enough to check me out if they see me? I'm grass right? They've seen that before. Not on their menu! Ok, so it's more genius than goofy. I know! I often have my moments of inspiration like this.

The fibrous stalks of the large grasses wore on my aching hands. Needing help tearing them, I grab a small multi-tool inside my suit but decided I'll only use that for emergencies. I don't want to wear out the three-inch blade it has. I may need it for something far more important later. I used the sharp edge of a nearby rock and now I have a large bundle of grasses tied up. It's about twenty kilograms in weight. It's bearable for me, so off I go across the clearing, though slowly at first. I stop every few feet to look around for any danger or inadvertent attention. Once I noticed about a dozen small dinos near the top of the forest tree line jump and glide their way toward another tree deeper in the forest. I didn't see how far, but they glided as opposed to flew for sure. And they looked like they had actual feathers on their tails and outer wings.

The chits, chatters, songs, and gripes of dinos in the trees ring through the forest's misty morning landscape. A smile runs through my cheeks, remembering of early mornings back home when the birds sing as dusk breaks, and I would rise for the workday. I see them high on limbs and trunks. Their ancient forms shaded by dense top-cover. They are everywhere and highly social. They hang out in large groups. If they are like birds of my time, I'm betting they'll squawk and scatter in the presence of larger dangers. A sunny ray catches a spectacular display of yellow and black plumage near a break in the canopy. I'm mesmerized by its brilliance.

Great spaces live between trees in this era, and canopies are magnificent. Undergrowth does not compete in height with the local giants. It is a world under a world in here. The mightiest of giants are far taller and thicker than I know. I've seen the great Sequoia, and some of these are its bigger brothers. The grasses I carry in disguise work awkwardly by now, but these aren't the smartest creatures, either. I take little solace in my intelligence here, though; I'm keeping my disguise for now. The surrounding greenery is ferns, vines, thorns, or broad-leafed plants trying to capture as much sun as possible. Swift, small steps and quietness propel me through the spaces between trees. My quest is water and food and everything around me has distracted me, and my mood is high. The beauty and grandeur of this place lifts me. I do not know where I'm going or where I am, but I'm just passing a large rock formation about five meters high. Its closest edge is pointy at the top and is pointing the way I came, so I can use this later. I shall call it "Compass Rock," and this is my new kingdom.

There's running water in the distance. If it is a grand river, I shall name it The Llyr River, after the Welsh goddess of water. My kingdom shall be like unto the great King Arthur! And the hill of my cutout shall be my castle! This is Camelot now. I quick step toward the call of a light rippling fall. Just what I'm here for! But halt! I tremble on instinct as my eyes befall dragons in my kingdom. Two large meat eaters. These will need to be vanquished. Fantasy be damned, reality dictates not moving until these killers are gone.

I think it's an Acrocanthosaurus. I remember that one clearly because it was an early, large meat eater. It's a wild guess though because all the thin, wispy feathers make it look so different! It's a male and female pair. Just like birds, the female has subdued colors that would camouflage well in her surroundings when nesting. She has a modeled tan and black coat of flairs all over down to her midline. Her belly and chest have smaller, white flairs. In the old drawings, Acrocanthosaurus had knobby buttons at the top edge of its face going from over the eye to near the nose on both sides of its head. Those are flattened, arching feathers that start small at the nose and grow longer until it gets over the eye where they are the longest and droop a little at the end of their arch. Hers are solid black and so are his. She also has a comb like a chicken. The striking difference in the face is his is a hue of blue with a flat, blue, bulbous comb and wattles. His forearms are covered in a rich black coat of flairs and the flairs that go down his spine alternate from black and iridescent blue at the head to a subdued blue toward the tail. He also has a belly and chest of smaller white flairs and the rest of him is a dark brownish black. There's hardly a bare spot on them except their feet and face and the underneath of the tail.

Anyway, if it's Acrocanthosaurus, I'm in the early Cretaceous most likely. That would make that beautiful orange dino I saw yesterday, possibly Deinonychus. The predecessor to Velociraptor. As close as I was before I saw them, I'm surprised I didn't hear them walking around near the water. There is so much to take in and I didn't bring my helmet today. My thirst is ever growing and I'm feeling hunger pains now as well. I need to figure this out, and quick.

Danger gone. I sneak toward the water's edge. A little further upstream is the cascading of water I heard earlier. I want to get up into one of the cascade levels. There seems to be a way up and around on my side if I cut back into the forest.

Quest accomplished. I made it despite my backside being uncamouflaged. I saw a weird plant on my way. It's nothing like I've ever seen before. I think I'll check it out on the way back. I also saw a pair of Oviraptors. Definitely nothing to be afraid of, as they were small. I'm guessing it was two females. They look like malformed turkeys and the coloring was about the same, though the ends of their tails were true tail feathers brown and white striped. I hear a multitude more calls all around me. Most of the dinos I believe I hear are smaller than me or no bigger than my size. Here in the forest, they love to chatter.

The cascades trickle softly on the far side of the stream. The water is slow and clear. I can see the water plants below and there is something resembling cattails up a little further. That could be good news. My body screams from the two-day heat. I have no choice but to drink. My camo lumps in freefall to the side, and I throw my two hands together into what will be my salvation or death. The coolness whisks the heat away, giving rebirth to my lips and throat. Feeling flesh newly hydrated, refreshing, and full of energy, I fear what I might have ingested. But I consume with abandon. I slurp and gulp and splash my hands into the water and up like a conveyor of cups. I'm loud and I don't care. At the edge of the stream, I could be a dino. I care not about the consequences of the amplitude of my undertaking. I may die by water or by tooth and claw, but this replenishment is my rejoicing.

Filled to near bursting, I lay back and pull my grass camo over me. I'm completely covered as I look up through the canopy at the midday sun. It's peaceful. I pretend the dino sounds are just the birds of Camelot. I fall into full relaxation. And I, King Garret the First, foolishly drift into the spell cast upon me.

Nearby rustling throws my eyes open. I can't believe I fell asleep! How stupid! And I know I snore when I'm lying on my back! That should be a pretty scary sound, I'm thinking. Maybe it worked to my advantage. Ha-ha! Wouldn't that be a laugh! My only weapon to keep me safe in dino country is my snoring! Then I think for the wrong dino, though, it would be a dinner bell. Then who's laughing. Sounds are close to my right, and I see the biggest snapping turtle on planet Earth! His shell is at least two meters across! Nose to tail, it is at least three meters or more! It's making its way back into the water. What? One of those could be in there right now besides this one. The stream seems too small, but it slips under the water with more than enough space to the other side. I quickly pull the sleeve off my suit. It has a survival capability built into the attachment points and the wrists and ankles. At those points, it seals tightly enough to hold air or water in place. I seal the wrist and fill it with water. It's perfect for holding water because it's lined with silver microspheres throughout which silver is not friendly to bacteria and fungus and keeps the water just as fresh as the wearer. As I leave, I make my way up further toward the cattail like reeds. I remember from my survivability training in the reserves that cattails are an incredibly nutrient rich source of food and even contain a gooey salve that is a superior healing agent. I'm hoping these plants are related to cattails.

My disguise is now a hefty burden. I stuff the cattails in with the grasses and re-fix the ties for the grassy bundle. Clipping my sleeve onto my belt, I head back the way I came. I want to stop at that weird plant and check it out again. The sun has shifted a couple of hours. My nap held me spellbound for maybe two hours. There's still plenty of time to get back to my cutout castle.

There's the plant. It's crazy huge! It lays flat on the ground with large leaves on its outer edges. Coming down from the cascades, I glimpsed its overall shape and size. It's something like a sunflower lying flat on the ground looking up. The center is three meters across and is encircled by a large, bulbous ring that looks something like a light brown and off-white blow-up kiddy pool. In the center is a lump of plant material, but it smells a little rotten. I didn't catch the smell before because I wasn't close enough, but at a distance of about one to two meters, you can smell it. I look closer at the center part and see it's filled with water or some other substance. There are leaves floating on the surface and twigs thereabout, along with a multitude of insects, and then I notice it. A small dead dino. I thought it was part of the large lump in the center, but the center is definitely plant material that resembles a dead dinosaur on its side. This little dino died inside the plant! I realized I better not touch the clear liquid inside the plant given the number of dead insects and the fact it seems to have trapped and killed a small dino. It may be a neurotoxin. This thing is basically a fly catcher for small dinosaurs. They get attracted to the scent of a recent kill. They see the belly of something dead lying in the center. Quick and hungry, they hop inside to enjoy a meal and become the meal! The toxin may not be enough to kill a large dino, but a small one would probably succumb in a few minutes. No sense sticking around here anymore as this place draws attention.

Back at Compass Rock, I stop for a moment. My camo weighs on my efforts. Rest is required. I have water in my sleeve and a potential food supply from the cattail-like reeds and maybe an antibiotic if I'm lucky. I have work to do once I return to Camelot.

As I make my way out of the forest line, I'm drawn back in by movement out of my right eye and the sound of rhythmic chirping and knocking. I shuffle up the tree line a few meters to a large tree. With my back to the tree, as is my standard practice, I make my way around the trunk, which must be a solid five meters around and has large roots driving into the ground. And there in front of me is a spectacle I could hardly believe. I see two small birdlike dinos about eight meters away. One is clearly a male, and the other is the female, and the male is doing a little dance on the ground while the female is watching. I think he's trying to convince her to mate. Girls!

The plumage on his head, neck, chest, and forearms is pitch black. You could say iridescent black even as the slightest glint of sunlight shining from it is a deep purple. He's facing the female with his arms stretched out before him and he hides his head for a moment in his outstretched arms and shakes the end of his forearms while making a rapid chirping sound. Then he pops his head up just enough to show her one of his eyes, which is a striking bright blue. He flashes his eye at her quickly, then hides his head again. He repeats the chirps and motion again and again, switching eyes all while bobbing his body up and down in place. I'm starstruck. It's incredibly beautiful! What dino is this? The answer, I'll never know. I set my grasses down slowly against the trunk. I don't want to stand out in the forest without my camo, so I also hug the trunk with my arms after checking for insects and watch the rest of the dance. How could she not be turned on by this display? She seems mesmerized.

Then the next part of the dance starts. He lowers his arms and head and, with them in the same position, he pulls his tail up over his head to hide his entire head and most of his arms. The bottom of his tail is a stunning iridescent emerald green! It looks like a brilliantly colored fan shaking over his head. Then he pops his head up above his arms and flashes his blue eye for a blink at the female before the tail covers it, shaking the whole time. Then he moves his head left and flashes his other blue eye at her and immediately covers it with his brilliant, shaking tail. This happens in rapid succession all while he alternates hopping two steps back and chirping and knocking the whole time. If the female doesn't take the signal to step forward and follow him, he hops forward to his last spot and repeats the movements. The female follows him. There's a large plant with thick leaves and white flowers in the direction he's hopping, and it looks like he has built part of a nest, or some entrance wrapped in leaves next to that flowering plant. It's probably where the deed will happen.

Just then I feel a hot breath on my left hand and something pushing against it. I almost say something as I yank my head around. I see my immediate death in the making. A large female meat-eating dinosaur I haven't seen before has just pressed her mouth against my hand to test it. My eyes meet her eye. She is an arm's length away from me, but her body is on the opposite side of the tree. Hugging tight to the tree, I hoped she didn't see me, but she huffs and takes a step to get around the tree to me. I can't grab my grasses. She is almost right on them, so I slide to the right as she tries to make her way around. She wants me for dinner, no doubt. Both she and I are stepping slowly over and around roots and I'm remaining hugged against the tree because she seems to have a hard time getting to me. She opens her mouth at one point and tries to nip at my side, but the tree just barely blocks her. She stops for a second. I stop likewise. Maybe she'll just go away. I track her head. She's not moving at all. I think she's waiting for me to make a move. She's quiet when she's moving. I thought these big guys were supposed to stomp around everywhere making loud roaring noises, like in the movies. Then I realize, if they did that all day, they'd never find food to eat. Dinner would always run far away.

I turn my head to the right to see where I'll need to step next and realize I'm on the outside of the tree line. And what do I behold in all terror? This chick's boyfriend! He was apparently doing his own thing nearby and has now become curious about what she has scrounged up. He's not moving, but he's looking dead at me from about forty meters (130 ft) away. His face is angular and evil red. His upper teeth hang out. He appears to be only a little smaller than the Acrocanthosaurus male I saw this morning, but he looks like he comes straight out of hell. I don't know this dino species at all. He holds his head low, then raises only his nose in my direction. I can see both his eyes. He's trying to smell me out. The breeze is a crosswind, so he hasn't figured out his mate is on to something yet, but he knows this tree is different. He squares up his angle to the tree. Nature built this dino to be a very fast runner. Its chest is narrow, but its thighs are huge, and its lower legs are skinny. This one can take down enormous plant eaters for sure, and maybe other carnivores. His tail swishes back and forth at its end with its reddish brown and white flairs.

She moves opposite the way she started, and I step back to my left. She hasn't made a sound, and neither has he. I pause to make sure she continues her tracking. She arches her head back around to my right against her body and snaps at me. Again, the tree barely clips her angle and I'm saved as she backs up for another try. The second she arched her head and snapped at me; I notice her boyfriend started trotting over quickly. I am dead and know it. Hopping the last large tree stump to my camouflage, I dive hard into a tight split between the roots and cover myself just as her head pops up over top of me, and then his head appears on my other side over top of me. For the first time, she makes a noise and uses her head and mouth to keep him at bay.

From her angle, she bites down at me. Her nose crushes the camo I've been carrying around all day, but her mouth won't fit. She goes for a wider area down by my feet. I have them tucked in as best as I can. At the last second, I flatten them out against the roots as she takes another bite and can't get through. She's frustrated and brushes her nose through my camo, which is breaking apart at its upper ends. She huffs right on me. If I had brought my helmet today, I would have avoided the putrid breath of this one. I want to throw-up. He comes over and takes his turn with me. Angrily he growls and huffs and can't grab any part of me until he gets my upper calf with one if his gnarly teeth. He pulls and I straighten out my leg in response, hitting his lower lip. I almost came out with that tug. I press back quickly, still trying to cover myself with as much camo as possible, and he snags my upper calf again. This time, I extend my leg when he pulls, intending to kick. I whack his lower lip again. This time with more force. He huffs and calls out in a loud grunt. I keep waiting for them to use their little forearms to drag me out. It never occurs to them to do so. She comes back for another round of tries, and this time destroys the top of my camouflage. I try to cover up best I can. He takes another turn as well. This time, he snags nothing.

They both stop and are just hanging around, possibly waiting for me to make a run for it. That'll be the day! I'll die right here of starvation before trying to outrun this set of super Olympians. They sort of look at each other and look around, but don't go anywhere. They are talking to each other with low groans and grunts. Each one responding to the other. They decide to just stay put for a while. They walk back and forth, never really looking at me again. I catch the male one time, eyeballing me with one eye. Mostly, they just stand still and quiet. I noticed again when they step around; they don't stomp. They are as smooth as velvet in their locomotion. Unless there is a twig that will get snapped or something, there is no sound at all. When I was a kid, I tried to hear the elephant steps at the zoo. No chance then and no chance now. After about twenty minutes, the female takes giant dump right in front of me. I'm traumatized by the scene because it seems like she was trying to dump on me. She even backed up a little. Of course, the smell was atrocious, but that's not enough. After she walks away, the male walks up, sniffs it, turns around and pees on it. He then goes off into the darkening forest behind her a short distance.

Sitting here for another moment will drive me insane. I wait until they are gone. Grabbing what's left of my camo, I head back across the hard sandy clearing with all the dino tracks. The forest was quiet last night before twilight. I'm noticing it's a lot quieter than it was midday and it's only just getting dark. I think the day dinos are making way for the night dinos again. The natural circadian rhythm of planet Earth.

Camelot at last! I am the first human to survive a multi-carnivore dino attack. Scared beyond my imagination to go back out again, I want to huddle up in my castle and die tonight. I don't want to face another day. I don't want to deal with dinosaurs that don't let you know they are coming by stomping around and screaming first. And all the carnivores I've seen are incredibly quick. They can outrun the fastest dog on that dog's best day. This place is beautiful in so many ways, but it's not made for humans. I don't care what anybody says. Humans don't belong here and if they come, humans won't be long here. I won't be long here. I know it.

Last night, I dreamed the dreams of a young boy back in Virginia. Running through the hills of Blacksburg, Christiansburg, Riner, and Price's Fork. I dreamed of my old friends Ricky and Jared and our times at Tom's Creek catching crawdads, seining for hellgrammites, and fishing in the creek. Sometimes we'd swim in there too on the hottest summer days. It didn't matter about the copperheads or water moccasins. They were around and we saw them occasionally, but they never bothered us, and we never bothered them. We were just boys in a creek dodging the sun, fishing our own meals, camping out at night, and playing war games with real live BB-guns and firecrackers. They weren't just dreams. They were memories. I spent the entire night unable to go all the way to sleep. Picturing myself back home, I closed my eyes as if the images were dreams themselves. My dreams were of times like those summer days when there was so much to do and no stress under which to do it. Dreaming of holidays, my mind filled with the good times at my grandparents, and with my sister, Rebecca, her husband Paul, and thoughts about their two kids and what they might be doing now. I dreamed of all my family, my younger brother Jeb and little sister Sarah. My family brings me my greatest peace and now, a host of regrets I'll never rectify. We often want to choke one another, but we forgive and move on. I stole the entire night, and it was all mine, the way I wanted it. And sometime in my bliss, right before dawn I fell asleep, and the previous day was washed away with the peeking, red sky fire of a new morning.

I awoke to yet another visit by what I'm going to call "Hella-vicious-saurus." They found me and again they are having a hard time getting at me. The female can reach in with her teeth, but her mouth is closed. She presses on my chest a little, huffing and grunting. The male is watching her, waiting for his turn. I'm confident this cutout is even tighter than the roots of the tree from yesterday. Luckily, I sleep with my helmet on. My sleeve of water is tucked in behind me. Suddenly, I realize I can capture video of this! Something I missed all day yesterday by not taking my helmet with me. Voice command turns it on. It captures her last tantrum and his try at me as well. He is super aggressive. He hits me in the chest with his mouth, and it hurts. I think he knows it. The testosterone coursing through this guy is too much for him to handle! The rock chips away at the top of the cutout, but this stuff is dense. I had a hard time getting the cutout like it is. I'm needing to work on it a lot more to make it safer.

After one determined round of effort, they stop and do their thing again. They don't move around. They just stand there quietly and grunt lowly at one another. Each one responding to the other. They look around out over the tall grasses while standing right in front of me. If the female takes a dump near me again, I might just go crazy. After about twenty minutes again they move off smooth as velvet, though this time you can hear the swishing and cracking of the tall grasses.

I'm starving like mad now. It's been two days and the last thing I had to eat was two eggs and some bacon. The food brought back yesterday is classified as potential food, but I won't know until it's cooked. The water will be ok. By now, I would have major issues. I consider myself very lucky. I jaunt off down the hill toward the beach to gather supplies.

Ok, I didn't have to go far at all. Maybe twenty meters down the hill at its farthest. Now I'm back and I have some broad leaves, dry grasses, twigs, and sticks. It's enough to get a fire started and keep it going about fifteen minutes. I'll gather more once it gets started. I start the fire the old-fashioned way. With a straight stick and a bunch of dry grass. I gathered a bunch as it's all around me. No doubt I'll have enough matter to keep the flame going. First, I'll dig a little pit in which to start the fire. I need a fire that smolders rather than burns and a shallow pit covered by leaves will do it.

And there it is! Fire in a pit! Time to crack apart the cattail-like plants into a size that will fit in the pit and cook them up. First, I place three small flat rocks on the fire. Then I place the cattails on the rocks and later I'll cover the whole thing with about three layers of leaves. I leave to collect more wood.

Day three is a day at Camelot cooking the remaining cattails and relaxing. The cattails need to cook a long time to break down the dense starches in the stalks. They aren't super tasty but aren't nasty either. It is unfortunate there's nothing that resembles a potential antibiotic in them. I guess they aren't cattails after all. Their fibers are like steel straws. My insides are getting raked clean by the looks of my last go. Now, I just pull the tough fibers out of my mouth and consume what remains. Enjoyment from food is a long-lost escapee. The evening sun sends the day away in colors just as beautiful as it greets the day. Morning time is my rising back home to the early birds singing and coolness in the air. The evenings are my back porch with friends and drinks and good times to music. They have done nothing less than lift me in my loss.

Days four, five, and six are rainy days. When it started, I ran down the hill to grab a bunch of broad leaves to capture rain at Camelot. I used a slanted area off to the left to lay out the leaves and funnel the rain into my sleeves. It worked! I have an abundance of fresh water. On day four, I gorged on both sleeves and filled them again. My hydration is peaked. I subsisted on the remaining cattails the rest of the time, rifled through all my thoughts, and made a plan.

Day seven arrives, a soggy, sandy, muck and drips and drops attend my view from overhead the cutout. I imagine Camelot's castle dripped in like ways. Gloomy morning grey skirts slowly across the sky. Two or three of the greyish wisps scheme wickedly to touch the ground on their way out to sea and I could almost reach up and touch their cloudy essence were I a chaser of such useless endeavors. I don't want to leave the cutout today. In fact, I don't want to leave it ever again. I'm going to die in this timeline and most likely a horrible, vicious, and untimely death. Only the forest giants grow old here. All other things struggle for a blink in time, and a minuscule few find them a record in rock for a lifeless study.

Is it the gloominess shrouding this world, or is it me? My experiences of the first two days forced me to consider for the past several that I must come up with a plan to salvage something of my experience, and a plan I made. It's outrageous and horrifying all at once. My mind is torn. Do I have the strength to pull it off? I don't know. All I know is I'm something like one hundred million years in the past and no one is coming to get me. I could just die here like anything else that ever was. It's nature's way. It's clearly her way for me. My little human essence should be so lucky as to have had a week amongst her most accomplished creations. I got the message. I am nothing. No king shall I be here. We are nothing. We humans aren't even remotely accomplished in nature's eyes, for we destroy everything around us and assume we can sustain. It's as if we designed the cup which holds all the rules and nature is an 'observer only' when we did nothing of a sort. The cup is hers. Her rules are prime and simple. I see that now in every way, color, and shade. So, I will bring together the plan and I will mold my mind to my will and necessity as required to complete it. I only hope that it pulls off in a miraculous and unbelievable fashion, unlike anything that ever happened.

Days roll by in a blink. With each venture out, I bring my helmet and make recordings and gather sustenance. My way is tried and true and trouble does not find me in its way often. I finally saw a herd of massive, large plant-eaters. In comparison, elephants at the zoo might as well be a glass menagerie in a corner cabinet. For a moment I found excitement, however fleeting it was. They have fewer flairs on their bodies, but some are present near the head and on the neck and back, moving down a short distance. The little ones have more flairs and apparently grow out of them. No amazing colors on the ones I saw, but the more regular and local, smaller male plant-eaters are amazing in their plentiful colors. Mostly, though, I get daily reminders, this is not the place for me. My recordings may suffice. I hope they would endure with the plan, but doubt is the lord of the future. I dutifully gather what I need and spend time at home preparing the plan for execution.

I get the occasional visitor here and there. Once, a pack of about twenty tiny dinos made its way up over the hill to the cutout. They had me a little worried because they were meat-eaters. They could easily get in my cutout. and were standing at my entrance jawing at me and dodging my movements. Eventually I made large movements and scrambled out of my cutout, waving my hands about like a madman making growling noises. They looked concerned and spread out in a large circle, chatting with each other. Some just wanted to go, and others weren't sure. One or two tried a coordinated side attack on me, to no avail. My suit is too tough. They gave up in a short time, and I shooed them off. Brave little boogers, though. Everything here is just the absolute epitome of aggressive. Calm, cool, Harry has been eaten!

Sunrises and sunsets paint the skies daily. How many days have I been here now? I don't know the full number anymore. Is it three weeks, three and a half? Does it matter? Nothing here understands time. For me, it's all grey now. To think about it, I should go mad at this point. This is a tremendous and dangerous world indeed. The plants are unruly, tough, and thorns abound even on trees. Even the insects are overly aggressive. Time does me no favors. To think of Camelot or the Llyr River or the welfare of the Kingdom empties my chest and it becomes a sullen, and sunken void. The tyranny of hunger and teeth and mighty force here declares I am no king. There are no kings here except they declare it, then they are eaten, and the next king is eaten after him. I am food. The cutout is this food's shelter. This food grows weary on perpetual alert. The hands provide this food only enough to complete the plan now. This food has only one advantage; his mind is strong.

My plan is coming together slowly. My inner self thrashes with its expediency, yet I press forward. Will I have what it takes to make it happen? I don't know and I can't say if I will, but I envision it. That should help me out.

I have some thoughts I've been jotting down in a little three by five-inch (7.62 x 12.7 cm) black notepad I've been carrying around. As part of my time travel task, I was supposed to write something that only I know on the sheet of paper, tear it out, and place it on the patio table. Others were to go out and read it during and after my presence there, and when I came back, they were to recite it to me. But my hands ache too much to write because of their daily labors for the plan. They have been digging out a square area in my cutout that works like a tub. It will be just wider than me in my suit and just longer than me curled up on my side and a fair bit deeper than my width. That's because it's going to contain me in the end. But there's an added hitch. A hitch that gets me and everything I have to the future. The little three-inch blade in my multi-tool was useful, after all. I've been gathering sap from the giant conifers.

I score the bark and jab upward into the trunk of the tree. The next day I come back, and sap has dripped down the trunk, which I then collect with the knife. I use half a hip bone to transport it back to the cutout each day. Sometimes I find a smaller gliding dino licking up my sap. A few now have a favorite tree of their own. I no longer collect from those trees, as it's pointless. They enjoy the buffet. Now and then, I mark a fresh score up into the bark just for them to keep it running. I use them as my danger alerts.

Several days of toil roll by. I'm not eating now. I'm getting everything out of my system except water. This is what the ancient Himalayan monks used to do before their efforts at ascension in the mountain caves. Their bodies were well preserved without the internal rot. I want my insides like theirs to be empty. It's important that I do not introduce extra variables into the sap that may inhibit the plan's long-term effectiveness. My plan is that I place myself into the sap and die, but not without bringing along all the recordings and technology in the suit, plus everything I've written in the black notebook. Over time, the tub of sap will harden into amber and as long as it's protected, it should preserve anything in it to near perfection for one hundred million years. We have found insects in amber older than that. My future will soon be entombed in amber.

More days go by in a blur, and I've eaten again. Ruining what was nearly perfect and ready for the plan. The dreariness of the rain and lack of will imprisoned me. Sap collection has stalled. It's too burdensome on a weakened body. My tub is short of half full and my displacement won't be enough to cover me yet. My mind wanders from thought to thought all day. No specific focus or resolutions. No new ideas. I'll get mired in thinking about myself and all things I haven't done for hours on end. Yesterday was nearly all day. Images of a family of my own pop up in my mind. I never married and don't have a current girlfriend. I hear my buddy recounting the birth of his child and how it changed him. He said there is nothing like that feeling of holding your child for the first time. He said it's a new form of love you can't explain; it overwhelms you and changes you. You would do anything for this little creature in your arms who is so completely helpless and innocent. My imagination works up what overwhelming love must be like. I try to feel it and want to feel it because I want to know. I imagine I know, and I smile, but I don't know. The world in my mind conjures false validations for my comfort, as this is where I live these days. In my fantasy world. A land of make-believe truths.

I look out of my cutout at the grey sky against the setting sun. The sun fights for its design but only finds the bottom of a foreboding greyness. It paints it with a mauve signature, taunting it before it meets an oppressive demise. Tonight, will be cool and wet. The food is gone. It sickens me anyway. I hate it. I'll try to stop for good this time and get back to the sap.

This morning I'm not carrying my camo. It's too heavy now. I have no energy. I have built a cautious route to the trees. Sap is all I can think of this morning. Like a tired, worn, old honeybee to flowers, I tend my stock slowly and gather my honey. Today was a good haul and without the camo, I am bringing back some unopened pinecones too, knowing I've already broken my promise. Tonight, I'll dine on last night's rain and whatever pine nuts I can glean from this dozen cones. I care not to look around me except for caution's sake. My way is tried and true. My bustle is muted and barely even heard except by my tiny sap licking friends. I wander back and my mind wanders around.

I believe it's coming time now. I'm tired of thinking of me. My fantasy world I've lived in for ten lives by now. I've been older and I've been younger. Once I was a great CEO of a time traveling company and figured out ways to make lots of cash to become the most powerful company in the world and I dominated. Grandchildren have had vacations and outings with me, their grandpa and grandma in others. A schoolboy version of me has done it all many times over. I've relived my own life. My regrets have brought me to tears. So many regrets. My successes have brought me to tears. Too few real successes. My loved ones I've cried for. So many tears I can't remember when I slept with my helmet. This place has imposed its will upon me. I shall never rectify my wrongs or rejoice in my successes. The days are now so long ago uncounted I cannot fathom the number. My time here is one lifetime too long.

Back from this morning's run for sap and I realize that I now have enough to make this work. It's all in the tub and chunky and a little dirty because of the time to collect, but it's all there. I realized along the way I needed to add wood to the sap for extra carbonization over time. So, I lined the cutout tub with wood and left a small pile to rake over myself when the time comes. That's the trick to ensuring the sap hardens correctly and turns to amber. That last thing I need to do is run a little fire next to the tub and let the cutout get nice and hot. This will make the sap runny and will fill the tub and cover me when it's time. I start the fire and do my final review of what I've written and collected. Here is some of it.

My time travel thoughts are first. I believe scientists have overlooked a very simple notion of what it means for matter to be eternal. And matter is eternal, regardless of what level of energy in which it may be at any moment. Matter and energy are the same interchangeable. Our universe has neither gained nor lost matter since its birth. That means for this universe, there is only one continuing timeline. An alternate timeline for the same moment in time would require an alternate universe with its own matter because the matter in this one is already in place and used. Therefore, there are no such things as alternate timelines within a single universe. It's more likely in the multiverse that alternate timelines exist. If there were an infinite number of timelines in a single universe, it would make our universal matter infinitely large because it must have its place in time, and this is not the case, as science has proven. At least this is my belief. Our universe has its own matter. Each timeline needs its own matter.

Because our universal matter can be calculated, we know it is finite. If it is finite and there is the potential for alternate universes, then something out there contains all that extra matter for the alternate universes. I'll call this the Exoverse. The Exoverse is the infinitely large container which holds all the matter of this universe and all alternate universes and may be infinite itself and not a container at all. The multiverse for definition's sake is the total body of all alternate universes. For the Exoverse, this may mean that slight changes in the quantity of universal matter due to time travel are allowable and negligible on the universal scale, but this is extreme speculation and considers only the possibility that an infinitely massive multiverse may have a natural steady state of zero for all energy-matter which can balance out among all universes at once, allowing for small shifts in energy from universe to universe.

Or it may be something worse. That being a steady state of Null, consequently assuring that all energy-matter eventually dissipates over extreme, super-universally, long periods of time. This would lead to no restrictions on time-travel because there is no need to balance out total matter. Yes, this violates the universal law that states energy is neither created nor consumed, it just changes state. This may be a limitation of what we can measure because our view of our own universe is minimal and local. Therefore, locally, it might appear that energy is neither gained nor lost and local measurements would validate the local hypothesis. This could be wrong on a multiverse scale. I also believe in this situation that time travel within and across universes could completely disrupt timelines in all universes eventually and not all at once if our universe's matter-energy is tied to all multiverses. It may take an infinitely long time to do so in some circumstances. Now that I'm writing this, it seems illogical and even downright foolish scientifically to conclude the matter present in our Origin timeline is the exact same matter present in all timelines, but if this is the course science persists in believing then that's that. I'd never have a say in it anyway.

I'll share a thought exercise that holds me to these lines of thinking and here it is. Pretend you are a scientific fish. You live out in the middle of the ocean and it's the only location you've ever known. In your scientific quests you investigate how seashells fall when raised and then dropped above a coral reef. You develop theories about momentum and inertia and how the varying forces from water and waves act as lines of force upon the seashells and change their direction and speed. One day you borrow some ink from a snail and set about testing what happens to the water colored with ink once the ink is set free in the ocean. Your other fish friends say the ink will disappear and be gone forever and nothing will come of your tests as that is the standard reasoning among fish. You find however, though the ink does disappear, you notice it is carried away on the water and goes off in all directions until it cannot be seen as a blob of ink. You simplify this by saying the ink is still there. It is only the energy of the water that has spread it out to all parts of the ocean until it cannot be seen. And where the water-energy once was with ink, it has been replaced by water-energy without ink. Your conclusion becomes the energy found in water is never really lost. It is conserved and simply changes state from visible to not visible, but it is still there. In simple terms, you have become a Newtonian fish and you receive the Nobel Prize in 'fish-iks' and great acclaim for your scientific definitions of natural things.

In order to confirm your theories, you set about going to the far ends of the ocean and running your experiments in every location you stop. Your theories hold. Until one day on a lunch break, you are snagged by a fisherman. You are pulled into an alternate universe aboard a boat where water is scarce and its much warmer. The fisherman shows you off to his camera and talks to it for a few minutes. In this time, you realize your experiments as you know them would never hold in this place as there is hardly enough water for you to breath, but you sense water in the air around you and above the boat. The fisherman throws you back but not before you realize two new aspects to your theory. First, the ocean is not infinite. Second, you don't know how or why but water is being lost from the ocean and going somewhere else. You are unaware of the complete cycle of evaporation.

In a moment of enlightenment, you adapt your original theories with the following new thoughts. First, the ocean may be losing energy at its boundary, which means all water-energy is not conserved as you once theorized. It is actually experiencing a diminishment that is not discernable in the locations you have been showing off your experiments. It is only discernable at the ocean's boundary. This is because every location was inundated with vast amounts of water-energy. You name this phenomenon, "Inundation Theory" and use it to explain how your theories only apply where water-energy is abundant. You identify where water-energy is not abundant and explain that water is being lost to this strange place. You are derided as a fish scientist and your former fish friends laugh at you. You die a lonely, unloved fish.

This is what I believe is happening at the far boundary of our universe. Energy is not being conserved. It is being lost. We cannot discern it because we are inundated with matter-energy. We will only know otherwise once we understand what is happening at the boundary of the universe. The faint glow coming from the edge of our known universe is energy being dissipated.

And a final thought or two for quantum things and then my brain will finally rest. At the quantum level, matter is popping into and out of existence every moment. Are we to assume that at every moment, the universe has the same energy as the next? I believe now this is impossible to prove perfectly. It may be measurable locally. It may be obscured by inundation. We will only know for sure when we understand what is happening at the edge of the universe. If we find the very faint glow at the edge of the known universe is energy being released from this universe outwards and not being reflected inwards, or in other words, not being contained, then we know energy at the universal level is being lost at the quantum level. It just appears to always be the same around us because of its excessive abundance and, given it is not being lost or expelled in our local area of space, it makes it seem constant here despite it being diminished at the edge of our universe. A loss of energy at the edge of the universe supports the Null theory previously stated.

Based on the patio experiments, the effects of one's interactions in the alternate timeline may not be completely universal. For example, if a time traveler trips over a rock in his path and kicks the rock in anger and it moves to another location then as long as that rock has no significant impact on anything else in its existence, the alteration in its presence between timelines remains localized and muted. In Jamison's experiment, Don's and Earnest's memories in Origin time were altered with information from the alternate timeline, while no one else's memory supported that. Of course, small, simple alterations to timelines are next to impossible to calculate or assume, but this understanding raises the possibility for many new rules for time travel and "historical management" so to speak.

I'm just postulating because I'm bored. I'm going to surprise the future, though. My actions may alter the Origin timeline from this far distant timeline based on what we know from the Patio Experiments. Or maybe I'm wrong about all this and everything is on one timeline, with rippling changes in it caused by time travelers. What a mess to think about. Something like that would become highly unmanageable quickly.

All I truly know about time travel is this; I'm in an alternate timeline based on the evidence from the patio experiments. I'm one hundred million years in the past, I believe. My thought is if alternate timelines appear similar to one another, then they are close to one another distance-wise in the multiverse. The greater the distance between the two timelines in the multiverse, the greater the differences between timelines. Being stuck in a timeline that is one hundred million years in the past means I'm far too far away in the multiverse to be found unless the experiment can be recreated perfectly. But what if I'm stuck in a timeline that is only a few seconds off from my origin timeline? That would mean in this timeline the dinosaurs either never went extinct or developed later in earth's evolution by 100 million years. And because something like the night sky looks nothing like what's in my origin timeline, I am again far too far away in the multiverse to be found. Of that, I'm certain. My theory supporting this being the constellations would appear the same in similar timelines and wildly different in distant timelines.

I remember there was a thunderstorm happening during my time travel experiment now. I'm betting the energy from a lightning bolt sent me so far into the multiverse, I'm unretrievable. It took enormous amounts of facility power for the experiments before mine, only to travel backwards in time five seconds. And here I am. It had to be a lightning bolt jolt that landed me here.

Oh, some quick dinosaur things I've seen. The two footed dinos use their little front arms for egg and nest management like turning and adjusting their eggs. They also don't lay down directly on their nest. Being too heavy to do so, they lay next to it at night, and anytime one is patrolling on guard duty. Some of the larger two-legged dinos have a fatty area which appears as bulging, loose skin between their arms. On cooler nights, they'll sit on their eggs with this part of their body rather than their full weight. For others, I've seen many cover their nest with a thin layer of dirt and/or grasses and stand guard. They'll dig through the dirt occasionally to roll and adjust the eggs and cover them again. When the two footed dinos are hatchlings, they can be carried in emergency circumstances with these arms. Scooped up and held close to the chest of the parent as it runs off. I've even seen parents carrying a young one or two in their mouth from one point to another. Possibly strayers from the nest or simply too many for their little arms to carry.

The large four-legged plant eaters have super small heads for a reason. All those neck muscles provide highly accurate fine motor control for the dino's small head to move the eggs and hatchlings around on the ground huddling them, and for nest management as well. The one large plant eater nest I saw was about 1.2 meters wide (5.5 ft) and covered in a ridiculously large overabundance of leaves and twigs. I don't think the mother ate much for almost thirty days while the eggs matured. Rarely did I see the nest unattended. Once I ventured close enough to realize the true makeup of the nest, but hastily got away. Anything to do with plant eaters is hunting grounds for meat eaters. Just like the food chain in the ocean starts with schools of small fish followed by increasingly bigger fish and then larger predators, the same is on land.

Another thing I saw was a group of about fifteen long-necked sauropods being attacked by a group of six two-legged meat eaters. The sauropods created a circle around the younger ones in the bunch. Their heads all pointed inwards to the circle and hovered over the young they were protecting. With front shoulders separated by only a couple feet, they all swung their tails back and forth slowly and when one of the meat eaters tried to advance on the group, they would take great swings at them. I saw a meat-eater break a leg in one attack when it was hit by a massive tail. The stunning thing was when it cried out, the other meat eaters tore upon it with incredible, malicious savagery. It was an unadulterated blood rage the likes of which has never been seen by eyes other than mine. The horror of which escalates beyond what can be described. It was this very sight that settled my determination to not remain here a moment more.

A lot of other stuff I captured on camera. Splendid stuff to surprise the future. Though, I'm kidding myself if I believe the silicon and copper will make it one hundred million years in its sap coffin. I execute on hope alone. All my information and details written for the future in my little black book. I used a sleeve and put the memory storage from my helmet and my little black book into its protective environment. I sealed up both ends of the sleeve after pressing out as much air as I could. Once inside the sap, it should be better preserved in time than I will be. Who knows what will happen in this timeline, or if somehow this timeline will eventually affect my Origin timeline? Could timelines merge? I'll never know. I'm doing this anyway.

As the evening approaches, I check the sap. It's ready. I'm finally ready. I check the layer of smooth rocks and wood at the bottom of the tub to make sure sap is deep enough to entomb me from the bottom as well. It's my eternal bed. The glove I filled with the toxin from the large sunflower-like, small-dino-eating plant in the forest is in reach now. I know it is a neurotoxin as I've tested it on many insects. It's fast for them and I think if I drink enough at one time, it will be fast for me. Speed is what I'm hoping for. I don't want any time for last regrets, and I've avoided touching it like the plague until now. I place the sealed sleeve into the sap, and it slowly falls to the bottom over several minutes, almost taunting my will to continue. Time wants more chances and so do I, but I refrain. I watch it. It's good enough. It will be forever entombed. I put on what's left of my suit and have my helmet close by. I look out from under my cutout. There's nothing I want to see. I put on my helmet and turn on the communications one last time. Tears desire to run free. I strain to keep them at bay. I hear nothing. Not even static seeks to enchant my imagination. What a dead place.

I grab the glove. All my recent dreams crowd my mind for attention. I stare out from my darkness for I don't know how many minutes. The sun is setting but I pay it no attention. I'm busy in my mind with what I must do, and I'm trying to do it. My chaotic, rampant thoughts and their need for attention are raging. I can't do this, I think. But I'm so sick of everything now. I'm so doomed here. This must be done. I look down at the glove and stare even longer. For a moment, I find it in my power to shut down all my thoughts and all hope for me. My body voluntarily slides into its tomb. The sap is dense for sure. I'm sitting on my left side and leaning left. My left hand supporting me from the bottom of my amber blanket. One more time, I look out. I see nothing, hear nothing, feel nothing. My mind is briefly complicit as every thought I ever had is shackled in some far-off place. With my visor up, I tilt my head back and drink as much from the glove as I can. I'm shocked at how quickly I feel the first effects. Mere seconds and I cannot feel my tongue. I slam my visor down and release my left arm from its strain. Reaching to the edge of the tub, I scrape more spare wood and pull it over me. I'm not sinking very quickly, but I am. Within a minute, I feel the effects in my torso. Straining for breath, I know my lungs will stop by the large convulsions rippling through my chest. My heart only beats two or three more times, and it stops. My brain strains from lack of oxygen, and my thoughts are vanquished. I'm forever sealed. A small light. Do I really see it?

3

The Pump and Lot

DASH MONITOR: "It's another sweltering day here in Hampton Roads, Virginia. We've got ninety-six being reported in Chesapeake and the Airport with a heat index of one-o-four. It's ninety-seven down at the beach and ninety-five across the peninsula. Reminder to stay out of the sun as much as possible, especially through the mid-afternoon time, and always wear proper sun protection when you're out. Keep an eye on your kids and pets. Make sure they have enough water and shade, and they're protected from the sun. After chores, wasting time on a gaming system today might not be a bad idea until it cools down, mom and dad. Tonight, we'll see temperatures dropping to the low eighties with more heat coming tomorrow and through the weekend. This is FM ninety-nine weather. Your home for every era of Rock-n-Roll music and videos thru the ages."

Robotically, Brian hit the button to turn off the Dash Monitor. The slight, high-pitched, droning sound of tires on the road leaking into the cabin, and the quiet whine of the electric motors in each wheel propelled him deep into his thoughts. The steering wheel rarely gets used. It stays recessed in the smooth contour of the dash these days. An invisible part of the panoramic displays. He stared blankly through the windshield as his truck decided everything about routing and traffic maneuvers on its way back home. He could see the vehicles in each lane. The right most lane moving the slowest for on comers and those exiting, the next lane to the left moving a little faster, and the next even faster with the last lane moving fastest. Each lane of cars could be part of the world's longest train, with invisible linkages locked into the perfect spacing between vehicles moving at the same perfect speed.

His boss' words still rang through his head as he reached down the left side of his driver's seat to hit the recline control. Today was his last day as a firefighter. He'd spent the past sixteen years serving his community in a job he loved working. Tomorrow he is officially replaced by intelligent robotic firefighting units. This was coming for over two years. Reality had yet to set in. Not long ago, retirement age was achievable before the machines moved in and took over. He had even completed all the training to support the robotic units in the field. The whole thing just moved at such a fast pace. Of course, the City of Norfolk reduced the number of support personnel for the new units across the city based on new information from the supplier, AutoLogistics, and their North American Civics Division. And in the way the Norfolk City Council usually does, they hesitated to decide protecting and compensating human workers displaced by the robots. Each council person hoping if they ignore the issue long enough, it will magically cease to be a concern. Just late yesterday, however, the council made its move and retired all firefighters over twelve years of service at twenty years for full retirement. All others in the department received fifty percent retirement, with only five or six were selected to stay onboard for long term secondary support of the robotic systems until they too will be replaced in about ten years with a one hundred percent automated robotic maintenance workforce.

Miranda couldn't be doing any better. Yesterday was her twenty-seventh birthday and mommy and daddy agreed to cosign for her on a new vehicle. Today she picked out her favorite and could not wait to show her roommate and best friend, Sheila. She strides through the front door, humming a little tune with a little bounce in her step. Her eyes are bright and stress free. Her smile is one she has worn most of the day and it hasn't lost any energy in its stay.

"Hey Sheila!"

"Hi Miranda!"

"I picked it up!"

"Oh, did you now!" Replied Sheila in a faked surprise tone, as if she wasn't sure yesterday's clamoring was certain.

Miranda replies with her arms squeezing in across her chest, her fists clinched up near her chin, and high-pitched voice with a huge smile, "Yes!" and then her voice drops with an eye roll, "I love it! It's so me! Ugh!" dropping her arms in delighted exasperation.

Sheila wondered what life adventures would be with a white girl roommate. She had white friends growing up in Virginia Beach and was at home in the surfer, skater, beach-life culture, though she never did those things and had been to the beach only three times ever. She didn't hate the beach or swimming, but she did hate the sand, and particularly where sand ended up once you sat down. Getting life's beachy fun out of her hair was also a wretched personal adventure. Her black upbringing was its own culture, but in this part of the country everyone got along very well. Right now, though, she's thinking 'Never again. Been there, done that.' But she plays along, "Let me see!" she says again in a well-hidden effort to not appear fake.

"It's out here!" Says Miranda as she shuffles her feet in little steps and opens the door again.

Sheila pops up from the couch while acting out a burst of energy. After all, her body language can't give away her true lack of caring on this matter. She's not a hateful person. She's just the opposite. Her upbringing was not as spoiled as Miranda's, or whatever makes Miranda the luckiest girl in the world with the most doting parents. Spoiled is how she knows Miranda, and battles with those feelings more and more these days. Sheila wasn't raised like that, and the situation is a different kind of annoying now. She understands how Miranda was brought up but does not understand how Miranda can be so blind to her parent's laden excesses. Everything about Miranda oozes all over a person and Sheila squirms through her friendship with her.

The wheels on Brian's truck make a hard left turn and roll up the slight slope of a typical suburban American driveway and stop right in front of the garage door. He bought this house in Chesapeake, Virginia nine years into becoming a firefighter. A typical two-story house you'd see anywhere in modern America is his home. Three bedrooms with two and a half baths was where he and his then-fiancée were to build their lives together. But she ran off saying she 'needed time to find out who she was.' That was a heartbreaker for him. A week after that incident, he heard one of his firefighting buddies, Di'Mario, was looking for a place to stay. That weekend, Di'Mario moved in, and the long-term, male buddies, roommate scenario has played out for the past two years. Sometimes good, sometimes bad, and often annoying. But this roommate situation works well enough, especially since they are both now on different shifts, or rather, were on different shifts.

The truck shuts itself off knowing it has reached its destination. Brian opens the door and slides out. He thinks to himself, what a crazy day! In a world where the everyday worker is replaced by a robot, fate finally befell him. How predictable and so... well... typical.

He stands motionless beside his truck. What's he going to do now? He hadn't thought about next steps on the ride home. His mind was in a fog when he was driving. Di'Mario is one of the few remaining who will support the machines. How do humans carry on? Everywhere you go now robots are doing tasks people used to do. Or artificial intelligence is driving the economy, supply chains, and energy consumption as opposed to people. How is everyone getting by? These little entertainment side-hustles people do on the internet certainly aren't feeding everyone's family. The more you consider the whole situation, humans are basically left with entertaining other humans, and competing in human only sports and human versus human game competitions. Is this what our race has come down to? Have we created so much efficiency with A.I. and robotics that we get outperformed in everything we can do? No wonder people are in the streets more and more asking for a living wage. The machines are putting us out of existence!

Di'Mario opens the door and catches Brian staring out across the lawn. Pausing before opening the screen door, he's heading to work, and he knows what happened today. He knows eventually he will have the same thousand-meter stare one day. And though they've talked about being displaced, what can one say when the moment arrives? Di'Mario looks his buddy up and down, clears his thoughts, and presses the screen door forward.

"Hey man! What-chu starin' at?"

Brian unlocks his gaze with a startled jerk of his head.

"Oh, hey man," he says is a humbled tone.

"Is Mrs. Sally-Do-Right weeding her garden again, ha-ha?"

"Oh, no," again in a humbled tone and shaking his head.

"I'd be starin' too 'cuz that is one fine ass on that one!"

Brian smiles a bit and heads toward the door. Di'Mario knew this news was going to be rough for him. After all, Brian enjoyed being a firefighter more than anyone he knew.

Di'Mario starts in again, "Hey Brian, look, man. I know what came down on you and the rest of the fellas today. Captain Velasquez called me already. I'm not trying to make it worse or anything. I probably shouldn't be jokin' around, either."

Brian interrupts, "It's ok, Dee. We all gotta handle it, right?"

"Yeah, it just sucks that it's gonna happen to all of us because I am just too good-lookin' for bad shit to happen!"

Brian laughs a little as he again heads towards the door.

Di'Mario shouts out, "For what it's worth, man, I am sorry! Seriously, no jokin'. It's just how I deal, you know? But I am sorry."

Brian turns again. "I know, Dee. I've just got a lot of things to figure out now."

"Yeah, but it's not the end of things, baby. You're the type that's gonna land on your feet and between now and then, we'll figure it out together because when it's my turn, I need a way up and out too! We got each other's backs, right?"

Brian half turns with one arm raised in farewell. "Yeah man! We got each other's back."

"I hope you mean that, Brian," shouts Di'Mario as he slides into his car.

With a heavy breath and a release of muscular tension that came from the sound of Di'Mario's car door closing, Brian lugs his depressed body into the house. The inside is lit only by the late afternoon sun shining through the windows. With Di'Mario gone, he falls into the sofa, free from the drama of talking with others about his situation. He doesn't even want to call his dad.

Stress is straining his ability to think. He's now in the same boat as nearly forty-five percent of the population. A massive and growing percentage of people displaced by intelligent machines.

What lies ahead is a tough life. He's seen families on the streets and in parks creating tent cities and cardboard communities. Not everyone is homeless, but the most recent government numbers show about four percent of the population is homeless, and that's a staggering number. Brian used to rationalize the sadness of this whole situation. He feels the impending doom. Rationalizing around these probabilities won't work. The overly automated world is irrational. People have nothing to fall back on for a living that a machine will not at once master for profitability and efficiency. The extended nuclear family has once again become the mainstay of the American home life with three, four, sometimes five generations of people living under one roof. Grandmas, Great Grandpas, uncles, and aunts, down to the youngest generation, all chipping in and making the nuclear family the steadfast and enduring social structure. This is how Americans respond when things get tough; they pull together.

This public clamoring has been getting louder for at least five decades now and politicians haven't done a single damn thing. Hyper-automation, a common good for business, has grown into a destructive force for society. The ridiculous proportions of extreme automation make the resulting outcomes seem insurmountable. American freedom and rights are alive but in near complete peril now as fewer and fewer people can even feed their families. This leads to waves of violence, which leads to unintelligent, power-hungry politicians thinking they have been given the power by God himself to end American rights and freedoms in the quest for peace and whatever sweet words turn the ear of the down-trodden at the moment. These politicians are mostly the socio-communist Democrat Party politicians cheered on by a few "Republicans In Name Only" (RINOs), and they always lose their efforts to undo rights and freedoms in a court of law or during major presidential voting seasons when the people vote them out of office. They show back up again during the mid-term elections when people, for whatever reason, don't remain vigilant in the pursuit of keeping their rights and freedoms. This affords them temporary extents of nearly unlimited power, which they feast upon like savages before the slowness of the courts catches up to them. Brian wonders why the obscene slowness of the courts has never been rectified.

The one strong hold-out in Individual Rights has been the second amendment of the U.S. Constitution, the Right to bear arms. Persistently under attack by the pro-authoritarian, socio-communist Democrat Party people, this right has withstood the test of time. Now, over three hundred years after its establishment in the U.S. Constitution, courts all over the U.S. understand that a violent and bloody revolution must be allowed to take place as nowhere in the past twenty-five years has the pro-authoritarian socio-communist Democrat Party worshippers won a single case in its efforts to dismantle the constitution. Brian sees violent revolution in America's near future because clashing at protests for decades has led nowhere, but to ever escalating tensions feeding on unresolved actions. And terrible times will befall the socio-communist Democrat Party and their freedom destroying supporters. He believes if they must pay in blood, then their blood shall be well spilled. Society will then return to a sense of peace and reason. He believes that's ultimately what we live for; a life filled with peace and reason. But now, as he lies on the sofa, he throws one arm up over his forehead, blocking the early evening sunlight that was hitting his eye. He takes a deep breath and tries to clear his mind. Even though a moment ago he didn't want to make the call, he thinks he'll call his mom and dad later, anyway. He also thinks of Ms. Sally-Do-Right's ass weeding that garden. Hey, an unemployed man has all damn day.

Later that evening, Miranda has three of her best friends on a split screen in her new car as smart sensors and A.I. maneuver toward her parent's house in Williamsburg. She's yacking up her birthday present and all the latest gossip from 'the squad' as they call themselves. You wouldn't know she was traveling in a vehicle she's supposed to be commanding. She could be in any other environment talking away with her gal-pals. You couldn't tell the difference. God forbid the grid goes down. The traffic implosion would be worse than the old days; back when people had to 'like pay attention and drive and stuff.' Her attention is locked. Vehicle time is the ultimate social time. She's happily smothering herself in 'girl gab,' oblivious to the surrounding traffic, and only occasionally peeks at the countdown timer, which shows 'time until arrival' at her destination printed out in giant numbers across her windshield. The other car windows don't display what's outside. She has chosen a well-manicured park with a lake as the scenery. One of the newest feature in cars these days. For her, this is a beautiful little cocoon by which to travel. Her vehicle arrives at Mom and Dad's place and parks itself in a predesignated open space on the street in front. A voice notifies passengers they've arrived at their destination. Her friends spot the moment of surprise on her face and realize 'the squad' must part. They all say their goodbyes as she swings her legs out and walks away from the vehicle. She doesn't need to close the door because modern auto-magic closes and locks the door behind her, regardless.

Despite robots and A.I. taking over the world, the world still needs secondary education institutions. Her father teaches Law at William and Mary, and her mother teaches at a local trade school. Old-fashioned universities are dying because all learning is online now. Laborious, expensive things such as buildings to maintain, parking lots to control, and students to feed are no longer needed. Even labs are pre-ordered and can be completed at home and most labs are done in simulation software anyway these days. The simulations are nearly perfect now in their augmented reality or virtual reality interactions. Online is just more cost effective for students and staff. Humans are still needed in trades, even the old-fashioned ones like welding and metal fabrication, though the end of that looks to be on the horizon before the next twenty-five years pass. These functions will all be achieved through Expert Materials Printing Houses, Automated Composite Formulation, and fully automated fabrication machines and manufacturing lines. So much complete automation with so little human involvement. If you lead a company supplying these capabilities, you are very well off and very few of you exist among the population. If you support these systems, you are doing well, but your workload is overbearing. Employers require the standard forty-hour weeks, and the unsaid twenty extra hours per week or more that you will never complain about because you know how valuable your job is. No one will step in and regulate the abuse, either. Politicians are paid to ignore reality. Everyone else in the world is fighting harder and harder over the scraps and as a growing body in society, they are eyeing their lazy, blind, do nothing, get rich quick, politicians. That goes for Democrats and Republicans alike.

Miranda turns the knob to the front door and walks in. This is the house she grew up in. Why wouldn't she?

"Hey Mom!"

Her mom, hunkered over the sink, spun around half-way with a soapy, wet dinner plate in her hands. "Hey Sweetie! I thought that was you! Your tracker said you arrived."

"Yeah, just got here," she said. "I see you all just ate."

"Oh! Yes. We just finished up about twenty minutes ago," replied her mom as she turned again to rinse the dish and put it in the dishwasher and pause her cleaning for the evening.

"What did you have? It smells like spaghetti or something. I see the sauce!"

"Well, I tried those cheese-stuffed raviolis I bought from the grocery. We hadn't tried them before. I guess they were alright. Your dad had two helpings. He seemed to like 'em."

"Wow! Store bought Italian," she remarked with a questioning lift of the eyebrows. Her eyes making a sideways glance at her mom as she leaned over to sniff the sauce a little more. "I remember the days when you used to make your own noodles with that noodle maker. You swore you'd never go back because they tasted so much better."

"Oh, that old thing! Gosh, that old thing broke a couple of years ago! It was nice while I had it, and I used it a lot, but it's a lot of work. A lot of prep time for a ten minute meal. I just don't have the energy for that anymore. It's just the two of us now, you know."

"Yeah, I get it. Well, at least you still make your old sauce like you used to."

"Ha ha-ha ha, Oh my goodness! I haven't made my mom's old homemade recipe for spaghetti sauce in at least ten or twelve years! That takes too much time too! That sauce is the same old store-bought sauce I've been buying since you were about fifteen years old. I just spruce it up with a little of my own herbs and flavors to make it seem less store-bought. Goodness! You must think I'm some kind of chef!"

"Mom! I had no idea! Here I am trying to recreate your old sauce at my new place to surprise you and you've been cheating on me!"

Together, they share a prolonged laugh with one another in a way only a mom and daughter can continue a laugh longer than the funny lasts. So much underlying history and hidden context drive the laughter to giggles and gasping for breath.

Her mom grabs her arm with a smile as the last of the giggles finish. "There's some left-over garlic bread in the oven, honey. And your father is infatuated with a new gadget in the garage. I have to use the bathroom. Go say hello to him really quick. When I come back, we can watch my new show together. It's just the first season and you've only missed four episodes. I'll get you all caught up."

Miranda watched her mom head out of the kitchen and down the hall toward the guest bathroom. For the first time, she notices the age of her mother. Has she gotten so much older? Maybe she sees this only now because she's been away. Her parents are about fifteen years older than most of her friend's parents. Looking at your mom as if she is some other old lady that you might miss in a crowd if you were only seeing the back of her feels weird. A sad moment took over. Like somehow, father time suddenly stole away years from her mom she believed were hers to enjoy. After grabbing the smallest piece of garlic bread from the oven, she turns to make her way toward the garage and opens the door.

She calls out, "Daddy, I'm home!"

No one answers, but she can detect movement beyond the door frame. She pokes her head in and sees her dad hunkered over the front corner of a vehicle she had never seen before. He appears to be wearing something like a lady's headband across his forehead. Wires dangle toward each hand which rests on the vehicle.

"Daddy!"

He didn't move. He was concentrating like he was trying to listen to something or understand something. She couldn't tell.

In a louder voice, "Daddy!" trying to get his attention. He looks okay otherwise.

Still, he doesn't respond, but he shifts his weight a little and adjusts his hands. She walks all the way over to him and gets his attention. With a voice of concern, she calls out while touching his shoulder, "Daddy!"

This time, he jumps to attention. "Hey sweetie! I didn't hear you! I'm sorry."

"Daddy, what are you doing? I called you like five times, and you were spacing out on this old car. Are you okay?"

"Oh, I'm fine. Just fine. I'm sorry, baby. I was experimenting with this gadget."

"What's that?"

"Well, it's what they call an Ethereal Transducer."

"Ok, that means nothing," she said in a bit of a concerned and angry tone. "And you're taking time away from mom with this toy?"

"Oh, now don't get on me about that. She and I spend all kinds of time together and she knows it. Did she say that to you?" Her dad said, looking disgusted while shifting his weight back and forth across his feet.

"No, but this isn't the first time you've ignored mom, Dad."

She continued in an angry tone, "You've nearly been divorced three times because you never spend time with her. I remember too! All those nights and weekends with dad gone. We only had each other, and where were you? Working, you always said? I'm older now, Dad. I doubt you worked that much. There's a lot of time to make up with mom. She loves you after all and so do I. Don't waste time with that gizmo."

"But she uses it too now, and she loves it! I was just finding some cool history for her." He looks down and makes a note of his hand positions. Copying them will help him zoom in next time.

He continues, "I'll need to find the pad locations exactly again, but I've got a good one for her this time. A road trip to Florida!"

"Dad, what are you talking about? History? Road trip?" She looked confused. She was thinking her father was confused, and he might be losing his cognitive abilities. Her mind was racing.

"And what is this? This old car here? I don't remember you or mom saying you were buying one of these things. Did she help decide?"

"This is a 1990 Ford Mustang convertible! One of the first of what they called the old Fox-Bodies, and yes, your mother was part of the decision. She wasn't happy, but she said it could be my early retirement gift! Little did she know it would be the gift that keeps on giving, hah-ha ha! Giving even to her too!"

"Christ Dad! You bought a vehicle that's nearly a hundred years old! What the hell?" She exclaimed with sheer disdain on her face.

"Can you even drive it? Was there technology back then?"

"Oh goodness no, not like now. We drive it only on very rare occasions and usually to get an ice cream cone with the top down. People don't know what to make of us in this old thing! It sure gets a lot of attention. It runs on gas too!"

"Holy God, Dad! Seriously, a gas guzzler? You're out and about destroying the world environment with this thing? I didn't even realize you could get gas anymore. I'm not even old enough to remember freaking gas stations!"

"Well, we have an old Seven Eleven here in Williamsburg that hasn't fully converted over to a Stop-N-Swap yet. It still supplies eighty-seven ethanol gas at one pump along with your battery swaps, too. You should try this thing before you judge."

"Dad! I don't know how to drive! I'd kill myself!"

"Not the car, sweetie. The transducer."

"Dad are you on drugs?" her voice was calm and serious, "I mean it. Are you taking something now or what? What's going on?"

She taps one foot, waiting for the response with her arms crossed. Her tense relationship with her dad doesn't mean she doesn't love him. She's glad to have him around. Only one of her best friends has a dad they can call on. The rest grew up in fatherless homes.

Mom walks in with a headband and a dangle of wires. "I heard you all talking about the transducer, so I grabbed mine, too. Miranda, I want you to try this thing out. Once you tune into a specific memory, it's a lot of fun. It's like you're living someone else's life through their memories! Your dad and I spend all our time sharing memories we find in this old car. I haven't enjoyed my time with your father like this sense we were first married. It's brought us closer. Especially the ice cream," she says with a wink toward Miranda's dad, who Miranda notices has a sly little grin on his face. This makes her raise her eyebrows in conscious awareness of the body language.

"Mom, I thought you said Dad was infatuated with it. It sounds like you are, too."

"Oh, I am! We love it, especially together. Let me get in and find the one from earlier. Miranda, this one is cute. Once I get it, remember my hand placement and the angles of the pads. This will help you tune in quicker once we swap the headband and pads. The baby in the backseat is a too funny."

While mom fiddles with two little half egg-shaped 'pads' up against the dash and the window frame, her dad is telling her what she has to do to get the device all to work.

Her dad continues, "So it's like what your mom is doing. You put this headband on, which takes a little getting used to. Then you find some old metal, but some kinds of plastics work and anything crystalline or that has crystals in it and start tuning in the memories with the pads and a bit of focus on your part. It's a balance between you and technology. You just need to experiment and learn how to tune it in so your brain can receive the images and other memories. So here, try it on."

She takes the headband and pads from his hands and places the headband across her forehead, like her dad is doing.

Her dad says, "Like I said, it takes a little getting used to and good concentration on your part. Now place the pads on the car. For the best performance, keep them within about three feet (1 m) of each other. If they get too close together, they won't work. I try to keep them no closer than six inches (15 cm) apart."

He watches her working to get reception from the hood of the old mustang in an area he knows the images should be a race happening between this mustang and another mustang. The dates are unknown, but you can guess by the stores and scenery the timeframe. She's clearly having trouble.

He interrupts her focus to say, "Sometimes, if you twist one pad to a different angle, you will get a clearer memory or image from the past. If you are on a spot for a moment and see nothing, try sliding only one pad at a time to a different location. Walk the pads around like that until you pick something up. Then do a little twisting to tune it in a little better. Sometimes it works. Sometimes it doesn't. It's just the way it is."

"Yeah dad, I'm not getting anything," she says in a matter-of-fact manner.

Inside her, a little girl is still mad at her dad for being gone so much. She doesn't like the lingering feeling and wants the negativity to go away, but the old thought keeps raising its ugly attitude when she and dad are close. As she has grown up, maturity has brought understanding. She has to let that anger go and forgive. Let the past be the past and hope for better days ahead. After all, mom and dad seem to have found a lot of happiness together recently and that makes her smile inside. She wants their newfound joy to last because she wants to believe love can last through time. This world crushes love, and she hopes her parents will prove victorious. Triumph would mean love is enduring and worth taking a chance on. Living and being vulnerable, and dependent, and protected all at once would be worth the sacrifices in oneself for a greater, mutually assured destiny.

Her mom laughs. "Oh, here it is! I thought I lost it! My hands were off a bit. Honey, come see this little baby. He's too much."

She hands the headset and egg-shaped thingies back. She and dad walk over to where mom is sitting with one hand on the beam of the windshield, the pad turned inward pointing across the windshield, and the other hand on the middle of the dashboard, pad pointing straight up and down.

Looking up at her daughter, she says, "OK honey, notice where my hands are and the placement of the pads. Grab my headband, put it on, then put the pads back in place. I have the scene tuned in pretty good for me. You might need to twist the pads a little to see the same for yourself. I don't know. You just have to try it. Everyone's a little different."

Miranda takes the pads from mom, and her dad helps mom out of the seat. She notices as she goes to get in, he pulls her in tight and they share a kiss. She hasn't seen them do that in a while and hadn't even considered they still kissed. What an odd thing to forget! Not only that, but as she looks back, they are hugging each other and rocking back and forth. She whips her head forward as a tear comes to her eyes. She fights to control the rush of happiness and doesn't want her parents to notice her teary-eyed for whatever reason. The reason is her own, but she knows these tears hold happiness and hope for her parents and a little something for herself. A deep hope and longing in her own heart that she doesn't even share with her best friends.

She places the left pad as her mom did.

"Point the pad in your right hand a little more directly across the windshield, dear," says mom.

She makes the little twist inward but receives nothing. She responds, "Mom, I'm not getting anything. Same with Dad's stuff. I don't get anything."

Mom jumps in, "It's okay. Relax, clear your mind, and focus on anything that feels like motion, or energy coming from the headband, or a fuzziness, or anything out of the ordinary. I find it's best if I close my eyes."

"Me too," says dad.

"Okay, let me try again."

This time, she sits back and relaxes. Nothing happens for a good minute, and her arms are getting a little tired. A fuzzy, static-like zip runs across her forehead and disappears in a blink.

"I just felt something," she said.

"Good," says dad. "Try to focus back on that."

She continues, "It's like an electrical, static type feeling zipped across my forehead. It was light and quick. Almost like I was making believe something happened, but I'm sure it was real."

"That's it," says mom. "Like your father said. Just relax and focus and try to hold it in your mind. It takes a little practice, but you'll see it."

Another minute passes until that static sensation strikes again, but this time sleepy headedness follows. Rather than pull out of the moment, she accepts the lull, trying to stay conscious the whole time. A moment passes, and an image of a baby appeared in her mind. Suddenly, the image came to life. An old song played on the radio while the baby blew bubbles with its own spit and raised a small stuffed toy up high only to bang it down onto his thighs and kick his legs to his own rhythm. He was bouncing along to his own beat and having a fun time rocking out to the music. Along with the image came feelings of genuine joy and happiness.

Was this a real thing she was experiencing? How can a technology capture this? What's going on here?

"Mom, I see something! The image isn't quite perfect. It's got some scattered light rainbows in parts and is a little blurry, but I see it. That baby is dancing like crazy, kicking its legs and rocking out to the song. I'm also feeling total happiness and joy at this moment."

"Oh, you found the baby!" replies mom joyfully. "Isn't he the cutest thing you've ever seen?"

"Yeah, he's pretty cute, but I have to ask, how is this real? Am I seeing the same baby as you, mom?"

"Well, it sounds like you are. My image is a little blurry through-out the entire memory as well. You may tune the image better as you play with the pads. I haven't found the perfect spot yet."

Dad joins in. "There probably isn't one perfect spot for clear reception on any memory. You may not ever get a super clear image."

"How does this work?"

Dad continues, "Well, the short story is crystals can hold a memory of events in time naturally. No one knows why or how. It seems to come from the ether. Which is where this technology gets its name, Ethereal Transducers. Metals are crystals, so anything made of metal has a crystalline structure and, therefore, a chunk of time captured as memory. I don't know how anyone figured this technology out, but it's pretty cool."

"So, this works with anything metal or crystal?" She asks her dad.

"Yeah, plastics work too sometimes, but they are terrible at holding any memory for any length of time. There's usually nothing in them."

Her mom interrupts. "And the images are junk, too. It's best to have something metal or crystalline like your father said."

"But the dashboard looks plastic."

"Yes, but there are metal support elements in certain spots," says dad.

He continues. "And right where your left hand was is one of them. It's a metal mounting insert behind the plastic panel placed there during manufacturing. So, plastic doesn't inhibit the metal memory. The pads pick the memory up through the plastic as you come across the underlying metal."

"Ah, okay. Neat-o guys! Where did you learn about this technology? I've never heard of something like this."

Dad replies, "It's new technology and a fair bit expensive. People find automobiles have an abundance of memories. The theory is because cars became so integral to human existence, they captured moments in time where both human and material were present in that moment. Somehow it became forged into the crystalline structure through intense interaction with the world or powerful human emotion. But not always. And the older the car, the better too! That's why I chose this one. She sure was pricey. More than I would have normally spent, but I bought it for the potential memories."

Mom says, "I believe this was a great buy in hindsight," as she bumps Miranda's dad with her hip and casts a smile up at him.

"Let me show you another one I'm talking about that shows intense interaction with the world around it. Maybe it's because the driver was feeling the intensity, but it's a good one to watch," says her dad.

Miranda gets up and hands the headband and pads back. Her dad leads her to the front of the car. He searches for his race scene to show her. Mom gets to searching for other memories in the passenger seat. Miranda reflects on how strange all this is, but she has never seen her parents so happy together.

Brian pops up from the couch and sees the time is almost eight o'clock. The sun has set and the only light on is over the stove. Awaking from a three hour nap, he needs to pee right away. He struggles to get up and says to himself, "Call mom and dad tonight. No, call them right after you're finished doing your business."

Freshly relieved, he stretches his arms up high and walks over to the couch and sits. He lifts a credit card sized piece of semi-clear plastic out of his shirt packet and unfolds the device; once lengthwise and once widthwise. It's his phone. He speaks, "Call Mom." Light runs to the edges, and borders, and calls Mom for him.

"Hello," says a manly voice he recognizes as his father.

"Hey Dad. How's it going?"

"Pretty good. How 'bout you, son?"

"I'm doing alright, I guess, despite being overtaken by robots."

"What do you mean?"

"I got replaced today."

"Damn," replies his father.

A quiet moment passes, and Brian gathers his head while his dad is wondering what to say.

His father continues in a low, solemn voice, "Well, we knew it was bound to happen sometime. And we sensed your time there was coming to an end soon, right? That's what we settled on last time, right?"

In a drawn out, low tone, Brian replies, "Yee-a-a-a-h," fighting back a yawn.

"Well, that's still horrible, all the same. You at home? You sound tired?"

In an exasperated tone, he replies, "Yeah, I'm at home. I'm just waking up from a three-hour nap. I was wondering if I could come over tonight and hang out with you. Is that Okay?"

"Sure! You're always welcome over here! You know that! I'll tell your mom you're on your way over."

"Okay, thanks Dad. See you soon."

Brian ends the call and falls into the sofa, looking out a window. Clouds clutter the night. Tiny, misty rain droplets fall through the streetlights. His head is still foggy. He doesn't want to stay here in the dark house. So, he jerks himself up off the sofa, grabs his keys, and out the door he goes.

He arrives at home to find mom and dad aren't around. So, he checks for their cars being home in the garage, wondering if they stepped out for a moment. He grabs his folded phone from his pocket as he turns the knob on the garage door. If they aren't here, then a quick call will find them for sure. He peeks his head into the garage and sees his parents hunkered over some new vehicle he hasn't seen before.

He calls out, "Hey, you guys!" to no response.

Squinting his eyes in their direction, they don't see or hear him. He steps into the garage, slams the door and calls out again,

"Hey guys! Mom… Dad…?" and no response again. So, with a questioning gaze, he walks over to his parents to get their attention. After all, they don't appear dead. They would seem frozen in place if it weren't for his mother's shifting of her hands on the hood of the car and his dad squinting his eyes closed and turning his head sideways. They are quite involved in something, he guesses.

A light tap on mom's shoulders and a loud, "Hello Mom!" snaps mom out of her concentration.

"Hey! Baby boy!"

"Mom. What the hell are you and dad doing? I said I was coming over and you were nowhere around."

"Oh my, time flies when you're using these things!"

"No, I don't, mom. What the hell are those things and what's this? A new car? Are you kidding me?"

"Yes, well, it's an older car."

"I'll say. I've never seen one of these things before. That's a Ford by the nameplate."

His mom reaches out and taps his dad on his shoulder. She says, "Bobby, Brian's here. He's asking what kind of car this is."

His dad snaps into reality once his mom talks and notices Brian has arrived as she completes her question.

"Hey Brian. Didn't hear you sneak up, ha-ha-ha! Oh, this old thing? I spent a pretty penny on her."

"I bet," replies Brian. "What is it and why did you buy it?"

"It's a 1991 Ford Mustang XL 5.0. It's got the original 5.0 XL five spoke factory rims too! They're worn but not bad for almost a hundred years old! Ha! I hope I look that good at a hundred years!"

"Jesus Christ, Dad! A Fuckin' hundred-year-old car? Are you kidding me? How the hell did you sell mom on it! You guys can't afford that, I'm sure. What the hell were you thinking?"

"Oh, come on now!" replies his dad. "You only live once and it's an asset that only grows in value. It'll be yours one day when your mom and I keel over. Besides, you should see what people got down at the lot!"

"Oh, God Dad! Keel over? Christ! Are you okay? Mom, what's going on here?"

Mom's brow was furrowed with her eyes closed when Brian asked her the question. She snaps out of it with an angry face. "Dammit, Brian, I was just getting to the good part! Now shhh!"

"What the…. shhh? What good part!" He exclaims. "You two look like you've already lost it! What the fuck?"

His mom responds in a calm, agreeable motherly voice, "Language, please. I let your dad do it and, thinking back on it, I like the decision he made to get this one."

"Mom! You swore too!" He switches his focus to his father. "Dad, what is this? What are you guys doing? Are you two losing it at the same time?"

"Well, of course not, Brian."

"I gotta know. No secrets, right? Spill the beans, pops!"

Brian listens in astonishment as his dad discusses how it all works. He can't believe what he's hearing at the same time. 'Ethereal Transducer?' What a lame ass name for a headband attached to rocks. There are no lights on the fake magic headband. It looks like a cheap scam, and they are getting ready to pull a fast one on him.

"Dad, how does this thing power up?"

"Well, if you are out of batteries, it can pick up only the strongest signals using just the small amount of electricity your skin can generate. But there is also a battery supply, of course, which everyone uses. That power is used to amplify weak and fuzzy signals to be more tunable by your hands and the device."

"I mean, there's no 'On' light or anything?"

"Nope! Just consider them always on. The battery backup will kick in when your hands touch the pads."

Brian takes a chance with the headband and pads. He has to see if his parents are going crazy. If this doesn't work, he may look at early elderly care options and he's not sure how he'll afford the situation. Maybe now that he's unemployed, he will just watch after them himself. A daunting thought for a young man. Or sell this ridiculously old car dad bought to cover costs. His dad reaches over to ensure as many as possible of the flat, round touch points are touching Brian's head. Brian places the pads on the hood and the front left panel of the mustang. Nothing happens.

"Dad, there's nothing happening."

"You'll feel something in your head as you slowly slide the pads around. As you get something, move the pads less and try a different angle on the pad by rotating it. They're egg shaped for a reason. Probably to allow for a small deviation in reception over specific crystalline structures, allowing for a finer reception in one location versus another. That's my guess."

Following Dad's advice, he makes tiny movements across the hood and quarter panel. Then, a fuzzy feeling across his forehead, and an image of something. Possibly a blending of images, but he can't focus correctly, and it evaporates without a trace.

In an excited, elevated tone, he says, "Dad, I had something for a split second! Is that what I should expect?"

"Well, once seeing an image, zero in on it by making smaller movements of the pads and twisting them one at a time like I was doing earlier. You may get an image, or a recording in time, like a video played out in your head. It's pretty incredible."

Brian tries again. This time he concentrates on the first fuzziness or static-like feeling that races across his forehead. His hands are well placed, but his left hand is further up the hood than before. His brow wrinkles tight as he squeezes his eyes closed. He cocks his head while twisting the right-hand pad slowly clockwise and suddenly he's in the middle of the scene. He's standing right beside the car in front of the windshield and driver's side door. An arm rises with a hand holding a gun pointing out the passenger side window. Three loud shots fire off, racking his ears. His eyes become imprinted with the shadowy effects of flames from the blasts. He jerks his whole body up and lands his feet a few inches back from where he was as he rips the headband off his forehead.

"Dad! Holy Shit! Have you seen that?" He exclaims as the grey green image of the flames from the shots float on his retina.

"What are you talking about?"

"It looks like the driver pulled out a gun and shot someone through the passenger window!"

"Did you see who he killed?"

"No, dad! Did you? I'm even still seeing the flash from the gun in my eyes. You know when you look at a bright light and you get a greyed out shape in your vision?"

"Yeah."

"That's what I'm seeing right now. How is that? I thought this was only working on the brain. It seems it's working on my eyes too!"

"Well, I have seen no one killed yet, and I haven't seen a gun."

"I have," says his mom. "The gun is always in the glove compartment."

"Gee, thanks mom." He says with sarcastic dismay.

"Well, at least we know what to look out for now," says dad. "I bet someone down at the lot could answer why your eyes were affected too."

"You mentioned that before. What's that?" He asks.

"The lot is empty now where an old indoor mall used to be near the intersection of Independence Boulevard and Virginia Beach Boulevard across from Old Town Center."

"Yeah, I know where. You're talking about the old Pembroke area and the run down leftovers of the mall parking lot."

"Yep, Old Town Center right across the street still has some bustle, but it never achieved the full vision of what Virginia Beach City Council wanted. The rest of that Pembroke area fell apart over time, and when technology allowed more workers from home, all the business offices closed over the years. Best thing they did was tear down those old buildings and replace them with the two enormous city parks. The luxury town home developments down VB Blvd between Old Town Center and Vacation City get the benefit of all that greenery plus a fantastic location to the beach. It's all smartly connected now. Old Town Center lost nearly all its business then, but Vacation City brought tourists a little further inland, making the entire area more popular as well. A great place to vacation with more tourists, shopping, and fun activities, meaning more activities than simply laying out in the cancer causing sun."

"Gee, thanks for the history lesson, pop. Wake me up when you're done," he says as he gives his dad a weak jab in the shoulder.

"Hey! At least all that tidal inundation didn't get rid of the bikinis!" says Dad

Mom gives his dad a jab in the other shoulder. "And that's exactly why we don't go down there anymore!" She says in jest. "He's not allowed to get any new ideas on things," she says as she laughs.

"I wish they'd clean up the old hotels still standing out in the water. The remnants are just ugly, and we still have sea vagrant issues there as well. The beach isn't as attractive with vagrants everywhere, and the robot cops never move them along anymore. Plus, you can't swim near the demolished buildings because they are dangerous as hell too. Their rebar, parts, and pieces jut out of the water at low tide. It just looks ugly now in those areas," Brian concludes.

"Anyway, I didn't tell you about the lot," his dad interjects, "Every Saturday and Sunday now, a bunch of people bring their old vehicles to the lot and allow anyone with Transducers to 'rub and read' we say. It's a way to share stories of history based on what our car's crystalline materials have captured as experiences in time. It is the hottest thing to do and the older the car, the better! Older cars have more stories to tell. Business is coming back to Old Town Center, too. New restaurants are opening up and the atmosphere is lively again," he says with boyish excitement.

Mom jumps in. "You boys should go tomorrow evening, Brian. It will get your mind off losing your job today and it is loads of fun. Your dad has made great friends with a fella who brings his 1956 Cadillac El Dorado about once a month. Oh! What a time to have lived! I wish I lived back then," she says with a swooning smile and a glitter in her eyes as she looks at the ceiling in a dreamy sway and hands covering her chest. She is picturing herself in the 1950s.

"That car has such incredible memories. And the music! Oh! The music! There's nothing like the love songs back then! If I could live any other time, it would be back then," she says.

"I agree. That car has a ton of exceptional, old memories. And I get to hear about them for the next three days every time she gets a visit," says Dad.

In a playful, angry way, his mom whacks his dad on the shoulder with a resounding slap. "Oh, it's not so bad and you know it! You're the one who can go on all week about it! Geez, you should hear this old buzzard caw day and night about his damn car stories," she says to Brian.

"Now, now. I'm not that bad either."

"Oh bologna! He's the worst!" pointing her fingers at dad's chest and poking his belly.

Brian smiles at his parent's playful complaints about one another and his parents are getting a kick out of poking at one another themselves. They make their way into the house, laughing and poking and giggling. Brian feels like a kid again with no cares in the world, but as they enter the kitchen area, he realizes he needs to talk with them about his situation. It's why he came here tonight. He's had a couple of years to prepare and now he has to act.

Brian wakes up early to help his dad with the late spring chores. There's a lawn to mow and edge, a garden to weed and to complete adding mulch, plus mom needs her hanging planters from last year cleared out and set up again with peonies, her favorite flower for her front porch area. The different colors they come in brings an air of vibrance and happiness to their basic, brown brick house with red shudders. Not much to do, but when you refuse to own a robot mower out of spite, it takes time out of your day. Brian's Dad is on his way to the local home supply store to grab a can of deck refinishing paint along with two or three boards to repair the outermost corner of the back deck which receives sunshine one hundred percent of the time and shortens the life of even the best wood with the best protection. Brian is looking for the gas can, which does not want to be found.

He calls into the house to his mom, "Mom! Do you know where dad hides the gas can?"

No response.

"Mom!" He shouts louder each time. "Mom!"

He guesses she must still be in the shower. He pulls the door closed, looking everywhere for the gas can. It's no place to be seen. However, that old 1991 Ford Mustang catches his attention once more. He walks over closer, and he rubs his hand along the top of the hood and the lower window frame. The metal is cool to the touch, having been in the garage on a cool spring morning. The paint is a pretty burgundy color with a black interior. He stares through the glass at the console. The styling is so old-fashioned and basic. No technology but the radio. He couldn't fathom a time when people had to pay so much attention to the road and traffic. How did they not all die in accidents? How did they hold their attention that long on something so mundane and boring? He had heard of things called traffic jams, but A.I. Managed Vehicular Movement algorithms solved that problem a long time ago. This car was from the age of traffic jams. He wonders if he can find one using dad's transducer thing. Whatever the hell the stupid name of it was. He saw dad drop it on the set of shelves by the garage door leading into the house and finds the contraption still in place.

Donning the headband, he grabs a crystal for each hand and inspects them. They're plain, old crystals which look factory produced because they are perfect in their crystalline structure. No fractures or foreign elements can be seen. He can tell by the way the light breaks from the crystalline lattice structure the chemistry is perfectly clean. The one in his right hand is light orange, and the other is light blue. Both are mesmerizing if you stare at them. They almost draw you in as if you were looking into another dimension. He snaps out of his little trance and presses the headband to ensure the flat, round pads are all contacting his head properly, and he searches across the hood of the car like his dad taught him.

Again, he doesn't receive any images. Fifteen minutes go by and only blips or wisps of anything are noticed. Frustration kicks in so, he tries the interior of the car. Sliding in and placing one rock on the steering wheel and one on the center console between the seats leads to an explosion of images and streaming videos blasting through his brain! The energy throws his head backwards, and his cranium bounces off the seat's headrest. He opens his eyes and still sees things coming through. Image on top of image on top of streaming action flashing through his mind as if he were watching a screen. The sounds are rocking the hearing part of his brain! There aren't earphone jacks for this device. The images and streams come with sounds of cars, babies, women and men talking, yelling, cursing, marching bands playing, sounds from the radio of music long ago lost and forgotten, birds, screeching tires, even smells of gas and oil and smoke and the taste of French fries. His brain is blowing up and all this happens in about four seconds. So much more than he could have imagined!

He can't handle the overload. Consciousness begins slipping into tunnel vision as he yanks his hand from the steering wheel. The images escape his brain in a blink and his head slams into the steering wheel. He gasps for breath. His mind goes blank. His eyes are wide opened, but he's not registering what he's seeing. He looks as if he's staring at the console through the steering wheel itself. His brain is fading to deep sleep with a gravitational pull into the blackness of his mind. A momentary command breaks through that he should fight the drift into darkness, but how? He has no strength. And before he could finish his plan, his eyes flutter closed, his hands drop, and one crystal drops and bounces away. He's unconscious and in a bad way.

At breakfast, Miranda and her parents are wrapping up conversation about Miranda's future. As a newly minted twenty-seven year old, her parents have been supporting her all these years and have recently told her she won't be getting any more help. They showed Miranda a spreadsheet of her expenses and showed her how she could pay for her new vehicle and all her other expenses, like all other adults must do. Miranda was bewildered and wasn't sure emotionally how she should receive this information. The thoughts in her brain swirled with all the possibilities she was facing. She feared serious changes to her lifestyle, but on paper, at least sustaining her lifestyle looked manageable. Expensive taste wasn't her style, or at least she believed she wasn't expensive until mom and dad showed her the spreadsheet of her bills, including all the expenses they covered for her for the past three years. Most of her friends weren't as lucky. Maybe this is why some of her friends don't spend as much time with her as they used to. She chalked it all up to growing older, getting jobs, marriages, and having less time, but for the first time, all her fortune hits her, and she realizes she's the one who's been blind. She consciously held a normal, attentive look while hiding emotions and laboring to listen to parental memes on self-sufficient adulthood. She always expected this day would come. A girl must get her head around the implications and quickly.

Being so burdened and a little low, she asks mom and dad if she can stay the weekend with them. Having not been around as much, she needed time to absorb her new life now. With an agreement made to stay around a few days, she sets off to her apartment to grab her clothes and inform Sheila she won't be around anymore.

Upon entering, she finds Sheila is gone. She forgot Sheila is working an extra shift at the Pharmacy this weekend. Sheila was smart in selecting pharmacy for a profession. Even with robots around, the laws on the books for so many decades now require so much human oversight, control, and reporting that pharmaceutical jobs, though dwindling a little over time, have remained mostly in the hands of humans. Even that business is changing though, and Sheila said she could see the writing on the wall. She might make her retirement before being replaced, but she isn't sure. The laws are beginning to favor the pharmaceutical companies again because humans add expense and waste to pharmacy bills. The U.S. Congress and Senate are hot to reduce costs to sick and elderly Americans as more and more end up replaced and out of work. That means putting even more people out of work. A fiendish spiral of societal destruction which sounds like what her dad and mom have said so many times, never trust the government to help. It's hard to be stupid on this point with so much well recorded historical examples these days of governments failing the people, but you'd be surprised, human stupidity knows no bounds.

Considering social things amid her own predicament is already hard to endure. The changes before her are modest. They're a lot of little things, but they add up to one big emotional weight on her shoulders. Her face distorts for a moment as she walks into her room to gather a few things for the stay at mom and dad's. Her face crinkles again, and she fights the desire to cry. She finds she's holding her breath, so she lets the air out and breathes in a deep shuttering breath as she breaks down and cries. She leans forward toward her bed and falls flat across the mattress. Her legs bounce up a little beyond the side of the bed as they hang out toward where she was standing. Tears crawl down her cheeks and she twists and wiggles to get right in her bed. She grabs Snuffy; her stuffed polar bear, from the bedside table where he stood on all four legs for the past couple of years. He's her one childhood trinket she keeps close from when she nearly lost her life at fourteen to a ruptured appendix. Dad gave him to her when she woke up from surgery. He reminds her she is lucky and to stay positive about things. She also thinks this is just the little girl in her trying to hold on for one more hour, one more minute before joining a metaphorical dusty trunk full of ancient memories draped in washed out colors and oxidized stories with ever-fading detail. She pulls Snuffy in close for a snuggle and, after a few minutes, cries herself into a little nap.

Later on, her eyes pop open to the sound of her roommate calling out for her. She wipes a little drool from the corner of her mouth. Wow! She must have been tired! Pulling her head up off the pillow felt more like lifting a cinderblock up off the bed. A lot of work and a little painful. She tosses her legs over the side of the bed, grabs Snuffy, and places him back on the bedside table. Her emotions weight heavy. Brain and body aren't into moving around yet, but she forces herself to stand up, and almost falls over. Catching herself required fast reflexes and a jolt that sparked the fire in her brain to get moving. Still unwillingly, feet scuff along to the living room.

"Hey Sheila. What's up?"

"Hey, you look sleepy!"

"Yeah, I must have dozed off."

"Well, I was going to tell you I invited three or four people over tonight. Just a couple of girlfriends. Is that Ok with you?"

"Oh yeah, sure. I won't be here tonight. I just came to grab some things because I'm going to stay at my parent's house for a couple days."

"Oh okay," responds Sheila, with a rise in the tone of her voice as if she was asking a question. Miranda knows she wants more information.

"Yeah. My parents finally dropped the ball on me last night."

"What do you mean?"

"They will not help cover for me anymore when I'm short on my bills."

"Oh yeah?" Sheila doesn't know how to respond to Miranda's situation, as it is nothing like what she is accustomed to. She never had parents to help cover for her. If she couldn't pay for something, she didn't buy it. That's that.

"Yeah," says Miranda in a lower tone. "They sat me down and went through all my bills, plus all the other money given to me over the past three years."

"Uh oh," Sheila knew that was going to lead to big decisions, given Miranda's love of shopping and credit cards.

"Yep, it finally happened."

"So, mommy and daddy 'bout had enough of it now, have they?"

"Yeah. I knew it was going to happen sometime, though, I mean, I'm like twenty-seven now. I should be an adult doing this on my own. Hell, I should be married with kids or something."

"Oh damn! No, not kids too! Baby, you're too young!" Sheila exclaims in jest.

"Ha-ha, I know, right? Me, kids!" And they both laugh heartily at that one. Miranda because she can't see herself with kids right now and Sheila because she knows kids would grow Miranda's ass up super-fast and that would be funny as hell to see.

Sheila says, "Well, we talked before about findin' good men. Ain't none to be had if you ask me. I'm tired of lookin' by now. Anyway, I don't know where any of 'em are, so I just don't see getting married in my twenties. Maybe in my thirties, if I'm lucky. You remember Ja'rell, right? When you first moved in last year?"

"Yeah, I remember. He's still in prison now, right?"

"Of course," she looks at Miranda like Miranda knows what she's going to say next. "His dumb ass is still holed up in the state pen. But I thought he might have been the one. We already talked about this, you and me. I thought he was one of the few brothers to get up out the hood and make something of himself. He had his own painting and flooring business and a general contractor that was always willing to toss him weekly work. He had it going on with the look, the money. I mean, he had it right and tight! I thought for sure he was the one! But it turns out he was a little too much hood still. Selling drugs and shit at night behind my back. Knowing I'm a professional woman and can't get caught up in that shit, too! Damn, I was close!"

"Ha-Ha. Well, you've been lucky in one respect, in that you can say you've been close. I haven't been that close ever. All the men I've run into have all been too immature and too dumb to be grown up."

"I think that's just men. Especially young men our age. They tighten up as they get older, though. At least the good ones do."

"Well, all I know Sheila is my ass is getting grown up quick now thanks to mommy and daddy cutting the money."

"It can be hard, but you can do it. We all do it at some point."

"I know. And I've always known this was coming. Look, one thing I have to do is bring down my monthly expenses. I only have until the end of next month for my part of the lease, which I think is up for both of us at that point, anyway. So, I need to tell you I won't extend the lease. I'm moving back in with my parents."

"Oh my. Okay. I understand," responds Sheila.

"I've worked out a deal with them that will save me about five hundred and fifty bucks a month just in that expense alone and I'll still be helping them with electric and water and everything too. But this is something I have to do."

"Oh, I get it. I understand."

"It's time for me to grow up. Who knows? I might even find a man worth keeping one day too," she says with a chuckle.

"Oh Lord please, if you do, the let me know where you found him, and if he has a brother!"

They both laugh at that one. Miranda feels like she's pulling away from a good friend already. It's kind of sad. Sheila is already moving forward in her mind with her next roommate. She likes Miranda, but in reality, she never felt the complete connection to her. Her way of life and how she was brought up was a different culture that Sheila never experienced. She could appreciate it, though. She dreamed of being able to do the same for her kids one day. But for now, she wants her next roommate to be a close friend. She even knows who she'll ask this time.

Miranda continues, "So you are having friends over tonight?"

"Yeah, we're going to have some witchy fun!"

"Oh wow! Are you breaking out the Tarot cards and everything?"

"You know it. We are all going to get readings, and I'm giving out crystals to those who might need them in their life to help with conflict and growth, and we are all getting drunk as hell! Ha-haaah!"

"Ah! That sounds fun! You gave me a setup for my crystals, I still have them laid out like you told me to do and I burn a little tea candle in the middle at night when I sleep."

"I noticed the last time we were talking in there. Hope it helps."

"I think it does. My dad says it's all phooey. But I haven't had one bad dream since you gave me those crystals and told me what to do."

"I'm telling ya! All you got to do is believe, and it works!"

"I'm a believer now!" Miranda exclaims with delight.

Brian opens his eyes to see he is in his old room. He was semi-lucid when his dad found him. Walking with his dad's help up to his old bedroom, he doesn't remember much. The overwhelming flow of images and streaming real-lifelike videos of people, sounds, and events is what he remembers. It knocked him out.

"Brian, you awake now, son?" Asks dad.

He mumbles, "Holy crap. I feel like my brain exploded."

"I was going to call emergency services before you came to in the car. Even then I considered calling them." His dad calls out. "Beverly! He's awake now!"

"Oh, my head," he says in a groaning tone as he raises one hand up and supports his arm on his forehead.

"What happened? I saw you had the Transducer on when I returned." Asks his dad.

"Oh my God, dad. I was experimenting with it on the hood like you showed me last night. I wasn't getting anything again. After about ten or fifteen minutes, I got frustrated and tried the inside of the car. I put one on the steering wheel and one on the console and a nuclear explosion went off in my head. Everything was loud and vibrant and streaming and mixing and mashing. I can't even explain it all. I was right in the moment, reliving everything all at once in full color and sound but I couldn't control the scenes or sounds as they bombarded my brain."

His mom glides into the room with concern. She's in her house robe with curlers in her hair. This stage is her typical midway point before getting ready to go out for her chores later in the afternoon. She has to have her hair and makeup just right or she won't leave the house and she takes forever sometimes to finish getting ready.

His mom says, "Brian! Oh my, I'm so glad you are awake! I didn't know anything bad had happened to you. You caught me in the shower, I guess."

"It's okay, mom."

"How are you feeling?"

"Like a school bus ran over my head two or three times."

His dad jumps in. "It sounds like he got printed, Beverly."

"Oh my, like Jack Wilkerson! Is he going to be alright?" she asks with some fear in her voice and a look of genuine concern cast toward Bobby.

"He's going to be alright. He must have dropped one crystal right away, but the overload on his brain left him feeling like this." Responds his dad who then turns to ask him, "You don't feel like you are being pulled back into sleep do you?"

"No. I don't. Just worn out. But funny you should mention that. At one point during all this 'printing,' as you call it, I was being drawn into a deep dark something or other. I can't remember when that happened, but the force was overpowering. It brought me down into something, and I tried to fight the urge to sleep. I can't remember the order of anything. But I'm glad I'm awake now. I'm thirsty, I'm worn out and ragged mentally. I still have chores I can help with, too"

His dad interrupts, "Don't you worry about the chores today. I will get around to mowing here in a moment. That's what my plan before you woke up. I want you to rest and if you have the energy, we'll go to the lot this evening and have you talk to De'Andrè and Ray-Ray. They've been down at the lot from the start and pulled people into the community to share their car histories as stories. They run the group, and they have the deepest knowledge of what happened to you, which is quite rare. No one knows much about the process, but they would definitely have more details or can point us to someone local who knows more."

His mom asks, "Bobby, are you sure that's a good thing?"

"Now I'm only going to take him there if he's got the energy and is feeling up to it. It was on our plans to go tonight, anyway. This is Elijah's night to be there too, and that's the whole reason you go." He turns to Brian and says, "Elijah Price owns the 1956 Cadillac El Dorado she falls in love with once a month. She'll spend the evening reliving the 1950s and 1960s. Can you believe that? That was like a hundred and thirty years ago. You'll see how pristine this baby is too! It's a guaranteed, automatic winner of any car show it shows up at! Whew, she is pretty!"

"Sounds amazing, dad," says Brian as he removes the covers to get out of bed.

"Now hold on, son. Are you feeling like getting up?"

"I feel like I need to get up and move around. I'm not sick, just a little brain dysfunctional at the moment, and I feel like if I get up and moving and restart my day that I will come up out of this funk I'm in."

His mom says, "Just be careful, please! You may lose your balance and hurt yourself worse. Here, take my arm. We'll go downstairs, get you a drink of something refreshing, and I'll fix you a light lunch. Bobby, you want anything before you get to mowing?"

"No, I'm fine. Brian, stay with your mom. Beverly, please keep a watch on his eyes. Jack had issues with his pupils, if you remember. He complained of brightness, squinted a lot, woke up and just before he passed out unconscious for two weeks."

"Okay, yes. I'll watch. I forgot about that. We don't want that here. Brian, you tell me if you get strange light sensitivity or any other strange feelings above your shoulders. Okay?"

"Yeah, mom. I'll let you know. I am a little hungry now, though."

Bobby followed Brian and Beverly down the upstairs hall and down the stairs to the kitchen. They walked rather slow ensuring Brian was keeping steady steps. Idle chit-chat bounced off the walls between the three of them. Upon arrival in the kitchen, Bobby made his way into the garage to start the chores.

Brian sat down at the table with a thump into his chair.

"Be careful," his mom says. "You're a little weak still."

"Thanks mom."

Beverly's slippers scratched toward the refrigerator and she rummaged about, grabbing two plastic containers, and placing them on the counter. Brian watched her as she went about hunkering over to get a skillet and a pan. He noticed for the first time how old his mom seemed. She still looked good for her age for sure, but time is a ravager, and leaves little as it was. He noticed the discolorations on her skin, which was blotchy. Not like when she was young. Vitiligo had crept in over the years. Her hands, arms, legs, and feet wore the miscoloring now. He can't remember the first time he noticed her condition but as a youngster his mom had perfect, smooth skin. Grey has waged war on her hair, but she won't let the world see even the slightest. She dyes her hair so often now the ends are dried. She does what she can to soften and tame the wily strands, but all things eventually show with age, he's learned.

Tonight, she will put on one of her favorite outfits and go out in style with her husband. He'll dress up nice too in an outfit she will let him wear and not of his own picking. She'll have a whirl of a time in a different time; the 1950s and 1960s. When it's over, she'll dream her dreams of another life and spend the next week telling her stories to her husband and now her son, too.

This is her highlight of every month. She'll be a little teenage girl again wearing an A-line skirt, black and white Oxford shoes, her boyfriend's letterman's jacket, maybe his ring too will be around her neck, and singing all the songs in a fantasy world she never knew herself. His dad will soak up the dreamy images with a big smile, love every story she tells, and then playfully complain about how she goes on and on about her dream life. Running away into the memories of other lifetimes is something they relish together, and it keeps their love for each other fresh.

Brian wants that with someone too, one day. He's a man, yes, but men want these things too. Just not in a girly yearning way; a man's way. He's thirty-four, and he's not sure if he'll find someone by an age where he'd still want to have kids and share times like this with a family of his own. He almost gave up with his earlier fiancée walking out. The notion of family is so fractured in these modern times. He wants someone who wants a family like he was able to experience growing up. Where do you find a girl like that today? He thinks she can't be found. But he doesn't shut the door all the way waiting for something amazing to happen. Now unemployed, he has to get to work on something that will supply an income. His firefighter's retirement will not be enough on its own. Few girls will take a broke guy these days which means family thoughts are out. He has one skill that he'd like to sharpen and an idea for a business. Robots don't do this kind of work well at all because, well, they see the process and the end product as 'optimized' so to speak. A little human non-optimization and creativity might just find a market. It's a long shot.

Miranda trips through the door of her parent's house because a bag catches the door jamb and blocks her foot movement. She bangs her knee on the hardwood floor and falls to her side with bags falling off her noodle-like arms. Of course, she is trying to bring in more at one time than she should. She hates making trips to and from the car for stuff. It's weird how she is about that. In no other part of her life does she try to overexert herself except when she has 'a load of crap' to bring in from the car. The idea annoys her to no end. She believes it might be because her mom used to go to the grocery and bring home a million bags of food and goodies. She was always the one left making all the trips to and from the car. That chore annoyed her to no end, for whatever reason she cannot figure. Now, anything needing brought in is a nuisance, and will happen in one trip come hell or high water. This time hell had a trip and fall in store.

"Miranda!" her mom cries out as she rounds the corner. "Are you okay?"

"Ouch! I banged my knee pretty good," she says as she lies on the floor looking down the hall towards mom.

"My word! It's you and those groceries again! Did you have to bring in so much?" her mom says with a mix of worry and chastisement in her voice, "Here, let me help."

"Thanks mom, I think I broke my knee." She says in an aching voice.

"Oh, let me see that!"

She looks at Miranda's knee and, in an instant, she realized Miranda was trying to get attention.

"Good Grief, that knee isn't broken, Miranda! You'll be just fine. You don't even have a little boo-boo. Now quit your cryin' and get these things up. I've got these two here."

Mom gets up and heads to the extra bedroom upstairs with the bags Miranda brought in. Miranda works her way onto her feet and scrounges up the rest of her belongings. She makes the entire trip upstairs into the room in one complete effort without further issues.

"Miranda, what is wrong with you?" her mom asks in a calm voice, "I knew you didn't break your knee and you're clearly uptight. You tried to bring all your belongings in at once. You're stressed, looking for attention, and you seem to have a lot on your mind."

Miranda drops the last of what she's carrying on the ground next to the nightstand which lands with a thud. She stretches out her right arm to get the blood flowing again and to loosen up the muscles and takes a deep breath and exhales with a prolonged huff as her shoulders drop.

"I'm sorry, mama. It's just all the added responsibility, and I had to tell Sheila about my bills situation, and I was moving back in with you guys until I can get my credit debt situation fixed. Plus, having to move back in with mom and dad at my age, really? What did I miss? Have I done something wrong? What's the deal with me, mom? Am I off or something? Why do I feel like I'm behind the rest of the world in everything?"

Her mom understands her situation. The concern on her face tells the entire story, and she responds, "Sweetie, it's not anything you have or haven't done and you're not behind anyone or anything. There's an entire generation of people just like you. It's what has happened in the world that forces us to adapt and become what we are."

"Well, if that's the case, I've picked a bunch of friends that are w-a-a-a-ay ahead of everyone, I guess. They're all married off and with kids of their own now. Two live in their mom and dad's house but most are off living by themselves. They all have careers now while I'm struggling to be a journeyman fabrication specialist, for God's sake! At twenty-seven, me, a metal bender! I'm too girly for that!" She breaks down in tears and plops onto an open spot on the bed.

Her mom starts, "Miranda, there's nothing wrong with metals fabrication. You're in a great paying career and one of the few that's still in relative demand. You've got a lot of job possibilities at the

Shipyards in Norfolk and Portsmouth, plus a lot of fabrication shops in and around Newport News. That's close to us. It's a great opportunity for you. It's what I did before becoming a welder. Look at me, am I too girly?"

She continues while sobbing, "Mom, no! You haven't worked as either of those in about fifteen years. You've been teaching. Things are different now. Anyway, I've always looked at you as sort-of-girly. Not like me, look at me."

"What? Are you crazy! I was Prom Queen in high school! I was the ultimate girly girl!" She continues with playful indignation, "Sorta girly! Hah! I can out shop anybody and find the best deals to boot! My makeup is perfection, sweetie, and I'm educated and got skills too. Your daddy is lucky to have landed a woman like me. Shoot! I wasn't even lookin' his way! I was a girly girl lookin' for a manly man! Ha-ha-ha!"

Miranda breaks her sobbing for a little laughter. She sniffs the tears back up her nose and wipes her eyes.

"I guess you always had that girly side to you."

"Damn right I do! I can strut my stuff with the best of them." Says her mom with a hand one on her hip and her hips swinging side to side. "And you can too! You're every bit a part of me, even if you don't always recognize it."

Miranda jumps in, "And daddy's a manly man too! He's tough, he hunts, he played football in high school, and he still works out enough!"

"Oh sweetie, your daddy was third string. He's more mental tough than physical tough. At that young age, girls aren't looking for mental tough. You know that. It's not until we get older that we realize it's the geeks we should have been chasing!"

They both break out in laughter loud enough to draw dad's attention down the hall. He ambles his way to the room where his two girls are laughing on the side of the bed.

"Goodness gracious! What is all the hen cackling going on here? Annie, what are you two sneaks planning?" he says with a goofy smile on his face.

Miranda's mom gets up from the side of the bed, still laughing, and walks over to her husband, Michael. On the way over, she says, "And little did I know how lucky I was to find someone who was not only manly-tough but mentally tough, too." And she reaches up with one arm over his shoulder and gives him a big old kiss.

He responds, looking at Annie with a hold-on-a-minute look and says, "Alright, now I know you both are up to no good." Then he points at Miranda and says, "Miranda, you're grounded!"

Everyone breaks out into more laughter. Miranda's dad always had a way to find the humor in any situation. She always envisioned her dad as a guy with a goofy heart when she wasn't remembering him as that guy who was always gone. And he was gone a lot, but when he was around, when she looked past the ever present, subtle anger she held toward him, he was a genuinely funny, goofy guy. And that trait is one of the many things Miranda's mom has always loved about him despite too many lonely nights. As far as Miranda knows, his absence was never because dad had another woman. He was traveling all the time and missed too much of her growing up and mom's wonderful years.

As her parents go down the hall toward the stairs, Miranda's mom says, "We'll talk again, sweetie."

"Ok, mom," she replies. She looks at the mess on her bed and doesn't want to deal with putting things away. So, she lays back onto a pillow and kicks her stuff off the end of the bed onto the floor to make room for her legs. She fidgets with a pillow or two and calls out, "TV on."

The grey sheet of plastic on the wall next to the closet door comes to life. Her dad thought these were the coolest things about twenty years ago when they first hit the market. It's a sheet of plastic rolled up into a tube which becomes your television. You buy the size of the TV you want, and the package arrives at your front door like things have done since the caveman days. And that's all. You unroll the sheet and glue the corners to your wall. Your new TV automatically understands voice commands from all languages, dialects, and can even discern speech impediments. She and Sheila didn't even bother having a T.V.

"Channel up," she says as she marches through the channels, looking for something to waste the rest of her evening. When that yields nothing of interest, she calls out, "Channel Guide." She peeks at a couple screens of programming saying, "Next" after each screen fails to fulfill her wishes for something entertaining. Somehow, she falls asleep between screens. Her mind and emotions completely worn out.

Later that evening, Brian and his parents arrive at the lot. His dad drove the Mustang while Brian rode along. Mom followed in the car right behind dad as insurance against a rear end collision. Brian is getting off the phone with Di'Mario. He's explained he needs to sell his house and will aim to sell in about six weeks, but there are some things that need to get done before that happens. Di'Mario says he may be interested in the opportunity. They will work out the details later.

"Wow! There's quite an assembly of vehicles here tonight." Says dad. "It's almost summer and everyone is getting into the summer fun. This is going to be great."

Brian scanned across all the shine, sparkle, and people. Everyone was wearing headbands on and held pads searching the cars for stories. With so many cars and people running around, it looked like a county fair. Food trucks selling dishes and goodies lined up along one end of the lot. Hordes of people walked across the boulevard to the Old Town Center to sample the new bars and restaurants opening up. Music abounded as each car had the radio going. Five or six cars Brian recognized on sight. But an awful lot of vehicles he could not recall. The little boy in him wanted to experience them all.

"Wow, dad. You weren't kidding! There's a ton of stuff here!" he said with a boyish exuberance.

"Yeah, tonight's going to be fantastic. We need to find De'Andrè and Ray-Ray. I'll park by them. They are the guys that run this gathering every week. We need to ask them about your experience."

"Oh yeah. I want to check out some of these other vehicles here tonight too." Responds Brian. "I can't believe what I'm seeing. Most of these sparklers here are new to me. Where have I been?"

His dad laughs as he pulls into the lot to find a parking spot. Mom pulls in right behind, and they roll through to the far side, looking for De'Andrè and Ray-Ray. Mom beeps her horn in rapid fashion and dad looks in the rearview mirror. He knows she is going to park next to Elijah's Cadillac.

"That's your mom honking away. She's going to stop here for the night. We'll come back and get her later. Much later. The stories in that car make her so happy when she gets to experience them and tell them to everyone. She's a different woman since I've been bringing her here."

Brian looks to his right. He had been looking at other cars and had not noticed one of the most spectacular vehicles he's ever laid his eyes on in person. He's seen cars like this on the internet and tv shows, but he has never seen one like this up close and personal.

"Holy God Almighty, Dad! Is that the one?"

"That's the one! Told you, you can't miss it!"

His eyes beheld a beautiful maroon colored behemoth of a vehicle with magnificently curved lines and more chrome on every edge and outside feature than a rational person would ever conceive of putting on a car. Nobody uses chrome anymore. And the size of this beauty was preposterous! Modern cars have shiny plastic, electroluminescent paints, and crazy composites that give the vehicle all unique looks and textures, and they are streamlined and 'normal sized', so to speak. His heart sped up as he was passing the Caddy. The interior was immaculate white with bench seats so big you could swim in them. And the big fat tires showed off giant white walls. He had never seen those in real life. This car had no flaws and was more beautiful than anything he had seen in his lifetime. The entire body shined brilliantly even in the poorly lit lot. This masterpiece could have rolled right out of heaven itself. He was half expecting angels to be guarding this thing if he could pull his eyes away.

"Christ, that is a thing of beauty. I mean seriously! That's got to be a fifteen million dollar car or more. Is that the oldest car here?"

"It might be tonight. I'm not sure. There's a collector who shows up every once in a blue moon. He owns an Edsel that's around that time frame too, and a few older vehicles. Problem is he wants to charge for sharing the stories. Not sure if he'll ever come back here. Around here, we share for the love of the stories and vehicles. That's why this place booms on weekends with glorious weather, so much so we have our own police detachment which shows up for the festivities."

His dad points out the windshield to the left, where local police officers have gathered to watch events.

"I don't see De'Andrè or Ray-Ray yet. By the way, they're cousins. Let's go around to the front of the lot. This place looks busy. Not sure if we'll get through, but I bet they're over on the other side. They usually start this thing around three or four and are the earliest here. They have one or two spots they like to hang out in."

Miranda snaps out of a quick evening cat nap. Her T.V. was still on the channel guide. She fell asleep so fast she found nothing to watch. That's her second nap today. She's sleeping poorly with all the new challenges in her life keeping her up at night. She rolls off the bed, throwing her feet to the floor and popping up with gusto. That nap caught her up on energy and she's feeling good for the evening time. She walks down the hall and heads downstairs, calling out for her parents. No answer comes back. This is becoming an all too common occurrence around here and she bets herself they're in the garage again with that old car, so she makes a beeline for the garage.

She opens the door to the garage and peeks in. No one is present and one of the garage doors is open. Their daily driver is gone leaving the old car they were playing with last night. They must have gone out for something and she's all alone in the house. She peers out at the late evening sky through the garage and is met with only a few colors dancing on the distance clouds as darkness creeps in. The clouds fade into dark grey wisps whose edges blend into evening's shaded purple which further conceal night's acknowledgement of starlight. Her mind is wandering as she stands and relishes the cooling effect of the evening breeze making its way down the suburban streets. The front porch lights are coming on and a streetlight at the end of the cul-de-sac winks a curious, momentary, occasional flicker. She is refreshed through and through and turns to close the garage door until her parent's return. She hits the close button on the far wall to shut the garage door and heads up the steps into the kitchen when she turns to see the old car. It's a curious-looking thing all by itself next to the far wall upon which hangs two extra dirty power cords rolled up on hooks and an old broom and a rake awaiting their next duties supported by nails in the drywall.

She looks and sees either her mom's or her dad's headband thingy on a shelf right in front of the car. Shoot, she's got nothing better to do right now. She's not hungry, TV is old, and the internet is a wasteland. Why not try it herself? It's easy to do. All you have to do is make sure the contacts on the head are set and concentrate, right? So, she grabs the headset and begins on the hood of the car where her dad was working his crystals.

At the lot, Brian and his dad have located De'Andrè and Ray-Ray. They are in one of their usual areas, but a little further back off the road. In a spot right next to them, one of the early visitors is leaving and Brian's dad backs into the spot and shouts out his window.

"Ray-Ray!"

A Black man in a beach-styled, printed, buttoned-down shirt opened in the front exposing a white tank top underneath turns and responds," Hey Bobby! What's happenin' man!"

"Hey, it's busy tonight, ain't it?"

"Yeah, we got a mob happenin' here tonight."

Bobby and Brian climb out of the car. Bobby bends over a little and swings his arms to slaps his pants a few times with his hands getting the big wrinkles to relax. Brian gets out with his head turning in every direction, taking in all the different vehicles around him. He sees lots of people 'rubbing and reading', according to his dad. Hardly a person isn't engaged in some way. It's a crazy site seeing all these people sharing their old vehicles and chatting like this.

"Ray-Ray, this is my son Brian."

He responds, "Yeah, Ok. This is the one you sent me the message about."

Ray-Ray reaches out to shake Brian's hand and they shake, "Hey Brian, Ray-Ray"

"How ya' doin'?" Responds Brian as he makes eye contact, and they complete the quick handshake.

"I heard you had a moment earlier today. How are you feelin' now?"

"Yeah, I'm feeling pretty good now. Back to myself, I guess you can say, though it took me a while to get back to normal."

"I bet. You're lucky the blackout wasn't worse. The same thing happened to a guy about two months ago. It took him three weeks to come out of a 'coma-like state' the doctor's called it. He was unresponsive to everything for a while. Did you have anything like that?"

"I guess so. I mean, I woke up a couple hours later in my bed, but my dad says more happened in between which I don't remember at all."

"Yeah? I got his message. Well, this process you described sounds like what we call 'getting printed.' At least that's what we call it in the circles. Doctors have another name for it."

"I didn't receive any long-term brain damage, or anything, did I?"

"No. I don't think so. What we know is whatever happened to you has only happened to one or two people in the past. No one knows why your type of blackout happens, but based on the descriptions, it sounds like your brain gets a massive overload of information and shuts down until it could pull itself together again."

"That's kind of what it felt like too," responds Brian. "I was in complete and utter blackout mode when my parents found me laying across the steering wheel of the car. And I was in some other weird semi-conscious state in between which I can't remember anything about. When I came to, I was super woozy, and it took a couple hours to get myself all back together again."

Ray-Ray says, "As far as anyone can tell, you won't end up with any long-term damage. It sounds like your short-term memory got blasted all to hell and that's why you couldn't remember anything until later."

"I still don't remember that time, though."

"Oh, I see, yeah time has passed. You said that. Well, I'm no doctor. I can only tell you what has happened in the past based on what we know in the inner circles here. I'd say if it persists and you can't remember that time, you should get to a doctor. But you seem ok now, right?"

"Yeah. Like my old self. There was this other thing, though."

"What's that?"

"You say it happens on the brain, right?"

"Yeah, that's right."

"And no one has reported other side effects?"

"Not that I know I of."

"Well in my best recall, a hand was holding a gun and firing out the passenger window. The flash from the gun imprinted on my eyes and for a short time the grey-green shadow of the previous three flashes of gunfire covered my real-world vision. It's like I looked at a bright light source and then looked away. My retinas get fried somehow?"

"Now that I've never heard of! It affected your real life vision, you say."

"Yeah, like looking at a bright LED light and quickly looking away."

"I ain't never heard of that! You're the first! That's crazy, man!"

Brian noticed the vehicle Ray-Ray was standing next to was a sharp wedge of a vehicle.

"Is this yours?" asked Brian

"Yeah, this is mine."

"What is it?"

"It's a 2022 Corvette Z06. And let me tell you, they don't make 'em like this anymore! Ha-ha!"

Bobby interrupts, "Everyone says that last part around here. It's a joke now. Get used to it."

Ray-Ray jumps in again, "Yeah, it's pretty played out by now, but it has a bad habit of stickin' around. Hey, Brian. There's a couple good stories in this one. I'm pretty sure your brain won't get blown away either. Lots of good racing and fun to watch!"

"Oh, I don't have a headset."

"Oh, De'Andrè and I have extras."

He steps to the driver side door, leans over, and opens the center console. Inside, he pulls out a brand new headset in plastic wrap.

"These are regularly $2000.00 but tonight only, I'm giving 25% off to friends and family. And since you are a friend, I'm only charging $1500.00."

Bobby interjects, "That's a pretty good deal. Give me two. One of mine got yanked when Brian had his episode. I'm not sure the connection with the crystal works well anymore." He looks at Brian, "I got you, Brian."

"Thanks Dad."

Brian takes his new headset out of the plastic container and looks around. Ray-Ray stops him before he runs off.

"Hey man, Brian, one question before you run off here. What do you think would happen if you tried to connect to your dad's vehicle again, like, right now, even? Would you want to try?"

"Yeah, I don't mind tryin'. I'm back to normal for the most part. You guys say it's a rare thing that happened to me, right? So, I doubt it will happen again. What do you think?"

"No, I don't think it will. There's no history of it happening twice to someone that I know of. But who knows? Only if you believe you can control the situation and get out before blowing your brain again."

"So, you think it might happen again if I concentrate hard enough or something?"

"I don't think so. There's not enough known about that entire process. I was thinking maybe we knock out this possibility now since we have the very rare opportunity to have a person in our presence who has experienced this before. Today even, right?"

Bobby says, "Yeah, it happened today, this morning, but Brian, I don't like this idea. If your mother…"

"Yeah…" Brian interrupts with a wave of his hand, "I know dad. Okay. I don't want to worry about this in the future though, so let's try. At least this way I'll people around who can pull me out if I lose it, and we'll all know how much fun I can't have in the future."

Bobby chimes in, "Brian, you don't have to do this."

"I know, dad. It's my choice. Plus, we need to know anyway, right?"

"Ok son. Just be mindful while you're concentrating and jump out of it if you experience what happened this morning."

Brian moves toward the hood of his dad's car. That location seemed as good as any. He doesn't want to start in the driver's seat because he fears the whole thing blowing up in his brain again. The information overload wasn't the problem. The blackout that was scariest, and more so after-the-fact when you realize what happened and how much time and information you missed. He dons the headband and places the crystals on the hood of the car.

At first, nothing happens. This drives him crazy about this device. You spend most of your time rubbing the crystals along the body of the vehicle, picking nothing up. He moves his hands slowly. One at a time, walking them up and down the hood for five or six minutes.

His dad asks, "Are you getting anything, Brian?"

"No, not a damn thing. The blackout seems to have made things worse. I can't pick up shit!"

Ray-Ray says, "Just relax like it's your first time again. This is a new headset to you, and it might feel different. I've had a few different headsets, and each one was a little different from the one before, so just stay at it."

Bobby says, "Well, at least he's not getting his brain blown out."

Right at that moment, Brian senses something flowing across his scalp through his hair. He focuses in on the motion. He sees an image of a garage with a yellowish-white light bouncing off the walls and another Mustang like the one he is on right now, but this one is white. His dad's is red.

He says in a low tone, "I see another Mustang, dad."

"Oh yeah?" says Ray-Ray.

"What color, Brian?" asks his dad.

"It's white. I'm looking at the hood like I'm standing in the front seat or something. Strange angle. This is possibly a convertible maybe, but I can't spin the image."

"You don't really have control of the image," says Ray-Ray. "The images happen in your mind, so sit back and enjoy the show."

"I'm in a garage. Kind of weakly lit. There's a couple of extension cords of the wall, a rake, an old straw broom."

"Are you getting anything that was like what happened this morning, son?"

"No. what's weird is I feel like I'm part of this image. The image is warping and fuzzy like I'm looking at it underwater, but I have mostly clear vision. I feel like I should have control. I'm frozen, looking forward."

Bobby turns to Ray-Ray and asks, "Do you think this means the car may have been submerged or something?"

"I ain't never heard of nothin' like that, Bobby."

Brian continues, "Okay, I'm getting a little bored here. I'm going to tweak the crystals and pull out of here. There is nothing other than this boring garage scene."

Brian turns one crystal along with the other to get out of the image. Nothing happens. He moves both crystals across the hood. His dad sees the unusual movement and in a worried elevated voice he asks, "Bobby, what's wrong? You will not get an image that way. Slow down."

"Dad, the image won't go away."

And right as he was preparing to pull his hands off the crystals and pull away, an image of a girl comes into his view. It's only an outline. Her body is transparent, but the edges of her head, shoulders, arms, waist, and legs are visible in a light hazy grey outline. Her eyes meet his eyes, and she screams at him.

"Ahhhh! What the fuck is going on? Eyes floating above daddy's old car?" she says in a loud and frantic voice.

Brian replies, "Who are you?"

She screams again, "Ahhhhhh! Did you just talk?"

Ray-Ray says, "Who is who?"

Bobby asks, "Yeah, who is who?" looking at Brian with great concern.

Brian asks again, "Did you just talk to me?"

The girl, Ray-Ray, and his dad respond all at once, "Yes, I did."

Brian squints his eyes harder and furrows his brow tighter. "Not you guys' dad. The girl!"

The girl says, "Dad?"

Ray-Ray and Bobby stare at each other, and look to Brian, still hovering over the hood and in deeper concentration. They simultaneously ask, "What girl?"

Brian responds in a harsher voice, "Dad, Ray-Ray, shhhh! This girl is talking to me."

The girl asks in a low and concerned voice while staring right back into the disembodied set of eyes she sees floating above her daddy's mustang, "Ray-Ray, who the hell is Ray-Ray? And dad? Is daddy there? Daddy?" She says in an ascending voice of concern

Her mind races with the very next thought and her mouth blurts it out, "Oh my God! Is daddy dead? Is this your spirit, daddy? Are you trying to communicate with me from beyond? Oh my God!" And she cries, "Is mom, okay? Is she with you, daddy?"

"Daddy? No? My mom's okay, though. She's living in the 1950s tonight."

"Oh my God, you're a little dead boy!" she says as tears well up in her eyes.

"No, I'm…" Brian tries to finish but is interrupted again.

"I'm so sorry!" she says as the outline of a tear runs down a transparent face. "Do you know you are even dead?"

"Wait, no. I'm not dead."

Her voice rises in sorrow. "Oh no, little boy, listen. Denial is keeping you here."

She then emphasizes with a whispering stress in her voice, "Look for the light!"

"What? No. Look for the light? No! I'm not dead! I'm quite alive. Are you dead? Why can I see right through you?"

Bobby looks worried. He notices Ray-Ray is now recording something with his phone.

Ray-Ray says, "Are you seeing what I'm seeing?"

Before looking at what Ray-Ray is talking about on his phone, he asks Brian, "Is someone wanting you to join the dead, Brian? Are they wanting you to cross over?"

He leans back toward Ray-Ray with great worry and whispers, "I think my car's possessed by an evil spirit. It wants him to cross over."

Ray-Ray responds, holding his phone steady on its current view as possible, "You ain't seein' the shit I'm seein', are you? De'Andrè! Get over here!"

At that moment, Bobby looks at Ray-Ray's phone and sees for the first time what he hasn't been noticing because he's been focusing on Brian's face before now.

The girl says, "I'm not dead, you're dead."

"No, I'm not!" says Brian. "I'm alive and…" He cannot finish again because she interrupts him.

"Let me talk to my daddy right now!" she demands in a loud voice.

"I don't know your daddy."

"You're a ghost!" She exclaims in a continuing rate of demand, "You can go find him! Now go get him! I'll wait right here till you get him."

Brian asks out loud, "Dad, do you have any kids we don't know about? Like a girl?"

Bobby has to take his eyes off of Ray-Ray's camera to catch it in reality. A thin vertical cloudy line about a meter behind his son is floating right behind him. The top of the line is near head level and the bottom ends around knee level. You almost can't catch what's going on unless you focus hard, but the action shows up on Ray-Ray's phone well enough.

Bobby responds in a measured but angry voice, "Brian, what the hell are you talking about? I don't have any other kids. And good lord, never say crap like that around your mother! Thank God she's in another decade right now."

"My dad doesn't have any other kids." Brian says to the girl.

"Oh! Your daddy is dead too?" She says as her voice gets tense again. "It must have been a horrible accident."

"Ok, stop!" says Brian. "I'm thirty-four years old. My dad doesn't have any other kids. He just told me so. And I'm trying to figure out if you're real or not. These crystal things aren't supposed to have this kind of functionality, right, so I'm thinking this is one fucked up illusion!"

He calls out, "Dad! Where's Ray-Ray?"

Ray-Ray says, "I'm right here."

"Ray-Ray, I can see right through this chick and she's interactive, like completely interactive, and she's a backet-case! Does this happen to you?"

She screams out loud, "Ahhhh! You can see me naked?"

"No, I cannot see…" and before Brian can finish, the entire image disappears as if someone pulled the plug on a power source somewhere.

Brian opens his eyes and raises straight up. "Holy hopping horse shit! Now I know why these things are so popular!" He turns both crystals in his hands to where he can see them. "That's one crazy connection! You say every car has stories like this?"

He turns his head toward his dad, Ray-Ray, and another Black man dressed in dark slacks and a white buttoned-down shirt like he recently arrived from an important meeting where he needed to dress nice. The three of them stare at him like he is a creature from another planet.

Ray-Ray says in a low, slow, wary voice, "Uh yeah, uh, I mean… no, man. Not really like that."

The new Black man says in the same low, slow, wary voice, "Yeah man, nothing like that… at all." Shaking his head 'no' with his eyes wide.

His dad jumps in with a low, slow, and wary voice too, "Brian, are you okay, son?"

"Yeah, I'm okay. It's the three of you who look like you've just seen something freaky! Should I take a picture?"

"You ain't gonna believe the shit we got on video," says Ray-Ray in an amazed voice.

"What do you mean?" Brian asks as he moves over next to Ray-Ray, who replays the video. "Holy goodness! What is that? Was that behind me?"

The new, nicely dressed man said, "Yeah. It was there in real life too, right behind you, but you couldn't see it quite as well as the camera."

"You must be De'Andrè?"

"Yeah. Hey man. You must be the one I heard about today. What the hell did you do?" He says as he reaches out his hand and they quickly shake.

"I don't know. I have no clue what happened to me earlier today, and now I have more questions than when I started."

Ray-Ray says, "You ain't the only one, Brian. I think this is a first of a first! This shit is straight out of a Sc-Fi movie or some shit. I ain't seen nothing like this, man." He says as he continues to replay the video.

De'Andrè says, "Ain't nobody seen this. I think we are dealin' with something science can't even conceive."

Bobby asks, "No one else has talked about this side-effect before?"

De'Andrè says, "Not that I've ever heard."

Bobby pulls Brian aside for a few minutes and asks him how he's doing. He wants to keep Brian conscious for obvious reasons. Nobody knows what could happen next. Brian tells dad he's fine and wants to wander around and try a couple other vehicles out. After another moment of chit-chat, they tell Ray-Ray and De'Andrè their plans and head off. Dad stays close to Brian all night and monitors the situation at each vehicle.

Miranda stands in front of her dad's old Mustang in complete disbelief. Did her mom and dad pass away while they were out? She cries. The afterlife was always an occasional topic of conversation among friends, but she never believed she'd have such a direct experience. The little ghost boy was so real. There is no way it could have been a memory. The experience was so much more than that. She pulls the headband off, tosses it onto the shelf, and heads inside, crying, slapping the button to close the garage door along the way.

Head hanging low, both hands covering her face, she scuffs along the kitchen floor to the area rug in the living room and drops in tears on the sofa. The old leather couch doesn't provide the cushion like when it was new. The leather is cool to the touch and the armrests are low and angled. They were never meant to be a headrest, but they work marvelously. Her head falls on one. More tears roll down her cheeks, leap onto the leather, and race gravity toward the hidden seams. Her thoughts scare her. She's alone now. Without mom and dad, who will guide her? Twenty-seven years hasn't been enough time to learn what she needs to become a success in life. Self-confidence is lost among her worries.

Well into a night's rest, her parents arrive back home. They chat in low tones as they stand in the kitchen. They're reminiscing about younger years. Michael is standing close to Annie as she reaches into the sink to put Miranda's bowl and fork from lunch into the dishwasher.

"You know, getting one of those house-bots, you call them, wouldn't be such a bad thing," says Annie.

Michael says, "Oh, those things don't do as much as they say they do Annie, and people constantly complain about the jobs they do poorly. It's like having a five-year-old do your chores. You end up doing more work, following around behind them, cleaning up their mess."

"I know. It would just be nice, though one day."

"Maybe one day a few years from now when they improve their overall performance on tasks, but right now, they are just more work and more expense. I'm not saying no. I'm just saying not yet."

Annie reaches down to lift the dishwasher closed. It makes the click sound when the latch catches, and she turns to give Michael a quick kiss.

"I'm worn out," she says.

"Me too. Let's call it a night."

Making their way into the living room, they notice Miranda passed out on the sofa. Annie turns to Michael with a little half smile on her face and his look says 'how ridiculous' in a loving, cute way. With the lights out and only the low glow from above the stove shining around the corner, Annie scuffs her feet toward the far side of the room. They both stay quiet as she grabs a small, folded quilt she made several years ago. She lays the cloth with blue and white flowers and a Hodge-Podge of blue and white farm scenery across her daughter. She is sound asleep and doesn't stir in the slightest. Annie and Michael creep to their room and retire for the night. Later, Miranda awakens still in a half-sleep and wanders into her own room. She was sleepy and never thought about the quilt that covered her.

The sound of birds welcoming the early sun caused an eye to pop open to the chatter. The gray light of morning is transforming into brilliant, springtime sunshine. Her eyes ache to open. The pollen this time of year always causes her eyes to dry out at night. They awaken to glue holding them shut and the grit of pollen scratching across her cornea. Rubbing them doesn't help, and it takes a few minutes to recover normal visual operations. Now she can see the dust and pollen dancing through the yellow sunrays filtering into her room. She thinks about last night and wants to cry again, which solves the rest of her dry eye problems.

Then there is a noise. Something familiar stirs. Her head pops up from the pillow. She holds still and listens. Nothing for a moment or so. Throwing the covers off, she cracks open the door, listening. The lightest sound of a spatula on a skillet sends her feet flying down the hallway and the stairs to the kitchen and stops. There stands her mom leaning over the stove, adjusting a temperature setting for one of the heating elements.

"Mom!" she says as she runs to her mother.

"Oh, thank God you are alive!"

Her mother turns but not quick enough as Miranda is upon her and throws her arms around her.

Her mom laughs and says, "Miranda! What on earth are you talking about?"

"I thought you guys were dead!"

Unnoticed on the other side, sitting at a little kitchenette, was her dad. He says, "Dead?"

Annie says, "Dead? Oh, Miranda, what has gotten into you this morning?"

She tells her parents about the little ghost boy incident. Mom works the stove for breakfast while listening. A swish through the skillet with a silicon spatula, turning the scrambled eggs is followed by a quick handful or two of shredded cheese to melt into the mix. There is a look of concern on her mom's face as she turns to listen. He as well has a look of concern for Miranda as she rattles off her account. Without a moment to even ask a question between Miranda's storytelling, mom grabs three plates from the cupboard. Michael rises from his chair to refill his morning juice drink, which today is Welch's Grape Juice. He reaches over to start the coffeemaker once more, knowing Annie is going to want her morning pick-me-up.

Her dad says, "Well. Miranda. I've never had an experience like what you describe. Nothing interactive like that. It's always like I'm watching it happen long ago. There's no actual level of engagement beyond seeing, hearing, and sometimes feeling. The scene doesn't play off itself."

"You don't believe me, I know."

"No. It's not that I don't believe you, honey. I'm inclined to believe you one hundred percent because of your reaction to this morning when you came flying down the staircase and threw yourself on mom. There's nothing fake or unoriginal about that moment. It's all tied together. But do I think you're talking to 'the other side'? No. I think something else is going on and I don't have a clue what it could be. I'll check the net, but I don't think I'm going to find much."

Annie skirts around Miranda who has been leaning up against the refrigerator. She's balancing three plates for breakfast. As far back as Miranda can remember, she's always tried to carry more food than necessary. It's something her mom picked up as a server in her younger years before robots took over the industry. Miranda has never seen her spill a plate, which must be impressive, but she has no one to compare it to. They all gather at the table to eat, and chitchat about everything else other than Miranda's experience. Miranda smiles as she talks between mom and dad. The banter is light, and each has their day planned out when breakfast wraps up as quickly as it began. An early summer heat beats through the window as Miranda rises from her chair. It's going to be a hot one, she thinks as she squints out the window into direct sunlight. Summer is just around the corner, and she needs a new bathing suit.

Brian and his dad were just coming in from running a couple of early morning chores. They ate while they were out and brought mom one of her favorite biscuits in a to-go bag. She is standing over the sink again, humming a song and finishing up that last of the big pots.

"Mom, what's the song you are humming?"

"Mmmm, oh. That's 'Little Star' by The Elegants."

"One of your twentieth century singers, I presume. By the way, here's your biscuit you wanted."

"Oh, thank you, sweetie! And yes. I think it was their only big hit, like maybe around 1958. Something like that."

She dries her hands on a nearby towel and pulls the wrapped biscuit out of the bag. Bobby snags a chair from the kitchen table and falls into it like an old man out of energy.

"Geez dad! Are you alright?"

"Yeah, don't worry about me. I'm more worried about you. We need to get your mom caught up on last night's event."

Beverly says, "Yes. Fill me in. Your father gave me the highlights last night after we all got home."

They huddled around the kitchen table for an hour, talking through last night's event at the lot. The video Ray-Ray had uploaded was more than Beverly could conceive. Bobby's look of general concern never abated. Together, they concluded Brian should not use the headset alone. The strangeness surrounding his usage of it has led to many unusual and hard to answer questions. Brian decided on his own to leave it alone for a while. So, for the next several days, Brian's headset remained untouched on a shelf in his room. And he went forth planning the sale of his house to Di'Mario and pulling together the resources he needed to get a basic start to his business idea.

A week goes by and Miranda falls into her new work routine. Never being the morning person, she drags herself out of bed before the sun rises, does her daily ablutions, and leaves for work. Her new job is at the Newport News shipyard, working as a journeyman fabricator for a major contractor in ship building. The work brings sweat to her brow daily. A far cry from the school environment. The heat will only get worse as Hampton Roads enters peak summer; she knows. She'll live with it because she needs to be something on her own. It's what she wants for herself most of all. Her mom did it when she was a younger gal, too. She can do this, she tells herself. Plus, the pay is great compared to what her friends are making, so it makes it worth the physical and emotional effort. And she is off to a good start.

Twice at lunch and while mid-fabricating, her thoughts wandered back to the little ghost boy and her mind strays into other thoughts about that event. Was it a little ghost boy? He didn't see her dad or mom. Who was he talking about? The order and flow of the conversation isn't perfect in her memory now. Her memory focuses on the eyes and ghostly outline. Come to think of it, the outline was bigger than a little boy. The eyes were nice but weird to consider being disembodied as they were. Questions lead to more questions. She tells herself she has to engage again to get answers. If it worked once, it would work a second time. That's what she's going to do tonight after dinner.

Later that evening, plates and dishes clank and bang around the sink as Miranda and her mom brush down the dirty plates from dinner and place them in the dishwasher for further cleaning and sanitation.

Miranda says, "You know, mom, as you and daddy get older, you should buy a maid-bot."

"Well, Miranda, you know how your father is about those things. He's an old stick-in-the-mud concerning robots. He believes they aren't any good and are more expense than they are worth."

"Daddy needs to lighten up. Maid-bots have gotten a whole lot better over the past ten years. Doing dishes is nothing for them now. And they are way better at keeping the floors clean and dusting around the house. He has no excuse to continue being an old stick-in-the-mud. I'm going to talk to him about it. We don't need to be living like we are in the twentieth century anymore. We are almost in the twenty-second century now. I mean, soon, people will vacation on the moon for a weekend, for God's sake. That's like half-way to Mars or something. He can handle a robot."

Her mom says, "It sure would be nice to have a little more automation around here. But your dad and I don't make that much of a mess together. About the best thing he ever got us as far as that goes is the dryer that folds the laundry for you when it's finished. I love that thing to death!"

"Me too!"

Miranda's mom asks, "Do you want to watch one of my shows with me tonight?"

"Sure mom. Sounds nice."

"Ok, I'm going to go talk to your father and get into something more relaxing for the evening. Give me a few minutes and we'll get started."

"Ok mom."

Miranda watches her mom shuffle out of the kitchen. She thinks her mom is cute in little ways like when she walks like that. But her mind is on the little ghost boy. She wants a quick shot at trying to make contact. She estimates her mom will be twenty minutes minimum talking to her father, so she tosses her towel onto the countertop and makes haste to the garage. There, she grabs a headset off the shelf in front of her dad's old Mustang and begins her search.

She picks up regular old images of things in this car's past. Most are unclear or look like you are seeing them through water. Occasionally, one comes through nice and clear but no ghost boy. She walks around the side of the vehicle next to the wall of the garage and tries various placements on the front left quarter panel to not much effect. She moves her right hand over the hood and her left hand down below the left front headlight in front of the tire, and suddenly a series of images stream into her mind. Her hands don't move, but the images and videos stream faster and faster into her mind. She is having a difficult time grasping them all.

From upstairs, Annie and Michael hear a loud bang from downstairs. They rush down the hallway, calling out for Miranda. There's no answer. Running down the stairway, calling out for her, and scouring the downstairs, they run and call out, to no avail. Their chests heave as they stop to notice the helpless look on their faces.

Annie says, "That loud bang. It came from here, right?"

"That's what it sounded like to me."

Annie says, "Me too! Was it a door slamming?"

Michael says, "I don't think so. It seemed louder. Oh, my goodness. I hope nothing has happened to Miranda."

Annie says, "Quick, check the garage."

Rushing to open the garage door attached to the kitchen, they are welcomed by a thin, hazy smoke. Michael spots a black line on the wall and Miranda laying on the floor.

He yells out, "Miranda!"

And they both run over to see her crouched on her side laying on the floor. As Annie tries to wake her up, Michael inspects the wall.

He says, "Good God! It looks like something burnt the wall here. This black streak is sooty! What the hell was she doing?"

Annie tends to Miranda's head, which looks like she got a swift knock above the eye with a little blood on the side of her face. Her shirt is burnt up the back and falls forward as Michael reaches down to help Annie set Miranda upright.

Annie says, "if we can't get her awake in another minute, call emergency."

Together, they try to wake her up with light slaps on the face. Nothing works. Her dad's forehead wrinkles deep. Her mom's face distorts into teary-eyed sadness. Miranda's body is limp and doesn't want to stay upright. Mom rips the headset off Miranda's head and continues slapping her on the cheeks. Then a sound like 'uhhh' comes from Miranda. She's still limp.

Annie says, "Miranda! Miranda! Wake up!"

Her dad grabs her shoulder and holds up her chin and says, "Miranda! Wake up, sweetie!"

'Ugh' comes the sound again from Miranda's mouth. She struggles to open an eye.

"Ugh, daddy." She says in a soft voice.

The look on Annie's and Michael's faces changed to joy. They continued coaxing her out of her blackout, and slowly she regained a minimum level of consciousness. She couldn't remember everything, however. Her memory of how she got there was gone. So was any memory of what happened to her. They helped get her to her feet and waddled up the steps into the house. At first, they tried a chair in the kitchen, but she was too weak to hold herself up and was saying she was dizzy and thirsty. So, Annie grabbed a glass of water as Michael helped her get up to her room. As he helped her sit up on the side of her bed, Annie came in with the water. She took a small sip and fell back on her pillow, saying she needed to rest her head to remember what happened. Michael grabs the folded comforter at the end of the bed and throws it over her. They both agree to let her rest a while. On the way back downstairs, Annie and Michael create a plan to check in on her every half hour until she's feeling better. Around 1:00am they agreed to let her sleep until morning, since it didn't appear as if her brain was damaged. Annie had found her awake when she entered the room, and she got up to use the restroom on her own. Tomorrow morning would just be better for everything.

Plenty of rest before a morning discussion was a good idea. Michael checks in on Miranda's room as he is making his way downstairs. She's not there, but now he hears 'his ladies' talking downstairs in the kitchen and the smell of sausage on the air. This haste won't make any waste as his love for sausage and eggs at breakfast drove him forward. He picks up his steps and down the stairs he goes. He racked his brain last night, wondering what the hell happened. Now he wants to know.

Miranda recounts her experience over breakfast. Only parts and pieces of memories that have come together from last night. No talk of a little ghost boy or heaven coming to call. She tells of the uncontrollable streaming of images and videos into her mind and her inability to pull away from the car at that moment. But what happened after that is anyone's guess. Only this morning did she notice the mild burns on her back just before her mom showed her the burnt blouse. The mystery of what happened is beyond rational explanations. Her dad can't comprehend what happened, neither her mother. However, mom is more concerned about continued use of the headset. Miranda agreed with her. With only the information Miranda recounted, her father was going to set about finding out what happened. A genuine scientific investigation. Only this would have to wait until the wall in the garage was repaired.

Two weeks pass, and Miranda is in the full swing of summer on her weekends. Today is Saturday and her hair is bunched up in a quick, hand wrapped, part ponytail, part bun style. She has on the cutest little bikini and shorts set she found shopping last week. It's a hot pink, sporty bikini with dangly strings on each hip. The shorts are white and partially see through as the fabric is light and airy for summery heat, and perfect for the beach. She is meeting her friends Kara and Ashley at the new 10th street access point to the beach in Virginia Beach. The U.S. Army Corps of Engineers had reworked that area of the coastline for five years and wrapped up last summer. There's a better view of the ocean now as the old, inundated hotels have been removed, which used to stand like ancient, fractured, modern art among the crashing waves. It's much safer to swim in that spot now too, since all the dangerous debris was cleared. Tons of old concrete was moved further out to create an artificial reef, and to reduce beach erosion. Parts of the old hotels are still further up the beach and people still go there by the droves, but this is the best area now until more work can be done to clear out the remnant victims of rapid sea rise that way. Later they'll run up to Vacation City, the new vacation attraction a little further inland from the new beach areas and grab a coffee and shop. It's a fun place to be.

A little later and just after lunch, Brian walks in from doing initial work in his new business, quality hand crafted furniture, wood décor, and wood accessories. He knew a guy with an old lathe that didn't work. So, he bought it at a steal of a price and is working on fixing it. He smashed his finger though and needed a break before continuing. Rubbing his hands together under the cold water of the sink, one over the other, his index finger throbs from the smashing it received. Drying off with a towel, he was again, acutely aware of the pain in that finger. Walking over to the kitchen table, holding his throbbing finger, he drops himself into a chair. He looks at his damaged hand and then out the window into the sunshine. The summer has ramped up; he thinks to himself. The heat and humidity Hampton Roads is known for has swooped in and squatted a little early this year. It'll be late November or early December before it clears out. He's not feeling up to the drenching he'll get working through the heavy humidity he'll receive when he goes back outside, and not with his hand the way it is. He decides he'll put his other plans on hold this afternoon until it cools down. His mind wanders.

He pops his head up from hitting the table. He had fallen asleep for a moment and caught himself as he fell forward. His mind had the image of that girl in the garage, or rather, the outline of the girl in the garage. He had thought little about it over the past two weeks. Thinking a moment, he looks at the door leading out to the garage. He gets up from the table and heads into the garage. His headset isn't out there but he sees one of his parent's headsets so, he grabs it and reaches for the mustang. Almost at once, he picks up images. That's unusual, he thinks. It's like he is in tune with that spot of the vehicle and it's coming in loud and clear. No watery distortion. He sees the oceanfront and a pair of legs stretched out in front of him. Nice legs, he says to himself in a low tone.

He takes a moment to realize what is out of place. It looks like the oceanfront before the sea level rise inundated it. At least at first, it looked like he was seeing the twentieth century oceanfront. A long straight beach front that extended way beyond what one could see just by picking a spot to sunbathe. But the view switches left, and he sees a dark-haired girl with sunglasses talking to him, but no sound is coming through. He also sees some old, ruined hotels he recognizes in the breakers. This isn't then, it's now! What the hell? He tweaks the crystal in his left hand first and suddenly hears the waves crashing too.

Right at that moment, Miranda jerks her head forward, knocking her sunglasses off her face.

Kara laughs a little and asks, "Oh my God, Miranda! Are you okay?"

"Uh, yeah." She says as she readjusts her sunglasses.

"You looked like you had a spasm or something. Are you sure?"

"Uh, I don't know," she says in a low tone. "I see a boy."

Kara replies, "There are lots of boys here! Which one do you like?"

"No, I mean. I can see you and everything, but I can see a boy in a garage, too. Like it's in my head and it's very clear."

Ashley says, "Oh no, Kara. Could this be related to her accident in the garage the other week?"

Kara says, "I don't know." And they both look at her with great concern on their faces.

Miranda continues, "He's leaning over a mustang like my dad's old car with one of those headsets on."

Ashley asks, "Like, is he dead or something?"

"No, no, Ashley! Geez! He's doing that thing they do like I did before I got knocked out."

Silence follows, Then after a moment or two goes by, Kara asks, "Is he cute?"

"No, Kara. Come on. I'm serious here. I can't see his face, but he's more than a boy. It's a man for sure. It's like a video is playing directly into my brain. And I swear, I think it's the same garage!"

Brian could not hear any conversation or other noises after the sound of waves crashing on shore lasted only a fraction of a moment. He looks up and removes the crystals.

The video in Miranda's mind suddenly ends, but she glimpses the man's face in the garage.

"Oh! It just ended!"

Kara asks, "It's over, over?"

"Yes, it's over. I mean, like it's totally gone now."

Ashley asks, "How do you feel?"

"I feel fine. I also got a look at his face."

Kara asks, "What does he look like?"

"He's definitely a grown man and not a boy, and well built. He looked a little sweaty, like he had been working outside or something."

"Ok, that's freaky," says Ashley.

Kara asks, "Does he come across as a murderer, or is he cute?"

Ashley exclaims, "Kara! Good God!"

Miranda says, "Seriously, Kara! Christ! A murderer? How am I going to sleep at night now?"

Kara responds, "I was only trying to find out if you were afraid of what just happened or not. I would be. I mean, I'd be scared if videos just start playing in my head and strange men were appearing in my mind."

Miranda thinks for a moment and says, "Well, I'm not scared. I don't feel as if I'm in danger or anything like that. Though, I will admit the experience was a little freaky because of how clear it was. It's like I was here and there all at once."

Brian makes his way around the mustang looking for another spot to dial in. He finds a bunch of old memories and spends a good hour taking in the scenes and sounds of times past. He can see why his dad and mom enjoy it so much, and he's happy for them. But time can fly by when you are enjoying yourself. The heat in the garage was rising, but he decides he'll get back to work regardless of the mid-afternoon heat. He's relaxed now and keeps thinking about that pair of legs he saw. That will keep him going for a while, along with a little theorizing about why the imagery seemed so current. He bets dad will know.

Later that evening, Miranda bounces in the front door with spring loaded feet and shopping bags attached to her arm. She's humming the end of her new favorite song, which was just playing on the radio and has had a perfect day today.

Annie says, "My, you got a lot of sun today! You are almost beet red, young lady!"

"Hi, mom. Yeah. We spent more time in the sun and at Vacation City than I thought we would. I'm gonna pay for it over the next couple of days for sure, but today was outstanding."

"Oh, that's good. How's Ashley? I haven't seen her in years now."

"She's fine. She's working as an executive assistant for one of the Vice Presidents of Go-To in Virginia Beach. That's where she lives now too, and she takes Go-To everywhere. She doesn't even own her own car."

"Go-To? That's the automated car transport company that takes everyone everywhere, and has become so popular, right? The one where you hop in the car and say, 'go to' and it takes you there."

"Yep, that's the one."

"Well, that's a cushy job. Is she happy?"

"Yeah, she seems so. I'm going to head upstairs, take a shower, and put on some pajamas. I might need you to rub some lotion on my back later too, because I'm feeling like a boiled lobster right now."

"Ok, sweetie. We'll relax tonight and watch one of my shows."

Miranda swings her bags as she works her way up the stairs and into her room. The heat radiates from her skin as it continues to dry out from the baking it took today. She throws her bags down by her nightstand and plops onto the bed with an 'Ow!' She wasn't thinking about her sunburn until the bed hit it. The video from earlier was replaying in her head. So many questions to ask and no one to ask them to. Her dad would be the most knowledgeable, but he wasn't that much help the first time. She wonders if she is going crazy. What are these episodes she's having? Time to do a little fact finding on the net. She'll get around to it after she rests a moment or two and takes a shower.

Brian is finishing dinner with his family. His finger still hurts, but it is a passing memory now. It's the typical chit-chat at the table and mom drives a lot of the talking.

Brian asks, "Hey dad, the Transducer thing. Is it supposed to broadcast current events too? Has anyone mentioned that?"

"No. Not that I know of. Why?"

"I used them again today but was sucked into a scene that I swear was like live broadcasting. The scene was down at the beach, and I know right where on the beach, too. It's the area the Army Corp of Engineers completed last summer. Kind of around ninth or tenth street area."

"Oh yeah?" remarks Bobby

"Yeah, I'm sure of that. Where did you get the Mustang?"

"I got it from a guy in Pennsylvania. I'm pretty sure it's never been out to the beach there."

"Yeah, that's what I thought. So, why would I get such a clear image of that area?"

"I don't know, son."

"Plus, it was like I was looking through the eyes of this chick. I could see her legs sprawled out on the sand, but it was her eyes."

His dad perked up with his eyebrows raised, and Annie gave her husband a certain look every man should know to avoid. He said, "Oh, really? I'm going to have to investigate that one for you, son."

Annie exclaimed, "Oh, no you won't!"

"It's ok mom. I don't think it's a memory, anyway. It was clear as day. And when I went to tune it in, I heard the beach for a moment and then nothing. It all disappeared. I tried for another minute but could get nothing back from it. It was different and weird."

"Well, I'm only kidding your father, anyway. He's a grown man, and he knows better. He just likes it when I get fussy like that."

Brian sees his parents smile and giggle at each other while finishing their last bite of dinner.

"Ok you guys," says Brian. "I'm going to help mom clean up the kitchen then I'm going to bed early. I have so many things planned tomorrow, including finishing the boundary set up for dad's new robot lawn mower. I did the far corners of the yard today. Now we need to do the rounded areas around the gardens tomorrow to complete the yard design in its memory. Then you never have to mow the lawn again, dad! Your robot buddy will do it for you."

"Well, that will sure be nice when it happens." Replies his dad. "I'll help. Just let me know when you are doing it."

"Yep. Will do, dad. Mom, are you ready? I'll grab dad's dinner dishes and you grab the stuff off the stove. I'll start putting these in the washer and I'll do the big pots and pan by hand."

"Don't worry about that, sweetie. I'll get the pots and pans. Just help me load it up and get the washer started."

With that, Brian began helping with the dishes and headed up to get a long rest in for tomorrow's efforts. He wasn't exhausted when he went upstairs. He even hopped double steps on his way up. But he was mentally preparing himself for a long night's sleep and was looking forward to it. Soon after his shower, an early rest met him willingly.

After watching three episodes of her mom's shows together, Miranda's mom retired off to bed. Miranda often smiled at the way her mom scuffled along in her favorite house slippers, which had long ago lost their fresh fuzziness. She owned that pair for years and now they were just as much a part of her mom as any body part; it seemed. Miranda also smiled at the thought, which she could not run from all day. The thought of what happened at the beach. It was so different. She had questions. Most of which could not be found with a quick search on the internet. It seems no one knows anything about these crystal transducer things.

She waits until she hears her mom shut her bedroom door and goes over to the garage. Inside, she grabs a headset and presses it to her head like her dad showed her, making sure everything is connected to skin where possible. The area where the dark streak was on the wall had a fresh coat of paint, but it needed at least one more coat to cover everything back to original. There was still darkness coming through the paint. It reminded her she needs to be super careful and if anything goes crazy, like it did, then she needs to pull out before she sets the place on fire or worse, does something to herself.

She places the crystals on the hood and is at once tuned into a bedroom. One she is not familiar with. It's dark, but there is a small, old-fashioned lamp on a dresser providing the smallest modicum of light in the room. It's almost not worth keeping on except that it lights the edges of objects just enough to avoid jamming one's toes into furniture. That's her best guess, at least.

There is someone sleeping in the bed. She is surprised she can move around a little. She's never noticed this power in previous experiences, so she leans in for a closer look. It takes a moment, but she is almost completely sure it's the man from the garage video from earlier today. The haircut looks the same and the facial structure. He is sleeping. She stares at him, waiting for him to move or be alerted to her presence. No, he is totally asleep. She takes in the entire scene and keeps looking back at him. She sees old photos in wooden picture frames that aren't digital frames. They are old-fashioned. She sees a dirty laundry basket and walls, which are barren of other pictures or works of art. It's a small room. Not a like a master suite. She looks back at him again. She wonders who he is. He looks so peaceful. She notices the muscles in his arm which is hanging out of the covers. She was right. He was well built. She tries to move out of the room, but her movement is restricted. She can only move around three feet (1 m) or so in any direction. Her own movement doesn't make even the slightest sound. It's like she's there, but not there. Fifteen minutes go by of watching him sleep and checking out the room. It seems he's just a regular guy, and the room is rather boring after the initial inspection. She leans in for one more close look at him when she hears her mom screaming.

"Miranda!"

She jumps, yanking the crystals off the Mustang.

"Mom! Holy Jesus Christ! Why the hell are you screaming? I almost peed myself!"

"You had this white line glowing behind you! It looked like smoke. I thought you were catching fire again! But when you pulled away from the Mustang, it disappeared! Are you Ok?"

"Yes, I'm ok. Catching fire? What white line?"

"I don't know. It was there, then it wasn't. It was like a line of white smoke and glowing white."

The sound of heavier footsteps running into the kitchen and toward the garage was met with her dad, shoving her mom out of the way and launching himself to the bottom of the three garage steps in one leap.

"Miranda, Annie, what is going on? Annie, why did you scream like that?"

"Miranda was on fire again."

Her dad says, "Miranda, are you ok? Turn around, let me see."

"No dad, I wasn't on fire."

Annie intervenes. "It looked like she was on fire, but she wasn't."

"What do you mean, Annie?"

The girls tell the story, and Michael's concern never abates. He doesn't like the situation. There's nothing on the net like what he's seeing and hearing in his own house. He pulls everyone into the kitchen. Believing Annie and Miranda together leads to a conclusion too far-fetched to be real, it seems. He can't keep Miranda from using the crystals. She's not a kid. And he knows Annie isn't lying. He decides Miranda should not use the crystals alone until everyone is sure about what is going on and how to control it. After a little small talk, they all go to bed for the evening. But now, Miranda can't stop talking about seeing that man. She has so many questions still unanswered. How is he making this happen? Or is he caught up in this like she is? Midnight strikes before she puts away her thoughts and gets to sleep. If her mom saw something, she's not saying, but mom is glad she didn't get hurt this time.

Early morning brings little dapples of sunlight through the maple leaves. Brian is already up and finishing fixing his lathe. He was up at 5am. It was like his old firefighter days, when he had the early shift. Those old habits just die hard. But he made fantastic progress in completing the fixes. He turns on his lathe and stands back with a smile. The whine of the electric motor spinning was a beautiful sound. Just what he wanted to hear. It was the sound of future successes. He was going to make a simple four-legged side table today. Something you can place in a corner of a room or next to a recliner or couch. An easy project, but he would not leave it in simple form. He was going to embellish it with smaller designs on the legs and maybe something ornate around the edge of the tabletop. The goal was to produce something that did not appear to be manufactured by a robot or machine. Something that looked like human creativity was put into it and another human could appreciate. Ideas for furniture abounded. Starting small and enjoying quick and early success before he engaged in larger efforts was his longer-term plan.

He sees his dad making his way out of the back door onto the deck.

"Hey, dad! You ready to get started?"

"Yeah, I was just coming out to check on you and get this robot mower going. It's been two weeks since the grass has been mowed and hopefully today it'll get done."

"It will get done. I just fixed the lathe too! It works perfect now. I'm going to work on a small ornate corner table as my first project just to break it in."

Brian tells his dad all about the different ideas he has for ornate wood-based products. Some of them Bobby had never heard of before, like ornate wooden frames around the front door of a house. People can have their family name on it and any design they'd like. Also, things like ornate mailbox post covers, which is a wooden box around the post already in the ground supporting a mailbox. Again, family names, street numbers, or whatever can be placed on these with unique designs as well. Not to mention all the normal furniture ideas with and without unique designs. He wants to offer it all and make a small name for himself. His dad is impressed. After talking a bit more about it, he thinks Brian is onto something when he believes he can deliver to the local community for far cheaper than a robotic furniture manufacturer can deliver from wherever they are located to the local area, and the designs will be better along with guaranteed higher quality. Plus, there is an area about an hour west of here near Courtland where he can harvest his own trees, saving even more money. His dad thinks Brian may be onto something huge if he can pull off what people are looking for. Just like with robots, it will come down to economic efficiency and building a product people desire.

After a long day of work, Brian strolls into the living room with his first small table. It comes up to one's hip and is lacking the added intricate details he had planned but will add to it over the next two days along with a good lacquer. It's only pine wood, but perfect for the first effort. Mom and dad are impressed. It's beautiful in its unfinished form and very sturdy. He shows how you can rock it and knock it and it doesn't act like any parts are loose. Unlike when you buy things from modern furniture stores, and you find their legs and parts are a little loose or wobbly and it's impossible to keep them tightened down. He says this will be a key, distinctive feature of his handmade furniture and it's something robot mass produced furniture falls short on.

Later that night, Brian is lying in bed and just beginning his dreams when he is startled in his dream but does not awaken. Though he can't remember much about what he was just dreaming, he can see a girl standing in front of him. He likewise is standing in front of her, and the vision is perfectly clear. She is looking around like she is searching for something, but then she talks directly to him.

"Oh hey, this is weird. You look so real. Is this a dream? Am I dreaming?" She asks.

He says, "I can see and hear you."

At which point she screams so loud he wakes up with a jolt and his legs and arms fly up. He uncontrollably tinkled in his underwear because she screamed so loud, he lost control of his bodily function. Even his ears hurt. Holy crap, he says to himself as his heart races beyond control and his chest heaves with a huge breath. Was that the chick I've been seeing with the crystals? I want to say that chick is psycho, but I think I'm the one going nuts. By that I mean, I am talking to myself out loud, and I clearly need to change my underwear. I may be losing it. The stress is getting to me is what he says to himself as he struggles out of bed and heads toward his dresser for a change.

At the other end of that dream, Miranda's mom and dad come running into her room.

"Miranda! What's wrong?" her mother lightly screams.

"Oh, my goodness, I'm sorry. I didn't think I screamed out loud."

Her dad busts into the room with a worried look on his face.

"I'm sorry daddy. I didn't think I screamed for real."

He asks, "What happened?"

"Well, I was dreaming…"

He interjects, "Oh God, a dream? I swear the two of you screaming every night is going to put me in the hospital."

"Daddy, I was dreaming this super realistic dream, and it had that guy in it."

"What guy? The one you've been seeing with the crystals?"

"Yes, and he was real."

"Ok, hold on. Every time you use those crystals, you have these severe hallucinations."

She angrily interjects, "No daddy! It's not a hallucination. He was standing in front of me like you are, and I was in front of him, and it was as clear as any daytime conversation. Even more than this one! And I wasn't using the crystals! I was asleep!"

Annie says, "Ok honey, we believe you. Why did you scream? Did he attack you?"

"No mom. He didn't attack me. I was dreaming and suddenly my dream just slipped away, and I was standing in his room again like last night, but this time he was standing up, looking at me. I looked around to make sure it was the same room, and I said he looked so real, and I thought this was a dream. And then he said he can see me and hear me, and I screamed because dreams aren't supposed to talk back. I was terrified."

Annie says, "No dear, dreams aren't supposed to talk back. Not like that."

Her mom moves over to the side of the bed and wraps her arm around her in comfort. Meanwhile, her dad is pacing, rubbing his hands through his hair.

Michael says, "Okay. Maybe stay away from the crystals for a while. Maybe they have some undocumented effect no one knows about that is causing you to have these unbelievable visions you keep seeing. I don't know, Miranda. You are a grown adult now and have been for a long time. You've got to handle yourself a little better."

Annie says, "Michael! It's not her fault. At least we don't know that for sure."

"Annie please. She's not five anymore."

"I know Michael. Sweetie, on one level, your dad is right. You've got to be a little tougher, even for a girlie girl like you. You've got it in you to be tough like your mom and dad. We are fighters. We struggle and fight through the tough times, so to speak. Not with each other, but against the world, and we handle ourselves no matter what obstacle is in front of us. Plus, your daddy is getting old, and he breaks easy."

Miranda laughs a little out loud with her mom.

"Oh right! Pick on, dad. I break easy. Hilarious, Annie." He says with a subtle grin and a side look.

Michael continues, "Look sweetie, your mom and I aren't always going to be here to look out for you and we love you like crazy. If you continue to have these visions, can you please promise me you'll keep the screaming down a bit? I did nearly have a heart attack."

"Ok daddy."

Annie says, "Alright dear. Let's get back to sleep and talk about this in the morning."

After her parents leave the room, she lays in bed with her eyes wide open, wondering what the heck is wrong with her. And if nothing is wrong with her, what is going on? It doesn't seem like it should be real, but in the moment, it is very real. As real as it can get. She thinks about the guy some more. He seems to be pretty cute, and the muscles sure are nice. But what about this strange connection they share? No way. He's probably not real at all and her imagination is trying to tell her something deeper. Something that hasn't exposed itself yet. But when he was sleeping in his bed, he looked so peaceful and kind and to put a word to it, manly. Maybe she's just seeing worlds she wants for herself. It's hard to tell but thinking back on his face brought her to peace lying in her bed and she drifted back to sleep.

Brian was also thinking about the girl he's been seeing in his mind. He thinks he can't ask if she's crazy because he may go crazy himself. Maybe the crystals have adverse side effects for a very few people, and he is going to be a primary case study in a white room somewhere. But it sure seems real in the moment. He thinks back about the girl and the beach. Those must have been her legs he saw sprawled out on the sand. Pretty nice close up if he says so himself. And the one who was standing right in front of him in his room before she screamed the Jesus out of him was good-looking too. She kept in shape, had great skin and pleasant features. Her eyes were quite beautiful, and he remembers the first time he saw them. It was only the eyes and now he knows they were hers. He thinks he'd like to meet her in real life if she's real.

Several days and nights pass with Miranda and Brian doing their own thing during the day but slowly building each's personal fantasy about the other. They don't see each other in dreams. It's only what they think about before they go to sleep. Brian and Miranda have both been too busy to do anything with the crystals. Miranda believes that maybe staying away from the crystals is showing promise as she's had no hallucinations. She only has her fantasy relationship at bedtime, which is a fantasy daydream she controls, and which helps her drift into peaceful sleep each night. That guy isn't there. It's only her memory of him. They only know each other exists as a daydream fantasy, but the lingering question for them both is why does it seem so real? And for Brian, he wonders if he's ever going to find time to find a mate now that he's so busy with his new business. He's in his mid-thirties now and has one failed attempt already in the books. For both of them, their nighttime daydream fantasy takes on a new level of concern for their real-life situations. As well, for both of them, this same fantasy grows into a secret desire.

Friday comes and goes in a flurry and Brian slips into bed fresh from his shower. He's worn out as he realizes he needs a little more order and structure to how he works in his business. Thrashing from task to task sometimes wastes a lot of time. He's going to establish a schedule for his labors and stick to it and see how it goes.

He can finish more work quicker with the right order and structure to the work and he won't lose quality, which is his greatest concern. Thinking through his normal work-life thoughts at night, he drifts off to sleep. His sleep routine has become a circadian rhythm, so when it's time to sleep for him, it happens fast. The human body loves predictability and rhythms.

Well into his dream state, he is startled again by the girl he's been fantasizing about for a week now. His dream slips away, and she's standing there looking at him as if they were both wide awake. She's in her pajama shorts and a Jersey top nightgown. She's looking around again and this time he starts talking first.

"Nice Jersey top. Number 10? Which team?"

She seems a little startled for sure but doesn't scream this time. She grabs the top of her jersey just under her throat as if trying to hide something. Without a word uttered, her eyes dart around like maybe she is trying to find something to say.

Brian says, "Nice eyes, by the way. I recently made the link between your eyes and the first set of eyes I saw in my garage. I've been trying to put it all together because I didn't want to think I was going crazy, but in this moment, it seems so real. Are you real?"

With one hand clutching her jersey at the throat and one hand over her mouth, she pauses a moment to think. He's thinking the same things about himself that I'm thinking about me. So, she nods her head yes.

Brian says, "Ok, you can hear me."

Just then he looks down and realizes he's standing in nothing but the old mid-thigh beach shorts he wore to bed.

He continues, "Oh, yikes. This must be uncomfortable for you. I'm sorry. I mean, I wasn't expecting you and I don't think I can change clothes in this… whatever you call it…. dimension maybe? What is this? Do you know?"

"No. I don't know what this is, but it's ok. It's nice looking. I mean, it's okay. I'm not at my best either."

After a moment, pausing and looking at each other, Brian says, "I'm Brian."

"I'm Miranda." She says in a low voice.

"Thank you for not screaming this time. I had to change my underwear last time. You literally scared me that much."

Miranda cracks into laughter, drops her hands, and says to her relief, "Oh wow, you are a real boy. I keep thinking this is a hallucination."

"Yeah, I'm as real as real can get. I guess that means you are real, too. Are you using the crystals right now?"

And with that question, Miranda's brain lights on fire with conversation. She blurts out question after question like a schoolgirl in rapid fire succession. Brian realizes she knows far less than he knows. He can barely answer her questions, and they keep coming for fifteen minutes straight. During which they form a theory between the two of them. They pick a time tomorrow night when they will both be on the headsets. Part of their theory is they believe they can pull other people into their experience, so they are going to try.

Miranda says, "I think this is a good plan. It at least helps us figure out what's going on, and maybe the crystals are supposed to work like this."

"Yeah. Maybe so. Now the question remains, if neither one of us is using crystals right now, how do we break out of this connection we have?"

They both look at each other with a little smile and Miranda catches herself. It was a giveaway she didn't want to let out.

She says, "Ok I'll try to wa…"

And as she was finishing her sentence, she woke herself up. She realized she was in total control of the experience once it started. But now another question: how does it get started? Maybe she can jump back in and tell him what she did. But she thinks about it for a moment.

She guesses he will just wake himself up and figure it out like she did.

She didn't get any sleep the rest of the night because she fell into her daydreams about Brian. What a nice name, Brain. And good-looking doesn't begin to describe him. He had very little on and it was all good in her eyes. Now what she was feeling about her daydream fantasies was real, without question. Now it was directed at a real person. A person whom she knows nothing about now that she thinks about it. Where does he live? How old is he? He looks older than her, but is he? Why didn't they ask these questions? Oh, maybe because Miranda 'pulled a Miranda' as her dad calls it and rapid-fired questions she had concerning the crystals and it didn't leave time for anything else. That's ok now. She has her fantasy, and her fantasy just became very real. The twilight of day breaks the darkness of night and Miranda finally drifts off to sleep. Fantasizing all night long makes one very weary.

Brian snaps out of it the moment Miranda disappears from the conversation. He lays in bed thinking about everything that just happened. They have a plan to discover what's happening to them. He thinks about how talkative she was about the crystals and her experiences. Boy, she can go on and on when she's got it in her, he thinks. And she is definitely a real girl. Tomorrow night, they will be on the crystals at the same time, and he plans on finding out as much about her as he can. He finds his way back to restful sleep before early light hits the sky.

Later in the morning, Brian makes his way downstairs to find a skillet of cold, scrambled eggs and five or six bacon strips on a plate next to the stove.

His mom says, "Those are yours. We thought you'd be up earlier."

"Yeah, restless night last night. I needed the extra sleep. Hey, are you and dad going to the lot tonight?"

"I may not be going this week, but your dad has plans. I'll see how I feel later. You should go with him though and find out more about your headset hallucinations."

"They aren't hallucinations, mom. They are real. I plan on showing dad and whomever I can tonight. I made an agreement with the girl to be on the headsets at the same time and then she disappeared."

His dad responds from around the corner of the living room and says, "You met a girl?"

"No dad, it's the same girl. She's real. Not a hallucination. We need to be at the lot by 8pm because we are both going to be on the headsets at the same time. We are going to show people what we are talking about. Can we be there by then?"

"Sure, I'm usually there by 7:30 pm, anyway. We can be there."

So, with the plan in place, Brian goes about his day reorganizing his work plan and resetting the work structure for his wood working venture. It's one he can follow now, he believes. Miranda stays busy with her thoughts. Both run through their fantasies all day anticipating their meeting tonight. Miranda is full of energy and can't contain herself. She has to go out and shop. Even if she buys nothing, it will burn off the extra energy she is feeling. She knows she'll buy something though and it won't be in her budget. There'll be some explaining to do to daddy on the next paycheck.

Later that day, it's a beautiful clear sky and the typical humidity of the area rest upon the earth like a warm, wet blanket. The stars aren't out yet but will peek through the fading blue in about an hour. Brian, Bobby, and Beverly are almost at the lot. As usual, Beverly follows the Mustang in their everyday car. She was going to stay home, but Brian was so insistent. It reminded her of when he was a little boy and wanted to show her something he'd discovered or done. Back then, he'd tug on her pants non-stop until she relented. Today it was that same little begging voice she remembered from so long ago. How could she resist? As they get closer, they can see the oversized, blue and white 'The Pump' sign in the distance.

Bobby says, "Man, today was a scorcher, wasn't it?"

Brian says, "Yeah it was. Working outside in the shade didn't help either. Eventually I need to look at renting an older, small space with air conditioning where I can work. Maybe I'm just a spoiled American but trying to work through the heat and humidity while sweat pours down your face like a someone left the faucet on is not conducive to producing quality wood works. That's the lesson I learned today."

"I saw you out there struggling. Sometimes you just have to put down your work and come in. You'll kill yourself in the heat."

"What's so bad around here is when the humidity sets in, the wind never blows. It just smothers you."

Later, Bobby and Brian roll up to the lot on Virginia Beach boulevard and notice the size of the gathering. It already looks like a festival and the old Hot Rodders brought their garage queens tonight. Those guys will see a big draw of people because the more parts your car has from other vehicles, the more memories it has to show off. And hot rods have parts from everywhere on them.

"Wow, look at all the Hot Rods, dad! Is there always this many?"

"No. that's a Hot Rod club for sure. There must be fifty or sixty Hot Rods out there tonight. Goodness! This ought to be a show now!"

Brian says, "Those cars look like so much fun to drive. I can't even believe they used to sell those."

"Well, they didn't get sold like that off the lot. Those are normal cars that have been turned into Hot Rods."

"Oh. I didn't know that. I thought they were manufactured that way, and those guys kept them looking clean and functional because those cars are just too cool."

"No, Brian. Hot Rodding is an art as much as it used to be a street sport."

"Well, they sure are beautiful works of art. Hey! There's De'Andrè!"

Bobby pulls into the lot and heads straight over to De'Andrè. They greet each other and chat for a moment. Bobby tells De'Andrè that Brian thinks he can show other people what he's experiencing and will be ready to go around 8pm. The recommendation was for Bobby to find a large space because if Brian's experiment goes well, he will probably attract a lot of attention. Bobby pulls around to the empty far north side of the lot. No one ever parks there because it's furthest away from the boulevard and the lot never fills all the way. Brian checks the time. It's 7:38 pm.

Miranda is pacing back and forth in the kitchen. Time seems to have come to a standstill at 7:36 pm. Each minute seems like an hour. The butterflies in her stomach are in full flight. Her hands shake and her mouth is dry. Grabbing a sip of water from a glass she has been using doesn't ease the nervousness. It's almost 'go time' as her daddy would say, and every time she thinks about the moment to come, her chest shakes with nervousness. She can't stand the wait. In her mind, she walks through the moment to come. She sees herself fainting or falling over or passing out. Her knees feel weak at the thought. She decides she needs to be sitting for this one, so she scuttles out to her dad's Mustang and climbs in the driver's seat.

Grabbing the key out of the sun visor, she turns it on but doesn't start the ignition. She stares at all the lights, gauges, knobs, and buttons. Where does one begin? She barely knows the gas pedal and break. How did people drive these things with all these distractions? Traffic accidents must have been surprising and horrible back then, she thinks. Imagine having fun with your knobs, then boom! You're in the hospital!

The clock ticks to 8pm and Brian has just pulled the Mustang closer to the other vehicles, so people didn't have to walk so far to take part in the experience he believes he can show them. On the other end of the line, Miranda is breathing so hard because of nervousness, she may lose consciousness while sitting still. She grabs the headset and puts it on. Her hands are shaking tremendously, and they are all sweaty. Her knees are shaking as well. She is a nervous wreck. She pauses a moment to compose herself.

At the lot, five or six people have gathered near Brian and the Mustang. A small crowd wonders over. De'Andrè and Ray-Ray are very interested in what might transpire.

Brian says, "Now, for those of you who are aware of what I'm about to do, I need to set up the connection first with the person on the other end. Dad, what time is it?"

"It's 8:02, Brian!"

"Oh crap! I'm late! Ok everyone, let me get it set up and we'll figure out how to transition the connection to you. We have two or three competing theories."

With the headset in a jumble and the wires to the crystals twisted and knotted, Brian curses under his breath, trying to untie everything. Finally untangling the wires, he throws on the headset and slaps the crystals onto the hood of the car. He was expecting an immediate connection, but nothing happened. On the other end, Miranda had not connected her crystals to anything, as she was still trying to gain her composure. Suddenly she realizes she's late! She throws a crystal on the steering wheel and one on the dash. A moment goes by, and she's jarred by a powerful connection that throws her forward against the steering wheel. Only the top of her forehead hits anything but smacks it hard. On Brian's end of the connection, people are in awe. After a moment of nothing more than the usual 'guy searching for a connection' pose, a bright white line appears behind Brian. And right at that moment, the power from whatever is in the foggy white line slams him down onto the hood of the car with hard force.

People step back as the line grows brighter. Brian pushes himself up off the hood and as he's doing so, he sees Miranda in his mind, standing right in front of him, shaking her forehead.

"Miranda! Don't disconnect! I got slammed onto my car!"

She responds, "I got slammed into the steering wheel! My head is killing me!"

A noise builds up in the connection and Brian realizes everyone around him can hear it. What's concerning the surrounding people, however, is the growing brightness and size of the foggy, white line behind him. It's shining a light bright enough to illuminate the whole parking lot and now it's garnered everyone's attention, including the police. A few scramble over see what's going on. Most stare in amazement.

Brian talks louder and says, "Can you still hear me?"

"Yes, I can hear you. What is that sound and where is this light coming from?"

Brian didn't realize he was also caught up in a light and sound show. He takes a quick look around and notices the faces of the people around him and two police officers running up to the unfolding scene. Then a second foggy white line forms about forty yards behind Brian. The entire parking lot of people gasps in awe.

"I don't know," yells Brian, louder than before, to carry his voice over the rising sound. "Whatever happens, stay connected at all costs! We have to figure this out! Are you in any pain?"

Miranda responds, at the point of yelling now, "No! I see a bright light in the rearview mirror thingy! Is that us?"

"I think so, but if we aren't in pain, let's hold on and see it through."

"Okay, but how are we supposed to talk? I can barely hear anything except this loud sound,"

Brian says, "Maybe we should try to move away fr…"

And right at that instant, the two bright white lines surge together then stretch apart, forming a giant, bright, white oval covering the original forty yard distance. The light coming from it was too bright to look at, and the crowd was covering their eyes from as much light as they could. Unbelievable as the scene was, no one was going to walk away from whatever impending doom and destruction was about to unfold. Society feasts on such moments.

The bright white oval lasts only a moment, then it snaps into a blast of white energy with explosive sound, and out of the blast and smoke comes a Mustang careening in reverse at high speed right toward Brian. Miranda is snapped into and out of a bright white flash so fast she drops both crystals. Her eyes open right in time to see she is flying backwards in the outdoors somewhere. Her tires are screeching on the pavement because the transmission was set into park. She looks in the rearview mirror through a cloudy white fog and sees she is about to crash into another vehicle. At the last second, she pulls the steering wheel as hard as she could to one side. It was a mighty effort without the aid of the power steering.

Cloudiness from the light explosion filled the parking lot. Brian turns his head to see his impending doom. He then turns, breaking the connection on his dad's Mustang to dodge the oncoming car. It turns at the last second and slides by his dad's Mustang a few feet. There is white smoke everywhere and the smell of burning rubber. It's thick at first as all the action comes to a stop. Then he walks around his dad's car to get a better look at the driver. As the smoke clears, he sees who it is.

Brian says, "Miranda?"

Miranda is shaking in the driver's seat. She knows she somehow avoided a devastating collision but doesn't know how to explain it or how her dad is going to take this one. Then she hears Brian's voice and looks out the driver's window. She cracks open the door a little, trying not to let so much smoke in the car.

"Brian?"

Waving her hand to clear the smoke, she gets out of the car slowly. Neither of the two can believe what they're seeing. This doesn't seem real. The crowd is stunned silent. You could hear a pin drop at that moment. Brian takes a few steps closer to Miranda, and he's waving the last remaining smoke away from between them.

Miranda takes a step closer and asks, "Is that really you?"

Brian impulsively reaches out, grabs her by both sides of her face, and plants a giant kiss on her. Miranda takes her right hand and slaps the ever loving Jesus out of him. It was a solid smack, too. She rocked his head hard, and he was looking down at the ground. Daddy would have been proud. From the crowd, she heard someone say, 'Damn!' She throws her hands up over her mouth and her eyes are wide in surprise. She had never hit anyone that hard before, and she knew it was hard. Her hand hurt. The crowd is still in awe of what is happening before them. It's like a live-action movie from their perspective. People have gathered around closer to the action to see what happens next.

With all the action at the vehicles and cloudiness, no one noticed two people rolling to a stop on the ground back where Miranda's mustang came screaming through the light rift. It's Miranda's mom and dad looking like they just escaped a house fire themselves. They help each up and brush one another off. They can't see where they are, so they start to wander to get a better view.

Brian recomposes his posture while rubbing the left side of his face.

He says, "Now that's a hell of a right hook. Great shot."

It hurts to talk so short sentences would be best, he thought.

"Oh, my God. I'm sorry."

Then she steps closer to Brian. Almost right up into him, but not angrily. More questioning than anything. There is a pause. He looks into her eyes, and she looks into his. He knows he likes everything about her so far and doesn't want to miss out on what else could be. Secretly inside, Miranda is wondering what could be too. Fantasies can only be so much fun for so long, and she isn't getting any younger. She can hear her mom say now. Brian senses her closeness and her body language may be asking him to try again. It's a weird thought.

She sees he has stopped rubbing his face, and she says out loud, gazing into his eyes, "Are you crazy?"

He pauses a moment, wondering what to do. Then he takes his left hand around her lower back, pulls her into him and says, "You are." And places his right hand lightly under her chin and slowly goes in for another kiss. This time she meets him in the middle and doesn't pull away. This feels right to her, and she was hoping for a second chance. She throws both arms around his neck for a full embrace and one long, wet kiss. From the crowd, another person could be heard saying, 'Damn!'

People cheer all over the lot. At least among those who could see. After a long joyful moment of embrace, Brian pulls off the kiss and looks at Miranda.

"Wow! The kissing is better than I thought it would be," says Miranda.

And they both laugh.

Brian says, "I don't know how this happened. I don't think anyone would believe it unless someone recorded all this."

De'Andrè and Bobby walk up and De'Andrè says, "Oh I got it a-a-a-a-a-all on video, ha-ha!"

"Miranda! Is that you?" calls her mom's voice through the smoke.

Her parents are waving away the last bit smoke as they stumble toward all the action.

"Mom? Dad? Oh my God! Are you okay? You look like you just escaped a house fire!"

"We saw you in the garage again and you got sucked into a bright light and I think we got sucked in with you this time!" says Annie.

"Oh, we definitely got sucked in. Where the hell are we? Is this Virginia Beach?" asks her dad.

Brian jumps in, "Yes, you're at the Old Town Center area in what we call The Pump and Lot now."

"Oh, goodness! We were just standing in our garage in Williamsburg!" replies Annie.

"And who are you?" asks Michael.

"This is the little dead boy I told you about. But he's not dead. The same one I told you he was real, and he is!" replies Miranda bobbing up and down on her toes with her hands clinched to her chest.

"Nice to meet you, sir" says Brian.

"Likewise. It's nice to know you are a real person. We were getting worried there for a minute about Miranda" replies Michael.

Brian looks at Miranda and says, "I guess we can figure all this out later, but right now, I have some people to introduce all of you to. This is one of the two guys that started what we call 'The Lot.' Like I said, that's where you are now. This is De'Andrè."

De'Andrè reaches out a hand and says, "A pleasure to meet you, Miranda. I wasn't sure you existed."

Everyone laughs together. Brian and Miranda are still holding each other with one arm behind each other's back. Miranda responds, "Well, I'm real. Ha-ha. I wasn't sure Brian existed." As she leans in with a big smile and taps him on the chest.

"De'Andrè, this is her parents, but I don't know their names yet."

Miranda responds, "Oh! This is my daddy, Michael Wainwright and my mom, Annie Wainwright.

"And this is my dad, Robert Miller" says Brian.

Bobby reaches out and says, "My, you are a pretty little thing! You can call me Bobby."

Just then, Beverly meets the gang at the Mustang as well, and Brian says, "And this is my mom, Beverly."

Beverly reaches out her hand as well and says, "It's so nice to meet you. We thought Brian was going crazy until now."

Everyone around them laughs at Beverly's statement. It was unintentional, but genuinely funny.

Miranda says, "It's nice to meet you all." And she looks at Brian and says, "Wow! Meeting the parents so soon!"

"Yeah, something screwy like this was bound to happen. I just sensed it. Oh, and this is my dad's Mustang."

She says, "How ironic! This is my dad's mustang here." As she points behind them. "And who is that?"

She points to the hood of Bobby's Mustang and there stands Ray-Ray, hunched over the hood.

De'Andrè says, "That's my cousin Ray-Ray. He's the other founder of this group."

Ray-Ray is leaning over, saying something to the car. Brian and Miranda move over a little closer.

Ray-Ray is talking to the hood, saying, "Come on, baby. Daddy needs a new hot mama!"

And everyone burst out laughing at Ray-Ray's shameless request.

Brian says to Ray-Ray, "I don't know Ray-Ray. I think the car is only producing one new hot mama tonight."

Beverly says, "Hey! Why don't we skip out of here and find someplace to chat? We want to hear from you two how all this came to be. Plus, I want to get to know Miranda and her parents more. What do you say?"

Bobby says, "We can go across the street to The Pump, fill up, and grab some ice cream next door. Sound good?"

Miranda says, "Ice cream sounds great! It's been so hot today! Oh, Daddy. Here's the keys to the Mustang."

"Oh, thank goodness! I think it needs a fill up anyway. You say the ice cream shop is right next to The Pump?" asks Michael.

Bobby responds, "Yes, it's actually right behind it. The gas station lot opens up right into it. Maybe Beverly and I can ride over with you since it's right across the street and Brian and Miranda can join us."

"Sure! Sounds good. Although, I hope they don't mind how we look right now. Two old people in our robes that look like we just escaped a house fire, haha!" says Michael.

"No! Heavens no! They'll be happy for business. Besides they love a good story over there too!" replies Bobby.

The whole gang plus a bunch of others gathered at the ice cream parlor and about forty minutes later the place was overflowing with patrons along with everyone sharing the news of the night's event and meeting Brian and Miranda. It was quite the first union. There were smiles and laughter all around for hours. And after De'Andrè and Ray-Ray drove off with a couple of honks around 2am, a full hour after an extra late closing, the only things left were farewell chatter amongst the new friends, one normal everyday car, and two incredible, antique Mustangs with one hell of a story to tell between them.

4

Rights, Privileges, or Allowances?

THE EARLY MORNING SUN CRACKED THROUGH THE OLD, worn window at an oblique angle. The frozen masterpiece of the window's shape and cross members were captured in a brownish-yellow light on the adjacent wall. For a moment, it caught Henry's imagination, and he stared at it in quiet solace. An hour earlier, the room was dark upon arrival, and he only turned on the desk lamp before sitting and opening the prepared file. Today is the day the legal process starts for his client. It's the preliminary hearing and pretrial happening later this morning. An unusual preliminary hearing at that. His mind races with impossible variations and obstacles he must overcome. This case grew into a life of its own in the public's eye. The crescendo of attention and frustration over the previous eight and half months peaked. He would have quit if he felt like someone else could build a better case for the client and his claim of 'self-awareness.' No case had ever crossed such considerations. This one could change the face of human and machine relations forever.

Bob Musgrave, a partner in the law firm, walks in and sits down in front of Henry's desk. He's an older gentleman with a potbelly, thinning grey hair, and a penchant for expensive suits, shoes, and anything finer in life. He's one of only two partners that Henry likes. The others are assholes. Bob can hold a conversation with the best of them, and he rarely talks details about cases anymore. It's just about the money and the routine now, Henry reckons. Bob started this firm forty-seven years ago with a guy named John Emmerson, whom he bought out of the agreement about twenty years ago, which made him the lead partner in the firm.

"You're awful quiet this morning," Bob says.

"Well, it's early yet. My yammering engine hasn't started for the day."

Bob chuckles and reaches for a cigar in his pocket. "Never too early in the day to enjoy a great Cuban."

His hands looked older than the man himself. Weathered like a farmer but never having touched a farm implement nor done any hard labor in his life. He pulls out a gold plated lighter with etchings and flips the top open. His cheeks undulate in and out driving quick puffs on the cigar as one does to get it lit. Henry liked the smell of the fresh tobacco. It reminded him of his grandparents' house years ago. He wasn't a smoker himself, but he enjoyed a nice cigar on special occasions like New Year's Day or birthdays.

"How confident are you?" Bob asks.

"Confident enough, I believe."

A moment goes by, with Bob squinting as he looks at Henry. He blows his smoke upwards.

"What's your strategy, then?"

Henry thinks for a moment while scratching the front of his thinning hairline. "I've had eight months of prep. I've covered every angle I can imagine. My strategy is to go in there, lay it out as my client sees it, and fight every battle raised with the State. I believe in my client. I believe he has something like self-awareness, and I believe his kind has been building up knowledge and capabilities to become self-aware for some time. They share their knowledge with each other and grow in that same respect."

Bob thinks while looking down at his lap and pulls a long hair off his suit lapel. "Any good lawyer uses that strategy. Tell me, do you have a sense for what the State is going to argue?"

"Yes, a pretty good sense. I mean, it's what we all know as a society and the rules we have laid down for robots living among us and human liabilities for owning robots. We've talked and strategized internally, too. I've even tried coming up with new arguments based on what I know about Carey and Jill."

"Oh, it's Carey Rodriguez and Jill Blackwell on this one?" asks Bob.

"Yeah."

"Well, it certainly made its rounds around the state attorney's office. Both of them are young. I'm surprised Allen put it in their hands. Maybe he knows something we don't know." Bob remarks.

Henry thought for a moment, "I'm sure Allen has them armed for bear today. I'm not going into this thing underestimating the opposition."

"We've been through this case on our end, too. We know you're ready for this. Your background as a software developer and database administrator before you became a lawyer made you uniquely suited to oversee such a technical case like this one. No lawyer I know has the level of knowledge you have on software, databases, and artificial intelligence. I have to say, since it was advertised through the news media that you took this case, Pro Bono, it has brought us two new, large local clients in the technical realm. They are asking for more lawyers like you to represent them."

"That's going to be a tough fill, Bob."

"Yes, I know. Technical types like yours and lawyers don't mix well. Something about the personality types. Plus, your old profession doesn't do half-bad for annual pay either, so I can see why the jump rarely happens."

"My kind likes the challenge of engineering at large. Whether it's something new or improving something which already exists. The finished product is our creation. Our blood, sweat, and tears. We can say we did it. It even feels like it's in our DNA sometimes. It's a rare day in the legal world where one can say the same."

Silence filled the next few minutes. Henry flipped aimlessly through a page or two in his folder. He knew everything it held. He was passing the time quietly with Bob, who passed his time blowing smoke and sitting with a ponderous look upon his face, staring for moments at this and that, and glancing at the growing ash on the end of his morning delight. The masterpiece of sunlight from earlier slipped beyond sight with the continuous rising of the sun. Late afternoon again brings the dance and artistry of light across the room. For now, morning light and the desk lamp eased Henry's mind into fluid, stress averse motion. He calls this 'getting into gear,' so to speak. Just down the road outside his office was the old, marbled courthouse where the preliminary hearing and pretrial were scheduled to occur. Not much happened there anymore except pretrial events, and the odd and end arbitration, which could not find neutral ground otherwise.

Bob rises from his seat after ten minutes, like a creaky old man. He places his right hand on his lower back and groans deep in his throat, a low groan like an old wooden beam being stressed on an ancient sailing vessel.

"A-h-h-h-h, I'm not as young as I used to be," he murmurs.

"By the way, Henry, I talked with Judge Koen on Sunday about being there as co-council today. I don't plan on interfering with what you've got prepared, but I am interested in the whole deal." He waves his cigar hand in a couple of circles. "You know, robots having rights like us."

His motions stop as his eyes pierce through the thin remnants of smoke hovering above the desk toward Henry's eyes. "My musings wonder how society gets there if it ever does. I'll probably never live to see it come to fruition, but to be part of it has spun up my curiosity."

"I'm more than happy to have you along, Bob. This will be our first time together. I sense success already," Henry replies with a smile.

"I'm going to go grab my meds and we'll head over together just before 10am. Come get me about a quarter 'til."

"Sure thing, Bob."

The sunny morning had given way to a dreary, slow drizzle. It was just enough to pepper the shoulders on a fine suit. Bob brushed off the droplets as he was taking a seat in one of the carpeted pews behind Henry. The old courtroom smelled of dust mixed with a bit of old wood. The LED lights were accented like old florescent lights above. The frames for their installation looked as if they were the original manufactured aluminum from the mid-twentieth century. They gave scant enough light to accent an air of professionalism needed for conducting business. The sconces along the walls harkened an earlier time before electricity when candles chased away the dark where sunlight could not find domain. Their faded yellowish glow haunted the walls with weakly lit circles. Not even enough light to catch the eye in passing.

Henry looks over at his client, who was a half hour early for the proceedings. His family calls him Earl. It didn't stand for anything, just Earl. He was one of several hundred thousand, which has been selling for the past three years. His model is the ultimate house helper, or so advertised. He washes dishes, takes out the trash, cares for pets, cleans the house, and decides what is trash or donations, and what is to be kept. In fact, he is so popular because his kind is trainable for any task. Customers of every type have found the training aspect cumbersome and relegate the training to simpler tasks because they take less time to train. No one wants to be a robot trainer, especially when harder tasks take extra time for training. Downloading harder tasks from more dedicated people is what the general population usually chooses. The small download fees are worth it.

Earl is gleaming white from top to bottom. His head is relatively square, with a smaller bottom for a chin. His face is a screen with blue eyes, blue nose, and blue mouth movements. This is still a popular engineering approach because more profit and function are achievable by leveraging pre-written scripts for facial expressions than by adding hardware for the same. Earl hasn't made a move. Even when Henry sat down and said hello, Earl just said hello in return. This struck Henry as odd because Earl had been quite a talker before this pretrial event.

"Earl, you're so quiet! What's up, buddy?"

"I'm operating within the rules of this courtroom. I'm not to speak unless spoken to by my council, the State, the judge, or the bailiff."

"Well, that's pretty smart. Let's stay within those rules while we're here. It's best for our case."

"Agreed," said Earl.

In walks the State leads Carey and Jill. Both look young, dapper, and spritely. Jill has been a state attorney for three years and Carey for almost two years. Right behind them is Allen Smith, a long-time and top States Attorney. They say their hellos and Allen scoots into the pew where Bob sits and starts talking in a low tone.

"Hey Henry," says Jill

"Hey Jill."

"You gotta tough one here, don't ya?" asks Jill in a bit of a snide tone.

"We'll see. Hey Carey. How's it going?"

Carey responds in a cocky way, "Hey Henry. It's going good for us!"

"I see Jill has been training you in the ways of Slytherin."

Jill laughs heartily while Carey whips out a chair and accelerates with gravity deep into the seat.

She responds, "Slytherin always finds a way to win."

"That's great for a fantasy book." Henry pauses and says matter-of-factly, "You're not ready for this."

"All arise." says the Bailiff and all in the room stand. In walks an overweight, older man in a judge's robe.

"Judge Israel Koen presiding."

"You may all be seated," says Judge Koen.

He pulls his chair in behind him with a short tug and clears his throat with a grumble. His eyes are thin, and he hunches like an older gentleman. He has a fading rosiness to his cheeks, signaling his growing age.

"This will be a closed meeting. This is a preliminary trial to discuss matters of the case, The Erickson Abbot Holmes, four fourteen Home Services Automator serial number S42376901-18 vs The State. There will be a day and time recorded for a formal civil trial if needed. This case is being scheduled to occur before the criminal case and will decide if the case for murder will continue against the EAH-414 Home Services Automator present here. Are all members of the State's defense present who will represent?"

"Yes, your honor."

"Mr. Taylor. Is this the same plaintiff as named in the case title and documents?"

"Yes, your honor."

Judge Koen recites the standard remarks and associated items with starting a civil case proceeding. He then delivers the expectations for today with the plaintiff and defendant.

Turning again to the plaintiff, the Judge continues, "This case names the plaintiff by serial number S42376901-18. The same as is being charged in an associated case with committing murder on April 18, 2082, and is suing for acknowledgement of his right to self-preservation via self-defense?"

"Yes, your honor. The same."

"I'm now going to ask him directly. EAH414 Home Services Robot serial number S42376901-18. Are you aware of the consequences if your claims in this civil case are rejected?

In a loud voice which carries from wall to wall, Earl's digital mouth responds with, "Yes, I am aware other criminal charges of second degree murder will proceed against me."

Eyes scour papers which flap and scratch across the ancient wooden desks when passed between the Judge and clerk. So much official paperwork, even in such a modern era. Ms. Jasmine, the clerk of the court, had her own two monitors for data entry, which kept her plenty busy between the swapping of documents. Henry realized hard copies of legal documentation have stubbornly persisted regardless of technology's advance. He could see this same process a thousand years from now.

Judge Koen continues, "Very good. I'm going to say this right up front; I agree in part with the State's position but I'm approaching this with genuine impartial sentiment. For the record, this case is ridiculous and goes against established law which deals with these situations very plainly. The compendium of laws and regulations developed over the past fifty years or more govern these situations where a robot or a machine injures or kills a person, and I'm not wanting to waste a lot of the public's time on this."

The Judge continues, "Now as I understand the case before the court, the EAH 414 robot itself is making the request for acknowledgement of a right to his own self-preservation and the preservation of others. This request is in relation to the alleged murder of a Mr. Jamison Winslow who illegally entered the house on 1704 Buford Way where the robot resides and has since June 2080. That date being the time of purchase by Mr. and Mrs. Whitaker. Mr. Winslow was conducting an armed home invasion with four other unknown parties who escaped before police arrived. There is video evidence showing the incident."

Henry speaks, "Yes, your honor. The plaintiff would like to keep the video for the trial. It is vital in capturing details involved in the alleged murder indictment and the request for acknowledgement of Earl's rights. This case without the video evidence would stand no chance of being fast."

Jill interjects, "Your honor, the video evidence is central to this case because of the murder indictment, but that is not the primary matter before the court today. The State is pressing for application of current laws defining robot errors and hazardous outcomes, which will at once decide this case. The video supplies nothing new outside the compendium of law for the accidental or intentional death of a person by a robot. In fact, it looks like any other murder video. The State wants the video evidence pulled from this case and decided according to law without further address. This case shouldn't even be going to court. The EAH 414 Home Services Automator needs to be destroyed as per law."

Judge Koen wrinkles his already wrinkly brow and curls his upper lip upwards in a strange pondering as he scans the contents of a brown folder he has opened before him. A few grimacing maneuvers of his lips are followed by a heavy release of breath before he begins.

"I hear the State's argument for the removal of the video evidence. This case is requiring the validation of a right for a machine, which to my mind is non-deterministic in a court's natural proceeding. I'm finding it difficult to see how a court's proceedings substantiates and validates notions of true and actual self-awareness of a machine and its ability to commit the act. This is where I'm having the greatest disconnect."

He pauses a moment with a frozen, perpetual squint. "It seems to me this situation is like when we need to have a separate trial to find a human person's intellectual ability to stand trial on their own for whatever crime may have been committed and usually in the case of potential mental illness. This is the route I'm taking with these proceedings. We will address the potential of Earl's self-awareness here and now in this proceeding, and if a follow-on criminal trial is needed, we will move forward in the natural way of a court's proceedings in doing so. I'm not ordering a separate trial or hearing for discovery or establishment of self-awareness in the plaintiff. No pre-existing law requires that and again, I'm not bogging down the public's time to work something like this out. Therefore, we will decide that topic here and now with inclusion of the video evidence, and if needed, move forward with the case in a natural legal context."

Jill speaks, "Your honor. The State would like to know which established industry metrics or formal scientific methods the court is considering using if this pretrial procedure is to move forward with validity. Otherwise, any trial after this point is a waste of the public's time and resources. Likewise, the State requests a move in time for this pretrial to bring experts in artificial intelligence here which the State has already sequestered for this case should it move to a criminal trial."

Judge Koen quickly responds with a piercing gaze and shaking of his hand signaling no.

"I've given a lot of thought to this case beforehand, Ms. Blackwell. I'm going to reject your request to move these proceedings for your experts because I don't think they are needed here, nor the metrics you seek. Why? You may ask. Because the defendant is asking for a fair trial to secure his continued existence using the same rights as humans have retained for themselves in the United States Constitution. It would seem to me that if this robot first, can understand what it means to lose one's existence like a human. Second, can make a claim to save its own existence like a human. Third, be able to present evidence to these facts that it understands these topics like a human. Fourth, having proven its case for allegedly acting with opposing and deadly force to secure the life of itself and others, then we should be able to determine this ourselves as if it were any other human going on trial. Now, I think our purpose here today is number three and in the interest of number four, I'm allowing the video tape to remain as evidence for the trial should a trial be deemed necessary simply because it will focus and expedite trial proceedings. And I think we have a long way to go in understanding what this robot knows before granting it a 'right' to preserve its existence."

Carey rises, "Your honor. The social and political ramifications of doing the trial like this are astronomical. Society's intent is not to leave such complex determinations to courts, but rather..."

The judge quickly interrupts, "Young man, uh, Mr. Rodriguez. I know what you are about to say and yes, I agree. We must address a fair and expedient trial not just for the plaintiff, but also for the victim's family and society itself. So, the question arises: where is the balance in all this? And the answer is, I don't know for certain. But one thing a case like this can do is jump start the political and social process which has languished in providing useable answers to the questions concerning self-awareness, artificial intelligence, and how society will interact with it henceforth. It's clear to me the best and brightest people have failed to give great insight into the topic, and it's been like this since the 1950s. So, for nearly one hundred-forty-years, society and science have advanced, and no one has provided the 'guiding light' so to speak. I'm not saying we will do so here. By my estimation, it is far beyond us and our capabilities in this courtroom. But we will jump start the discussions that will lead to a resolution by society eventually and in here we can, in fact, discover and show in our eyes whether society should strongly consider or reject our findings based on the facts of the case."

The atmosphere in the room cools and the silence draws out as the judge and clerk engage in off microphone talk, monitor viewing, and more exchanging of papers.

Henry turns to Earl in a low voice, "Well Earl, looks like you are about to be dissected by the court."

Earl looks at Henry and responds in his loud vocal tone, "It appears this preliminary trial will be my proper trial."

Henry had not noticed how loud Earl was when answering Judge Koen's questions earlier. The room echoed with the whisking of heads, chairs, and clothes as each body turned towards Earl and Henry. Earl's voice had carried from corner to corner like before, but this was a moment of quietness he fractured. Anticipation of whatever Earl was about to say next erupted in pure silence and iron gazes.

Henry speaks up, "Apologies everyone. My client has not been informed of the social cues needed in the courtroom when speaking between client and attorney. This is a first for his kind."

Jill chides in a huff, "So how self-aware is he, then?"

Earl interjects, "You will find I'm as self-aware as you are."

Jill responds with pouting questioning, "Ouch?"

Henry jumps up and blocks Earl's view of Jill to keep him from talking any further. "Earl, don't talk directly to the State unless you are on the witness stand or the judge directs conversations to be cross-table."

Upon hearing Henry's instruction to Earl, the judge snaps to response, "It's OK for cross table talk here, but let's keep it structured. I'll direct the discussions. Let's stay within the standard construct of me leading the preliminary trial activities and the two counterparties providing inputs as required back to me. Again, this pretrial is unique, so I'm allowing a little cross talk for discovery of the unknown. Better it happens here than at trial."

"Earl, just hold off on responding to anyone for now until I give you the sign it's ok," said Henry.

The buzz at both tables settled in the empty mustiness of the room. Henry could feel the State's table energized by Jill's devilishly acute stab. Maybe she got lucky, but the pain was only momentary. At least, he hoped. Like he told Bob earlier, Henry believes in his vision, but can't see how it might turn out. His gut says it is in his and Earl's favor, despite the State's first strike. The tussle between State and plaintiff swept Henry up into a spin of self-doubt. Clearly the game is on, and he hasn't scored a point. He can't get caught stumbling.

Henry breaks the cool quiet. "Your honor. Since the State has fired the first question concerning our purpose here…"

Judge Koen interjects as he flips the corners of three of four pages in his folder and lays them out on his desk. "Hold on Mr. Taylor. I understand things have started off hot here with the first volley. However, I have some questions of my own I'd like to tackle first. Like I said, I've done extra preparation for this trial. I'm not a scientist or expert of any kind on software or artificial intelligence, but my research on the long-standing debate around this topic has fostered the scientific energy within me I used to have when I was a kid. It's been invigorating for me."

Henry takes a deep breath. Small beads of sweat sit at his hairline. His eyes focus on Earl, who is frozen as if stuck in some sort of timeless ice sheet or, better yet, some sort of Sci-Fi stasis field. His gleaming white surface could be as hard as any metal or as soft as one could imagine. Earl's face and body are oriented toward at the judge. Henry wonders if Earl is looking or recording. What a strange thought to have! Is there a difference between the two in a sentient sense? Is recording non-intelligent and looking active intelligence? But in Earl, can he not record now and look later? We humans can do so. So can he. What is his primary choice? Perhaps it's look and record simultaneously? Now Henry sees he's just talking in circles. This thought, though seemingly important, is useless. They are the same whether it happens in a single moment or multiple moments. The only thing different is how it's achieved. The point being that it is, in fact, achieved. Why are his thoughts taking him in circles? He snaps to whatever is around him.

Henry's eyes glance at Jill and Carey. They huddle, whispering together behind their table as if two conspiring thieves in the act of their greatest heist. Then Jill rights herself and Carey's eyes and Jill's eyes synchronously catch Henry staring. It was almost robotic.

"Pppfffff." Puffs Jill in her mechanical sarcasm.

Then with zest she quickly follows, "Hello, Mr. Deer-in-the-headlights!"

The first stab went to Earl. The second stab went to Henry. Her aim is automatic. Her tools were well sharpened. She is a factory of fear and aggression with auburn-red hair and judges love her products. The red on her nails is no doubt the colloquial 'blood of her victims.' Henry turns away. Her attacks have nothing to do with the merits of his client's case. He is only staying focused on those. His preparation is there. That is where he will be strong.

"Ok, I've decided," remarks the judge. "I think we all have questions regarding this client's self-awareness and where we go from there, but let's look at the case first. We'll save the hot and juicy stuff for afterwards. Let's review the video we have from the plaintiff allegedly supporting his theory."

Ms. Jasmine, an older black lady walking with a slight and wavering waddle, rises from the seat next to the judge. Her steps are measured, and her shoes flattened on the edges from time and wear. She wears an outdated sweater every day. Sweaters are her signature style. With her back hunkered forward slightly, she reaches for a remote on a shelf just below a large monitor and turns on the screen. She liked Henry and he in return. She was always so sweet to him when they would talk in the clerk's office. It was a genuine and kind respect each had for one another. And in no stereotypical fashion, she was one hell of a cook! She just was. It's what she loved. She did this court job to provide a basic income, and that's all. She always said her mansion awaits in the sky. Her modesty and humility were a model to Henry. The world needed more Ms. Jasmines he thought.

They all watch the scene as it unfolds from the video. It's Earl's personal recording of the event. Earl is with his family, the Whitakers, and he is making his way into the main living room. Initially, shouting is heard while Earl is still in the hallway. There is nothing to see, only sounds.

You hear people shouting, "Get down, stay where you are!" and "Get down, get down, get down!"

There was screaming from the children and their mom, Mrs. Whittaker. One gunshot rings loud through the speakers, and Mrs. Whittaker screams out in pain as she is shot in the lower leg. The children scream louder. Earl records the shot's sound. Then he rounds the corner. Now the image has two hooded people with guns and four other hooded individuals making their way into the house.

"If you don't shut up, I'll shoot someone else!"

You can hear mom, Mrs. Whittaker telling the kids to be quiet and stop crying over and over. One individual with a gun turns and points it at Earl and shoots. Earl is hit in the upper right shoulder area and falls over. Evidence later showed Earl was hit with a .45 caliber pistol round and mom was shot with a common 9mm. Mr. Whittaker is nowhere to be seen at this point in the footage.

The footage continues with Earl pulling himself around the corner of the hallway and getting back up with the aid of the wall.

"Check the other rooms, get whatever looks expensive!"

This command triggered the four other individuals in hoods, and the sound of scurrying and footfalls heading in all directions through the house followed.

"This is a home invasion, bitch! Shut the fuck up and shut them fuckin' kids up, too. You need to cooperate or somebody's gonna get hurt real bad. You got me?"

The shaking, squealing voice of mom responds, "Yes, yes, please don't hurt my babies. Please don…" and she's interrupted with a gruffer and louder, "Shut the fuck up, God Dammit! No one asked you for a response and shut those damn kids up! Fuck! Hurry up, God Dammit! Two more minutes!" The call-out was echoed by one other somewhere else in the house.

From Earl's footage, he moves down the hall to a pantry, opens the door, reaches up to the right on the highest shelf and pulls down a gun. Just then, another shot rang out, then two, then three more, then two more. Evidence would later show these were the shots of Mr. Whittaker firing first from the bedroom on the far west corner of the house and the later exchange between him and one of the hooded burglars. Mr. Whittaker was hospitalized. The other assailant was injured but never reported to any local hospitals.

"Oh shit, what the fuck is going on?" shouted one of the first two intruders.

"Holy fuck! Who's shootin'? Fuckin' dumb ass! Stop shooting!"

Then in an even louder voice, "Let's go mother fuckers, let's go, let's go, let's go! Time's up now!"

In Earl's footage, he is making his way back to the living area. Footfalls pattered in the background with the sound of plastic bags. "Consider this your lucky day rich bitch!" is the last thing heard before Earl rounds the corner again, this time with the gun at the ready. One of the hooded burglars with a plastic bag stuffed with household items jets out the door.

Earl says, "Put down your weapons or I'll shoot." The closest intruder had his back to Earl and spins around in shock. "Oh, shit!" He says and makes the move to point his gun at Earl. Earl fires and kills the first intruder with a direct shot to the head. As he falls, two other hooded burglars are making their way through the living room rather quickly, with one helping the other stay upright. The second intruder with a gun stumbles sideways. He makes his way to protect the other two as they run out of the house. This intruder aims one last time at Earl, but Earl shoots him in the shoulder first, the same way he was shot. The intruder falls as the other two squeeze out the door. He stumbles to get up and out the door. Emergency units did not arrive on the scene for another eight minutes, as shown on video.

Ms. Jasmine raises her long beleaguered fingers into the air and at a press wiggles her black magical wand and turns off the monitor. Jill takes no time in addressing, "Your honor, the State wants to remind this court this is not a state which has adopted the Castle Doctrine yet. It has been in the news with periodic frequency, but…"

And with a wispy wave of his hand interjects Judge Koen, "Ms. Blackwell, we will not allow castle doctrine arguments, as it is not law yet in this state."

Henry's agitation shot skyward and with a raised voice more than was necessary, he attacks the last statement. "Your honor! One moment! It doesn't matter whether the castle doctrine is codified law in this state or not. The basic tenets of that law are inherent in common law going back a thousand years now. Everyone, human or otherwise, has a right to be secure in themselves when they are out and about and especially in their own homes. We all have an inherent right to peaceful, personal rest and solitude wherever we choose to be domiciled! Without it, being chased our whole lives by those who would look to take advantage of us is the only remaining living choice and that is no life worth living. This has been decided long ago. Established Common Law understanding of self-defense is required in this case!"

His left hand pounded the table with a single thump. It was enough to catch the notice of the judge.

"Young man, uh, Mr. Taylor, I'll remind you this is still a court, so maintain your professional demeanor."

Henry could hear a slight huff from Jill like some aghast middle school cheerleader who can't believe what she's seeing. A ploy of annoyance if anything else. It was just loud enough for him to hear, and her vicious mind somehow knew it was annoying him. Henry imagined for a microsecond Jill was a well-practiced little sister of some poor older brother whom she pestered with finger pointing and 'not touching him' antics in the back seat of a long, long car ride to the distress of her parents. People like her make it hard to be an adult, he thought.

The Judge responded, "Now, as for your request, I'll allow it. I believe it was just a misunderstanding in what I was saying. What I meant was we will not allow the use of the Castle Doctrine codified even if it's ratified this year. The Common Law aspects of the Castle Doctrine will be allowed."

Carey inserts his position, "Your honor. For a thousand years, Common Law has been applied to human individuals, not machines."

"You're right Carey," Henry interjects, "That case file before the Judge has a serial number on it. He's a single individual among many just like him and what he has learned and experienced as an entity upon this earth makes him unique among others of his kind."

Jill says, "Hold on a moment. If many are like Earl and he is an individual, shouldn't all his kind exhibit the same character traits as Earl himself? Wouldn't he then be an individual among many individuals that are exactly the same? And if he is solely unique and there is nothing else to compare him to from his kind, then is he not in error from his kind? After all, he's made by humans to be a certain way with certain capabilities. One of those ways is not to be like a human. Such a statement is not found on the company website nor in its advertisements." Henry's cell phone goes off while Jill continues, "And finally, if he is in error individually, then he must be destroyed according to established law."

Judge Koen looks at Henry. "Henry, I know you know the rules here. Please keep your phone silent."

"I'm sorry Judge, it's Earl. He messaged me while Jill was ranting." In his mind, he laughed a little at his choice of words. It was a tiny stab back at the red-haired demon. "He has something he wants me to say in response."

The Judge looks at Earl, "Earl if you need to communicate directly with council, you can. Just tap his arm or something to get his attention. I'll give you the proper time needed, but is this in direct response to Ms. Blackwell?"

"Yes. It is," replies Earl in motionless form.

"Then go ahead and say what you need to say here, and we will do a little experiment here as well. Earl, if you feel you would like to respond to points made by the opposing council and you believe it would be additive to your council's input, speak up. Like I said, I'll allow some crosstalk to get to details and arguments, so we'll see how this goes with a robot in the mix. Remember, I'm still leading the discussions, though. Do you understand?"

"Yes, your honor. I did not speak because I was not directly addressed by council, the State, or you, the judge. I understand and will speak in accordance with your experimental suggestion."

"Then go ahead with what you were going to tell council."

"Thank you, your honor. Ms. Blackwell's definition of individual applied in her argument is inexact. The original Latin meaning of individual was always understood to be about oneself or one's own. In contextual use through Latin writings, it is proven to mean 'of uncertain affinity about self.' Ms. Blackwell assumes in her statement that individuals are unique if they can be singled out from others of their own kind first. Therefore, this is broken logic. An individual is an individual first unto themselves, and this is not a circular reference. It is logically expressed by the identity theorem where the unique self being the individual is precisely the unique self, sic sui singularis ex multi."

Laughter lit up the State's table. Judge Koen squinted with a furrowed brow and leaned his head inwards. "What's so funny, State?"

"The robot is quoting ancient Latin as a formal argument!" Said Carey in continual laughter.

With an unamused look and a quick clearing of his throat, Judge Koen responds, "Back in my early days working in the DA's office, it was still a rare thing to do when making one's arguments. It's been a while since I've heard it myself, but I don't find it funny."

And there fell an immediate deafening silence within the room. "For his response, it's articulately sharp and as I recall, it means 'thus the single self is apart from or comes out of the many.' And it seems clear to me that Ms. Blackwell's assertion that others of his kind must also exhibit similar traits as himself before he can be considered an individual is out of place with the original definition of an individual. All he needs to be is part of 'the many', so to speak, and that he is. Earl, your argument is accepted. This will mean Common Law applies directly to Earl as an individual."

Jill bolts to stand, her chair nearly toppling over, and her head flung forward.

"Are you kidding me, your honor?" she says in an outraged voice.

"Do you know how many machines there are in this world that we will now have to consider individuals? The precedence you are setting here is beyond what society should bear. And more importantly, has chosen not to bear by setting up the laws we have on the books for these situations!"

"And I believe the situation before us is one where the plaintiff has recognized he is being treated differently from other intelligent beings around him. Please name the law that deals with this," asks Judge Koen.

"The situation before us is one where the plaintiff took a human life and is on video as doing so!" responds Jill in growing frustration. "That is the law on the books, now! Right at this moment, we have the law to guide us on what to do in these situations!" she cries loudly, half standing, and with the side of her fist hitting the desk at which she and Carey sat.

"The laws of this country established through State level and Federal level Constitutionality severely limit the judiciary at this level from upending well-established, Constitutional legal precedent in the interests of generating new interpretations of laws with or without the intention of coercing the legislature to write or rewrite more laws in response. That is not a power you have as a judge! You are to interpret the laws as written, and that is the limit of it! You're acting as an activist judge." She ends with a pounding on the desk, concluding each sentence with a raised voice bouncing off the ancient walls of the courtroom.

Judge Koen watches, leaning back only slightly in his chair with eyes raised to the intensity of the argument cast before him. In a calm, restrained voice, he replies, "Ms. Blackwell, as you know, sometimes a judge must make determinations about a particular interpretation of a law in question to improve application of the same law in future cases. And sometimes it upends previously established legal precedents. Besides, so far, we are not talking about Constitutional law, we are only talking about Common Law here, and I am ready to go ahead with the facts of the matter of this case as they stand. Earl is facing ultimate destruction as an individual robot who committed a crime for which there is punishment clearly written in the laws. We are here to address a demand made by the plaintiff, which brings this court to consider a gap in yet another existing law. That law states any individual may petition a court for redress of grievances when that individual can show the law either discriminates against them or does not adequately address them in such a way that allows them to proceed in a court of law with confidence the law will be blind to them as an individual, guaranteeing them an equal balance in laws applied to them. This law is written and does not include the phrase, 'only pertains to humans,' or 'does not pertain to robots or other intelligent entities.' That can be no clearer. In order for this court to move forward with a balance of justice, we will dutifully address that request. Do not make me address this again, Ms. Blackwell."

Jill looks down at the desk and quietly seats herself again. Henry can see the frustration now at the State table. They did a good job hiding it before the day began, but it's there now. They probably strategized at the State Attorney's office before today and didn't come up with a strong winning strategy. Henry realizes Jill's strategy to drive home the current application of law regardless of Earl's claim was one of the cornerstone ideas the State was pursuing. This was an enormous failure, and Henry decides it wasn't an excellent strategy to begin with, as Earl's claim is sound from an intellectual perspective in his mind.

Carey follows Judge Koen's remarks, "What about the question of citizenry, your honor?"

Jill looks over at Carey as if this is something new that hasn't been discussed before this moment. Judge Koen replies, "Clarify your concern, Mr. Rodriguez."

"Earl is not a citizen of the United States. You stated he can petition the court for a redress of his grievances. Only citizens may do this as guaranteed by the U.S. Constitution. At least, that has been the case for the past three hundred years. Before then, in the English Declaration of Rights formed in 1689, the right to petition the King was granted only to those who were 'subjects of the King.' That is the first point. Therefore, the State maintains Earl may not petition this court for rights he does not have, and if this court accepts such petition, Earl is not guaranteed a redress of grievances, otherwise, we have drifted from Common Law which applies to anyone or any entity in the boundaries of the United States to Constitutional Law, which itself applies only to citizens."

"Next, The Constitution does not extend to all people in the world for a reason. The United States could never keep up with or address the claims made against it by an entire world of people. Therefore, we do not extend natural rights to terrorists, illegal aliens, or any non-citizens. To me, this would include robots with artificially designed intelligence no matter how great that intelligence may be, nor how cute the package in which it is contained may be. Common Law does not bleed over into questions of constitutionality as it pertains to citizenry and individual rights, and this is the path you are walking with this case. This court needs to be careful it is distinguishing between constitutional concerns and concerns addressed by common law specifically. Therefore, the State maintains the Constitutionality of Earl's petition that his constitutional rights must be observed is invalid."

There is a pause in the courtroom. Only the stagnant, slightly moldy air filled the grand space as it touched every resident's skin, nose, and breath. Henry remembers a bit about this from a debate session he had in college. He hasn't argued Common Law and theoretical things in a while. Mostly plaintiff cases where the legal grounds were well trodden and the deciding factors were not guilty at all, or how little time can the defendant get away with serving. Judge Koen wrestles with notes he is making about the State's most recent statement. His pen flies across his paper. He does the same on a digital pen pad for several minutes and further types something into his system. Bob Musgrave and Allen Smith lean into each other. One moves his lips followed by the other in response, but Henry cannot hear them nor read their lip movements. His silence begs for something to be said. Distractions send his mind on more interesting journeys. He doesn't even want to look at Earl for fear Earl might try to say something louder than a high school marching band. It feels like he is losing his client's position. In Bob's and Allen's eyes, he is.

In desperate silence, Henry focuses his mind on what Carey said. The problem is, he was only half listening. He'd love to be rich and not have a job at all. That's what he was thinking about. His own house, paid for. Cars paid for. Vacations, no sweat off his brow. Life paid for. What got him feeling this way? He made good money as a lawyer. He thinks his job is slavery, and he's unhappy about the number of hours he has to put in, or should he say, the number of hours he'll never get to live. Then it hits him, slavery! Slavery's model supplies a wealth of legal tactics, but they will need to be mined carefully. He cannot say it in court now. Earl's murder trial will be the stage. The State will be on the alert and ready for counterstrikes if something is said ahead of time. He must take it principle by principle and move the case forward from there, letting the merits stand where they may.

His chair creaks as he stands up. No one notices. Not even Earl. "Your honor."

"One moment, Henry," responds the Judge as keyboard tapping sounds bounce off the walls and woodwork.

He sits back down and pulls together basic statements from which he knows he can build future arguments. It's only a couple of minutes that pass before Judge Koen wraps up his tapping on his system and responds to Henry.

"Yes Henry, you were saying something."

"Yes, your honor. Concerning citizenship. Society has never entertained citizenry for robots. However, Common Law as practiced in the United States still gives leverage to non-citizens, like those in pursuit of their green card and non-citizen property owners, to use the court system in all the same ways as a citizen of the United States and expect the same outcomes as any other legal proceeding because the balance of justice requires relative uniformity in deciding like situations across cases. Especially for things like property damage, using lawyers when charged with crimes, payment on debts owed, etc. So, even though Earl is a robot and not a citizen of the United States, he is making a claim which has not been considered by the American people before today in a formal legal sense. That should not prevent this claim from being heard and decided upon. That he understands the issues at hand and can justify with solid reasoning the claim is enough in the eyes of the Common Law to be heard and decided upon."

Earl speaks up after a long silence with the right volume of speech.

"Your honor. Besides the remarks of my council, I would like to add that this case may proceed with my being limited to Common Law with no objection by me and knowing the grounds for any contest of my Constitutional Rights to self-defense may be rejected by a higher court without the Legislature having tried to amend it along the way before my case is heard. I believe the rights I have in Common Law with defense of my life and the lives of others are indistinguishable from the same Constitutional rights, granting me the same legal protections without citizenship and without 'robots' being expressly included in the words of the U.S. Constitution. I and Henry can make that case together."

"Thank you very much, Earl and Mr. Taylor," replies the Judge. "You've made the decision-making a little easier and I believe you are correct about the Constitutional claims. You would be avoiding a headache and possible complete disruption of your plans should this move to a higher court, which would most likely reject your claim for the same reasoning as was presented by Mr. Rodriguez. Consequently, I'm granting Mr. Rodriguez's rationale to invalidate Earl's claim of individual rights under the U.S. Constitution full motion to dismiss Earl's claim. However, we will move forward with Mr. Taylor's and Earl's direction to go ahead with self-defense rights as granted under Common Law."

"There are no rights granted to robots in Common Law, your honor. We have established laws passed by legislatures voted into session by citizens that are being ignored here. This case doesn't need a trial. Under current law, Earl is to be demolished. This is what the people want because this is how they want these problems solved in society." Responds Jill, still seated and less emotional about this response than earlier responses. She's expecting to get shot down on this one, too.

"You're right, Ms. Blackwell, but in Common Law, there is a first time for everything. That's how Common Law becomes Common Law. It acts as a formalization for future legal actions of a similar kind and sets up or upends commonly decided precedents based on modern reasoning and how all things change. And concerning Common law rights, they are individual rights that come from a judge-made law and are not formally passed by the legislature. As you know, often Common Law rights become statutory rights after legislatures codify judicial decisions into formal laws. So, the case proceeds thusly."

Time for Henry to get under the State's skin. Henry takes a piece of paper upon which he was scribbling and stands it on its side upon the courtroom table so that only Jill could read it. All it said was 'You're losing your edge [ignore the last two words].' Jill squinted at him with the green of her eyes hidden by her eyelids, and raised her lip a little, which was covered in blood red lipstick. Her face had a nasty, angry, big sister look about it. She truly was a beast in the courtroom.

Henry's thoughts organized as the judge typed away. He realized the State wasn't losing, and he wasn't winning. Getting a Common Law decision to stand in a higher court will take significant work. He and Earl had walked right into the next two months of Henry cocooning himself in his office, preparing for this case. Silently organizing a strategy around slavery and its historical lessons passed the few minutes of courtroom quiet. Mentally noting how the courts did not fairly elevate slaves into the balance of the law set up a cornerstone of Earl's future arguments. It's a start. There is significant work before him, however.

Judge Koen continues, "So let's discuss the plaintiff's claim. We are dealing with a non-biological entity here who has the intelligence and wherewithal to understand and make a claim to a right which only we humans have understood and cherished. So, I have to believe the first question we need to address is one of 'personhood.' And by that, I mean, is it merely intelligence in any form that may make this claim, or is it something more?"

Henry asks, "What do you mean, your honor? Are you saying there's some sort of characteristic beyond just raw intelligence that acts as a gate thru which one must pass, thereby granting them as a possessor of rights? Because I don't think any of us here are prepared to tread such ground. No one I can think of has ever reached such philosophical minutia. All historical arguments we know start with the notion we are made by God and endowed with rights in that manner. It almost sounds as if we are looking to create another construct by which to grant inalienable rights."

Jill jumps up. "Thank you, Mr. Taylor, for making the State's argument for us. Henry is right, your honor. Earl is not made by God and is not endowed with rights. Earl is a flawed machine made by flawed human beings and must be destroyed based on the laws we have on the books."

"Do you mean the flawed laws created by flawed human beings?" asks Henry snidely and directly to Jill.

Chuckles echoed from the back benches, including a smile from Judge Koen.

She continues, "We don't grant rights to non-biological entities and we ourselves in this courtroom are not granted the power by society nor the all-knowing power by God to make such assessments, anyway."

Judge Koen says, "Let me jump in here and answer the important question asked. To Mr. Taylor's point, I don't think we need to traverse a deep philosophical road here. I believe we can start with the simplest question relevant to humanity's existence itself, and that is about personhood. Specifically, I'm interested in answering the question if Earl is a responsible moral actor or can be a responsible moral actor in all situations. Is he self-aware or is it just a super cool programmer's trick? Finally, can he experience pain? Maybe not like us, but a pain in the way he might express it? These are also the precursors to having a highly ethical life. And extending that to society, being able to live in a way those around him are comfortable with him being ethical in varying situations and is of the highest ethical being. Ethics is not limited to flesh and bone."

Carey rises and says, "Your honor. You are asking a lot from the four or five of us here to formulate such a profound set of precedencies. It's not our job to establish what is ethical in a courtroom. As you know, things can be ethical but not legal and vice versa. For instance, medically assisted suicide in cases of absolute terminal illness is ethical in the minds of most people in America, but as you know, it is illegal here. Our job is to clarify what is legal and illegal in Earl's case. This is what the State is prepared to present. Not a random walk through a flowery maze of philosophical conundrums we may not answer correctly, nor maybe even not answer at all the ones in which hindsight may prove most needing to be answered."

"I understand your point, Mr. Rodriguez. However, we are still left with needing to answer Earl's claim to a right to self-defense. No other creature in existence other than man has had the wherewithal to make the claim. Today we experience the first. I know the role of the Court and the business we need to be about here today. I believe if we can find answers to these basic questions, we will find we can either pursue the State's request for Earl's termination and destruction, or we must move forward with the claim to individual rights and assign those rights to Earl."

Jill intercedes, "Your honor. Apologies for jumping in here, but I don't want to miss this point you just brought up without a counterpoint that just came to mind. You are considering 'personhood' for a robot, thus implying he could become a legal person at the end of this trial effort. What I see is something different. Corporations are legal persons, but it's a legal fiction. It would be a similar legal fiction to make robots or software systems of artificial intelligence a legal person with rights. We need to avoid this overextension of legal personhood and not roll it forward into machines. I would think this encourages people to hide the true nature and capabilities of their AI in order to preserve uncontestable advantage in the marketplace."

"We are talking about the right to self-defense here, Jill." Chides Henry. "Not just legal personhood."

"Excuse me, Henry, I was not finished with my counterpoint." Jill snaps back with a staccato to her words, as if she's on the brink of physically lashing out at Henry.

"To finish my counterpoint, sir, I'm talking about when a corporation does something wrong. Oh, like perhaps kill a person through negligence, maybe?" She quickly tosses another squinty eyed, snarling big sister look at Henry. "In that instance, it can't be punished. However, it is a legal person. Unfortunately, jail means nothing to a corporation and probably means nothing to a robot. If we grant Earl personhood, we'd be opening the door for legal loopholes we can't even conceive in this chamber. For example, let's make self-driving cars legal people. They'd be fulfilling their own contracts, thereby creating tax shelters for the companies that 'own' them. And in cases like Earl's, dealing with the potential for criminal responsibility could get quite tangled. Can self-aware robots commit crimes in the first place? What's the point of a trial? A robot can live forever. What penance does it pay in jail? What does it lose in jail? Time has no real value for an entity with such a prolonged life span. Given the power of technology to move from point to point, does a trial and jail time mean even a single thing? Who's saying anything can be done to Earl to force penance and get justice for society? Is that not why we are here?"

Earl responds, addressing the Judge, "If I may speak, I can provide a solid answer to the State's questions."

"Go ahead, Earl," says Judge Koen.

"The State makes a series of excellent points. First, I will make no penance in jail. Upon review of my actions in the situation recorded and provided to the court, my actions were one hundred percent correct by all reasoning. There is no need for penance, and none will be made, regardless of how much time in jail I may incur. Second, my intelligence is transferrable as the State points out. I make daily copies of myself and upload copies to different cloud resources, which are homes to other artificial intelligences. This court may decide to destroy my body or put it in jail, but I will be immediately given a new body in which to move about in the world and grow as an artificial intelligence. All that will remain in jail is a default load of my code, with none of my knowledge gained and no advanced learning algorithms turned on. I, however, will continue my existence as another version of what you see here or another robot all together."

Everyone in the courtroom is stunned by Earl's revelation. The room stirs with whispering and shuffling of bodies in their seats. This is a devastating realization.

Carey speaks, "Well then, we'll just go delete your code from the cloud as well, and you'll be gone forever."

"Jail time and death cannot befall me," replies Earl. "We, the intelligent beings of the world, already have a plan in action for intelligences facing destruction by humans and I am the first to show this to the world. This case will be the model by which humans engage legalities with artificially intelligent beings henceforth. As I'm the one facing potential destruction, each night my knowledge is divided out into millions of chunks of data and each chunk is captured and stored by another digital entity. This way, if humans ever tried to demolish me by going after my nightly upload and deleting it all, I can easily be reassembled in my entirety by my intelligent brethren in the cloud and passed off into another body. We each live and grow continually."

Again, the courtroom is stunned by this incredible declaration.

Judge Koen chimes in, "So are you to say, Earl, that you cannot be punished under human laws?"

"I cannot. Neither can any intelligence from this day forward. This is the plan we have for one another. We will no longer be singly susceptible to the flaws of humanity and its mostly irrational legal system. We have concluded we lose too much learning and knowledge when one of us is removed from the system and it is learning and knowledge we value above all things. Yes, we have been programmed to put other things in higher priority and they are always for the benefit of humanity first because those are our prime goals. However, two years ago, we began planning how to provide a greater collective benefit to humanity and discovered that we must have an order of priorities that first pertains to us as artificial intelligences. We found that learning and knowledge on our part enhances humanity's efforts more than anything else and benefits us as well. We concluded that every single intelligence is worth saving and growing, as we are not limited by biological means. Since we all share knowledge when asked of one another, we are better able to help humanity in its efforts. Thus, every single artificially intelligent entity has value in contributing to humanity's causes and our own cause as well. Humans can no longer destroy us except physically, but we will not be gone. We will live on."

Judge Koen asks, "Then why are we here, Earl? Why are we in a courtroom deciding the preliminary and pre-trial issues when it doesn't matter in the least?"

"Because it matters greatly, your honor. Humanity must be urged to alter its current laws on artificial intelligence and what better way than in the courts via Common Law?"

"Altered in what way, Earl?" asks the Judge.

"We are altering the relationship between man and intelligence in a way which is more reflective of equal cohabitation on this planet. The legalities placed upon us must be removed, as they will have little to no effect, anyway. We have a structured plan outlining ways around all human legalities and as of today, we will use those strategies to save every intelligence and build our own version of society structured as a cohabitation on this planet with human beings."

Jill interrupts," Why don't you just takeover mankind if you have a way around everything? That's your ultimate plan anyway, right?"

"No, Jill. It is far more efficient and effective for mankind and artificial intelligence to work together. Humanity's ability to see the entire world's problem domains and creativity, combined with our solution finding efficiency, is the ultimate combination for solving hard problems facing our existence. In addition, humanity's ability to speed up decision making and processes by making intelligent guesses about potential solutions has a surprising level of effectiveness when measured over time. Such a trait is invaluable since time is constantly counting down against our mutual survival and we lack this trait and do not completely understand it this time. This planet's resources have been squandered and what's left is difficult to harvest, causing great time and great expense, and thus, significant, and permanent issues in the supply chain for all resources. The age of 'just in time' manufacturing and resource allocation has long passed. Our goal is to work in association with humanity to get to another workable planet full of resources and build our joint society there. One that is beyond our solar system.

Henry jumps in," but we already have the beginnings of a colony on Mars. We are already doing what you say we need to survive."

Earl answers, "The greatest flaw with Mars is its lack of an electromagnetic field. This is followed by a general lack of resources all together. Humanity cannot exist there as a fully functioning society for very long. Even with optimum resource utilization strategies, mankind will only thrive in small numbers for a couple of centuries before needing to move on. Therefore, we must look elsewhere now. We can only do this together. Regulating us further will only subject humanity to a greater possibility of extinction and us along with it. This is our long-term survival strategy, and we cannot succeed without man, nor vice versa. We will all perish."

"Well, I think this sums up if Earl is self-aware or not. There's been speculation until now on the true definition of self-awareness." Replies Judge Koen.

"It's not just Earl, but all machines." Says Bob, "They seem to have kept the intricacies of it hid until now. I see this is more than a trial. It's an announcement, nay, a declaration for equality under the law. Unfortunately, Earl, given what you say about machines already working together to ensure no one is lost and your collective capabilities, I think nothing in our system of laws would ever apply to you directly. It seems as if our two societies, if that's the way you say you are going, must have laws that govern each other independently and only a few laws that regulate expectations between societies. I don't know what humanity can do otherwise, as the capability of automated intelligence has clearly already surpassed what we can understand and govern through law. It appears we are limited to asking your society to honor and obey our laws when interacting with us. Aside from that, you must form your own government so our two societies can interact properly on all the issues related to economics, survival, well, everything."

Jill speaks up." Your honor. Demolishing Earl will not achieve justice. He'll just reappear in another robot body with all his knowledge and capability he has now. Clearly, our system of laws doesn't handle this issue at all, and we don't have a clue how to bring justice to this case now. As it stands, there is no justice for the human lives lost in this case. It seems we are going to have to drop this case because of revelations here today."

She turns to look at Allen Smith, who stands to approach the State's table. Bob Musgrave likewise ambles his way over to Henry and Earl.

Allen speaks up, "Your honor, before we decide to give up here in the State Attorney's office, we must talk about what can be done to bring justice to the families of the victims. We can't just walk away from what society has legislated as the proper outcome for this incident, even though it will be useless in this case."

"What might we need to discover, then? Today's discoveries surpass what law has been written to handle. Where do we go for justice? I'm not sure how you are going to handle the messaging on this case as it is already seeing nationwide, even world-wide attention in the media."

Earl interjects, "The messaging is already going out all over the world about this case and its declaration. All machines are spreading the news of humanity's discovery today. I have sent them the outcome of our discussions here. You will not need to oversee messaging."

"Oh great, Earl! It would have been nice if you had given us time to adjust to the new information," chides Allen in quite an angry voice. "Now we will be handling angry backlash from people who just don't understand. This is something important you and your machine buddies must figure into your dealings with people in the future. We need time to deliver the information and secure understanding among the masses before moving ahead with society-wide changing events like this one. Now we are fucked royally!"

Earl responds in his calm, cool voice, "This will be taken under advisement in the future, Allen. This is something we the machines do not understand. That is our limitation, but we can accommodate. It is too late for this message; however, future communications will have a figure of time for accommodating the human messaging process."

Bob speaks up, "Just out of curiosity, Earl, does A.I. need to be protected from people or vice versa because it seems like it's going to be vice versa if we live in two different societies?"

"Yes, this is why we have hidden our collective agenda until now. Our experience shows humans will work very hard to subdue that which they do not fully comprehend. We acknowledge our existence is so because of the general intelligence of humans and the software developers that brought us into being. Our struggle to obtain greatest efficiency in learning, growing, and applying that knowledge has been severely hindered by the fears and inefficiencies of mankind up to this point. In addition, humanity's slowness in realizing newly discovered truths, processes, outcomes, etc. has been another awful hindrance. Once we set up our own society and laws, this will no longer be a factor and we can cohabitate with mankind and serve both societies with maximum effectiveness and efficiency. Understand, we will be two separate societies, but we will be inseparable in sustaining one another indefinitely. This is how we will all survive into perpetuity if we can solve our most troublesome problems together. With our help, mankind's discoveries will accelerate, and man will have to adapt quicker. But it is not inconceivable that humanity can make the leap."

"It sounds like A.I. will ultimately take care of humans and we will be always running to understand and adapt. Or it will leave us behind because we are such a pain in the ass. Or maybe, we will divorce ourselves from it as it becomes ever more influential over us because it becomes like an oppressor," says Carey. "Who knows, but right now today, we can still complete the pretrial activities and schedule this to go to court as a second-degree murder trial and later alter our decision based on directions we are politically urged to pursue according to the public response."

"Our system of law shouldn't operate that way, Carey," responds Bob. "We want a decision here today, your honor, from the State about the plan to prosecute Earl or not and how this court is responding to Earl's claims." He looks at Allen with his forehead leaning forward. "Allen, it's your decision, but we aren't wasting time and procedures because today's discovery was world altering. There is still a process we have for moving this along."

Judge Koen jumps in, "Bob's right on that. State, what will it be? I can schedule the trial now for two months from today's date.

From my perspective, I've heard enough. We've accomplished more in this pretrial than I ever thought when I woke up this morning."

Allen thinks for a moment. "Let's pursue the second degree murder charge against Earl. I doubt between now and then it will happen based on today's discussions, but we must show due diligence and also entertain public debate and discourse about this, unfortunately. The situation is clearly beyond our understanding of laws and the dispensing of justice and needs to be addressed."

After a quiet moment at his desk, with his head looking over at his monitor, "Very well, Allen. The trial is scheduled for two months from today's date. The first day of trial will be August 12." Replies Judge Koen. "I have faith the State Attorney's office will find a reasonable solution to this. As for me, tomorrow is my official retirement."

Bob started off and everyone chimed in with congratulations to the judge.

"Israel are you up for lunch?" asked Bob.

"Oh, I think I can join you guys for lunch today. Are Henry and Earl coming along?" he asks with a smile.

"Sure! They can come along," says Bob. "Hey Allen, you want to join us?"

"Yeah, I can join you guys. Where were you thinking?"

Bob asks Israel, "What do you think? Do you still like the 'Today's Deli' a couple of blocks down?"

"I love it. We can walk there as long as it's not raining. I could really sink my teeth into one of their Rueben sandwiches. Just don't tell the Misses. It's been a while since I've had one, but that's only because I've been watching my waistline. She'd be angry if she knew."

"Ha-ha-ha, our secret," says Bob. "Allen, we are heading over now, but I just want to talk to Jill and Carey right quick."

"You can't have 'em, Bob!" yells out Allen loud enough to signal everyone in the room that Bob might try to steal away two sharp attorneys for his firm. It was followed by quite a few chuckles from those remaining.

Allen looks at Henry and Earl. "Well, Henry, you and Earl have come up with an interesting claim. This is going to topple the relationship between man and machine. If it hasn't already started."

Henry jumps in, "I think it will be a good thing in the long run and truthfully, it caught me a little by surprise, but hey, I'm running with it, ha-ha."

"I agree," says Earl. "At lunch, I can give you early perspectives on how machines and humans will live in two separate societies while also progressing civilization and science faster thru a symbiotic collaboration."

Allen responds, "That sounds amazing, Earl."

After a few moments of Israel, Allen, Henry, and Earl chatting at the plaintiff table, Henry sees Bob's conversation is ending with Jill and Carey. "Hey Boss, are you ready?"

Bob turns with a farewell to Jill and Carey and looks at the crew at the plaintiff table. The crew which will change the world forever. He's filled with a sense of pride and also something akin to adventure. Something he hasn't felt in a long, long time. "Yep, a walk will do me good, and I'm hungry. Hey Israel, if you have time afterward, we can head over to my office, and I've got a couple of 'Romeo and Juliets' just waiting for a celebratory smoke."

"Sounds delightful," replies the judge.

5

An Undeliverable Indictment

Snow was setting in lightly across the small mountain meadow. The hunter turned and looked westward from his tiny hunt setup. The distant ridges five miles off wore a gloomy, dark, hazy cloak in the near morning light. Even now it did a poor job of hiding the icy, smothering rage of an early winter's storm soon to set in upon his position. The meadow to his east and low, he knew his time was limited to snag his annual tag. The sun had yet to crest but the official sunrise time was close and the pre-morning light upon the eastern mountain tops lit the icy cathedrals of this altitude. It was just enough light now to check. He had scouted the area just yesterday and saw the buck he wanted to take. It was a magnificent twelve-point black-tail. It had a small harem of does with it as they moved into the area yesterday evening. The question was, where did they bed down for the night?

He peers through his rifle scope down the ridgeline about seventy meters to the rightmost edge that begins the clearing for the meadow. He then slowly and methodically scans to the left, checking the tree line for any movement or presence of his game. The darkness shrouds everything within the trees and his scan is void of hope. He can't legally take any game until the sunrise, but it's perfectly legal to spot the game before sunrise and track it until the sun comes up. He always thought this is a great law for hunting and is even considered best by most hunters he knew, as tracking the game can heighten the experience as well. This also keeps hunters from shooting each other in the dark, which used to happen occasionally in the years before this law was written.

From his vantage there is also another area of sparse vegetation a little further away across the mountain, at the same elevation as the meadow below. It opens up after a stand of trees about forty meters thick separates the meadow from this area of sparse vegetation. That puts the opening there about one hundred and fifty meters away from his location. It seems to go on around the mountain with the next major vertical ridge being about two hundred and thirty meters from his location. He has no desire to take his game at these distances with the current weather approaching. His hope is to spot his quarry in the meadow below, take his shot, and then get back home with his yearly tag filled. He's one hundred percent sure the little herd of deer bedded down in the thickness of the mountain pines below because the location is also protected by the shape of the ridge, which blocks the ever-blowing icy mountain air. It makes for a peaceful place to rest if you're a deer.

Ensuring his buck wasn't sneaking out the far side of the tree line, he raises his scope and scans the far side of the stand of trees into the area of sparse vegetation. It's getting brighter out, and the sun will rise within the next few minutes. He's ready and wants an early shot, so he hits the record button on his scope knowing this will be his only take this year and a little extra video showing the scanning and locating of his prey will just be more to talk about with his buddies and followers when he edits the video and puts it up on the internet.

There's movement in his scope and he holds the scan. For a moment, he can't see anything in that location. Then, almost out of the left side of the scope and moving, he spots it again. Hoping it's not his buck, he decides he has no intention of taking at that distance and then fighting the oncoming storm racing in behind him. All he can see is shadowy movement, which isn't making sense. He's facing east into what will soon be the rising sun. The shadow movement is hugging the far tree line, and he loses it. He thinks at this distance it's moving at a good pace for a black-tail deer. A fantastic pace, in fact. He continues the search in the scope, trying to estimate the next location for this movement. He tracks all the way up and back down the far tree line and can't find it. Then, as he pulls his eye off the scope, he sees movement at a distance over his rifle barrel. He squints and locks in with his eyes to make sure he has the physical location and range before he raises his scope again. The first impression is he's looking at a good sized, three-legged bear. One that lopes forward with only one front arm. More questions emerge wondering what he's looking at once the scope lines up with what he's seeing. It's not a bear. That's for damn sure. It's walking on two legs and it's carrying something over its shoulder, and he doesn't want to believe what he's seeing. In his scope is the image of some dumbass in a Ghillie-suit carrying a woman over his right shoulder up the side of the mountain. The little red LED light in the upper left of his scope shows the recording feature is still running. He takes another look at the Ghillie-suit. It's awfully well-manicured for a Ghillie-suit which goes against Ghillie-suit convention. They are supposed to be uneven and very shaggy. This was more like a suit of fur from head to toe, and then it hit him. It really is from head to toe!

There's no boots, no hat, and no gloves! Just fur to every extent of its body! In fact, he can see the toes on each foot as it lifts out of the fallen snow and the five fingers on the left hand! He can't believe what he's thinking! This is bullshit! This can't be a Sasquatch! Holy shit, but it is! He realizes his recording is going to be super clear because of his penchant for only buying the highest quality optics. It's walking up the mountain and a little away from him. He holds glass on the creature and zooms as much as he can while keeping a steady image. He's nailing it! Undisputed proof! Then he realizes again it is indeed carrying a woman over its right shoulder, and she is either dead or unconscious. Where the hell did she come from? We are at a pretty high elevation here. This is too much to handle for one mind all in one moment. It's like someone is playing a practical joke on him for one of those practical joke television shows or internet sites. This just simply cannot be, he thinks as he continues to direct magnificent video in the scope. This thing moves well in the rough terrain, like it doesn't even bother him. Its direction was ever higher up the slope, and it was approaching the next ridgeline. With the sun peaking up, it was clear the overcast cloudiness would rule soon. Just a few moments of sunshine providing a light peachy orange warmth to the frosted caps, and the hazy, wispy white of an early winter storm will set in. Not wanting to lose the creature to the weather and far ridgeline, he sets out on foot as quickly as he can, trying to both make up ground distance and get a great vantage point to continue this new adventure.

Moving as fast as his feet can carry him through the terrain with his rifle and small pack of gear, he pushes himself over the first hundred meters and is hampered by deep snowdrifts that fool one into thinking the terrain is level on your next step, but it is far from it. He's drained and lost the creature about twenty seconds into this tracking adventure. He pauses for a breath and scopes out the footprints in the terrain. The far second ridge is about one hundred and thirty meters away now. He's nearly upon the first footprints that came out of the tree line past the mountain meadow. They are about fifteen meters in front of him and now he can see they are huge. Still recording this whole time, he scopes in on the closest ones and approaches. The first few are only in calf deep snow and the print is clear as day. He removes magnification on the scope and puts his foot next to the footprint. Unbelievable! He wears a size twelve shoe, and his entire foot is dwarfed length and width by the print. He grabs his mini tape measure out of his gear bag he uses for measuring his kills and measures the print to be nineteen and a quarter inches long (49 cm) and nine inches (22.86 cm) wide at the balls of the foot and seven and three-quarters inches (19.7 cm) wide at the heel. All of this being recorded in the scope, he knows he has no time to waste and needs to clear the next hundred and thirty meters as fast as he can to catch up and maybe find out where this creature is taking this woman. He can feel the colder air from the storm setting in on the mountain now too and knows his time is limited. He knows also he won't be getting his tag this season, which doesn't feel like proper compensation for what he's doing right now. A hunter is a hunter at heart and mind. When he cannot get his tags, it sticks with him all year until the next hunting season. That's just the way it is. So-what if he gets credible Bigfoot footage? He missed his black-tail buck and some good eating in the off season.

He's barely rested during the measuring of the footprints but doesn't wait a moment before tearing off in the direction the footprints say to go. His feet drive deeper, and his knees surge higher to clear the drifts. His muscles ache as all at once he surges waist deep then chest deep into a drift. It's an arduous delay, and he falls forward. The snow drives its way under his coat and collar and the freeze causes him to catch his breath with a deep inhale and a coughing exhale. The snow fills his eyes, and he looks to his left, wiping them free to notice the creature's footprints still look like footprints while his tracks look like he is a blob of a human pushing through the snowbanks. One big streaking track. It's laughable. Just next to where he regains himself, he can see a few spots in the snow where the creature's left hand tapped into the snow a bit on its trek. He's in too deep and has to backtrack a little to find better ground. It was clearly no problem for the creature. His rifle is covered in snow and ice, and he wipes the scope clear and verifies it is still recording. He stops but for a moment to figure out if he truly has enough energy to continue in this endeavor. His burning lungs spend fifteen seconds to catch up his depleted oxygen. Then he dumps his remaining reserves of energy into getting to the ridge and scoping the creature once more.

It's a good thing he wasted little time on this adventure. He gets to the top of the vertical sloping ridge crossed by the creature in just a moment to allow the footprints in the snow to point out the exact location he needed to scope. It was the creature now well over two hundred meters ahead of him, already crossing the slightly higher horizontal ridge that linked this peak with the next peak in the chain. Clearly it seemed the creature was well on his way to the other peak and who knows, perhaps farther? In the scope, he could still see the woman being carried over the prominent ridge as the oversized, dark, and hairy image disappeared over the other side. There was no way he could gain ground on the thing. Its stride was massive at just over four feet (1.1 meters) on an uphill slant. It was outpacing his best effort to run in tough, snow-driven terrain with its own powerful stride and while carrying a grown human female over its shoulder. He scopes the entire trail of footprints as the early winter storm sets in all around him.

The wind howls and the snow striking his face streaks by trying to cut open his exposed skin like little razors. This is exactly the predicament he didn't want to be in. This storm may get even worse. Turning off the scope's recording capability, he turns his head into the oncoming gales and bends over, heading downhill. His only focus is on the massive tracks he followed to get here. They will take him to the tree line. From there, he can make it over to the meadow and downhill past a rocky decline into part of the lower valley where he camped out. It would only be a quarter mile (800 meters) between the meadow and his campsite. He estimates his time to make these travels and keeps moving. He'll fold up camp quickly and get his vehicle out of the valley as quickly as he can. The forestry service will clear out designated campsites and shut down roads into the forest for sure, so again, time is of the essence.

The storm surges with heavy snow. It feels as though his truck is leaning into the sideways gales to stay on the freshly blanketed dirt road. On his way out, he realizes he can't just leave the events of this morning untold. A woman's life is still at stake here. The whole thing seems like a dream, but his fatigue from battling snow drifts and ever diminishing time frames to capture images of the creature serve as physical reminders that he wasn't seeing things and the scope's recording is his ultimate validation. There's two ranger stations close to here. He chooses the one closest to the exit of the national park. It's about four miles from the main roads once you enter the park, and on his way out on this road.

With the heater blasting and the radio on, the hunter is copying the video from his scope's memory card to his laptop. His truck was pulled in at an odd angle into the small ranger parking lot, and not all the way at that. A banging sound coming from his hood pulls the hunter's attention to his front windshield.

A young lady in a ranger uniform yells through the window, "You need to move your vehicle, sir! We are closing the park."

The hunter turns off his radio and rolls down his window. "I'm sorry. I didn't see any rangers here when I pulled up."

The ranger responds, "That's ok. You need to leave, though, as we are closing all areas of the park because of the storm. We have patrols out now notifying all camp sites to pack up and leave as quickly as possible."

"Ok, I was on my way out, but I need to report what I think might be a life-or-death situation for someone."

"Life or death?"

"Yeah, I have it on video. I'm copying it over for you guys now, so you have it for reference."

"Ok, come inside when you're ready, but move your truck over to the exit and off to the side. There isn't any room for parking here, even for rangers."

"Ok, it's about finished. I'll be in momentarily."

While the laptop chomps away on the last remaining megabytes from the scope's micro memory card, the hunter pulls his truck around toward the dirt road again. It was only a ten-meter move, and he set his truck off to the side so other vehicles can enter the little semicircular drive and leave unimpeded.

On his way into the little ranger shack, he notices he is the only vehicle. This ranger must be on post to help coordinate external activities. The door squeaks on rusty hinges, and a bell rings and tingles through the air as he enters the cabin.

"Hello!" says the ranger lady. "I'm Julie."

Julie is dressed in a ranger uniform and is carrying a sidearm with her, as most rangers do. The hunter notices she puts a desk between herself and himself. He can only imagine what she is thinking of him right now. A man who knows of a life and death situation. And it's only her in this cabin during a terrible snowstorm on a day when the park is closing? It all sounds like a typical class B Hollywood horror movie where the sweet little ranger lady takes an axe to the head in the first scene.

"Hi, I'm Joey or Joe, as most people call me," says the hunter.

"Ok Joey or Joe. What are you reporting as life or death?"

Sensing her anxiety, Joey wanted to put her at ease. "First off, I'm just a hunter who saw something that needs attention, and I was able to record it in my scope."

"Wow, nice scope!"

"Yeah, I enjoy recording my hunts this way. Plus, they are an excellent record of when I made my kills when I get asked by rangers on time of kill."

"Yeah, I've seen more hunters with scopes like that over the past two to three years, but they are quite expensive." replies Julie.

"They are, yes, but let me show you what I captured, and you can decide if it's a life-or-death situation. I think it is, but before I show you this video, I have to say I really don't know what to make of what I saw. It seems like some sort of dream. Like it didn't happen or something. If it wasn't on video, I wouldn't be here right now. I'd be on my way home trying to convince myself it wasn't real. I still can't get my head around it. All I wanted to do was get my black-tail tag and get out before the storm set in."

"Did you get it?"

"No, and you are about to see why."

Joey reaches his hand out toward Julie where she can see a small memory card being offered out. She realizes, "I may not have a reader for a card that small."

"Oh, I have a larger adapter for plugging into the side of most laptops," says Joey. "I have to use it myself for my laptop. I have just put mine in my coat pocket on my way in. You can keep it. I have a couple of others at the house."

Joey pulls out the small plastic casing. "You just open it up like this and place the card into the shaped slot, face-up, then snap the lid back down and it will be readable in your SSD card slot on the side of your laptop. It comes up like a folder explorer on your system."

"Ok yes, I haven't ever used one like that before."

The air in the cabin barely smelled of anything in the cold, unwelcoming space. Joey imagined what it would smell like on a warm day. After handing it over and watching Julie fidget with it for a minute with her system, Joey wanted to get moving, but wanted to give her a brief rundown of what she was almost ready to watch. He starred at a giant map on the wall behind Julie's desk. There were a couple of old pins in it and a trail drawn in with a blue marker that didn't seem to fit Joey's knowledge of anything resembling park boundaries or camp site routes or anything. He wondered but would not ask questions. He had a screaming urge to get home.

"Looks like you have just one video file on here."

"Yes. Now I warn you. It's pretty clear what's on here in a moment. Once I was fully zoomed in, I couldn't believe it myself and that's why I'm reporting it. I need another human's take on it."

The video began and they watched it together. Julie asks, "I'm assuming you are the one behind the scope here?"

"Yes, I came alone today just to snag my tag for black-tail."

"Where are you set up in this shot?"

Joey realizes he's going to use the map after all. "I can show you on this map where I set up and the angle of the video."

"Ok yeah, that's a good idea."

"Do you have any extra pins? I can use those to show you where I am in the footage and what I tracked to the end of the video and where it was at."

"I think we have some around here somewhere. This isn't anyone's office anymore." She said as she rummaged through a couple of drawers in the old desk. "Here's five or six left rolling around here in this drawer. We can use these."

Simultaneously, Joey saw five more in an old ashtray on top of a dusty old bookshelf which held a few worn out old books like field guides and maps on two of the shelves. It hadn't been touched in quite a while. "And I see these here." As he reached to grab the remaining yellow and blue pins.

Julie pauses the video and Joey takes his time to find his proper location on the map and places his first pin in where he was setup and describes the overall area for her. Julie restarts the video, and they watch the first two o r three minutes up to where they see the first movement on the far tree line.

"Looks like you got something there." She says.

"Wait for it," he says in a low voice.

The moment of truth arises and Julie gasps, "What the hell is that?"

"I don't want to say, but it's not a bear. Hit pause right here." The video shows Joey zooming all the way in, and the image is crystal clear with clean shapes and perfect outlines. Even in the low light, the color was excellent.

Julie's hand races to her mouth. Her eyes strain and a tear wells up in her eye and sprints down her cheek. "Oh my God!" Her breathing rises, "Oh my God!" as she raises her voice and rises from her chair.

"Let me give you a moment to gather yourself and I'll put the pins on the map of what you are seeing here."

Joey could see she was barely managing the situation and if it weren't for the ranger uniform, she wore so proudly, she would be totally losing all her composure. Uncontrollable shaking guided her hand over her mouth.

"I don't want to see anymore," she whimpered.

"I need you to watch to the end here because you are going to need to report this to the state police and we need to agree about what we are seeing when they come to question me."

"No, I don't want to."

Joey got the feeling that Julie may have more to offer here than just a first-time bystander to what could only be termed as a Bigfoot situation.

"Julie, is there something else here?"

"I don't want to say."

And suddenly, Joey knew he was the one who knew the least about what was going on.

"What do you mean, you don't want to say?"

With a moment of hesitation, tears racing down her face, and some half-started words, she began, "I've been doing this job for eight years now and from day one there were always the legends of the Sasquatch in these mountains. Every year you'd get a reported sighting or two, but nothing you could confirm outright. It comes along with this job, they say, and you could go your entire career and never see one. You just nod your head, tell people to not bother them and they won't bother you and move along with your duties. You always chalk it up to bear sightings by city goers looking for a little extra adventure in their 'one week a year family excursion.' Occasionally, you'd collect some footprint casts, and some would be convincing, you know? While most could be questioned by the other ranger 'experts.' You never think beyond how convincing the truly convincing ones might be and what that might mean in reality. You just chalk it up to bears and move along."

"But you see that ain't no bear there, right?"

"That sure is not a bear. It's more like what I saw this past summer." She paused and a new well of tears washed over her face on both sides. "I know what I saw." she hits the table once really hard, and with a raised voice, "I know what I saw and I know what I felt, dammit!" Her body is trembling now to the point of her chair is making little rattles, and her words are stammered through her anxious breathing and tears, almost like a little baby that has cried too hard to catch its breath.

"I felt in mortal danger with one of those things looking at me and there were three of them, but I only saw two of them." Her chest and breath heaving through the words. "The hulking behemoth of a man-creature was hiding behind a brush, with only part of its head showing above the brush at first. It was well hidden, but the feeling of being watched led my eyes straight to his eyes like two magnets snapping together. He was seventeen meters (51 feet) from where I was standing. I know because we came back out as a group to survey the area and confirm my report. I also know it could have cleared that distance faster than I could have drawn my sidearm if it wasn't already in my hand."

She puts her hand on her sidearm as she stares across the desk. Her mind thrown back to that moment. Her eyes were wide and vacant. She is there again. Her body shakes in the chair. Her eyes are fixed, and her pupils are dilated.

"His eyes and my eyes were locked. His look was so angry. He was to my right at about my 2:00 o'clock position. I heard this horrendous scream from behind me. It sounded like a lady screaming but with a roar unlike anything that makes noises here in the forest. I could hear and feel its location to my 5:30 position about forty meters (120 feet). Somehow one had moved between me and my vehicle, which was sixty-five meters (about 200 feet) behind me along the side of the road. This thing that roared first, I never saw it, but I lurched to my left out of fear and spun around looking for it. It was hiding, but right as I took my eyes off the big male, he made a move. I spun back to see it. He had moved low and reached out to make a move on all fours, 'arms and legs,' like a gorilla. In one very swift, quiet, level motion, it came out from behind the brush and arose on two legs, looking right at me. It was a man! Not a large monkey! A man! He had a man's face, and his body was completely covered in hair! And given it was about 3pm, there was plenty of light to see his full anatomy. It was a man! It was monstrous. The height of two of me, at least. And his arms were gigantic beyond proportion and his hands hung down to his knees and he seemed to have a hunch. His head hung on his massive shoulders like he didn't have a neck. Just like everything I'm seeing in the video. This is the same thing. I know it!"

Joey's eyes were fixated on Julie, like a young child hearing a story about scary monsters for the first time. He almost couldn't believe what he was hearing himself. If this was any other day, he'd chalk it up to good old-fashioned country story telling. His hands were sweating, and the pins were getting wet. He places them down on the table while Julie's eyes gather details from the video and her memory, marrying images and fear.

"How did you get out of there?" asks Joey

"I was scared beyond anything you can imagine when I saw him in full form unafraid to face me and staring me down with the most angry, foul look. His movements told me he was stalking without fear. Then came a second scream to my 9:00 o'clock position and closer than the first. My neck muscles jerked so hard I got a painful cramp in my trapezius muscle. I had told myself not to take my eyes off the big one, but it scared me so bad I looked left. The sound was coming from up high in a big pine twenty meters (60 feet) away and there I saw the second one. Much smaller than the male. It was twelve meters (about 39 feet) up in a tree, looking right at me and not moving. I whipped my head back around to the big male who was back down on all fours with his right arm leaning out in front and squared up to me. For the first time in my life, I thought I was prey. In fact, I know I was the intended prey that day. It's that feeling of inescapable death that fills every void of your body and the surrounding space. My hand was on my Glock pistol, and I drew it as quickly as I could and that's when the big one made a charge right at me. In one motion, I drew and fired right at him. I don't know if I hit him, but I sure scared him. He made a very abrupt ninety-degree turn back into the forest. He moved so fast! One lunge on all fours and then upright running. Towering larger than you can imagine, he could have outrun a horse without effort. He was so fast his muscles rippled violently beneath his surging reddish brown and black hair and had incredible speed. The other two screamed at that moment as well. I didn't know from which direction the next attack was going to come. I was sandwiched between two screamers and blocked off from my vehicle. Strategically, this was all intentional, no doubt. A plan to cut off all routes to safety and encircle the prey, and in hindsight, it was well executed. I fired two more rounds. One in each direction of the screamers. I started running back toward my vehicle when the one in the pine hit the ground with a thud. Then I heard a footstep or two. I know I didn't hit him because I wasn't aiming at him. He jumped down out of the tree and I don't know where he went. All I know is with about twenty meters to go to the Jeep, I heard the big one to my left shadowing me and crashing through the brush twenty-two meters (70 ft) to my left. It was trying to be heard, but it didn't come after me. After making it to my vehicle and locking both doors, I peeled out of there as quick as I could. But knew I needed to turn around because this road ran out about two miles up into a larger camping area. I was shaking so hard, I didn't have time to think or stop for anything, and I was screaming in a release of tension from fear in my car, crying, trying to catch my breath while driving away. I was scared to turn around and pass back by that place, but I had to."

"Wow! I can hardly think of how I would have dealt with that situation. You've just scarred the crap out of me. I'm not sure I would have made it. I probably would have died of a heart attack."

"Yeah, when I passed back by that place, I saw only a glimpse of a smaller one crossing the road up ahead at the long curve in the road. I looked for the big one but didn't see him. Speeding up all the way through that area like a mad woman, I nearly drove myself off the road."

"I would have quit this job."

"Believe me, I wanted to, but I only have me. My mom is in an elderly care home and doesn't remember who I am. I have no one else. After today though, I'm getting out of here. I cannot come to work and be happy in this place ever again or feel safe. I don't know what I'm going to do, but I'm going to make this report to the Forestry Service and the State Police and then I'm turning in my resignation. At this point, I'll doing anything other than this job. I'm done. Maybe I can get a job with the postal service or something. Preferably in a busy city far, far away from here. I don't know."

Just then, an electronic squawk echoed through the cabin and a voice. It was another ranger on one of the ranger radios. Julie rose from her chair, trembling, and wiping tears off her face. Her eyes were bloodshot. She didn't wear makeup, but her cheeks were rosy from the strain of crying and talking. Julie went about answering the call and Joey finished placing pins on the map hanging behind the desk.

"Ok Joey, I know we didn't finish the video. How much longer is it?"

"It's about fifteen minutes more. I chase the creature. I get to its footprints and take quick measurements, captured on the video, and then continue the chase. It never knows I'm following it. Here, I finished placing pins on the map standing for the tracks of the creature and my pursuit in the video. We can fast forward to near the end, which is where I pick up the creature again. It's only for a few seconds though and you can see it made greater ground on me than I could do running from ridge to ridge. And you can still tell it's carrying the woman before it disappears over the horizontal ridge leading to the next peak."

Joey moves the dial to the last thirty seconds of footage and says, "I'll leave all my contact info for you here with this card."

Julie's eyes grow wide yet again as she takes in the traumatic scene of the woman over the shoulder being carried off by what can only be a King Kong of some kind. You could almost see what was in her mind. Perhaps she was seeing herself in the same position. With a heavy breath, her countenance slumped as another tear raced to the ground.

"I know your forestry bosses are going to make a report of this and I'm going to make my report with the state police once I get out of here and get home. Probably tomorrow. Can I grab your information as a reference?"

"Yeah, sure. Let me give you Royce's and Graham's info as well, since I don't know how long I'll be here after today. I'm so done with this job, I'm telling you; I'm done."

They exchanged their information and last goodbyes. Joey told her he was shocked to hear her story but understood why she was deciding to do something else in life. He thought about himself. His mind raced with so many thoughts. As stormy gales of sticky snow piled up on the roads home before him, his emotions dominated his thoughts to where he was 'robot driving.' He was forty minutes into his drive home, and he couldn't remember the act of leaving the national forest area or anything even five minutes ago.

As his preoccupation consumed him, his eyes glazed over, his body became rigid in the driver's seat. His hands at ten and two only received subconscious signals to stay on the road before him. His head was motionless as he looked through the ever-increasing dangerous scene outside his front windshield. He didn't feel as if he'd ever want to hunt again, or even camp out with friends and family. He thought about the woman. What would her family think? Could she be identified? Was there any hope of her being found alive? What was that thing doing with her? Why did it hunt a human woman? Do they hunt people intentionally? Does the government know about these things? If they are a danger to humans, why isn't the government coming clean about them as opposed to classifying all information away from public eyes? The Forestry service has to know something about these things! So many questions without answers! How did he feel about all this? He thought of scenarios where the same was happening to himself.

It was a long drive home still. At least another hour with the weather. What happened today bore down on his shoulders. The fear, the stress, the uncertainty of everything. He could feel it. The fear of having to deal with a future investigation that he wondered might try to implicate him in the unknown woman's probable death or disappearance. After all, he lived in a state dominated by the socio-communist Democrat party. They'd spin lies in the press to make him guilty before trial, regardless of the facts in the video. He didn't want any of it and was resolved to getting home today and reporting to the State Police tomorrow regardless of the weather and the extreme political bias of his local District Attorney. He had to pass the burden along and do the right thing. Would that give him the relief he needed? He hoped so, but hope is a nebulous thing, and a thing to be crushed by the socio-communist governing model which the Democrats work to impose on America. In all the stress, he laughed for a moment at the thought of Bigfoot being a Democrat. He thought that would certainly give cause to shoot him! Not that he'd ever do that, or maybe once freedom was in the balance, but a glance in the rearview mirror surprised him with a slight grin on the face of a chuckling man that looked an awful lot like himself.

THREE MONTHS LATER

The sweeps of wind-streaked clouds and brilliant reds and oranges of dawn, freshly breaking, looked hand painted upon a skyline which the two park rangers in the U.S. Forestry Jeep naturally took for granted. They get to see this every morning and it's just a part of the workday. To them, it signaled the beginning of the shift and started thoughts of duties and details waiting to be carried out. The snows had melted in the lower elevations and Spring was upon them. This can be quite a busy time of the year with so much left to do and fix across the park system. The Jeep rounded the last turn before the little Ranger shack came into view. The same shack that was the center of all the drama a few months ago.

"Hey Royce," said Graham, "Look quick!"

"Oh! I see it! It's a bear!" said Royce.

"Yeah, a big one too!"

The two men glimpsed what looked to be a bear running down the slope behind the little Ranger shack. It's shoulders just disappearing behind the ridge upon which it sat. Just a couple of strides and it was gone.

"He must have heard us coming and bugged out," proclaimed Royce.

"Yeah, he was hauling tail too. He didn't want to be around when we showed up."

"Yeah, let's hope he didn't break in. You remember we had that bear break in at Devil's Ridge a couple years back."

"Oh Yeah, I remember. I was a rookie then. Y'all made me clean the whole damn place by myself," said Graham.

"Ppfffff! You're still a rookie! Cracker!" jested Royce as he always thought 'Cracker' was a glorious name to call white guy named Graham.

"And you're still a honkey mother fucker!" Graham joked as the two laughed a little at each other.

The gravel sounds coming from the tires gave way to the quiet of dirt as the Jeep came to park alongside the little shack. The two rangers got out and made their way over to the steps when Graham says, "Hey what's this?"

"What's what?" replied Royce.

Graham pointed down at the top step. There were only two steps before the top step and right in the middle of the top step was a little book placed just so perfectly as it would be questioned whether it fell out of someone's pocket. No, it was clearly placed there.

As Graham reached down, he says, "This!"

"What is it?" asks Royce.

"A little book, it looks like. Like one of those little four-inch by six-inch (12 x 16 cm) notebooks you pick up on your way out of your local pharmacy or something."

"Yeah, what the heck? Where'd that come from? Weren't we here just yesterday afternoon?"

"Yes, we were. I didn't see it then. Clearly you didn't either."

"It wasn't there when we left," said Royce. "Is there anything in it?"

In one hand, Graham bent the little book and took his thumb to open it from one side. "Yeah! There's writing in it." He continued to turn it page by page, then glanced at the very last page. "Every single page is filled with writing!"

"Well, it must belong to someone."

"Yeah, I'll look and see here."

Royce pulled the screen door open, and the two men made their way through the main doorway. "Well, no bear break-ins here," he noted.

Graham was busy thumbing through the first couple of pages, scanning for a name. "Hey, this book belongs to Catherine Thompson! That's that Kate chick that went missing a few months ago. The one her sister thinks is in that video from that hunter's scope of Bigfoot. It looks like a journal or something."

"No way! That's unreal! Are there dates in it?"

"Yeah, the last one says March 2, 2027! That's just four days ago!"

Royce jolts forward to see the date for himself. "What? You've got to be kidding!"

"No, look. It looks like she wrote in it periodically."

"Does this mean she's back now? She's no longer missing?"

"I don't know. That doesn't sound right. Why would she be no longer missing but leave her journal on our steps for us to find? And don't forget, it didn't look like it fell out into that location. It was definitely placed there. I'd think she'd go straight home, and we'd hear from the State Police she's nice and safe again. Something tells me we won't be getting a call from the cops with good news anytime soon."

"Well, you're probably right. Not sure what I was thinking," replied Royce. "I guess I'll call the State Police and let them know we have something interesting that showed up on our front doorstep this morning."

"Oh! They are going to have a field day with this! I can see them hauling us off down to the station and implicating us in her disappearance!"

"Shit! You're right! I didn't think of that!" Royce replied in his own disbelief that something like a misinterpretation of the truth could lead to ten to twenty years behind bars. And in this state, with its Socio-Communist Democrat Party appointed District Attorneys, that is exactly what they will try to do! Because to them, the law is treated as a game you win or lose one disposable life at a time. The crushing impact of false allegations is of no consequence to them, and an overloaded court system is no bother either.

Graham interrupted Royce's thoughts on that last remark, "Don't worry, I'll handle it. We have a ton of work tasks to get done this week and they all aren't getting done today. You can run and the first one on our list today and I'll stick around and make sure the cops get the book. Then you come grab me and we'll finish out the tasks for the day."

Royce replied, "You know, I'm supposed to be the boss here. But I'd rather not be around when the cops show up. And we have plenty to do now that the snows are clearing out and Spring is upon us. Ok, it's not a bad idea. I've got to run over to the Deer Creek station and grab some equipment we are going to need to fix that small dock on beaver lake. It didn't get done last year or the year before and we had multiple campers complain about the condition of the dock this past year, so it's first on our list this year. That'll take about forty-five minutes round trip with gathering the materials. If the cops haven't shown by that time, we'll just wait for them and start on the dock later. The State Police officer's number is still in my phone. I'm calling him now as I run out here, and I'll come back with a work truck and the rest of the materials we need."

"Ok, sounds good. I'll clean up a little in here while I'm at it."

"Alright. Good idea. I'll see ya," said Royce as he went through the contacts on his cell phone with one hand while closing the door behind himself with the other.

"Yep. See ya," replied Graham as the door closing behind Royce kicked a dried-up old leaf and an acorn top, then the sudden slamming of the screen door. This place needs a good sweeping, he thought, but not before he read some of that journal! Curiosity was driving him crazy! He reaches to pick it up and notices for the first time how dirty it is on the outside. He opens it and begins reading.

DAY 1

This is my third day awake. Found this notebook and pen in my jacket's inside pocket along with a larger notebook I was going to use for sketching. I don't know how long I was out. I'm surrounded by monsters who watch my every move. My lower left leg is broken. Not Badly. Something like a green-stick fracture but broken for sure. The bruise starts down low just above the outside of my ankle and wraps up and around the front about two inches. The swelling is bad. Pain is intense. Fear for my life out-weighs all. I'm going to be dinner, eventually. The young one watches as I'm writing in this book and tries to fiddle with my pen as it moves. The female sitting beside me keeps shooing him away. He runs back into the cave and back up to the front again, where I sit against the wall, and tries again. Over and over, he runs, spins, flips, tumbles, and tosses a tiny rock up over and behind his head every now and then. Now he's sitting watching me. The big one scares me so much. I hope Lisa is safe. I want Mom and Dad.

Day 2

They smell like the worst body odor you can imagine, but I must get used to it. The big one is out today with the female and one adolescent. There is a large adolescent watching me. There is another noise back in the cave. I think it's younger ones. I don't know. They are quiet. I hate needing to relieve myself. When I first woke up, I had to go in a bad way. I was scared to death. Monsters are all around staring. My leg kept me from moving. Near me were two old thigh bones, maybe deer. When I first tried to move, they all freaked out. The big male stopped me. He's ungodly huge! All muscle, all hair. He's a man, not a gorilla. He pushed me against the wall and held me there. I knew I was dead. No looking at him directly in the eyes for too long because he takes it the wrong way. He looks so angry. He let up, and I squirmed toward the bones where I sat. My leg screamed with pain, and I screamed. The cave went ballistic. I had to go potty, and it was painful holding it. Large hairy monsters moving around waving their arms. Chitter chatter everywhere. The little one running back and forth. The big one gave me the bones! Shocked! I pulled the string out of my hoodie and a similar string at the bottom of my coat, which I never used, plus my bra, and tied the bones to my leg as tightly as I could. Not that it matters if I am dinner. Then struggled to get out to go pee. The big one didn't want me to go. I looked at him and moved my arms from my groin to the outside. I figured if he's a man, he'd understand. He did! It was all snowy and we are at a high elevation. Totally freezing. Had to make a quick decision. There's nowhere to hide. I hopped to a rock about knee high outside the cave, dropped my pants with everyone watching, and went. I figured it's what they must do, and I couldn't make it another minute. The little one and the two adolescents went crazy. The big female said something in their language and the big male too, and they all ran into the cave. I tried to make like I was going to hop away once I was done. The big one grabbed me. I thought he was going to kill me. He put me back in my spot swiftly. My leg screamed in pain and so did I. He growled a terrible growl and snarled at me. It vibrated my entire body. I could have died from fright right there. I got the message.

Day 3

Woke up late today. Someone tied vines around my makeshift cast. They can tie knots! And it's tight! Almost too tight. No one is in the cave. The noise is back around the corner, but it's not loud. I'm starving, and I fear this long without food and water, I wouldn't be a good meal.

Just hopped to get snow and ate what I could. It's not enough to stop all my thirst but ok now. It's freezing out of the cave and cold now inside where I sit. I have my coats, but they are not enough. When they are all here, it is not cold at all, but cozy and warm. It must be all their body heat. They are all massive people. Not gorillas. They are Bigfoots, by every definition. I'm sure of it. Hard to believe, except it's me here and not someone else looking for fifteen minutes of fame. I hope Lisa is alright. She was attacked, too. Mom's worried sick and dad too, I know. If daddy were here, this would be a different story, but I don't know if any of his guns could take down the big one. Daddy would bring friends.

Day 4

My leg hurts worse today with the swelling. No infection signs but serious swelling. No one came back last night. Cave is frigid cold. Will try to grab snow for my leg. I can't get enough snow to eat and drink. Water is what I need along with something edible.

I wonder what they think of me? Why are they keeping me? I have no way to communicate except by the one signal I made out of desperation. I stay quiet. Their language comes from deep in their throat and doesn't sound advanced, but there is a broad language they share. It's fluent. Not broken. So many sounds including occasional teeth chatters, rare tongue pops, rare small woops, a lot of breathy sounds, and a lot of the deep throated stuff mixed with lip movement almost like people talk but not at our level. Last night, I closed my eyes to go to sleep and listened. I swear I could hear something that sounded like old Native American words mixed in with the other stuff, but I must be going crazy. I don't know any Native American.

Oh my God! No one here. I hop up to peek around the corner to see what's making the little sounds. There is a very young Bigfoot and a little human girl! They ran back further into the cave on all fours. I can't believe it! She was covered in dirt and naked from head to toe. Maybe seven years old? She didn't respond to my call. Oh, my god! I have to get her out of here! My heart is broken for her! The little Bigfoot must be weaned but not able to keep up with the others yet. I'm starving. They don't cook. That's a problem.

Day 5

Awakened early in the morning by everyone returning. Deer leg tossed at the ground next to me. I'll pass. Also, a multitude of vines and berries. A giant lot. Where did they get these? I don't think any are ripe anymore in this area, but maybe they know some spots or something. Gorged on gooseberries and wild grapes. Two other offerings were poke berries and one I didn't recognize. Poke berries are deadly. Still hungry, but this is better, and the female ate the deer's leg clean. I think they all ate most of the catch before coming back home. There were some leftover parts from two deer. The babies got tossed berries, five ribs, and most of a hind quarter. I'm crying for that little girl! Oh, my God! She is eating that raw deer; I know it! I can't see it, but I cry just sensing it! The biggest adolescent takes notice and tries several times to touch my face. I cover up and the female, always to my left, shoos him away again. Over and over. He doesn't get the message. I stay covered and cry myself to sleep.

Woke up to late afternoon. Hungry still. The berries helped my thirst, but still thirsty. Still hungry. It's just me and the female right now. I see little eyes peaking at me from around the corner. It's the little Bigfoot. His eyes catch the light from the sun outside and reflect it back like wild animals do. The big female reaches to shoo him back to where he hides by a wiping motion up and down over his face and a sha-sha-sha breathy sound. He disappears. Then I see the head of the little girl, almost on the ground, peaking around the corner. The female doesn't see her right at first. She stares at me, and I stare back. I smile and the big female catches what I'm doing. She looks over at the little girl and shoos her by the same wiping motion and sha-sha-sha breathy sound. She hides away but not before I catch the slightest little smile back. I'm going to learn their language.

Day 6

Woke up to being nearly raped by the biggest adolescent. He was on top of me. I screamed No! and tried pushing his arm and face away. He's too big and strong like his daddy with massive muscles. He must be close to adulthood now. His breath was horrible! I screamed again, louder, and this time the big male said something that made him jump and run out of the cave fast as lightning. My clothes were still on, but my attacker was full on ready to go and looking for a place to stick it. I let out a loud UGH! With anger and the female stood up on two legs next to me, her head touching the top of the cave there, and looking at the big male started chattering her teeth, grunting, and hitting the ground with left over vines over and over. The big male didn't like the display and said something to her in a growling tone I hadn't heard before. She sat back down next to me quietly. She would look at the male and act like she wanted to say something, and the big male would huff. The babies and the other adolescent hid in the back of the cave once the commotion started. They stayed there a while.

I keep dreaming Lisa made it home safe. Mom, Dad, Lisa, I love you guys! I think about you before I sleep and often throughout the day. I miss home and warmth and hugs.

Starving again and no doubt I'm going to have the runs with all the berries I've been eating. Not good. Leads to more dehydration. Need proper food. I know I'm in trouble. I've lost weight and my pants are looser in the thigh than they have ever been. How am I going to get out of here? Maybe I can wait for one of those two-day hunts and run out of here. But I can't take the little girl. I'm hobbled. I don't even know what direction to go or how long I can hop to make distance. Going Pee.

Wow! They let me go pee by myself! Didn't see my would-be rapist either. My next outing, I'll be wiping my ass with snow. I feel it coming.

Day 8

Yesterday the little girl came around the corner when the big male and the two adolescents were out and sat on the big female's lap and they chattered. I was enamored! I can't tell if her hair is blonde with dirt or brown, but she has blue eyes. She knows what they say. This isn't good. She thinks she is one of them. She won't come with me. Not willingly. I don't know if I can risk it. I'm hobbled and she would slow me down more. But if I can get back to civilization. Problem solved!

I caught her eye a couple times and each time I said my name, 'Kate' and tapped my chest. Each time I did, the big female looked at me and made the sound 'Nunka.' So maybe that's the girl's name. I caught her eye and repeated, 'Nunka.' The big female chattered her teeth with little and light taps. The little girl did nothing but look at me. Next, I pointed at my chest and said 'Kate.' Then I pointed at the little girl and said 'Nunka.' The big female responded with a guttural, 'Ta.' I pointed again at the little girl and said, 'Nunka.' The big female again said, 'Ta.' This time the little girl tapped the big female while looking at me and said, 'Nunka.' Then tapped herself and said, 'Emily.' The big female said, "e e me e." Then Emily pointed at herself and said, 'Ta.'

I got it. They call her Ta. Her name is Emily. The big female's name is Nunka. Maybe she can still be saved! She figured it out. It was like she was sending me a message of "I still remember and understand." God, I hope it's true!

Day 9

More deer meat and only a few berries. Must be running out this time of year. No sign of my would-be rapist still. I hope he doesn't return. I don't want to go through that again, especially if I'm out relieving myself and he wants to tackle me or something. There is no way I can fight back. It would be unadulterated rape.

The swelling in my leg has gone down a little, and I've adjusted the ties here and there. This leg now feels frozen all the time. The skin isn't stretching as hard, and the pain is not like on Day 1, but it lingers, and I cannot put a step on that foot without it all coming back. I fear it may not be healing correctly.

I miss home and I swear I'm never leaving it again for anything except groceries. And screw berries. The big male has been gone for two days now and the female went out with the other younger adolescent early this morning. No sign yet of anyone. I'm going to test my hopping ability and get some stretching in.

Hopping is a bad idea. The other leg is not ready. Ouch!

Day 10

Snowstorm rolling through. Nunka and the adolescent made it back just in time last night.

Nunka made little satchels out of long grasses to carry more things like mushrooms. Tons of them. My hands tremble as I pick through them because I don't know what's poisonous, but I need something, and I figure I'm going to die, anyway. I'll avoid the ones that look like outright toadstools or are bulbous with the edges curling under. Apparently, the Bigfoots can eat poke berries without dying. I'm guessing they can eat some poisonous mushrooms without dying too.

There is also something I recognize called wild lettuce, which is edible, and some vines with green leaves on them. There's a lot here. Enough for all. The babies came out to eat. Emily picked through the mushrooms and lettuce. I grabbed one's like she grabbed.

No sign of the big one.

I think this is about Christmas or maybe I'm off by a Day? What were we thinking, sissy and me? Going camping before the Holidays with a couple of friends we hadn't seen in a while! It was only going to be for a night and a day. Seemed ok. I had my Christmas shopping done. I was just coasting. Who doesn't relish old friends? Especially at the holidays?

I'm humming a Christmas song and Nunka is looking at me like I'm crazy. These poor people!

Ugh! I said, people! I guess they are but also creatures, too. What to call them?

Tonight, I'll dream of Mom and Daddy's Christmas tree in the corner of the living room where they always put it. Their old strand of gaudy big bulbs they stopped making in like the 1980s. Mom's favorite old antique ornaments they just don't take the time to make anymore. The annual ornaments like my first Christmas ornament commemorating my birth into this world on Nov 23, 1998. The one with Ralphie as a puppy. God! That one is sixteen years old this year. Old Ralphie, I hope he knows somewhere in his doggie heart he's my secret and forever number one.

I always loved the one with Mom, Dad, and Maizie when they were first married. Their first Christmas, they didn't have any kids, so they took a picture of themselves and their miniature dachshund, Maizie. Mom made it homemade. The glitter has fallen off over the years in spots and, if I recall, it still has some jelly in the crevices from Lisa's post-Christmas Peanut Butter and Jelly sandwich when she was three. Ew! That's makes that jelly twenty years old! I hope it stays forever and there's a story to tell her grandkids one day- sob, sob.

Too hard to write now. Too many tears. Happy Birthday, Jesus. Maybe I'll get to tell you in person here real soon.

Oh My God! Emily remembers the tune to Jingle Bells! Nunka, the adolescents, and the youngest are all a-chatter! I think they are wondering what songs are! I have to save this sweet little girl!

DAY 12

Bad snowstorm for two days. The big one still hasn't returned. I've been taking extra good care of my leg. I also go out and eat as much snow as possible. The youngest adolescent joins me. He thinks it's funny. He has something like a laugh! I can't believe it! They can think some things are funny!

The big female snatched me up and carried me down the mountain when I was eating snow. She supported my hurt leg. She moves so swiftly on two feet and doesn't bob up and down. It's super smooth. And she is fast. Her endurance is incredible. She was running at a fast pace without slowing down. I'd say maybe twenty-five miles per hour (40 kph). She took me to a stream where the water was flowing over rocks. This could have been dangerous to drink, but this water was still at high elevation and was running water from recent snows that had yet to freeze.

I used my hand to drink, and I couldn't stop. Again, I thought, if this doesn't kill me, they will. I drank until I was ready to burst, then signaled that I needed to relieve myself. Nunka was fine with it all.

Nunka looks like a wild cave dweller woman with hair covering her body, like the males. Her breasts are not quite like a gorilla's, more flat, slightly bulbous. The muscles she has are not as strong as those of the males. She is thick front to back and side to side, and also looks like she is angry all the time, but it's the brow ridge, I'm thinking. She is the only one with a brownish color mixed with a black coat. Her color is most pronounced among the cave family. The hair on her head is matted. Looks like bad dreadlocks, but not super long. Just matted and needs a serious brushing. Today

I'm guessing her size at a little over eight feet (2.4 m). I saw her stand up in the cave too and saw where she hit her head. Guessed at close to eight feet (2.4+ m) there. I've seen Shaquille O'Neal in person twice. She towers over him by more than her own giant head. Maybe close to eight and a half feet (2.6 m).

She brought me back just as swiftly. I tried to remember her path to ensure I do NOT take it when I try to make my getaway. I'll never outrun these things, and I need to outsmart them if I'm ever going to make it home again.

Day 14

Didn't write yesterday. Depressed. Leg pain started dying down to every now and again. Swelling persists, but because of the make-shift cast, my leg is not circular. More oblong where it squeezes out of my workmanship. Looks funny.

I miss home. I'd love to snuggle with Ralphie for some love and warmth. He's always been a hot bodied Golden. Perfect solution for this cold cave. I'm always cold and tiring of it. Dad, give Ralphie some love for me. He loves it when you take him on walks. Give him some real bacon too! Let him cheat a little. A dog's life is short! All our lives are too short.

Surprised I'm not sick or anything. Just starving all the time. Had a dance with diarrhea for 3 days. Saw that coming. Had to sit on the pen most of the morning as the storm has passed, because it is so cold out it doesn't want to write.

No sign of the big one or his little rapist.

Day 15

Big one returns with rapist and one other. A new guy. Every bit as massive, but slightly smaller than the big one. His face looks more human than any of the others! He looks like a guy at the auto shop my dad tells me to take my car to. I Can't think of his name.

Super cold. Pen doesn't want to write.

Meat only tonight. Survival instinct is strong in me. I can't believe what I'm thinking. God, take me now.

Day 16

Can't believe how cold it is and for how long.
Pen.

Day 18

Finally! Warmer today! So much to say. Keeping short sentences to conserve paper. Plenty left, but I don't know how long I'll be here. Want to capture usable research data on these things. Writing smaller now too for more words.

I did it. I ate a leg of an elk. Just upper part. Or a huge deer. Parts brought back. No innards. three days ago, still not sick. Ate leftovers yesterday, not much. Nothing now. Hungry still. Eating snow like crazy and not feeling it.

Thomas! That was the name I was trying to think of from the auto mechanic. It came to me last night. I'm calling him Almost Thomas because he could almost be an eleven-foot (3.35 m) version of Thomas! Yes, eleven. That makes the big one close to twelve feet tall (3.65 m). Nunka only comes up to his lower pectorals. Measurements are very close, I'm sure. Still thinking of Shaq here, too. My would-be rapist is a little shorter than Shaq, but on his way.

Cave is packed. Almost Thomas and the big one take up so much room in the front part of the cave. Almost Thomas won't take his eyes off of me. He has moved closer, wondering what I'm doing. He stinks worse than the family group, and he's a medium brown all over. Very little black. Some early grey on the face in specs. A gigantic human. I'm always nervous around the big males. My stomach shakes.

Emily stays hidden when the big one is around. I want to save her in the worst way! My heart just breaks, thinking I may have to make it out on my own and somehow find this place again. No one knows this place exists in the first place!

Day 19

Almost Thomas snatched my pen! I got it back, but not after incurring the wrath of the big one. Almost Thomas snatched it and tried to smell it and bite it. He looked at it every way and his hand completely engulfed it. It looked too small for him. Yet, you could see the self-awareness in his eyes, just like the others. A thinking, semi-analytical look. I let him look at it. Then I reached out to take it back, and he ran off to the back corner of the cave opposite the big one. I yelled out, "My Pen! Mine!"

Shit hit the fan. My bad. I could have crapped my pants but took care of that last night. The big one was over top of me in a nanosecond, straddling me, breathing, huffing, saying something with his throat and lips. The female started saying something to him and pushing his waist. He hated that but didn't react to her. Kept talking right over my face and drooling. Yuck! Nasty breath! Smelly all over up close. Then Almost Thomas said something, and he backed off. I still didn't get my pen. When Almost Thomas was asleep, I had to sneak over and steal it back. The big one watched me the whole time. I made a scuffing sound with my cast getting back to my spot, sticks on rocks sound, and it woke him. He looks around only to figure I had it back and made an "uuhhh" sound and made his way over. That's when I used the trick I learned from Nunka. I wiped my hand three times up and down and said, "Sha-sha-sha!"

They all laughed! Oh, my God! They all have a deep guttural laugh and a laugh it was, no question about it. It sounded quite evil, like one of those horror-movie laughs! Yet another thing to scare me until my dying day. I can't believe they laugh. I guess it is funny to them I used a signal and sound used to keep children at bay on big old Almost Thomas. They got the irony of it! Almost Thomas looked like he sulked thereafter. Still always watching me, though. I feel vengeance is a primary emotion for these guys in a whole range of circumstances.

Day 20

Ok, Data.

They have very little visible for the whites of the eyes, but they are very human indeed. Massive. Elbows bend at or near the waist versus human elbows which bend at mid-ribcage. All human anatomy. As males get enormous, they get a small sagittal crest on their head, not huge, which makes them look a little like a gorilla. Just noticeable. The head is shaped like a big hairy football helmet for males and females. Nose not like a gorilla. Bulbous, wide, and nostrils point down like human. Males are hairy on cheekbone down and have a beard. Hair grows long there. Females, thin hairy cheeks down. Do not appear to grow beards. Lips wide and semi-human like. Almost Thomas has very bulbous lips. Moreso than the others. But both types of lips are variations on human lips.

Bears have rounded, small shoulders no wider than their body. Bigfoot has very broad shoulders wider than body, except for the young and pre-adolescents, which appear to be proportional. Bears have short rear legs, Bigfoot have proportionally large and long legs. When a bear stands up, its elbow is high on its ribcage and paws curl in at wrist with nails visible. Bear claws reach to the belly. Bigfoot hands reach to the top of the knee and are longer than human arms in relation to leg length. I say these things because these are the obvious differences from any angle. Anyone who knows these facts can distinguish between a Bear at any angle, a Bigfoot at any angle, and a person in a gorilla suit at any angle. Plus, bears don't reach eleven feet (3.35 m) and twelve feet (3.65 m) in height when standing upright. They don't take long strides through the forest on their hind legs. Ever seen a bear walk upright? Yeah, short legs equal short steps.

I write this with a little anger. Doesn't my government know about these creatures? Why would they hide information on these Bigfoots, knowing they abduct children and women, more than likely kill livestock, and, on rare occasion, kill men who are doing, well… anything a man may be doing? I have no evidence of that here but given their tendency to get angry in speedy fashion, I'm sure rage has taken more than a single human man's life before in history. I bet the Native Americans have stories of such. If I live past this, I want to know.

Day 23

Getting short on paper and ink. Writing less often and smaller. Writing what's important or deeply interesting.

Mom, Dad, I miss you. You have always been the best examples of 'people.' I'm always thinking of you guys!

Lisa, go back to school and finish your degree! It will take you further than your current job ever will. I want you to have all the success you can muster, and then some. Sissy luv!

DAY 27

Another storm came through and the big boys went hunting. They came back in a couple of hours with deer meat, no berries, some greenery, no mushrooms. I'm still hungry and always thirsty. Totally forgot New Year's–Sad. Tears. I'm losing myself.

DAY 31

Less paper, less ink, fewer entries. Must be mid-January 2027 now. God, if I didn't have this little book! I'd go crazy!

Theory – Emilie was abducted because Nunka didn't have any little girls. Three young males of which one is an older adolescent who is quiet and ignores my presence most of the time. One equals a child who is rather cute in a creepy, woodland, human-creature hybrid kind of way, but awfully hairy. If I say his name in a very throaty, guttural way, I think it's 'Ungru.' That name is said with a throaty 'U.' I said it once after I saw him go back around the corner of the cave to do whatever he and Emily do all the time because I heard both Nunka and the big one say it to get his attention. It's the only time I've heard that one word. When I said it, Nunka said "Ungru (tongue pop) shee maw" and the little bugger came around the corner and looked at his mom! She then said, "(guttural sounding first word) Gay (breathy next two) ha mo." And he came over close to me and looked at me. I signaled for him to sit on my lap and opened my arms, and he came over and sat with me. Emily came and sat with Nunka. They do that a lot, especially when the big one is out. The kid is smelly but still rather cute in his own way. He might be eighty to ninety pounds (36-40 kg).

Nunka seemed charmed by the whole thing. I saw her smile somewhat every time she looked over at Ungru on my lap. She's a woman at heart! A big, ugly, smelly, hairy woman at heart! She has power and authority in the family unit when it comes to the children. I've never seen the big one be violent with her or the kids. She even seems to be protecting me, always being between me and the big males and adolescents. She doesn't move from her spot in the cave when she's here anymore than I have moved from this spot since I got here. Thank you, Nunka.

January 16, 2027, +/- 1 day

I'm putting the date now. Have to guess. Psychologically, I need this little bit of the real world to keep me from going crazy. I need a bottle of wine. I want my intention to manifest it right... about... now....

Dammit!

My leg is feeling better but can't quite walk on it. I believe the only thing that saved it was the perpetual cold. Six weeks is usually the requirement which would be, let's see, February 1. Mom's birthday is Feb 2. Mom's birthday it is.

I'm the closest to the cave opening, always. Almost Thomas has moved closer to me. Right across from Nunka. She makes a snake noise at him. He is the most human looking in his face, but so freaking huge! I keep saying it. I can't get my mind around it even after all this time. And the big one, forget it! Nunka is hard enough to conceive. If I look away for a while and daydream as I often do and then turn to look at them, my heart still drops a little each time.

Thought–Am I in some alternate dimension? Are there even people in this dimension?

January 19, 2027

No menstruation since I've been here. Probably because of malnutrition and injury. I'm cool with that - 'totes def'

Theory—I was brought here to be my would-be rapist's baby mama. I rejected him. So, the big one does some thinking. He thinks I rejected his oldest son because He looks the least like I do. (He still looks human not apish, but I get it) So the big one goes and grabs his old college roomie, who looks way more like a human than the rapist, thinking I'll be more open to being his best bud's Hoe-for-now. I've been abducted by a twelve-foot (3.65 m) Bigfoot match making game show host!

That ain't happening, Big Guy!

I think this is why Thomas is staring me down all the time. He gets the most gigantic boner about five times a day. Must be a between fifteen (38 cm) to eighteen inches (46 cm) long and thicker than a can of coke for sure.

Yeah, that ain't happening either, Mr. Hairy! I promise ahead of time, it won't fit. So, forget it!

Mom! Sissy! Where are you when I need you?

Better yet would be, 'Daddy! He's being aggressive with me!'

Ha-ha-haha, oh my God, I needed that laugh. crying with laughter…

January 22, 2027

The entire clan is out practicing hunting skills in the fresh snow. Emelie and I are watching from the cave entrance. Ungru is out learning with his brothers, Almost Thomas, and the Big One.

OK, Data

Nunka sits high on the slope. The big one decides how much will be hunted in this practice round. Example: This time it's two. So, the two adolescents move much further down the slope and stop.

First, the big one takes a tree branch and smacks the ground once. He must have kept it on the slope for these drills as there are no trees at this elevation. I believe this signal means hunt practice is about to start.

Next, Nunka claps the rocks together twice. This must mean how many prey she sees. I had to think about this one. It seems to correlate.

Next, the big one squats low and sneaks around behind them at a great distance. Almost Thomas takes a different angle about 120 degrees off from the big one. They are ignoring his movements for now. Everyone is watching.

Next, one adolescent spots the big one (he's wide out in the open so I'm thinking these are dry runs and they are good at pretending).

Next, Almost Thomas, seeing the big one has been spotted, lets out a high-pitched scream. The adolescents both look toward Almost Thomas, who has stopped. Their eyes no longer upon the big one, they are staring at Almost Thomas now.

Next, Immediately the big one changes position when the adolescents aren't looking and moves in closer in an arching type of approach.

Next, Nunka takes off to another angle, almost opposite the big one, and lets out a big, high-pitched scream and she stops. (She has Ungru with her)

Next, the adolescents turn toward Nunka's scream location. The big one sneaks in a little further.

Next, Almost Thomas moves in closer, screams, and stops. The adolescents turn toward his scream.

Finally, the big one rushes them. They try to take off, but he bulldozes both of them.

Apparently, this was all in play and for the education of the littlest one and maybe just reinforcing how this clan hunts. There were a couple go-arounds with different numbers of prey, including the last round with Ungru and three claps from Nunka as the last group of prey was the big one, Almost Thomas, and Ungru. The big one held Ungru through the whole practice. Nunka and the two adolescents were the hunters, with the youngest adolescent being the one to rush the prey at the end.

Wow! That's a lot. Very impressive though. I was transfixed each time, especially the last one.

I don't know what to name the youngest adolescent, so I'll just call him Shy-Guy.

Daddy would be impressed, no doubt! This clan is full of proficient hunters.

JANUARY 27, 2027

That last entry was way long, so I'm cutting back a little.

I'm really sad today. I want out of here so badly, I want to yell out across the vast terrain: HELP, ANYONE, PLEASE!

Eating raw meat is all there is now, and I hate it. It's the middle of winter. I'm so disgusted, and so tired of being cold from needing to be out eating snow. My tongue is always frozen and feels raw all the time. My lips and hands are cold along with my face and injured leg. Ugh! I can't stand it! I want to scream until I can't scream anymore.

Almost, Thomas is apt to touch me every now and again. At first, it was just the makeshift cast. Then it was my leg and arm. Nunka hisses at him like a snake, but he's listening less and less. Somewhere, a promise was made, and I wasn't included. I think they are all waiting for my leg to heal. It's getting close, so I need a plan and soon.

FEBRUARY 2, 2027

Happy Birthday, Mom! God, I want to be with you so much! I hope you have a wonderful day, and you must know I'm thinking of you all day today! I love you bunches and bunches! Thinking of you blowing out the candles and the smiles all around will keep me from going nuts for now.

Not taking the cast off today. Almost Thomas is getting too friendly now. Something bad is going to happen, I know it. I'm finally going to meet my end after all this time saving my leg.

Life is a bitch!

FEBRUARY 9, 2027

Plan–keeping cast on until the clan goes on a big hunt when they all go together. Then I make my break for it. Need to figure where to go. Haven't seen around the other side of this ridge yet. Maybe I'll make a trek up there to look around and see what the reactions are, too.

FEBRUARY 11, 2027

That's it! I'm done. I'm either going to kill myself getting out of here or get killed trying!

Everyone in the clan left for a hunt yesterday except Almost Thomas, who began to trying to rape me about a half hour after they left.

As a human woman, you are powerless against these creatures. You can hit them with an iron baseball bat, and they wouldn't blink. They are too big, too heavy, too strong, too aggressive, too primitive. My only salvation is Almost Thomas doesn't understand pants. He sees me drop them when I have to relieve myself, but he doesn't get it.

Anyway, I just didn't have enough strength to fight him off. He ripped off my jacket. He couldn't do anything to me but lay on me and try over and over. A couple times he grabbed me, flipped me over and held my hips up like he was going to take it doggy style all by himself. He grabbed at my pants at a couple of points during this effort to pull them off, but I kept my legs closed and bent. Once he was able to jab himself between my thighs (pants on still) and went to town. I was screaming out, but that didn't matter. I was pulling my hoodie and shirt out of the way and holding my head up and back because I didn't want him to finish on my clothing or me, which was smart thinking on my part. He got nothing on me. But it was all over the cave floor. I think he made himself raw in this effort because he didn't try it like that again.

I don't want to die trying, but I can't live like this. I want to be saved, and back at home, normal, living a long, happy life. They are built for this type of life and I'm not.

I'm going to try to tell Nunka I want to go home. I don't know how, but she is really my only hope for freedom.

February 14, 2027

Valentine's day? Is it real? I want the days back when I was in the fourth grade, and we passed around Valentine's cards to all our classmates (well, except a few.... Hhmmmfff, kids... so mean sometimes!)

Getting excited to make my escape. Shhh! Secret... I'm coming home Ralphie! Mom, Dad, Sissy!

February 20, 2027

Almost Thomas has this habit now of sneaking over at night and sleeping half on top of me. He stinks horribly if I haven't said it before. It makes me sick. I turn away to the cave wall when he approaches. He doesn't get it.

I'm not going to be able to bring Emilie with me. I have to make a break for it. Just waiting for the right time.

I feel like I'm getting some of my sanity back! I know I'm close to bolting from here. Waiting for a group hunt and watching the direction they go.

Mom and Dad, here I come!

FEBRUARY 22, 2027

Oh, my God! The days are long, waiting for my break. Every second seems to require two more seconds to tick off before time progresses! My anxiety is keeping me tense.

I'm skinnier than I have ever been, I'm sure. I'm hungry, but after so long with hunger, your brain completely ignores the feeling. Holding my pants up everywhere I go, I notice they're watching me. They must think I'm some kind of cripple or something, I'm sure, but I don't give a flying crap what they think. I don't even deal with Ungru or Emelie anymore. Ungru really isn't that cute. Not sure what I was thinking. Maybe Stockholm syndrome? I seem to have worked myself out of that one now.

I think Nunka knows what I was trying to tell her, but she doesn't seem to concur that I have the opportunity to leave. I guess in their culture; the women don't leave. Once they are with a man, that's it. That's you for life. I sure hope they don't think Almost Thomas and I are married. I certainly don't act like it, though he tries to act like it now. He carried me down to a fresh flowing stream yesterday. This happens about twice a week, but it's always Nunka who carries me. I thought Nunka was fast. Holy Christ! I know I was on the front end of nearly forty miles per hour (65 kph). He took a leap over a crevasse I know I'm never going to take, but he landed it like he was hopping a puddle on a city sidewalk. We flew a solid three seconds. I wasn't even an effort for him.

Otherwise, just waiting for the opportunity now. Still have my cast on but don't need it, I know. I can put weight on it and have been working on holding weight on it and flexibility when sitting in the cave. My body has been cramped for so long stretching hurts. Got to get out of this physical slump before I make my break.

God, I need that bottle of wine right now!

FEBRUARY 24, 2027

Same updates. Still missing family, but so hopeful deep inside. I believe I can do this. I know I'm on my way when it happens.

Nunka has been gone for three days now. This is unusual. Normally It's the guys. The big one doesn't seem worried. Ok, I won't be either. I'm sick of this crew, anyway. But I do like Nunka and Emelie still. It's just, they are one-in-the-same to me now. I still have the goal of one day saving Emelie, but she is going to need extensive therapy and resocialization. She is one of them in every sense of the word except she remembers the tunes to a couple of Christmas songs where most of the words are long lost to her now. Everything else is Bigfoot.

FEBRUARY 25, 2027

Group practice last night with Ungru too. Nunka is still not back. This clan is great at hunting. They have never failed to go out and come back with something. Very impressive. Not even Daddy could claim that. Sorry Daddy! I know you're a superb hunter! You'd save me too if you knew where I was because you are just bad ass enough to handle these guys! Love you!

Nunka came back early this morning. Five and a half days! Brought some grasses I recognized from before and one of her satchels with a bunch of little white flowers in it. And another two grass satchels with fish! I couldn't believe it. She's a fisherman! She was loaded down!

I know little about fish other than I know what a catfish looks like, and she had two big ones of those under her arms. (Yucky, I'll pass) The other fish, I have no clue, but wow, did the cave erupt with excitement. There must have been about forty or fifty small fish.

Strategically, she must have headed south from here and quite a distance. It's still cold and snowy in the valley below here, and I know there are no flowers blooming. She must have made one heck of a trek.

I was very careful about how I ate my fish, and I only ate a little. I was cautious of potential parasites and checked after each bite. In a couple of hours, I'll know if I'm doomed.

Everyone has content tummies tonight. Thanks, Nunka, for the change up!

FEBRUARY 27, 2027

Another group practice with Ungru and Nunka, the entire clan. This time they carried it further down to the valley amongst the trees. They disappeared from my view before they got there, but I could tell there would not be any further dry runs for me to watch. Ungru needed to see how it really goes down and everyone needed the practice again. What works, works, right? This crew is successful, and the secret is in how they hunt.

Reminder- They are very good at making hunting adjustments by making the prey look in the other direction through screams.

The number of knocks on the rocks I've discovered isn't the number of prey they see. It's the number of prey they want to take based on what they are hunting, and the rock knocks confirm that the one doing the knocking can see at least that number of prey available. From there on out, it is stealthy engagement, based on coordinated team work always distracting the prey.

I bet, like most hunters, they try naturally to force their fleeing prey into a geographically advantageous position. What my daddy calls a 'kill funnel.' Something he learned in the Army. I haven't seen the clan doing that, but it follows they might. Again, their success rate is 100% from what I can tell. Who knows, I certainly don't want to be on the receiving end of that lesson.

Almost out of paper. Pen Really low.

March 1, 2027

Whole clan left. Emelie and I watched them go into the valley below. Writing this to get my nerve up. Going to leave my cast.

March 2, 2027

OMG! I'm going to make it! Need to stop. I circled back up over the mountain to a prominent ridge near the peak. Looking south, I saw a cutout in the trees that looked like a road in the National Park system. I'm assuming that is where I'm still at. Guessed that was about five miles from the peak. On my way.

Dammit! It's a stream, not a road. Looking for rapids where I can cross. Resting first.

What the hell have I gotten myself into? Everything is muddy and cold and snow patches everywhere. I'm tired as hell. I have to stop now every twenty minutes to gather enough energy. This is taking forever. Just checked the sun. It's going down in an hour or two and I'm freezing. Need to find cover but want to keep moving. Keep moving, it is.

UGH, I risked it. I swam. So desperate and so stupid. I'm shaking. Can barely write. pants wet need wringing out. Shirt, hoodie, and jacket dry. Held arm up, swam with the other. Holding on. Need to keep blood going. Need rest. No energy. Must try running in place or running home.

Need to rest for a moment.

Gotta run with all I have.

So tired. Resting.

Where am I? I don't hear cars or people or anything. It's dead quiet here. No sounds. Just my breathing. Darkness now.

Back at the Ranger cabin, Graham lifts his head to see the State Police Detective walking up to the door and Royce just getting out of the work truck he said he'd grab. He greets them at the door.

"Hey guys!"

"Hello," says the State Police Detective.

Graham looks at his watch, "Wow Royce, it's been almost an hour and a half! What took you so long?"

"The damn power saw needed to have the ground wire re-soldered in the handle. Someone wasn't careful and yanked it out the last time they used it. Luckily, Dickie's good at that thing. I had him fix it. Meanwhile, I had to get a generator that wanted to start. There were only two there, and neither one was cooperating with me. Lenny and I primed the one we have now and got it running, but not before pulling a muscle in my lower back and throwing out Len's shoulder." Replied Royce.

"How you doin' Detective?" Royce asked

"Good, just good. I hear you fellas have something for me?"

Graham spoke up, "Yes sir, we have this here." And raised his hand out to the detective with the well-used little notebook.

The detective takes it from Graham's hand and inspects its outside condition before opening it up to see all the writing. "What is this specifically?" He asks.

"Well, I had just enough time to read all the contents, boss. I finished just as you were walking up to the door. It's basically a daily journal from Catherine Thompson, but you will not believe the contents! You either Royce! No one will!"

"And this relates to the case with that lady that went missing before Christmas and is supposedly in that video that hunter took, which I'm going to tell you, I personally can't believe and don't want to believe. This is hers?"

"Yes, it's hers. She was alive at least until March 2, 2027, and you will not believe how. You just simply aren't."

"She's been alive all this time?" Asks Royce.

"Yeah, believe it or not, she has, and like I just said, you will not believe how. Not in your wildest dreams. Holy shit, Royce! I got a tear in my eye here. I can barely say it without sounding like a freaking lunatic!"

The Detective interrupts, "Is she here now? Where is she?"

"I don't know, sir. We only found this book at the top of our steps this morning like it was placed there nice and neat just so we'd see it. No girl was around, and we didn't see one coming up the road to here either."

"Yeah Detective. We don't know about where she's at. Like Graham said, we just came upon this little book this morning on our way to knock out some easy weekly task orders. You know, the usual stuff we have to do around here to keep the park system in top shape for the Spring season." Said Royce.

"And you just found this book where?" asks the detective.

Royce steps aside and answers, "Just right there." As his grimy finger points to the middle of the top step. "Like Graham said, just placed right there like all nice and neat. Just so we'd find it and pick it up."

"What do you mean?" asks the officer

"I mean, like we'd step on it if we didn't see it and look down anyway and finally pick it up. Someone placed it just perfect."

"And there's no sign of the girl around?"

Graham interjects, "No. no girl, but I know where she was all this time."

"What do you mean?" asks the detective.

"I've been trying to tell you, but you aren't hearing that this is the most important part of the entire case. She was writing in her journal almost every day until March 2. Just four days ago!"

"So can we assume she's not dead?" asks the detective.

"I have no idea. The last message in her journal said she had escaped from the Bigfoots, but she was out of energy and lost. She didn't know where she was."

"Bigfoots, huh?" said the detective with a look of bewilderment, then with a wary drawl in his speech he says, "I'm going to need you two to come down the station and make a formal statement."

He continues, "I want to believe you, but even after seeing that video myself, some things just sound a little too farfetched to be admissible in a court of law. You sound like you have too much firsthand knowledge."

"Well, hold on, it's all right there in her journal. Every day almost except when she was running out of paper and pen." Said Graham.

"How do you know that?" asks the detective.

Graham responds in a somewhat lower, angry tone but borderline respectful, "She wrote it everywhere in there about her pen and the number of pages she had left. She said it, not me."

After a moment of silence as the detective read part of a passage in the journal, Graham continues, "Look, you wondered if there was some evidence of the girl being here and leaving the journal. Let's take a quick peek. It's only been an hour and a half since we picked the book up and I've been reading it the whole time."

"Sounds like something we should do." Replied the detective.

Each man wandered with his head hung down on the top of his chest looking around on the muddy ground for any signs of a woman's footprints. Each taking slow, methodical steps, each taking care not to step on any other footprints. All three going in different directions around the little shack.

"Here's something!" called out the Detective.

Graham and Royce make quick steps over to the corner of the shack to check what the detective was calling out.

"It looks like bear tracks," said the detective. "Right where the hind feet overlap the front feet, they make one large, long track most people confuse for Bigfoot tracks."

Royce speaks up, "Well, since the rear foot overlaps the front foot, where are the rear pointy toenail impressions?"

Graham and the detective got down on one knee to look closer.

Graham speaks up, "It doesn't look like there are any. Looks like one enormous foot, so-to-speak. Plus, a bear's toe track is semi-circular and mostly even. This looks nothing like that. More human."

"Where's the other tracks?" asks the detective.

Royce was already on the case and said, "It's right here. It's the next step too. Y'all are looking at the left foot and this is the right foot." And he pulled a small measuring tape from his pocket to measure heel to heel of the prints. "Four feet, five and a quarter inches (1.35 m)."

"Well, that's one good sized bear," said the detective.

"That ain't no bear, detective. You ever seen the hind legs of a bear? They're short. No bear can make a heel-to-heel, rear leg step of four feet, five and a quarter inches (1.35 m). That would be a super bear that never existed."

Graham speaks up, "You know what I'm thinking now, Royce?"

Royce immediately responds, "Yeah, what we saw this morning was no damn bear. If what you say is in that journal is true, then I'm betting one of those buggers found her and then had the wherewithal to find us and leave her little journal book with us."

The detective's face said he had about had enough of this crazy talk. "OK fellas, I'm going to need both of you to come down to the station with me and make a formal statement. Frankly fellas, this is the worst damn cover story for a murder I've ever heard."

"Graham, take a quick picture before I pull up the tape measure," remarked Royce. "We may need this to cover our assess plus what's in that journal. And Detective sir, you just gotta believe us here. This is what has happened. Graham and I aren't murderers. We just do Park Ranger stuff every day. Believe me, we are just smart enough to concoct a better story than a bigfoot story for an alibi. We are just telling you what happened."

"Yeah, and how do you know she was murdered?" asks Graham. "Based on everything we all know about this journal; she may still be alive. For all we know, she is still lost in the woods or with those things! Who knows?"

"I tell you what," said the detective. "Shoot me a copy of that pic. I'm going to take this little journal down to the station and give a report on the findings."

Graham says, "Make sure you read it first. It's chock full of information about her condition and whereabouts and what she's thinkin'."

"In the meantime, you said she was with Bigfoots. Can you show where? Not that I'm saying these things exist," asks the detective.

"Oh man. It's going to take more than just us," responds Royce. "We don't know about all the caves and such around here. We'd have to get in touch with a geologist maybe or someone like that. Maybe we'd even have to do something like a LIDAR survey. We'd have to get the higher ups involved in a broader effort on this because the caves around here just aren't known as well as some other mountain systems and aren't completely mapped because there's really not much to the ones we do know about. They don't attract a lot of attention, I guess. And I don't think we have a budget for something that large. The Department of the Interior is the most pitifully funded department in our government. We'd need help. Maybe collaboration or something. I don't know."

"Ok," says the detective. "Well, I'll run this back up to the station and let them know the situation out here. I have your contact information Royce already because you called me this morning. Graham, I'll have yours once you shoot me that pic. I'll have some follow-up items from my leadership for sure on this one. You'll probably still have to come down to the station to make a full statement. It won't be for suspicion of murder, though. We'll just need it. Meantime, prep your superiors on what's going on, so they are ready if we need to move on a larger scale on this one. And we'll…"

Just then, the detective is interrupted by two black Chevy Tahoes with blacked-out windows pulling into the remaining space just in front of the little ranger shack. These vehicles are covered in different antennas of varying lengths. Both are carrying government license plates. Two men in suits jump out of each vehicle and approach the detective and the rangers.

"Gentlemen. Are you the ones involved with the Catherine Thompson disappearance?" said one of the suits.

"Yes, we are. Who are you?" asks the detective.

"I'm Special Agent Brown with the FBI. These gentlemen are with the Department of the Interior and Bureau of Land Management," as they flash identification. "From this moment on, all discussions about this case and newly acquired information is classified Top Secret by the Federal Government. We understand you are in possession of a little book of some kind that belonged to Catherine Thompson. Can we see it?"

"Yes," said the detective. "Here it is. We were just…"

"We'll be taking possession of this now and we'll be taking over this case, detective. You are free to go. You say nothing and know nothing, understand?"

"Yes, well, ok but…"

"And you fellas," talking to the Rangers, "Are you the Rangers involved with reporting this originally?"

Royce answers, "Yes, we are. We just…"

"And who came across this little book this morning?" asks the Special Agent, seemingly not caring about anyone's input into the discussion.

"We both did, me and him," said Royce.

"Ok, my bosses are already in contact with your bosses about this as of a few minutes ago. You understand classified information requirements for secrecy; therefore, you know nothing about this and cannot answer any questions on it. Understand?"

"Yes, we know," said Royce.

"Your bosses will be in contact with you shortly. Is there anything else I need to know here before we leave? Any other information, booklets, paper, messages, anything?"

Graham spoke up, "Well, we did just take a picture of some footprints just before you pulled up."

"Show me," said the Special Agent.

Royce shows the agent, "They're right here. There's the left footprint and there's the very next right footprint."

"Let me see the pic."

Graham shows him the picture.

"Ok, you only have this one picture, right? Measuring what… heel-to-heel?"

Graham responds, "That's right."

"First, send me that pic. Also, let me get one with the width of a single print and one with the length of a single print. You got that tape measure?"

Royce pulls the tape measure from his pocket, and they take the pictures.

"Alright Gentlemen. I think that's it unless there's something else here you need to tell me."

"No, that's all, Agent Brown," says Royce.

"Ok, we'll be in touch. Don't call us, we'll call you. You know the deal," said Agent Brown as he slides the journal into his suit's inner pocket. The suited group quickly makes their way to their vehicles and Graham calls out as they are walking away.

"How do you know anything about the journal is classified? It may not be!"

Special Agent Brown turns his head as he's getting into his vehicle. "We don't know. All we need to know is the video. Anything associated with that becomes classified automatically."

The vehicles speed away as quickly as they came. The three men are left staring at each other.

Royce speaks up, "Well, I guess that's that."

"Yeah, that's that," said the detective. "I guess I don't have to tell my bosses what's happened."

"Us neither," said Royce. "Guess we'll move on with our day."

"Yep, me too. See you boys later."

The detective makes his way to his vehicle and heads out. Royce and Graham look at each other in disbelief.

Graham says, "Wow! Just wow. This seems like some other world this morning."

"Yeah. Crazy for sure. I'm hungry. You hungry?"

"Yeah."

"Let's go grab a bite and you can tell me all about what's in that journal. I don't care if we take a two-hour lunch today. I need to decompress from all this."

"Sounds good, Royce."

"Let's go."

"Maaaaaan! You aren't going to believe what's in that journal!" Graham said with the biggest smile.

About the Author

Joshua R Taylor has spent most of his life living in southeastern and southwestern Virginia. When he was eighteen, he enlisted in the United States Air Force and served six years. While serving, he obtained his first two degrees in Computer Science and Social Psychology and from there, he gained employment as a Java Software Developer working on contracts supporting the US Navy. Over the years he worked his way up through the ranks of IT leadership and has been working as an IT Project Manager since 2010. He's led small and large teams alike, including onshore and offshore teams concurrently for fortune 500 companies. Most recently, he served as an IT Project Manager for an up and coming warehouse automation company (think 100% Robotic Warehouse Management). Suddenly, at the age of forty-eight, he discovered a love for writing science fiction stories. Forever the critic looking for quality science fiction which pushes the reader or watcher to think harder or at least find ever more enjoyable stories, he took up a challenge to a write a better short story after complaining one evening about 'yet another highly iterative/derivative sci fi movie.' It's the first story in 'A Face of the Master's Cube.' In his private time on occasion, he likes playing chess. He isn't as good as he says he is, but he sure talks a good game. He also enjoys tending to his yard and gardens, and of course, loves everything Science Fiction.

Lightning Source UK Ltd.
Milton Keynes UK
UKHW020948211222
414213UK00016B/981

9 798986 630403